VOLUME 32

Ellery Queen's Magicians Of Mystery

Edited by " *Ellery Queen* "

DAVIS PUBLICATIONS, INC., 229 PARK AVE. SOUTH, NEW YORK, N.Y. 10003

COPYRIGHT NOTICES AND ACKNOWLEDGMENTS

CONTENTS

2 SHORT NOVELS

2 NOVELETTES

15 SHORT STORIES

(CONTINUED ON NEXT PAGE)

CONTENTS *(CONTINUED FROM PAGE 5)*

Dear Reader:

There is an affinity between magic and mystery—they go hand in glove and are as thick as thieves. When you think of magic—the magic of prestidigitation, of legerdemain—what comes to your mind? Misdirection, illusion, sleight of hand, bag of tricks, hocus-pocus—they are the warp and woof of magic, and equally, the blood and bones of mystery technique.

Consider: the mystery writer says one thing, means another—misdirection, but always performed with fairplay. The mystery writer scatters red herrings on and off the scene of the crime—misdirection and illusion. The mystery writer's words are quicker than the eye—misdirection, illusion, and sleight of hand. Then there are the cryptic remarks, the false trails, the cleverly planted clues, the shifting fingers of suspicion—the whole bag of tricks, the hocus-pocus and mumbo-jumbo of magic-and-mystery.

We open and close this volume, the 32nd in the series of semiannual anthologies deriving from *Ellery Queen's Mystery Magazine,* with two mysteries that feature magicians as characters—Raymond in Stanley Ellin's *The Moment of Decision* and The Great Merlini in Clayton Rawson's *Miracles—All in the Day's Work* (the perfect title to end a collection of mystery and detective stories); and in between you will find such world-famous criminological conjurors as Erle Stanley Gardner, Q. Patrick (Patrick Quentin), J. J. Marric (John Creasey), Nicolas Freeling, Michael Gilbert, Cornell Woolrich, and Julian Symons; and such mistresses of witchery and masters of wizardry as Patricia Highsmith, Phyllis Bentley, Nedra Tyre, Lawrence Treat, Joe Gores, Gerald Kersh, and Edward D. Hoch.

Now, take your seat, keep the bright lights on, and watch the curtain go up on 19 spellbinding performances—2 short novels, 2 novelettes, and 15 short stories—the enchanting entertainment of the mystery story, baffling, exciting, purely magical. . .

ELLERY QUEEN

7

Stanley Ellin

The Moment of Decision

This story won First Prize in Ellery Queen's Mystery Magazine's International Contest of 1954, and was first published in 1955. Like all Stanley Ellin's mystery stories, "The Moment of Decision" is characterized by texture and solidity in style, by substance and creative imagination in plot. For reasons we will comment on after you have read the story, this First Prize Winner has an especially powerful, yet subtle, impact, and a provocativeness in those larger meanings which deal with questions that, 21 years after the original publication, still have no easy answers . . .

Hugh Lozier was the exception to the rule that people who are completely sure of themselves cannot be likeable. We have all met the sure ones, of course—those controlled but penetrating voices which cut through all others in a discussion, those hard forefingers jabbing home opinions on your chest, those living Final Words on all issues—and I imagine we all share the same amalgam of dislike and envy for them. Dislike, because no one likes to be shouted down or prodded in the chest, and envy, because everyone wishes he himself were so rich in self-assurance that he could do the shouting down and the prodding.

For myself, since my work took me regularly to certain places in this atomic world where the only state was confusion and the only steady employment that of splitting political hairs, I found absolute judgments harder and harder to come by. Hugh once observed of this that it was a good thing my superiors in the Department were not cut of the same cloth, because God knows what would happen to the country then. I didn't relish that, but—and there was my curse again—I had to grant him his right to say it.

Despite this, and despite the fact that Hugh was my brother-in-law—a curious relationship when you come to think of it—I liked him immensely, just as everyone else did who knew him. He was a big, good-looking man, with clear blue eyes in a ruddy face, and with a quick, outgoing nature eager to appreciate whatever you had to offer. He was overwhelmingly generous, and his generosity was of that rare and excellent kind which makes you feel as if you are doing the donor a favor by accepting it.

I wouldn't say he had any great sense of humor, but plain good-humor can sometimes be an adequate substitute for that, and in Hugh's case it was. His stormy side was largely reserved for those times when he thought you might have needed his help in something, and failed to call on him for it. Which meant that ten minutes after Hugh had met you and liked you, you were expected to ask him for anything he might be able to offer. A month or so after he married my sister Elizabeth she mentioned to him my avid interest in a fine Copley he had hanging in his gallery at Hilltop, and I can still vividly recall my horror when it suddenly arrived, heavily crated and with his gift card attached, at my barren room-and-a-half. It took considerable effort, but I finally managed to return it to him by foregoing the argument that the picture was undoubtedly worth more than the entire building in which I lived and by complaining that it simply didn't show to advantage on my wall. I think he suspected I was lying, but being Hugh he would never dream of charging me with that in so many words.

Of course, Hilltop and the two hundred years of Lozier tradition that went into it did much to shape Hugh this way. The first Loziers had carved the estate from the heights overlooking the river, had worked hard and flourished exceedingly; in successive generations had invested their income so wisely that money and position eventually erected a towering wall between Hilltop and the world outside. Truth to tell, Hugh was very much a man of the Eighteenth Century who somehow found himself in the Twentieth, and simply made the best of it.

Hilltop itself was almost a replica of the celebrated, but long untenanted, Dane house nearby, and was striking enough to open anybody's eyes at a glance. The house was weathered stone, graceful despite its bulk, and the vast lawns reaching to the river's edge were tended with such fanatic devotion over the years that they had become carpets of purest green which magically changed lustre under any breeze. Gardens ranged from the other side of the house down to the groves which half hid the stables and outbuildings, and past the far side of the groves ran the narrow road which led to town. The road was a courtesy road, each estate holder along it maintaining his share, and I think it safe to say that for all the crushed rock he laid in it Hugh made less use of it by far than any of his neighbors.

Hugh's life was bound up in Hilltop; he could be made to leave it only by dire necessity; and if you did meet him away from it you were made acutely aware that he was counting off the minutes until he could return. And if you weren't wary you would more than likely find yourself going along with him when he did return, and totally unable to tear yourself away from the place while the precious weeks rolled by. I know. I believe I spent more time at Hilltop than at my own apartment after my sister brought Hugh into the family.

At one time I wondered how Elizabeth took to this marriage, considering that before she met Hugh she had been as restless and flighty as she was pretty. When I put the question to her directly, she said, "It's wonderful, darling. Just as wonderful as I knew it would be when I first met him."

It turned out that their first meeting had taken place at an art exhibition, a showing of some ultra-modern stuff, and she had been intently studying one of the more bewildering concoctions on display when she became aware of this tall, good-looking man staring at her. And, as she put it, she had been about to set him properly in his place when he said abruptly, "Are you admiring that?"

This was so unlike what she had expected that she was taken completely aback. "I don't know," she said weakly. "Am I supposed to?"

"No," said the stranger, "it's damned nonsense. Come along now, and I'll show you something which isn't a waste of time."

"And," Elizabeth said to me, "I came along like a pup at his heels, while he marched up and down and told me what was good and what was bad, and in a good loud voice, too, so that we collected quite a crowd along the way. Can you picture it, darling?"

"Yes," I said, "I can." By now I had shared similar occasions with Hugh, and learned at first hand that nothing could dent his cast-iron assurance.

"Well," Elizabeth went on, "I must admit that at first I was a little put off, but then I began to see that he knew exactly what he was talking about, and that he was terribly sincere. Not a bit self-conscious about anything, but just eager for me to understand things the way he did. It's the same way with everything. Everybody else in the world is always fumbling and bumbling over deciding anything—what to order for dinner, or how to manage his job, or whom to vote for—but Hugh always *knows*. It's *not* knowing that makes for all those nerves and complexes and things you hear about, isn't that so? Well, I'll take Hugh, thank you, and leave everyone else to the psychiatrists."

So there it was. An Eden with flawless lawns and no awful nerves and complexes, and not even the glimmer of a serpent in the offing. That is, not a glimmer until the day Raymond made his entrance on the scene.

We were out on the terrace that day, Hugh and Elizabeth and I, slowly being melted into a sort of liquid torpor by the August sunshine, and all of us too far gone to make even a pretense at talk. I lay there with a linen cap over my face, listening to the summer noises around me and being perfectly happy.

There was the low, steady hiss of the breeze through the aspens nearby, the plash and drip of oars on the river below, and now and then the melancholy *tink-tunk* of a sheep bell from one of the flock on the lawn. The flock was a fancy of Hugh's. He swore that nothing was better for a lawn than a few sheep grazing on it, and every summer five or six fat and sleepy ewes were turned out on the grass to serve this purpose and to add a pleasantly pastoral note to the view.

My first warning of something amiss came from the sheep—from the sudden sound of their bells clanging wildly and then a baa-ing which suggested an assault by a whole pack of wolves. I heard Hugh say, "Damn!" loudly and angrily, and I opened my eyes to see something more incongruous than wolves. It was a large black poodle in the full glory of a clownish haircut, a bright red collar, and an ecstasy of high spirits as he chased the frightened sheep around the lawn. It was clear the poodle had no intention of hurting them—he probably found them the most wonderful playmates imaginable—but it was just as clear that the panicky ewes didn't understand this, and would very likely end up in the river before the fun was over.

In the bare second it took me to see all this, Hugh had already leaped the low terrace wall and was among the sheep, herding them away from the water's edge, and shouting commands at the dog who had different ideas.

"Down, boy!" he yelled. "Down!" And then as he would to one of his own hounds, he sternly commanded, "Heel!"

He would have done better, I thought, to have picked up a stick or stone and made a threatening gesture, since the poodle paid no attention whatever to Hugh's words. Instead, continuing to bark happily, the poodle made for the sheep again, this time with Hugh in futile pursuit. An instant later the dog was frozen into immobility by a voice from among the aspens near the edge of the lawn.

"*Asseyez!*" the voice called breathlessly. "*Asseyez-vous!*"

Then the man appeared, a small, dapper figure trotting across the grass. Hugh stood waiting, his face darkening as we watched.

Elizabeth squeezed my arm. "Let's get down there," she whispered. "Hugh doesn't like being made a fool of."

We got there in time to hear Hugh open his big guns. "Any man," he was saying, "who doesn't know how to train an animal to its place shouldn't own one."

The man's face was all polite attention. It was a good face, thin and intelligent, and webbed with tiny lines at the corners of the eyes. There was also something behind those eyes that couldn't quite be masked. A gentle mockery. A glint of wry perception turned on the world like a camera lens. It was nothing anyone like Hugh would have noticed, but it was there all the same, and I found myself warming to it on the spot. There was also something tantalizingly familiar about the newcomer's face, his high forehead, and his thinning gray hair, but much as I dug into my memory during Hugh's long and solemn lecture I couldn't come up with an answer. The lecture ended with a few remarks on the best methods of dog training, and by then it was clear that Hugh was working himself into a mood of forgiveness.

"As long as there's no harm done," he said—

The man nodded soberly. "Still, to get off on the wrong foot with one's new neighbors—"

Hugh looked startled. "Neighbors?" he said almost rudely. "You mean that you live around here?"

The man waved toward the aspens. "On the other side of those woods."

"The *Dane* house?" The Dane house was almost as sacred to Hugh as Hilltop, and he had once explained to me that if he were ever offered a chance to buy the place he would snap it up. His tone now was not so much wounded as incredulous. "I don't believe it!" he exclaimed.

"Oh, yes," the man assured him, "the Dane house. I performed there at a party many years ago, and always hoped that someday I might own it."

It was the word "performed" which gave me my clue—that and the accent barely perceptible under the precise English. He had been born and raised in Marseilles—that would explain the accent—and long before my time he had already become a legend.

"You're Raymond, aren't you?" I said, "Charles Raymond."

"I prefer Raymond alone." He smiled in deprecation of his own small vanity. "And I am flattered that you recognize me."

I don't believe he really was. Raymond the Magician, Raymond the Great, would, if anything, expect to be recognized wherever he went. As the master of sleight of hand who had paled Thurston's star, as the escape artist who had almost outshone Houdini, Raymond would not be inclined to underestimate himself.

He had started with the standard box of tricks which makes up the repertoire of most professional magicians; he had gone far beyond that to those feats of escape which, I suppose, are known to us all by now. The lead casket sealed under a foot of lake ice, the welded-steel strait jackets, the vaults of the Bank of England, the exquisite suicide knot which noosed throat and doubled legs together so that the motion of a leg draws the noose tighter around the throat—all these Raymond had known and escaped from. And then at the pinnacle of fame he had dropped from sight and his name had become relegated to the past.

When I asked him why, he shrugged.

"A man works for money or for the love of his work. If he has all the wealth he needs and has no more love for his work, why go on?"

"But to give up a great career—" I protested.

"It was enough to know that the house was waiting here."

"You mean," Elizabeth said, "that you never intended to live anyplace but here?"

"Never—not once in all these years." He laid a finger along his nose and winked broadly at us. "Of course, I made no secret of this to the Dane estate, and when the time came to sell I was the first and only one approached."

"You don't give up an idea easily," Hugh said in an edged voice.

Raymond laughed. "Idea? It became an obsession really. Over the years I traveled to many parts of the world, but no matter how fine the place, I knew it could not be as fine as that house on the edge of the woods there, with the river at its feet and the hills beyond. Someday, I would tell myself, when my travels are done I will come here, and, like Candide, cultivate my garden."

He ran his hand abstractedly over the poodle's head and looked around with an air of great satisfaction. "And now," he said, "here I am."

Here he was, indeed, and it quickly became clear that his arrival was working a change on Hilltop. Or, since Hilltop was so completely a reflection of Hugh, it was clear that a change was being worked on Hugh. He became irritable and restless, and more aggressively sure of himself than ever. The warmth and good nature were still there—they were as much part of him as his arrogance—but he now had to work a little harder at them. He reminded me of a man who is bothered by a speck in the eye, but can't find it, and must get along with it as best he can.

Raymond, of course, was the speck, and I got the impression at times that he rather enjoyed the role. It would have been easy enough for him to stay close to his own house and cultivate his garden, or paste up his album, or whatever retired performers do, but he evidently found that impossible. He had a way of drifting over to Hilltop at odd times, just as Hugh was led to find his way to the Dane house and spend long and troublesome sessions there.

Both of them must have known that they were so badly suited to each other that the easy and logical solution would have been to stay apart. But they had the affinity of negative and positive forces, and when they were in a room together the crackling of the antagonistic current between them was so strong you could almost see it in the air.

Any subject became a point of contention for them, and they would duel over it bitterly: Hugh armored and weaponed with his massive assurance, Raymond flicking away with a rapier, trying to find a chink in the armor. I think that what annoyed Raymond most was the discovery that there was no chink in the armor. As someone with an obvious passion for searching out all sides to all questions, and for going deep into motives and causes, he was continually being outraged by Hugh's single-minded way of laying down the law.

He didn't hesitate to let Hugh know that. "You are positively medieval," he said. "And of all things men should have learned since that time, the biggest is that there are no easy answers, no solutions one can give with a snap of the fingers. I can only hope for you that someday you may be forced with the perfect dilemma, the unanswerable question. You would find that a revelation. You would learn more in that minute than you dreamed possible."

And Hugh did not make matters any better when he coldly answered: "And *I* say that for any man with a brain and the courage to use it there is no such thing as a perfect dilemma."

It may be that this was the sort of episode that led to the trouble that followed, or it may be that Raymond acted out of the most innocent and esthetic motives possible. But, whatever the motives, the results were evitable and dangerous.

They grew from the project Raymond outlined for us in great detail one afternoon. Now that he was living in the Dane house he had discovered that it was too big, too overwhelming. "Like a museum," he explained. "I find myself wandering through it like a lost soul through endless galleries."

The grounds also needed landscaping. The ancient trees were handsome, but, as Raymond put it, there were just too many of them. "Literally," he said, "I cannot see the river for the trees, and I am one devoted to the sight of running water."

Altogether there would be drastic changes. Two wings of the house would come down, the trees would be cleared away to make a broad aisle to the water, the whole place would be enlivened. It would no longer be a museum, but the perfect home he had envisioned over the years.

At the start of this recitative Hugh was slouched comfortably in his chair. Then as Raymond drew the vivid picture of what was to be, Hugh sat up straighter and straighter until he was as rigid as a trooper in the saddle. His lips compressed. His face became blood-red. His hands clenched and unclenched in a slow, deadly rhythm. Only a miracle was restraining him from an open outburst, but it was not the kind of miracle to last. I saw from Elizabeth's expression that she understood this, too, but was as helpless as I to do anything about it. And when Raymond, after painting the last glowing strokes of his description, said complacently, "Well, now, what do you think?" there was no holding Hugh.

He leaned forward with deliberation and said, "Do you really want to know what I think?"

"Now, Hugh," Elizabeth said in alarm. "Please, Hugh—"

He brushed that aside.

"Do you really want to know?" he demanded of Raymond.
Raymond frowned. "Of course."

"Then I'll tell you," Hugh said. He took a deep breath. "I think that nobody but a damned iconoclast could even conceive the atrocity you're proposing. I think you're one of those people who takes pleasure in smashing apart anything that's stamped with tradition or stability. You'd kick the props from under the whole world if you could!"

"I beg your pardon," Raymond said. He was very pale and angry. "But I think you are confusing change with destruction. Surely, you must comprehend that I do not intend to destroy anything, but only wish to make some necessary changes."

"Necessary?" Hugh gibed. "Rooting up a fine stand of trees that's been there for centuries? Ripping apart a house that's as solid as a rock? *I* call it wanton destruction."

"I'm afraid I do not understand. To refresh a scene, to reshape it—"

"I have no intention of arguing," Hugh cut in. "I'm telling you straight out that you don't have the right to tamper with that property!"

They were on their feet now, facing each other truculently, and the only thing that kept me from being really frightened was the conviction that Hugh would not become violent, and that Raymond was far too level-headed to lose his temper. Then the threatening moment was magically past. Raymond's lips suddenly quirked in amusement, and he studied Hugh with courteous interest.

"I see," he said. "I was quite stupid not to have understood at once. This property, which, I remarked, was a little too much like a museum, is to remain that way, and I am to be its custodian. A caretaker of the past, one might say, a curator of its relics."

He shook his head smilingly. "But I am afraid I am not quite suited to that role. I lift my hat to the past, it is true, but I prefer to court the present. For that reason I will go ahead with my plans, and hope they do not make an obstacle to our friendship."

I remember thinking, when I left next day for the city and a long, hot week at my desk, that Raymond had carried off the affair very nicely, and that, thank God, it had gone no further than it did. So I was completely unprepared for Elizabeth's call at the end of the week.

It was awful, she said. It was the business of Hugh and Raymond and the Dane house, but worse than ever. She was counting on my coming down to Hilltop the next day; there couldn't be any question about that. She had planned a way of clearing up the whole thing, but I simply had to be there to back her up. After all, I was one of the few people Hugh would listen to, and she was depending on me.

"Depending on me for what?" I said. I didn't like the sound of it. "And as for Hugh's listening to me, Elizabeth, isn't that stretching it a good deal? I can't see him wanting my advice on his personal affairs."

"If you're going to be touchy about it—"

"I'm *not* touchy about it," I retorted. "I just don't like getting mixed up in this thing. Hugh's quite capable of taking care of himself."

"Maybe too capable."

"And what does that mean?"

"Oh, I can't explain now," she wailed. "I'll tell you everything tomorrow. And, darling, if you have any brotherly feelings you'll be here on the morning train. Believe me, it's serious."

I arrived on the morning train in a bad state. My imagination is one of the over-active kind that can build a cosmic disaster out of very little material, and by the time I arrived at the house I was prepared for almost anything.

But, on the surface, at least, all was serene. Hugh greeted me warmly, Elizabeth was her cheerful self, and we had an amiable lunch and a long talk which never came near the subject of Raymond or the Dane house. I said nothing about Elizabeth's phone call, but thought of it with a steadily growing sense of outrage until I was alone with her.

"Now," I said, "I'd like an explanation of all this mystery. The Lord knows what I expected to find out here, but it certainly wasn't anything I've seen so far. And I'd like some accounting for the bad time you've given me since that call."

"All right," she said grimly, "and that's what you'll get. Come along."

She led the way on a long walk through the gardens and past the stables and outbuildings. Near the private road which lay beyond the last grove of trees she suddenly said, "When the car drove you up to the house didn't you notice anything strange about this road?"

"No, I didn't."

"I suppose not. The driveway to the house turns off too far away from here. But now you'll have a chance to see for yourself."

I did see for myself. A chair was set squarely in the middle of the road and on the chair sat a stout man placidly reading a magazine. I recognized the man at once: he was one of Hugh's stable hands, and he had the patient look of someone who has been sitting for a long time and expects to sit a good deal longer. It took me only a second to realize what he was there for, but Elizabeth wasn't leaving anything to my deductive powers. When we walked over to him, the man stood up and grinned at us.

"William," Elizabeth said, "would you mind telling my brother what instructions Mr. Lozier gave you?"

"Sure," the man said cheerfully. "Mr. Lozier told us there was always supposed to be one of us sitting right here, and any truck we saw that might be carrying construction stuff or suchlike for the Dane house was to be stopped and turned back. All we had to do is tell them it's private property and they were trespassing. If they laid a finger on us we just call in the police. That's the whole thing."

"Have you turned back any trucks?" Elizabeth asked for my benefit.

The man looked surprised. "Why, you know that, Mrs. Lozier. There was a couple of them the first day we were out here, and that was all. There wasn't any fuss either," he explained to me. "None of those drivers wants to monkey with trespass."

When we were away from the road again I clapped my hand to my forehead. "It's incredible!" I said. "Hugh must know he can't get away with this. That road is the only one to the Dane place, and it's been in public use so long that it isn't even a private thoroughfare any more!"

Elizabeth nodded. "And that's exactly what Raymond told Hugh a few days back. He came over here in a fury, and they had quite an argument about it. And when Raymond said something about hauling Hugh off to court, Hugh answered that he'd be glad to spend the rest of his life in litigation over this business. But that wasn't the worst of it. The last thing Raymond said was that Hugh ought to know that force only invites force, and ever since then I've been expecting a war to break out here any minute. Don't you see? That man blocking the road is a constant provocation, and it scares me."

I could understand that. And the more I considered the matter, the more dangerous it looked.

"But I have a plan," Elizabeth said eagerly, "and that's why I wanted you here. I'm having a dinner party tonight, a very small, informal dinner party. It's to be a sort of peace conference. You'll be there, and Dr. Wynant—Hugh likes you both a great deal—and," she hesitated, "Raymond."

"No!" I said. "You mean he's actually coming?"

"I went over to see him yesterday and we had a long talk. I explained everything to him—about neighbors being able to sit down and come to an understanding, and about brotherly love and—oh, it must have sounded dreadfully inspirational and sticky, but it worked. He said he would be there."

I had a foreboding. "Does Hugh know about this?"

"About the dinner? Yes."

"I mean about Raymond's being there."

"No, he doesn't." And then when she saw me looking hard at her, she burst out defiantly with, "Well, *something* had to be done, and I did it, that's all! Isn't it better than just sitting and waiting for God knows what?"

Until we were all seated around the dining-room table that evening I might have conceded the point. Hugh had been visibly shocked by Raymond's arrival, but then, apart from a sidelong glance at Elizabeth which had volumes written in it, he managed to conceal his feelings well enough. He had made the introductions gracefully, kept up his end of the conversation, and, all in all, did a creditable job of playing host.

Ironically, it was the presence of Dr. Wynant which made even this much of a triumph possible for Elizabeth, and which then turned it into disaster. The doctor was an eminent surgeon, stocky and gray-haired, with an abrupt, positive way about him. Despite his own position in the world he seemed pleased as a schoolboy to meet Raymond, and in no time at all they were as thick as thieves.

It was when Hugh discovered during dinner that nearly all attention was fixed on Raymond and very little on himself that the mantle of good host started to slip, and the fatal flaws in Elizabeth's plan showed through. There are people who enjoy entertaining lions and who take pleasure in reflected glory, but Hugh was not one of them. Besides, he regarded the doctor as one of his closest friends, and I have noticed that it is the most assured of men who can be the most jealous of their friendships. And when a prized friendship is being impinged on by the man one loathes more than anything else in the world—! All in all, by simply imagining myself in Hugh's place and looking across the table at Raymond who was gaily and unconcernedly holding forth, I was prepared for the worst.

The opportunity for it came to Hugh when Raymond was deep in a discussion of the devices used in effecting escapes. They were innumerable, he said. Almost anything one could seize on would serve as such a device. A wire, a scrap of metal, even a bit of paper—at one time or another he had used them all.

"But of them all," he said with a sudden solemnity, "there is only one I would stake my life on. Strange, it is one you cannot see, cannot hold in your hand—in fact, for many people it does not even exist. Yet, it is the one I have used most often and which has never failed me."

The doctor leaned forward, his eyes bright with interest. "And it is—?"

"It is a knowledge of people, my friend. Or, as it may be put, a knowledge of human nature. To me it is as vital an instrument as the scalpel is to you."

"Oh?" said Hugh, and his voice was so sharp that all eyes were instantly turned on him. "You make sleight of hand sound like a department of psychology."

"Perhaps," Raymond said, and I saw he was watching Hugh now, gauging him. "You see there is no great mystery in the matter. My profession—my art, as I like to think of it—is no more than the art of misdirection, and I am but one of its many practitioners."

"I wouldn't say there were many escape artists around nowadays," the doctor remarked.

"True," Raymond said, "but you will observe I referred to the art of misdirection. The escape artist, the master of legerdemain, these are a handful who practise the most exotic form of that art. But what of those who engage in the work of politics, of advertising, of salesmanship?" He laid his finger along his nose in the familiar gesture, and winked. "I am afraid they have all made my art their business."

The doctor smiled. "Since you haven't dragged medicine into it I'm willing to go along with you," he said. "But exactly how does this knowledge of human nature work in your profession?"

"In this way," Raymond said. "One must judge a person carefully. Then, if he finds in that person certain weaknesses, he can state a false premise and it will be accepted without question. Once the false premise is swallowed, the rest is easy. The victim will then see only what the magician wants him to see, or will give his vote to that politician, or will buy merchandise because of that advertising." He shrugged. "And that is all there is to it."

"Is it?" Hugh said. "But what happens when you're with people who have some intelligence and won't swallow your false premise? How do you do your tricks then? Or do you keep them on the same level as selling beads to the savages?"

"Now that's uncalled for, Hugh," the doctor said. "The man's expressing his ideas. No reason to make an issue of them."

"Maybe there is," Hugh said, his eyes fixed on Raymond. "I have found he's full of interesting ideas. I was wondering how far he'd want to go in backing them up."

Raymond touched the napkin to his lips with a precise little flick, and then laid it carefully on the table before him. "In short," he said, addressing himself to Hugh, "you want a small demonstration of my art."

"It depends," Hugh said. "I don't want any trick cigarette cases or rabbits out of hats or any damn nonsense like that. I'd like to see something good."

"Something good," echoed Raymond reflectively. He looked around the room, studied it, and then turned to Hugh, pointing toward the huge oak door which was closed between the dining room and the living room, where we had gathered before dinner. "That door is not locked, is it?"

"No," Hugh said, "it isn't. It hasn't been locked for years."

"But there is a key to it?"

Hugh pulled out his key chain, and with an effort detached a heavy, old-fashioned key. "Yes, it's the same one we use for the butler's pantry." He was becoming interested despite himself.

"Good. No, do not give it to me. Give it to the doctor. You have faith in the doctor's honor, I am sure?"

"Yes," said Hugh drily, "I have."

"Very well. Now, Doctor, will you please go to that door and lock it."

The doctor marched to the door, with his firm, decisive tread, thrust the key into the lock, and turned it. The click of the bolt snapping into place was loud in the silence of the room. The doctor returned to the table holding the key, but Raymond motioned it away. "It must not leave your hand or everything is lost," he warned.

"Now," Raymond said, "for the finale I approach the door, I flick my handkerchief at it—" the handkerchief barely brushed the keyhole "—and presto, the door is unlocked!"

The doctor went to it. He seized the doorknob, twisted it dubiously, and then watched with genuine astonishment as the door swung silently open.

"Well, I'll be damned," he said.

"Somehow," Elizabeth laughed, "a false premise went down easy as an oyster."

Only Hugh reflected a sense of personal outrage. "All right," he demanded, "how was it done? How did you work it?"

"I?" Raymond said reproachfully, and smiled at all of us with obvious enjoyment. "It was you who did it all. I used only my little knowledge of human nature to help you along the way."

I said, "I can guess part of it. That door was set in advance, and when the doctor thought he was locking it, he wasn't. He was really unlocking it. Isn't that the answer?"

Raymond nodded. "Very much the answer. The door *was* locked in advance. I made sure of that, because with a little forethought I suspected there would be such a challenge during the evening, and this was the simplest way of preparing for it. I merely made certain that I was the last one to enter this room, and when I did I used this." He held up his hand so that we could see the sliver of metal in it. "An ordinary skeleton key, of course, but sufficient for an old and primitive lock."

For a moment Raymond looked grave, then he continued brightly, "It was our host himself who stated the false premise when he said the door was unlocked. He was a man so sure of himself that he would not think to test anything so obvious. The doctor is also a man who is sure, and he fell into the same trap. It is, as you now see, a little dangerous always to be so sure."

"I'll go along with that," the doctor said ruefully, "even though it's heresy to admit it in my line of work." He playfully tossed the key he had been holding across the table to Hugh who let it fall in front of him and made no gesture toward it. "Well, Hugh, like it or not, you must admit the man has proved his point."

"Do I?" said Hugh softly. He sat there smiling a little now, and it was easy to see he was turning some thought over in his head.

"Oh, come on, man," the doctor said with some impatience. "You were taken in as much as we were. You know that."

"Of course you were, darling," Elizabeth agreed.

I think that she suddenly saw her opportunity to turn the proceedings into the peace conference she had aimed at, but I could have told her she was choosing her time badly. There was a look in Hugh's eye I didn't like—a veiled look which wasn't natural to him. Ordinarily, when he was really angered, he would blow up a violent storm, and once the thunder and lightning had passed he would be honestly apologetic. But this present mood of his was different. There was a slumbrous quality in it which alarmed me.

He hooked one arm over the back of his chair and rested the other on the table, sitting halfway around to fix his eyes on Raymond. "I seem to be a minority of one," he remarked, "but I'm sorry to say I found your little trick disappointing. Not that it wasn't cleverly done—I'll grant that, all right—but because it wasn't any more than you'd expect from a competent blacksmith."

"Now there's a large helping of sour grapes," the doctor jeered.

Hugh shook his head. "No, I'm simply saying that where there's a lock on a door and a key to it in your hand, it's no great trick to open it. Considering our friend's reputation, I thought we'd see more from him than that."

Raymond grimaced. "Since I had hoped to entertain," he said, "I must apologize for disappointing."

"Oh, as far as entertainment goes I have no complaints. But for a real test—"

"A real test?"

"Yes, something a little different. Let's say, a door without any locks or keys to tamper with. A closed door which can be opened with a fingertip, but which is nevertheless impossible to open. How does that sound to you?"

Raymond narrowed his eyes thoughtfully, as if he were considering the picture being presented to him. "It sounds most interesting," he said at last. "Tell me more about it."

"No," Hugh said, and from the sudden eagerness in his voice I felt that this was the exact moment he had been looking for. "I'll do better than that. I'll *show* it to you."

He stood up brusquely and the rest of us followed suit—except Elizabeth, who remained in her seat. When I asked her if she wanted to come along, she only shook her head and sat there watching us hopelessly as we left the room.

We were bound for the cellars, I realized when Hugh picked up a flashlight along the way, but for a part of the cellars I had never seen before. On a few occasions I had gone downstairs to help select a bottle of wine from the racks there, but now we walked past the wine vault and into a long, dimly lit chamber behind it. Our feet scraped loudly on the rough stone, the walls around us showed the stains of seepage, and, warm as the night was outside, I could feel the chill of dampness turning my chest to gooseflesh. When the doctor shuddered and said hollowly, "These are the very tombs of Atlantis," I knew I wasn't alone in my feeling, and felt some relief at that.

We stopped at the very end of the chamber, before what I can best describe as a stone closet built from floor to ceiling in the farthest angle of the walls. It was about four feet wide and not quite twice that in length, and its open doorway showed impenetrable blackness inside. Hugh reached into the blackness and pulled a heavy door into place.

"That's it," he said abruptly. "Plain solid wood, four inches thick, fitted flush into the frame so that it's almost airtight. It's a beautiful piece of carpentry, too, the kind they practised two hundred years ago. And no locks or bolts. Just a ring set into each side to use as a handle." He pushed the door gently and it swung open noiselessly at his touch. "See that? The whole thing is balanced so perfectly on the hinges that it moves like a feather."

"But what's it for?" I asked. "It must have been made for a reason."

Hugh laughed shortly. "It was. Back in the bad old days, when a servant committed a crime—and I don't suppose it had to be more of a crime than talking back to one of the ancient Loziers—he was put in here to repent. And since the air inside was good for only a few hours at the most, he either repented damn soon or not at all."

"And that door?" the doctor said cautiously. "That impressive door of yours which opens at a touch to provide all the air needed—what prevented the servant from opening it?"

"Look," Hugh said. He flashed his light inside the cell and we crowded behind him to peer in. The circle of light reached across the cell to its far wall and picked out a short, heavy chain hanging a little above head level with a U-shaped collar dangling from its bottom link.

"I see," Raymond said, and they were the first words I had

heard him speak since we had left the dining room. "It is truly ingenious. The man stands with his back against the wall, facing the door. The collar is placed around his neck, and then—since it is clearly not made for a lock—it is clamped there, hammered around his neck. The door is closed, and the man spends the next few hours like someone on an invisible rack, reaching out with his feet to catch the ring on the door which is just out of reach. If he is lucky he may not strangle himself in his iron collar, but may live until someone chooses to open the door for him."

"My God," the doctor said. "You make me feel as if I were living through it."

Raymond smiled faintly. "I have lived through many such experiences, and, believe me, the reality is always a little worse than the worst imaginings. There is always the ultimate moment of terror, of panic, when the heart pounds so madly you think it will burst through your ribs, and the cold sweat soaks clear through you in the space of one breath. That is when you must take yourself in hand, must dispel all weakness, and remember all the lessons you have ever learned. If not—!" He whisked the edge of his hand across his lean throat. "Unfortunately for the usual victim of such a device," he concluded sadly, "since he lacks the essential courage and knowledge to help himself, he succumbs."

"But you wouldn't," Hugh said.

"I have no reason to think so."

"You mean," and the eagerness was creeping back into Hugh's voice, stronger than ever, "that under the very same conditions as someone chained in there two hundred years ago you could get this door open?"

The challenging note was too strong to be brushed aside lightly. Raymond stood silent for a long minute, face strained with concentration, before he answered.

"Yes," he said. "It would not be easy—the problem is made formidable by its very simplicity—but it could be solved."

"How long do you think it would take you?"

"An hour at the most."

Hugh had come a long way around to get to this point. He asked the question slowly, savoring it. "Would you want to bet on that?"

"Now, wait a minute," the doctor said. "I don't like any part of this."

"And I vote we adjourn for a drink," I put in. "Fun's fun, but we'll all wind up with pneumonia, playing games down here."

Neither Hugh nor Raymond appeared to hear a word of this. They stood staring at each other—Hugh waiting on pins and needles, Raymond deliberating—until Raymond said, "What is this bet you offer?"

"This. If you lose, you get out of the Dane house inside of a month, and sell it to me."

"And if I win?"

It was not easy for Hugh to say it, but he finally got it out. "Then I'll be the one to get out. And if you don't want to buy Hilltop I'll arrange to sell it to the first comer."

For anyone who knew Hugh it was so fantastic, so staggering a statement to hear from him, that none of us could find words at first. It was the doctor who recovered most quickly.

"You're not speaking for yourself, Hugh," he warned. "You're a married man. Elizabeth's feelings have to be considered."

"Is it a bet?" Hugh demanded of Raymond. "Do you want to go through with it?"

"I think before I answer that, there is something to be explained." Raymond paused, then went on slowly, "I am afraid I gave the impression—out of false pride, perhaps—that when I retired from my work it was because of a boredom, a lack of interest in it. That was not altogether the truth. In reality, I was required to go to a doctor some years ago, the doctor listened to the heart, and suddenly my heart became the most important thing in the world. I tell you this because while your challenge strikes me as being a most unusual and interesting way of settling differences between neighbors, I must reject it for reasons of health."

"You were healthy enough a minute ago," Hugh said in a hard voice.

"Perhaps not as much as you would want to think, my friend."

"In other words," Hugh said bitterly, "there's no accomplice handy, no keys in your pocket to help out, and no way of tricking anyone into seeing what isn't there! So you have to admit you're beaten."

Raymond stiffened. "I admit no such thing. All the tools I would need even for such a test as this I have with me. Believe me, they would be enough."

Hugh laughed aloud, and the sound of it broke into small echoes all down the corridors behind us. It was that sound, I am sure—the living contempt in it rebounding from wall to wall around us—which sent Raymond into the cell.

Hugh wielded the hammer, a shorthandled but heavy sledge, which tightened the collar into a circlet around Raymond's neck, hitting with hard even strokes at the iron which was braced against the wall. When he was finished I saw the pale glow of the radium-painted numbers on a watch as Raymond studied it in his pitch darkness.

"It is now eleven," he said calmly. "The wager is that by midnight this door must be opened, and it does not matter what means are used. Those are the conditions, and you gentlemen are the witnesses to them."

Then the door was closed, and the walking began.

Back and forth we walked—the three of us—as if we were being compelled to trace every possible geometric figure on that stony floor. The doctor with his quick, impatient step, and I matching Hugh's long, nervous strides. A foolish, meaningless march, back and forth across our own shadows, each of us marking the time by counting off the passing seconds, and each ashamed to be the first to look at his watch.

For a while there was a counterpoint to this scraping of feet from inside the cell. It was a barely perceptible clinking of chain coming at brief, regular intervals. Then there would be a long silence, followed by a renewal of the sound. When it stopped again I could not restrain myself any longer. I held up my watch toward the dim yellowish light of the bulb overhead and saw with dismay that barely twenty minutes had passed.

After that there was no hesitancy in the others about looking at the time, and, if anything, this made it harder to bear than just wondering. I caught the doctor winding his watch with small, brisk turns, and then a few minutes later try to wind it again, and suddenly drop his hand with disgust as he realized he had already done it. Hugh walked with his watch held up near his eyes, as if by concentration on it he could drag that crawling minute hand faster around the dial.

Thirty minutes had passed.

Forty.

Forty-five.

I remember that when I looked at my watch and saw there were less than fifteen minutes to go I wondered if I could last out even that short time. The chill had sunk so deep into me that I ached with it. I was shocked when I saw that Hugh's face was dripping with sweat, and that beads of it gathered and ran off while I watched.

It was while I was looking at him in fascination that it happened. The sound broke through the walls of the cell like a wail of agony heard from far away, and shivered over us as if it were spelling out the words.

"*Doctor!*" it cried. "*The air!*"

It was Raymond's voice, but the thickness of the wall blocking it off turned it into a high, thin sound. What was clearest in it was the note of pure terror, the plea growing out of that terror.

"*Air!*" it screamed, the word bubbling and dissolving into a long-drawn sound which made no sense at all.

And then it was silent.

We leaped for the door together, but Hugh was there first, his back against it, barring the way. In his uplifted hand was the hammer which had clinched Raymond's collar.

"Keep back!" he cried. "Don't come any nearer, I warn you!"

The fury in him, brought home by the menace of the weapon, stopped us in our tracks.

"Hugh," the doctor pleaded, "I know what you're thinking, but you can forget that now. The bet's off, and I'm opening the door on my own responsibility. You have my word for that."

"Do I? But do you remember the terms of the bet, Doctor? This door must be opened within an hour—*and it doesn't matter what means are used!* Do you understand now? He's fooling both of you. He's faking a death scene, so that you'll push open the door and win his bet for him. But it's my bet, not yours, and I have the last word on it!"

I saw from the way he talked, despite the shaking tension in his voice, that he was in perfect command of himself, and it made everything seem that much worse.

"How do you know he's faking?" I demanded. "The man said he had a heart condition. He said there was always a time in a spot like this when he had to fight panic and could feel the strain of it. What right do you have to gamble with his life?"

"Damn it, don't you see he never mentioned any heart condition until he smelled a bet in the wind? Don't you see he set his trap that way, just as he locked the door behind him when he came into dinner! But this time nobody will spring it for him—nobody!"

"Listen to me," the doctor said, and his voice cracked like a whip. "Do you concede that there's one slim possibility of that man being dead in there, or dying?"

"Yes, it is possible—anything is possible."

"I'm not trying to split hairs with you! I'm telling you that if that man is in trouble every second counts, and you're stealing that time from him. And if that's the case, by God, I'll sit in the witness chair at your trial and swear you murdered him! Is that what you want?"

Hugh's head sank forward on his chest, but his hand still tightly gripped the hammer. I could hear the breath drawing heavily in his throat, and when he raised his head, his face was gray and haggard. The torment of indecision was written in every pale sweating line of it.

And then I suddenly understood what Raymond had meant that day when he told Hugh about the revelation he might find in the face of a perfect dilemma. It was the revelation of what a man may learn about himself when he is forced to look into his own depths, and Hugh had found it at last.

In that shadowy cellar, while the relentless seconds thundered louder and louder in our ears, we waited to see what he would do.

EDITORIAL COMMENT: *Now that you have finished Mr. Ellin's story, you realize that it belongs in the great tradition of "challenge" tales—in the literary stream of Mark Twain's "Awful, Terrible Medieval Romance" (1871), Frank R. Stockton's "The Lady, or the Tiger?" (1884), and W. W. Jacobs' "The Lost Ship" (1898). You also realize that Mr. Ellin's story does not merely re-create a riddle of the past, or simply offer a new variation. Actually, it is an extension of the great tradition—a 1955 version which reveals one of the most serious dilemmas of our time.*

Mr. Ellin's story calls for more than the usual "reader participation." Entirely apart from the question of whether Raymond did or did not have a weak heart, we are left with this speculation: What did Hugh decide to do? To win his bet—at any cost, possibly of his very soul? Or to lose the bet—

and thus become a man of heart and conscience as well as of brain?

In the sense of posing a problem and giving no solution in the story itself, Mr. Ellin follows in the footsteps of Mark Twain and Frank R. Stockton. But "The Moment of Decision" is not a pure riddle like "Awful, Terrible Medieval Romance" or "The Lady, or the Tiger?" Those earlier classics presented the reader with unanswerable questions; Mr. Ellin's riddle is answerable. Readers have but to look into their own hearts: for it is really your dilemma too—the dilemma of people everywhere—the dilemma of nations, even of civilizations, in this new atomic, men-walking-on-the-moon age . . .

J. J. Marric (John Creasey)

Gideon and the Pigeon

*Another in J. J. Marric's (John Creasey's) series about Gideon,
the Commander of the* C.I.D. *(the Criminal Investigation Department of Scotland Yard)—the story of a jewelry-store robbery, and a 16-year-old first offender, and of Gideon's understanding of his job . . .*

Detective: GEORGE GIDEON

Jimmy Morris was terrified. He had never been in the hands of
the police before, never committed a crime before. Now policemen swarmed everywhere. One stood towering over him as he sat,
pale and shaking, on a chair in the corner of the jeweler's shop.
Another waited by the door leading to the street, near the place
where the injured man had lain. Two plainclothes detectives, one
red-haired and hard-looking, the other fair and plump, were by
the smashed glass of the window.

If only he had never thrown that brick!

Two more policemen pointed cameras at the broken window,
and at the watches, rings, clocks, and jewelry that littered the
floor. The cameras clicked and flashed. A baldheaded man was
brushing powder over a section of the long glass counter.

Jimmy felt like a very small mouse, cowering among the paws
of giant cats.

He could hear, from the street, the noise of passing traffic, but
the stretch of pavement in front of the jewelry store had been cor-
doned off, and there were no footsteps except those of the two
policemen on guard outside. A few minutes ago a shiny white
ambulance had screeched to a halt at the front door, and he had
watched the stretcher bearers push the injured man into it.

Was he dead?

If he was dead, it would be murder.

Jimmy felt his lips quivering, in fear, in shame, in remorse.

The telephone rang, and he jumped. The red-haired policeman walked quickly behind the counter and plucked the instrument from its cradle.

"Smedley's," he said quietly. His tone was even. He might almost have been a shop assistant answering a customer's inquiry. Then Jimmy saw his manner change, heard a new note of respect in his voice. "Yes, sir . . . Yes, I'll see that's done. Very good, sir."

He hung up, then turned to the others. "Gideon himself. He'll be here in half an hour. He wants everything finished by the time he arrives."

Gideon? Who was Gideon?

Although Jimmy did not know, he was immediately aware of the effect of the name. The men in uniform and the plainclothes detectives suddenly began to hurry, almost to hustle. Jimmy shivered. What kind of ogre was this man Gideon who could scare even *these* men? The officer standing over him spoke to the one at the door.

"The Commander of the C.I.D. Ever seen him?"

"Twice."

"Third time unlucky. You know something?"

"What?"

"Gee-Gee wouldn't come unless it was murder."

Murder! Dear God, what madness had he got into?

As minute by minute ticked slowly by, Jimmy Morris, slight, frail for his 16 years, battled with the urge to burst into hysterical tears. He hadn't *meant* this to happen. Didn't they *know* that he hadn't meant it? His lips trembled.

The policemen glanced at him and fell silent.

Someone was chalking an outline on the floor, in the shape of a sprawled body. That was where the manager of the jewelry store had fallen, after he had been struck. To Jimmy Morris it was as if he were still lying there, the blood still trickling from his forehead.

The baldheaded fingerprint expert drew back from the counter. "Well, *I've* finished, anyway."

"So have we," said the photographers, obviously with relief.

Jimmy moistened his lips, pushed his hands into his pockets, then pulled them out again. His hands felt hot and clammy. No one took any notice of him, but a certain edginess was shown by the way all the men kept glancing toward the street. This Gideon must be a terrible person.

Suddenly a voice called out, "Here he is."

Jimmy started, twisted round, and stared out of the window as a long-nosed car drew up and one of the policemen on guard hurried to the rear door of the car. After a moment a man's gray head and broad shoulders appeared; the next moment the man was standing by the side of the car, looking toward the store.

He was very big. Something in his expression, seen at a distance, was forbidding, almost fearsome. His face looked as if it had been hewn out of rough, brown-colored rock, and his eyes shone very brightly. When he moved it was with a deliberate manner, as if he meant to push everything out of his way.

He appeared at the front door, paused, looked down at the floor, then stared about him. Jimmy shivered, stirring miserably in his seat as that penetrating gaze reached him. It lingered, then passed on. One of the officers moved forward.

"Good morning, sir."

"Morning, Chief Inspector." Gideon's voice was deep but, unexpectedly, not frightening. "How are things going?"

"I think we're on top of them," the Chief Inspector said cautiously. "Everything's done here; all we have to do now is size 'em up and catch 'em."

"You still think it's the Castleton gang?"

"Pretty certain, sir. Same tricks, same pattern, and the seventh job in five weeks."

"That's why I wanted to see for myself," said Gideon. "So you're pretty certain, huh?" Without actually saying so, he gave the impression that this wasn't good enough. Turning toward the chalked outline on the floor, he rubbed his chin slowly, pensively. The Chief Inspector asked the question burning in Jimmy's mind.

"How's the victim, sir?"

"Being operated on," answered Gideon. He moved away, studying prints and scratches through a magnifying glass, aloof, unperturbed, noncommittal. Jimmy Morris wanted to close his eyes, but couldn't. This man seemed to mesmerize him; but then, he appeared to have the same effect on everyone else.

Suddenly Gideon swung round toward Jimmy and moved closer. Jimmy had never before been stared at so closely, never before felt as if he were under a microscope. Then quite unexpectedly the strong, stern face broke into a smile.

"Didn't know what you were letting yourself in for, Morris, did you?"

Jimmy stammered, "No—n-n-no, sir, I didn't."

"Why did you do it?"

"I—I don't know, sir."

"Of course you know." Suddenly Jimmy's mind was carried back several years, to a headmaster he had both feared and respected. "For money? Excitement? Which was it?"

"Mon-money, sir."

"How much?"

"Five pounds!" Jimmy blurted out.

"What did you have to do for this five pounds?"

"They—they told me to be outside the shop and wait until their car drew up—it was a red Mini, sir—and then throw the brick."

"How often have you done this for them before?"

"*Never*, sir!"

"How well do you know the men?"

"I've never seen them before!" Jimmy gasped.

He sensed disbelief in Gideon's eyes, sensed a feeling of derision among the others. He knew this reaction to his words only too well. As a child he had once, and only once, told his father a lie. His father had beaten him for it, and he had never told another—but since then he had always been known as a liar. "More lies, Jimmy?" his father would say, reaching for his belt—while his mother pleaded with Jimmy, in the maudlin tones of an alcoholic, to tell his poor Ma the truth.

Now both his parents were dead and he lived with his sister Grace; but the old tradition persisted. He was a liar. He always had been, And so his sister cuffed and slapped him, in a misguided effort to make him tell the truth which he already told.

He was telling it now, yet this huge man, whose hands were so big and strong, would be like all the others: he would not believe him.

"If you'd never seen them before, why did you do as they asked?" demanded Gideon, and Jimmy stared, astonished that, for the first time, the truth had not been flung back in his face.

"You must have had a reason. You knew it was wrong, didn't you?"

"Yes—yes, sir. I—I needed the money. I lost ten pounds at the dog track last week—I *had* to have it, sir."

"I see. Did these men say why they approached you?"

"No. No, they didn't."

"How *did* they approach you? Exactly what did they say?"

"They came up to me last night, when I was going home. It was in the alley near where I live with my sister, and they frightened me stiff, sir. Then they told me they'd give me five pounds if I promised to do this, and—and another five tonight. Ten pounds in all," he added, desperately anxious not to lie. "It would have been ten pounds, not five—"

"All right, I can add five and five," said Gideon brusquely. "Now, what did they say to you? Try to remember their exact words."

They had told him what they wanted him to do, what time he should do it; and they had told him to run away the moment he had smashed the window. And he *had* run, but had slipped and fallen. When he had been caught, the shop manager was lying inside the doorway, bleeding, and policemen had appeared as if out of the air, and the nightmare had begun. Jimmy told the story stumblingly but vividly; by the time he was finished, no one in the store looked at him with derision; it was more like pity.

"What about your parents?" Gideon asked; and Jimmy told him about them, and also that he had a mattress in a corner of the kitchen of his sister's flatlet. Friends? He had no friends, not really.

"All right, Morris," Gideon said. "Wait here for a few minutes." He looked at one of the uniformed men. "Get him a cup of coffee and a sandwich. He looks half starved."

Jimmy Morris stared at the back of the man whom he had thought would be an ogre, but who was one of the gentlest men he had ever met.

Gideon led the way to the back of the store, followed by the two plainclothes detectives, who closed the door and so cut off the boy from sight. Gideon pondered for a few minutes, and they knew better than to question him. At last he began to talk, ruminatively, as if he were thinking aloud.

"He's too frightened to lie, so it's all true. He's only a dupe, a gull, a pigeon. But no one would have picked on *any* boy—they'd have to be sure they could rely on him. And if they didn't know Jimmy, they must have known someone else who knew him. Someone who told them where they could find him last night— and that he was pushed for money and ready to do almost anything for that ten pounds." Gideon frowned. "Begins to add up, doesn't it?"

"Add up to what?" asked the Chief Inspector blankly.

"Only someone who was on fairly intimate terms with the boy *could* have known all these things. He hasn't any friends, his mother and father are dead, but—he lives with his sister."

"Sister!" exclaimed the others, as if some great truth had been revealed to them. "Of course, his sister."

Later that day Grace Morris stood glaring at her younger brother as they faced each other in Gideon's office.

"You told them what I'd said about these men. You *must* have told them. You beastly little liar! You promised me you wouldn't say anything!"

Ashen-faced, Jimmy Morris stood silent and afraid.

"All right, Grace," Gideon said. "You told your brother to do what these men wanted him to do and he did it. Now who are they, and where can we find them? There's no point in refusing to tell me—we'll catch them soon enough whether you tell me or not; and you'll only make things worse for yourself if you don't."

She told him, still glaring at her brother in vicious anger, still convinced she had been betrayed.

The men were arrested that night, the haul still in their possession.

They were charged with robbery with violence, which charge would be changed to murder if the manager of the store died.

They confirmed that they had never seen Jimmy before, but that they knew his sister well.

"Now, Jimmy, I want you to understand this," Gideon was saying the next morning, just before the court hearing. "Tell the magistrate the truth and he will believe you. You're young enough to be put on probation. Your sister will go to prison for her part in the crime, but you won't. The probation officer will find you a job, and a hostel where you can live, and if you don't get into any more trouble you'll be all right. Do you understand me?"

"Yes, sir."

"Do you believe me?"

"Oh, yes, sir!"

"That's fine," said Gideon. "So stop worrying."

He put a reassuring hand on Jimmy's shoulder; and something of Gideon's compassion, of his warm-heartedness and confidence, passed itself on to the boy.

Nicolas Freeling

Van der Valk and the Two Pigeons

Another in Nicolas Freeling's series about Van der Valk, Chief Inspector of Amsterdam's Juvenile Brigade . . . the story of two pigeons, one soft and downy, the other venturesome and vivacious, and how Van der Valk, like his London counterpart Gideon, proves himself anything but a cold-blooded, hard-hearted policeman; and like Gideon, Van der Valk knows the true meaning of his job . . .

Detective: VAN der VALK

C hief Inspector Van der Valk had been in England on business, and he first saw them on the night-ferry train which trundles its slightly dirty way from the dismal hubbub of Liverpool Street to Lethe's muddy shore at Harwich. Neither is what you would call a place to make you fall in love with England's green and pleasant land, and he wondered why they were crying so desolately.

It was high summer. The train was crowded with purposeful Germans gathered round their cheerleaders, and smaller, grimmer groups of sturdy Britons; but all were staggering under fearful burdens—huge lumps of shapeless textiles, great clattering bundles of ironmongery. One could barely move. Smells of beer and sweaty jollity rose above the English-railway scent of dust.

Van der Valk was pinned down under a table in the swaying, gibbering car, watching the two girls fill in their immigration forms. They were Dutch, looking isolated in the hearty mill of holidaymakers, the more bizarrely since they went on gulping and weeping into grimy handkerchiefs.

One was the prototype of the country girl—a big pink shapeless thing all soft and downy, with that wispy hair that is neither blonde nor brown. The other was smaller, thinner, with a close cap of brown hair and gamine good looks; her vivacious features would be pretty when not smeared with crying.

He watched them limping with pathetic suitcases along the icy, drafty platform at Harwich, their backsides sticking out in dirty blue jeans. He saw them again in Hoek van Holland, under the horrid blue notice saying *Welcome Home* where starched, bedizened military police examine everyone for signs of subversion. They did not cry at being welcomed home, but looked utterly forlorn.

He saw them again, shuffling toward the exit of the Central Station in Amsterdam, the dumpy one stumbling along more uncoordinated than ever from sleeping in the train. But the slim girl had a remnant of tautness in her bearing, and she was shouldering a discolored canvas bag as though she would not easily loosen her grip on youth, on enjoyment, on life itself. The two pigeons, thought Van der Valk. But in the story, surely, only one pigeon went away. The nervous one had stayed at home. Yes, but in his mind there they were—the two pigeons . . .

It was a month later and he had forgotten them, but despite the change he knew the pigeon at once when she came forward to serve him in a dairy, over in the dingy quarter between central Amsterdam and the docks. Now she was fresh and rosy, almost pretty in a clean white apron, wholesome as the smells of cheese and yoghurt. She had a country accent, an earthy thickness in her speech; he had known she would.

"Where's your friend?" asked Van der Valk cheerfully.

She looked startled, but she had the round-eyed, perpetually bewildered look of her type.

"What friend?"

"I saw you last dragging your bags along in England, the two of you."

"Oh . . . I don't know. She went away, I think. I—I had just met her, that's all."

Why was he so sure she was lying? And why should she lie?

Sure enough it was in August, barely ten days later, that he saw the other one, the venturesome pigeon, in the street, not a hundred meters from the dairy in the Oude Schans. Shiny slim legs twinkled under her pale-lilac miniskirt; the smooth cap of hair was now bright blonde, and she swung a jaunty little handbag.

Van der Valk should have been delighted with this pleasant sight; instead he frowned. He made a half-hearted step as though to follow her, but it was eight in the evening and he was tired. He put a cigarette in his mouth and compressed his lips so that it jumped up and down and touched his nose. Then he shrugged and went home. The Oude Schans, a lifeless and dingy canal, was some distance from the tourists' red-light quarter, but not as far as that; and when a day later he was in the Warmoestraat, which is the district bureau for the old quarter, he asked the desk sergeant if anything was known about the two pigeons.

"Short blonde hair and a lilac mini? Doesn't ring any bell but I'll keep an eye out. I can think of several—but all nearer forty than twenty."

"This one," said Van der Valk dryly, "is the wrong side of twenty—my side."

It was odd—he was worried about his two pigeons. Naturally, hundreds of teen-age girls go through the hands of the Juvenile Bureau every year, but he knew nothing to justify a professional interest. It was somehow personal. Had he not seen them crying in the train leaving England, dirty and bedraggled from a night on the North Sea Ferry, but with that odd spark of verve? He had his files of missing girls searched, a thankless task in August. Nothing.

But when toward mid-September he got a call from the Criminal Bureau, and an address near the Oude Schans, a thundercloud of foreboding rolled over the streets of Amsterdam so clean and bright at the dawn of a lovely late-summer's day.

"Teen-age girl, Van der Valk—I think you'd better look at this one."

The only surprise was that the dead girl was not the gay one in the lilac miniskirt. It was the milkmaid, and she was no longer rosy; her face showed the vile bluish color of strangulation. Lightning had struck the stay-at-home pigeon.

He climbed a narrow dark staircase to a third floor and found a youngish Inspector, not very experienced, who had plainly called in the older man for fear of making a mistake. Van der Valk looked round the room, with its tumble of clothes and possessions, the primitive washing arrangements, the dingy curtain down the middle that could be drawn to give privacy of a sort. He knew these down-at-the-heels houses in the older quarters, warrens of one-room flats rented cheap with a few sticks of junk furniture to students, married couples with no money, girls who work and men who do not. Nobody knows anyone else; questions are considered in poor taste; people come and go. The Inspector was looking at handbags, papers, letters, and making notes.

Van der Valk pointed to the other bed.

"Find her yet?"

"Holy cow, I just got here."

"Better find her quick—or you might find her in the river. Who reported it?" It was barely six, and few people were about as yet.

"A fellow who goes to work early. He saw the door open, thought it funny, and looked inside. Street door shut, of course."

"But is left open half the day."

"I guess so."

"I know these girls by sight. I think this will prove to be an open-and-shut case. We must find the other girl, and quickly. I'll get a description broadcast. She'll be easy to find—a waitress, some temporary job of that sort. She's certainly in trouble—and she may be in danger."

A noise in the open doorway made both men glance over their shoulders, for though it was a small noise, like a breath suddenly drawn in, it startled them. Van der Valk laid a hand on the other's arm, but the clown was already bawling, "Stop. Come here. Hey, you."

Van der Valk looked at him and uttered a short bitter monosyllable. "You frightened her off."

Both men made for the door. Van der Valk tripped on a ragged piece of carpet, bumped into the other, and lost several valuable seconds. He had to go gently on the dark worn stairway if he were not to break his neck. Nobody was at the street door; he cursed the policeman who should have been there, looked up and down, saw nobody, and said furiously, "Take that way, and hurry!" A street with canals on all four sides!

He forced himself to look carefully at doorways, alleys, and shadowed patches. Amsterdam hereabouts goes to bed late and nobody was about. He was very afraid. He stopped at the corner, listening above the silence and the distant grumble of the stirring city, and then he heard the sullen noise of a heavy object striking water, and ran, but he had taken the wrong turn. When he saw the movement on the scummy water he was breathless and in a sweat, but still able to curse: disgusting foul water, fool of a girl.

He took his jacket and shoes off, trying to slow his clumsy

movements, and went in with a bellyflop. He blew a foul taste out of his nose and mouth, swam like a wounded hippo, tried to judge distance, dived, wondering if he would ever come up and muttering, "Please, not both."

Five minutes later he was sitting giddily on greasy pavingstones, throwing up. Two Amsterdammers whose windows had been open—they are never greatly surprised at persons or things falling in the canal—were holding another figure carefully, helping it to throw up too.

"Police car," gasped Van der Valk, lurching to rubber legs.

"When did you have your last typhoid shots?" a bored intern asked at the hospital.

"Is the girl all right?" He got up, hitched a brown ambulance blanket to stop it from falling off, and looked to see if everything was still in his jacket.

"She'll be all right. We'll keep her, naturally, a day or two. She's in shock—large dose of sedative."

"Keep her carefully." He looked over at the Inspector, who was standing there staring as though Van der Valk were the monster from ten thousand fathoms, all gray ooze, (look like it, and sure smell like it, he decided).

"As soon as she can talk get a description of all the men she's been with—one of them killed her little friend."

"A psychopath?"

"How the hell should I know? Is there a cup of hot coffee around?"

"Two pigeons," he said slowly. It was the next day; he was sitting in his office; two sets of distraught parents, arrived from the backwoods, were gibbering at him. "They were always together, and one was the natural leader, always. It was her idea to go to England—am I right?"

"But we thought they were still there. We've had letters—"

"Slowly please. Two girls went to England, to the usual 'au pair' jobs. Where was it, by the way?"

"A place called Scarborough."

"We'll have to get in touch with the police there. One left her job. But she didn't want to go back to Holland, which is dull. She liked England. I saw them, crying, on the boat train. We don't know yet—perhaps she got into mischief. Perhaps her permit was canceled. It was something they did not care or dare to admit in their letters. Forced to leave, they came back as far as Amsterdam, and decided to stay there. It was exciting. They wrote to acquaintances in England, enclosing occasional letters to be given an English stamp and postmark. To keep you from inquiring.

"Now, I'm afraid, we have a sadder tale. They had to find jobs here. In the summer that is not difficult. The quiet girl found a job in a dairy—simple, pleasant work. A docile girl, easily led. The other wanted life—thrills. Work is not thrilling. We learned she took a job as a hotel chambermaid. Poorly paid, but the evenings were free. You must not blame her if she slipped into bad company. Many of these girls slide onto the fringe, surreptitious pickups in the bars and cafés. In the summer, with the town full of tourists, this becomes very difficult to control. One cannot upset and frighten visitors with unending identity checks.

"The other, we may guess, wanted no part of that life, but she had no resource but in her active friend. One day, perhaps, the other brought a man back to the room in the side street. She had to learn to pay no attention, draw the curtain, and go to sleep. One man—we have him, by the way—remembered the address and returned one night. The street door was still open—they often are, up to midnight. The people who live in these houses are honest, but casual, irresponsible, and feel they have little to lose and much convenience to gain.

"The man was quite drunk. He had no vicious purpose—he had no idea except to find a girl who had pleased him. He found the wrong girl. Probably she lost her head and began to scream and it is quite likely, as he claims, that he wished only to silence her. She was not assaulted. He was frightened and ran away, leaving the door open. Nobody saw him. I am sorry—it is not a pretty story.

"The other had stayed out all night. In the early morning she came back to change and go to work as usual. She found the dead body of her friend and overheard a scrap of conversation between two policemen. Incoherent with terror and remorse, her one idea was to seek death herself. She has suffered, and will suffer, much more than her friend."

"You yourself, Chief Inspector, saved her from death." The girl's father was a prosperous shopkeeper from a small provincial town, not at all a bad or even a stupid man.

Van der Valk looked at him. "But I did not save the other. I saw her in the shop, looking quite happy. I thought nothing of it.

I caught a glimpse of her friend, with her hair dyed, in the street. And I thought little enough of that. She had not been noticed in bad company. After this month she would have been. But the police are overworked in summer. A regrettable fatality."

"You cannot be blamed. We blame ourselves."

"Try not to blame her."

Van der Valk accompanied the two worthy couples to the door and went to see Commissaire Boersma.

"Such things happen every day," Van der Valk said after the business had been covered. "Why should I be so upset?"

The Commissaire looked at him, shifting the pipe in his teeth.

"The lightning struck the wrong pigeon," he said, "and there's something about those night ferryboats that brings out the romantic in you. Next time I'll go myself to England."

Erle Stanley Gardner

The Clue of the Runaway Blonde

There were forces in Rockville—the political bigwig and one of the newspaper publishers and other leading citizens—who wanted to oust 70-year-old Sheriff Bill Eldon. Despite Eldon's popularity, they considered the sheriff an old fogy in his crime-fighting methods—an old fossil who didn't know "modern scientific stuff." But Sheriff Eldon, with his slow drawl and whimsical sense of humor, with his warmth and kindness, and especially with his understanding of the townspeople in particular and of people in general, had his own detective method—a method that has never grown old or old-fashioned, that is always as new as the latest electronic gadget. He knew that the solutions to the deepest mysteries of life lay not in physical clues (notwithstanding the title of this story!) but in the hearts and minds of people, in human nature and human character . . .

BONUS: Something you don't usually expect in an Erle Stanley Gardner detective story—an "impossible crime." The victim was found stabbed to death in a freshly plowed field with no footprints going in any direction—not even the victim's! How can a person walk over moist, loamy soil and not leave any footprints?

A fast-moving, shrewdly plotted short novel complete in this anthology . . .

Detective: SHERIFF BILL ELDON

C old afternoon sunlight made a carpet of long shadows back of the eucalyptus trees along the road as Sam Beckett opened the gate of the old Higbee place and drove his tractor into the eighty-acre field.

45

Things had been moving swiftly. Only the night before, the Higbee heirs had finally quit squabbling long enough to agree on a selling price. John Farnham, the realtor, had made a hurried trip to see Beckett the next morning. Within a few hours Beckett had gone over the property again, and the heirs had signed on the dotted line, the money went into title escrow, and Sam turned his horses into the Higbee place to pasture. Now he was starting plowing. He'd work until midnight, or longer if he didn't get too sleepy.

Out in the center of the field the old homestead was hemmed in by big shade trees. The dirt road ran to it in a diagonal line from the gate. But Beckett had no use for the big rambling house. It would cost more to renovate it than it was worth.

He lowered the plow and started up the tractor. As he plowed up roads and green sod with utter impartiality, the rich black soil rolled out in smooth billowing streams. The welcome smell of moist, fertile earth filled his nostrils.

Low sullen clouds drifted by overhead and to the east. Only in the west, where a wind from the ocean was temporarily pushing back the heavy clouds, was there a strip of blue sky. And the setting sun, glinting through under the clouds, turned the lower dragging wisps of moisture to a reddish purple which held a trace of orange, a color peculiar to wintry sunsets in Southern California.

The monotony of the tractor's motor, the steady strain of watching the furrow, lulled Sam Beckett into a state of half hypnotism where minutes marched by unnoticed.

The long shadows dissolved in dusk. Sam Beckett switched on the headlights and kept going. His eyes were fixed on the strip between grass and plowed earth, keeping it lined up just to the left of the right front wheel.

The chill night air flowed past his legs and stung his cheeks. His hands grasped the wheel until the knuckles felt numb, but his eyes remained automatically fixed on that slowly moving strip of ground, green on one side, black on the other.

The horses he had let out to pasture seemed unusually restless, because of the new environment, the green grass and the springy soil, perhaps. They galloped and snorted, chasing each other around the field. At times they plunged over into the heavy going of the plowed land.

Over at Beckett's place a cow was pleading for the return of her calf, an intermittent, mournful bellowing repeated at regular intervals.

Sam Beckett paid no attention to these things. He kept himself absorbed with his plowing, grinding steadily around the field, turning neat, straight furrows.

Somewhere back of the clouds was a moon, a day or so past the full. After it came up, enough light filtered through the cloud-bank to disclose the weird outlines of objects in a colorless, ghostly world.

Something over there on the right looked like a sack of potatoes.

Sam Beckett jerked his head, rubbed his eyes, looked again. Then he pushed out the clutch and reduced the motor to idling speed. He climbed stiffly down from the seat and stumbled over the furrows toward the object, expecting it to disappear at any moment, an optical illusion of the night and the fatigue of too much work.

But the object didn't disappear. As Beckett approached, it seemed darker and more solid. Beckett saw a pair of high-heeled shoes, legs, a skirt, somewhat disarranged—and then he was kneeling by the side of the limp body of a young woman lying face down in the freshly plowed earth.

"Hey!" Beckett shouted, his ears dulled by the after-noise of the tractor engine. "What's the matter?"

He touched her. She was warm to his touch, but there was a peculiar, inanimate lack of response, and Beckett suddenly withdrew his hand.

The hand felt sticky and seemed dark in the weak moonlight filtering through the cloud-bank.

Abruptly Sam Beckett found himself running back toward the tractor. He climbed to the seat, raised the plow, and turned the tractor around. Opening the throttle he started jolting and lurching over the freshly plowed furrows toward the gate, his mind trying to shake off the weariness of his physical fatigue, trying to adjust itself to this startling development.

Even then, it didn't occur to him to notice the exact time.

Sheriff Bill Eldon finished the office work on his desk, rolled a cigarette, and settled back in the creaky swivel chair to glance through the paper before going home. Occasionally he worked nights at his office in the courthouse, and he always remained late if his wife's sister, Doris, was a visitor at the house. Doris was there tonight.

The sheriff could get along all right with Doris because he made it a rule to get along all right with everyone. But he was careful to take her in small doses. Doris felt that her brother-in-law was far too "easygoing," and she lost no chance to air her convictions. She had a suspicious nature, a hard, driving personality. Her shrewd, glittering little eyes were as impudently appraising as those of a bluejay, and her tongue was constantly in motion.

The passing years had turned the sheriff's hair white. They had accented his slow drawl and his whimsical sense of humor. These things were a constant source of irritation to his energetic sister-in-law, who thought a man should have some "git-up-an'-git" to him. Of late she had been referring to him as "the old man" whenever she had occasion to mention him. This was on an average of a dozen times an hour.

The sheriff skimmed through the headlines of the *Gazette*. The Higbee heirs had worked out a partial compromise, he noticed, by which title could be conveyed to the old homestead. It was reported that a sale was in process of negotiation.

Bill Eldon knew that the purchaser must be Sam Beckett, who owned the eighty acres directly across from the Higbee place.

The sheriff browsed through the front page, turned to the inside page and read the "Personal Mention Column" with that detailed knowledge of the community which enabled him to get a great deal more news out of the column than was actually printed. He noticed that Elsie Farnham had gone to the city for a visit, and the sheriff's brow puckered. That meant she and John had split up. Elsie's visit would be duly announced as a separation after a few weeks—

The telephone rang.

Mechanically Eldon reached for it, picked it up and said, "Hello," before it dawned on him that in all probability this was his sister-in-law calling to tell him that it was high time for him to come home; that if the County expected him to work overtime, the County should pay him for it; that he was too easygoing anyway and people were always taking advantage of him; that—

"Hello, Sheriff!" The man's voice was excited. "This is Sam Beckett. There's a dead woman down at my place!"

"Who is she?"

"Don't know."

"How long she been dead?"

"I don't know."

"How did she die?"

"I think somebody stuck a knife into her. I just found her."

The sheriff said, "Don't touch anything. I'm coming right out."

He left the office on the run, climbed in the County car and drove rapidly down Chestnut Street, which paralleled Main Street. He didn't use the sirens. To cronies he sometimes explained that using sirens in a small city was mostly "showing off." He said that you could make just as good time by taking the side streets and driving steadily and carefully as you could by hitting the main street and scaring everyone to death.

But the sheriff did switch on the official red spotlight, and once outside of the city he sent the car lurching forward in a swift rush of gliding speed.

It was ten miles to Sam Beckett's place, and the sheriff made it in ten minutes flat from the time he had started the motor on the County car.

Sam Beckett, looking shaken and bewildered, was waiting for him. Mrs. Beckett was standing beside him, making the fitful, useless motions of a frail, nervous woman under the influence of great excitement.

"You all alone, Sheriff?" she asked, apprehensively, almost incredulously.

"Yes, ma'am."

"Land sakes, you two hadn't oughta go traipsing around there all alone! You can't tell *what's* over there."

"What did you see, Sam?" Eldon asked.

"This girl lying face down, right in the fresh plowed ground. She's sort of blonde-like. Ain't much more than twenty, I'd say. Nice clothes and—this hole in her back. Looks like she'd been stabbed."

"You make any tracks around the place?"

"Just where I walked up to her."

"Okay, let's go see."

Beckett said nervously, "I was plowing and she was lying there right on the plowed ground, and no one had left *any* tracks. If somebody killed her, he must have—"

The sheriff climbed on the tractor and stood with his feet braced on the drawbar. "Let's go over in this," he said.

"Now you be careful!" Mrs. Beckett fired a shrill warning after them.

"We'll be careful, ma'am."

The sheriff felt his belt.

"Got your gun?" Mrs. Beckett asked.

Eldon laughed. "Wasn't looking for my gun. I was looking to see if my flashlight was hanging on my belt. It's okay."

The sheriff opened the gate when they crossed over to the old Higbee place. "Keep right in your same tracks, Sam," he said, "just as well as you can."

Beckett nodded and drove back across the plowed ground, keeping in the same tracks he had made before. By following those tracks it was easy to return to the place where the headlights illuminated the huddled, inanimate object lying on the plowed field.

"Those footprints," the sheriff said, "are they yours?"

"They're mine."

"There aren't any other footprints at all, Sam?"

"That's what I noticed," Beckett said uneasily. "I was telling you there wasn't any tracks."

"She just didn't float down here, Sam."

"The way I figure it," Sam said, "is that she must have been stabbed and then probably started running. She ran across the field, and the first furrow she came to, she pitched forward and fell on her face, and didn't have strength enough to get up. She died right there. Then I came along with the plow and didn't see her the first time around. After that it was easy to miss her."

"How come you missed her the first time?"

"That was before the moon came up, and I was watching right where the front wheels were going. I kept looking down."

The sheriff climbed down from the tractor, being careful to step in the same tracks Beckett had made. He bent over the body. His flashlight sent its beam up and down the still figure. His fingers felt for a pulse, but he was careful not to move the body. Then he stepped back to the tractor and said, "Back up, Sam. Keep in your same tracks. When you get to hard ground, stop."

On hard ground the sheriff once more left the tractor and with his flashlight close to the ground he moved slowly along, giving each blade of grass a hawklike scrutiny.

"No blood," he said.

"I *could* have plowed up the blood."

"You *could* have. But if this girl had been running after she'd been stabbed, the blood would have dropped down on her skirt. It's only on her coat."

"By gosh, that's so!" Beckett exclaimed. "I never thought of that."

The sheriff went on, "Tell you what you do, Sam. Go back and telephone Deputy Quinlan. Tell him to get a photographer and to get in touch with the coroner. Looks to me as though we're up against something mighty puzzling here. Me, I'll stay here and kinda watch that things aren't disturbed. Tell Quinlan I've got the County car. He'll have to come out in his car."

"Okay," Beckett said, the relief in his voice indicating that he was only too glad to get away.

"Okay. After you phone George, better come back with your tractor. I want to have the photographer stand up on the tractor and take a shot looking down at the body just to show the way it's lying, and that there aren't any tracks."

"Except mine," Beckett said.

"Except yours," the sheriff remarked tonelessly.

Beryl Quinlan, the nineteen-year-old daughter of the deputy, had been sitting within reaching distance of the telephone for more than an hour. Roy Jasper was scheduled to call from Fort Bixling. And it spoke volumes for Beryl's feeling toward Roy that she would wait for an hour in any one place simply to talk with him over the telephone.

In the living room Beryl's father was having a mysterious low-voiced conference with three of the town's leading citizens. They had no idea that Beryl was waiting for her call. Seated in the big chair by the telephone, she was too completely engrossed to concern herself with the import of the occasional snatches of conversation which drifted out through the curtained doorway of the living room. But she did recognize the voice of the real-estate agent, John Farnham, generally known as a "crusader," and, later, the voices of Edward Lyons and Bertram Glasco.

"I couldn't do it," Quinlan said in a low voice which lacked finality. "Bill Eldon is my superior officer."

"Bill Eldon's crowding seventy," Glasco said from the smug complacency of his fifty-two years of well-fed prosperity. He was a political bigwig, caring only for power, and was reputed to be able to make or break any man in the County politically.

"Well, now," Lyons interposed quickly, conscious of his own sixty-two years, "it isn't his age that's the matter with him. It's the general way he does things. He's old-fashioned. He's too unchangeable—too dated. That's it, he's dated."

Lyons beamed at the astuteness of his own diagnosis. Publisher of the *Rockville Gazette*, he was also a political opportunist whose entire influence had been built up by a shrewd ability to forecast the trends in local political opinion. He had a habit of being on the winning side. And after identifying himself with the winner, he managed to impress on the uninitiated, and some few of the cognoscenti as well, the vote-getting importance of the *Gazette*.

"Your duty," Glasco suavely pointed out to Quinlan, "is to the County and its people. You're drawing pay from them. Personally I don't think Bill should run again, and I don't think he would if he were faced with a hot fight."

"It might not be a hot fight," Quinlan said.

Lyons cleared his throat. "The *Gazette* would make it hot."

"See here, George," Glasco hastily interposed, "if, in the next important case that breaks, you'd just ride along and not make any suggestions, Bill Eldon would dig a hole for himself and fall in it—flat on his face."

"Is it your idea that I should lay down on the job?"

"No, no. Not at all," Glasco protested hastily. "Just follow his instructions. Do whatever Sheriff Eldon tells you to, but don't go out of your way to make suggestions."

"I don't think I'd like to do that," Quinlan muttered.

"The point is," Glasco hurriedly went on, "suppose old Bill *does* make a botch of some big case. Then he wouldn't run again. Then the question is—would you run?"

"Oh, sure—if Bill wasn't running."

"But suppose he became obstinate and did run. Would you be willing to resign a few months before election, and then give the voters a chance to say whether it hadn't been because you were so efficient as a deputy that they'd been keeping Bill in the sheriff's office?"

"I wouldn't want to run against Bill."

"It isn't what you'd want to do. It's what—"

At that moment the telephone rang, and Quinlan, pushing back his chair, showed he welcomed the interruption. Beryl Quinlan promptly lifted the receiver and said, "Hello," in the dulcet voice she reserved for boy friends and important company. The sound of her voice so close at hand froze the little group in the living room into surprised immobility.

The operator said, "I have a long-distance call for Miss Beryl Quinlan. Is she there?"

"Speaking," Beryl said.

"Just a moment."

Roy Jasper's voice was eager. "Hello, hello!"

"Roy!" Beryl exclaimed.

"Oh, darling I thought—"

The crisp voice interrupted, "Drop twenty-five cents for three minutes, please."

Then Beryl's end of the line went dead, and she had to wait agonized seconds until once more she heard Roy's voice. "Say, Beryl! Have I got news for you! I'm going to be able to make it! Yes, sir, your GI's coming home!"

"Oh, Roy!"

"Going to be glad to see me?"

"*Am* I!"

"How's everything?"

"Oh, fine—especially now."

"You were right there at the telephone, weren't you?"

"Well—yes."

"Honey, I think I'm breaking down their resistance. I *may* get a discharge."

"Oh, Roy, you wouldn't try to kid me, would you?"

"No fooling."

"When?"

"I can't tell when. Pretty soon, perhaps. But I'm getting off for a two-week furlough. I'll see you tomorrow. You'll save a date for me?"

"*One?*"

"Dancing?"

"That will be lovely!"

"Know something?"

"What?"

"I'm crazy to see you."

Beryl's youthfully clear voice, held low in an effort to insure privacy, was, nevertheless, distinctly audible to the anxious group in the living room. She said, "It'll be nice—seeing *you*."

Glasco growled irritably, "She wasn't out there all the time, was she?"

"I don't think so," George Quinlan said apologetically. He went to the door of the living room and stared moodily out at the telephone. Then in an aggrieved gesture to emphasize his desire for privacy, he pulled the heavy curtains closer together. Beryl's voice continued to penetrate through the curtains.

The four men sat uncomfortably silent while the cryptic conversation went on, until the operator's businesslike tone advised the talkers that the three minutes were up.

Roy promptly said, "'Bye, honey," and hung up. Beryl clung to the receiver for a moment or two after the connection was severed, as though loath to relinquish the channel over which Roy's voice had come. Then she hung up.

Almost instantly the phone started ringing again.

Beryl eagerly snatched up the receiver. "Hello, hello!" she said. "Hello, Roy!"

A man's heavy voice, sharp with excitement, said, "I want George Quinlan right away. It's a murder!"

"Just a minute," Beryl said. "Father, here's a call. The man says it's a murder."

Quinlan jerked back the heavy curtains and strode to the telephone. He picked up the receiver, listened to Sam Beckett's hurried voice. The deputy asked a couple of routine questions and then said, "I'll be right out."

He hung up and walked back to the living room. His face was without expression but his eyes couldn't keep from showing his relief. "Woman murdered out on the old Higbee place," he said. "I've got to go. Bill Eldon's out there. It's an impossible case on the face of it. Sam Beckett found her lying face down on a freshly plowed field with no tracks. They want me to go out right away. I've got to get a photographer and notify the coroner."

Lyons' eyes sparkled. "I'll be right along," he said.

"Don't let on you got the tip from me," Quinlan warned. "Bill might not like it."

"Bill never gives *us* a break," Lyons observed.

Bertram Glasco rubbed his hands. "This may be *it*, George. A body lying face down on a freshly plowed field with no tracks. That sounds as if it might be way beyond Bill Eldon's range."

Lyons said, "Let him show the voters what an old fogy he is. It'll serve him right."

Quinlan interposed, "If you boys will excuse me I'll have to rush for it."

Farnham said, "I have every confidence in the ability of Sheriff Eldon to solve crimes. My objection is that he tolerates gambling. I wish you a good night, gentlemen. No, no, George, you have work to do. Don't bother to show me out."

He slipped out through the curtained doorway.

Quinlan said angrily, "It'd take an army to stop *all* the gambling in this county. And suppose you broke up the little poker games that run in the lodge rooms around the country—"

"Forget it, George," Glasco said. "He's just the front for our campaign."

"You can't ever satisfy him," Quinlan grumbled.

"We know it," Glasco soothed.

"I've got to go, boys," Quinlan said. "Sorry, but you know how it is."

Quinlan shot out the door. Lyons turned to Glasco. "Can't depend on George," he said. "I told you so."

"He'll come around all right," Glasco said. "It might be a good thing to play this murder up big, Ed. And you might be able to work in a little stuff about how old Bill doesn't have any knowledge of fingerprint classification. You can mention that he depends on George for all the modern stuff. Let it creep in between the lines that Bill's getting to be an old fogy. Then if he slips up on—"

Lyons interrupted testily, "Hell's bells, I'm two paragraphs ahead of you. When it comes to politics don't ever forget that the *Gazette* has been in business a long time. Candidates the *Gazette* supports get elected. Well, I'm going to rush out there and cover this story right from the start."

Glasco watched him out of the door, then said in a low voice, "You mean you support the men who are going to get elected, you damned old buzzard."

He heard the sound of a quick intake of breath, whirled, and saw Beryl Quinlan sitting motionless by the telephone, lips slightly parted, watching him with wide startled eyes.

Glasco hesitated for a moment, then walked past her, saying nothing, because there was nothing to say.

The little group examined the huddled figure in the light of the floodlight that Sam Beckett had rigged on the tractor. They all agreed there were no footprints. The photographer took flashlight photographs from half a dozen different positions, placing his tripod on the light trailer which Sam Beckett had put on the back of the tractor in place of the plow which had been there.

"Well, Jim," the sheriff said to James Logan, the coroner, "guess you can move her now. Poor kid, she can't be over nineteen or twenty."

"Stab wound in the back," Logan said, crisply businesslike, "and the knife isn't there. You got a murder case on your hands, Bill."

"Uh huh."

The coroner was plainly puzzled, slightly impatient. "You can't murder a girl in a freshly plowed field with soil as soft as this and not leave *some* sort of tracks."

"Uh huh," the sheriff announced, then, raising his voice said, "I want everybody here to remember that when they go out, they're to go out on Sam Beckett's tractor. I don't want any footprints in this plowed ground, no footprints at all. You understand?"

No one said anything.

The sheriff turned to Quinlan and drew him to one side. "What do you make of it, George?" he asked.

"Well, it looks to me—" Quinlan cleared his throat.

"Yeh, go ahead," the sheriff invited.

"Well, it's a murder all right," Quinlan said somewhat lamely. "I'm just wondering—"

"About what?"

"About Sam Beckett."

"What about him?"

"That body couldn't have got there the way he said."

The sheriff fished a sack of tobacco from his vest pocket, skill-fully curled a piece of rice paper around his left forefinger, shook grains of tobacco into the paper, and caught the drawstring of the tobacco sack in his teeth to pull it shut. "Go ahead, George."

"Well, Beckett must inadvertently have stepped right in the murderer's tracks. That's the only thing that *could* have happened. And then you came along and walked in Beckett's tracks and—well, that's the only way it *could* have been. And *that* blots out the murderer's tracks."

The sheriff tilted back his sweat-stained sombrero to scratch the grizzled hair around the back of his head. "Well," he said, "maybe we can look around a bit, come daylight."

Quinlan moved away. The sheriff caught Sam Beckett and drew him to one side. "Sam, take everybody out of here on your tractor.

Don't let anybody walk out." And then he added in a lower voice, "Come back in about an hour and pick *me* up. Don't tell anybody I'm staying. Make a couple of trips. Take the body out in the first trip."

Beckett nodded and Bill Eldon moved away in the darkness, the tip of his cigarette glowing now and again, then dropping to the earth and being extinguished.

Sam Beckett's tractor moved slowly across the plowed ground to the gate, following the ruts which had now been worn in the soft soil.

The sheriff sat squatting on his heels, cowboy fashion, watching the activity at the gate as parked automobiles roared into noise, headlights splashed on, and tail-lights glowed in sinister blood-red, meteorlike trails.

Slowly the calm of silence descended, broken here and there by little night noises. The field became dark and silent as it had lain for many months while the heirs of old Marvin Higbee squabbled among themselves.

Somewhere behind the sheriff a horse snorted.

Bill Eldon straightened. He turned toward the vague patch of blackness which marked the trees around the old Higbee homestead and walked slowly, the green springy grass muffling his steps. His legs moved with that peculiar high-kneed motion which characterizes the best hunters when they are stalking game. He carefully refrained from using his flashlight.

A few minutes later when the big gloomy house loomed just ahead of the sheriff, the officer loosened his gun in a holster worn shiny with age. He catfooted along the shadow of the trees, found an advantageous place, and once more squatted on his heels, waiting.

An owl boomed suddenly, puncturing the silence with its weird cry. A faint rustling sounded in the dead leaves on the ground over to his right. The sheriff cocked his head slightly to one side, the better to listen to that rustling. Then as the sound became the unmistakable scurrying of some small animal, he turned back toward the house. For some twenty minutes he sat motionless, until the noises made by small nocturnal animals reassured him. Then he straightened to his feet and went forward.

The doors of the big house were closed. The windows had been boarded up. A *No Trespassing* sign had been nailed to the front of the house.

The sheriff cautiously switched on his flashlight as he inspected the front door and then moved around to the back door. Both doors were closed and locked.

A side door on the east caught the sheriff's eye. There were spider webs on the side of that door which had been freshly broken.

The sheriff turned the knob.

The door creaked open, rusty hinges squawking at his intrusion.

Stale, musty air assailed Bill Eldon's nostrils. His flashlight illuminated a small hallway thick with dust and hung with spider webs.

The sheriff pushed across the hallway and entered what had at one time been the living room. A rat, caught in the beam of his flashlight, gave a frightened squeak and scurried for shelter.

Old Marvin Higbee had died over a year ago. Since then the heirs had been engaged in such bitter quarreling that none of them had ever lived in the house or tried to keep it up. Now the living room presented a weird sight. Rats were nesting in the upholstery of the davenport, while spiders were entrenched in webs spun from chandeliers. The floors were thick with dust, and the pictures on the walls hung at crazy angles.

During his lifetime Higbee had been chairman of the board of one of the local banks and had amassed a comfortable fortune as a highly successful contractor. The Higbee place had been the scene of much hospitality. A widower, Marvin Higbee had no children. But he left a sister, Carlotta, and two brothers, Oscar and Robert, when he died after a brief illness. His will bequeathed $10,000 to Oscar, $10,000 to Robert, and the balance of the estate to his sister, Carlotta Higbee Lane. When the will was offered for probate, however, Mrs. Kidder, who had been Higbee's housekeeper, calmly advanced the claim that she was, in reality, Mrs. Marvin Higbee. There had been a common-law marriage, she said. Because she had not been provided for in the will, she maintained that she was entitled to the rights of a wife.

There had followed a period during which dirty linen had been aired in public. The two brothers, Oscar and Robert, contended not only that Mrs. Kidder was an adventuress and a liar, but also that Carlotta had exerted undue influence on Marvin at the time he made his will. The result had been a legal Donnybrook Fair in which the big country home had become a forgotten side issue.

The sheriff stooped to hold his flashlight near the floor. As he did so, the oblique illumination disclosed prints which had theretofore been invisible.

The officer studied the dust-covered carpet carefully. He could make out the prints of a woman's shoes and those of at least one man. They had walked back and forth, intersecting each other's paths. They had made a veritable crazy quilt of tracks, seemingly as purposeless as the tracks left by kangaroo rats dancing wildly about in the moonlight.

The old mansion could tell many a tale, the sheriff meditated. Higbee had been a deep one—with women, in politics, and in business. For a while Farnham, the crusader, had been after Higbee's scalp, claiming collusion on the big school-construction job. Glasco had been trying to get the *Gazette* to demand an inquiry, but suddenly the whole thing had been dropped. Higbee's charm, fascinating to women, had seemed to be as effective with his political enemies. And Higbee, big, vital, breezy, had gone on his way until death had intervened. No amount of backslapping, the sheriff reflected, could make death change its mind.

Moving cautiously, the sheriff entered other rooms of the house. Everywhere, when he dropped his flashlight to a lower angle, he found the same pattern of zigzagging, intersecting footprints in the dust.

Dust had been carefully cleaned from a table in the kitchen. On that table the sheriff found waxed paper, bread crumbs, a lipstick, and a hammered silver cigarette case. At one end of the table there was a charred streak some two inches long and bordered with gray ash, whish had apparently been made by a burning cigarette.

The sheriff examined the linoleum floor. One burnt match was lying underneath the table, and also on the floor were two cigarette stubs, both of which had been pinched out. One held the telltale red of lipstick.

Eldon picked up the cigarette case and turned it over. He saw that a heart had been engraved on the side, an arrow intersecting the heart. There were two initials on the arrow, R at the feathered end and B over the point of the arrow.

After studying the cigarette case thoughtfully, the sheriff placed it back on the table just as he had found it. Then he turned around and to the accompaniment of squeaking boards and scurrying rodents he left the house as he had entered it. He took care to close the creaking side door behind him.

It was nearly eleven when the Quinlan telephone rang stridently, insistently.

Beryl threw a robe around her shoulders and ran from her bedroom. "I'll get it, Mother," she called as she passed her mother's door.

"Thank you, dear."

Beryl fairly flew down the stairs. She raised the receiver and said breathlessly, "Yes, yes, hello. This is Beryl Quinlan."

The drawling voice of the sheriff came over the wire. "Your father there, Beryl?"

"Why, no. Isn't he with you? He hasn't come back yet."

"Hasn't got back yet?" the sheriff asked.

"Why, no, he went out to investigate that murder."

"I see."

"Can I take a message?"

The sheriff said, "If you will, please. When he comes in tell him I want to get in touch with him right away. Someone left a silver cigarette case out here at the Higbee place and I want him to look it over for fingerprints."

"I'll tell him, sheriff."

"Tell him to bring that fingerprint outfit of his and to be sure to bring his camera. It's a silver cigarette case with a heart engraved on it and an arrow through the heart. There's an R on one end of the arrow and a B on the other. You tell him, will you, Beryl?"

"I'll tell him—Goodbye." The words came haltingly. And the hand that slowly lowered the receiver back into place seemed to have turned to ice.

The cigarette case she had given to Roy for Christmas!

And then another thought, which for some time had been uneasily asking for attention, suddenly popped out to the front of her consciousness. The long-distance operator had told Roy to deposit *twenty-five* cents. If he had been at Fort Bixling the rate would have been eighty-five cents.

"Beryl," her mother called from the head of the stairs, "what is it? Nothing's happened to your father, has it? Your voice sounded—"

Beryl's laugh was harsh. "Good Heavens, no, Mumsie! Go back to bed. I've—I've got to go find Father."

"Find Father? Why, Beryl, what's the matter? What's happened? Tell me. Don't try to keep it from me."

"Don't be a goose, Mumsie. It was the sheriff. He wanted Dad, that's all, wants him to take some fingerprints right away."

"But your father's *with* the sheriff."

"No, he left."

"Well, the only thing you can do then is wait for him to come in and—"

"Oh, I think I can find him," Beryl said casually, dashing upstairs. "He'll probably be at the *Gazette* office."

"Then why don't you telephone?"

Beryl's cold fingers were frantically divesting herself of her pajamas, picking up lingerie. "He might not be there, Mumsie. He might be some other place where I could just run onto him. I'll drive up and down the main drag, and see if the car's parked somewhere. Remember, he took his own car. I can spot it as far as I can see it."

"I wish you'd telephone, dear."

"No, I'll jump in my little whoopee and have Dad located in no time. You be a good girl, Mumsie, and don't worry. And if Dad should come home, tell him I have a message for him."

"Can't you tell me what the message is, and I—"

"I'll tell him," Beryl said. "Tell him to wait for me," and she went streaking down the stairs.

It was nearly midnight when the sheriff drifted in to the coroner's office.

"George here?" he asked.

"Yeah, he's in back with the doctor."

"What did the doctor find?"

"Stab wound in the back—left side. Think it went straught in."

The sheriff said, "I've been trying to get hold of him. I—here he comes now."

George Quinlan stepped out of the back room. "There isn't a drop of blood on the skirt, Bill," he said. "It was a stab wound. Missed the heart, but severed one of the big blood vessels. Death was almost instantaneous. She might have lived for a matter of seconds. It's hard to tell."

The sheriff nodded. Then he beckoned the deputy to one side. "Been lookin' for you, George. Did you see your daughter?"

"She got me on the phone a few seconds ago, said she'd been

driving around looking for me. Said you had some fingerprints. I was just starting for the office to pick up the fingerprint outfit."

"I told her to try and get in touch with you," the sheriff said. "There's been a couple of people in the old Higbee house, walking back and forth across the floors, sort of zigzagging, and out in the kitchen I found where some sandwiches had been eaten, and there's a girl's lipstick and a cigarette case. I thought there might be some prints and—"

"You didn't touch those things?" Quinlan asked.

"Well, just sort of picked them up and looked them over," the sheriff admitted.

"Let's hope you didn't smudge any fingerprints. Gosh, Bill, I've told you a dozen times that you've got to be careful handling things that—"

"I know, I know," the sheriff said, "but I thought it was pretty important to see the other side of that case. Had to turn it over to do that."

"How about the lipstick?"

"I didn't touch that."

Quinlan said, "Let's go. I'll stop by the office and get my fingerprint outfit."

"You got your car here?"

"Uh huh."

"I'll meet you out there," the sheriff said.

"You want to take a look at the body?"

"Oh, I don't think so. Not right now. Get prints of her fingers?"

"Yes."

"What do you make of her?"

"Natural blonde, blue eyes, smooth skin, a beautiful girl, somewhere between nineteen and twenty."

"Too bad," the sheriff said, and then added after a moment, "I'll be seeing you out there."

There was little traffic on Main Street at this hour, so the sheriff swung out close to the center of the street. He opened up the County car, but didn't use the siren. This time it took him nearly fifteen minutes to get to the Higbee gate.

The sheriff got out of the car and opened the gate. Then he paused as his headlights disclosed tire tracks superimposed on the tracks left by the tractor.

Quinlan drove up to find the sheriff down on hands and knees studying these tracks with the aid of his spotlight.

"What's the idea?" the deputy asked, jumping out. "You found something?"

"A car's been in here," the sheriff said.

"You mean since the tractor came out?"

"Yes."

"It didn't get stuck?"

"No. The tractor had packed down the earth hard enough so a car could drive in all right."

"Well, now, that's something," Quinlan said. "Wonder who it could have been. Probably some of the newspaper people snooping around. It wouldn't have done any harm to have put a lock on that gate."

"Or left somebody here," the sheriff said.

Quinlan's silence showed that he felt very definitely someone should have been left in charge but that it had been a matter for the sheriff to arrange.

"Tell anything by the tracks?" Quinlan asked.

"Not much. Tires worn pretty smooth and only occasionally you can get a bit of the pattern. And if you'll look over here on the left you can see where the front wheels swung just a little bit out of the ruts. Now, that must have been when the car was going out, because they're the last tracks that were made. So this'll be the right front wheel on the car. And you notice that little nick out of the tire, on the side? Better remember that, George. We may run into a car like that again if we keep our eyes open."

Quinlan said, "Hadn't I better get the photographer and have a picture taken of these tracks?"

"Can't you do it?"

"No. I've got a fingerprint camera and that's all. Anyway, that's a little beyond my technique."

"Well, just make some measurements of that gouged-out place in the tire and sort of sketch the pattern you can see," the sheriff said, "and we'll get going. I want to do some more work in that house."

Quinlan said, "If that should turn out to be important evidence—"

"Well," the sheriff said, "I guess you and I can remember those tracks well enough to identify the automobile, can't we?"

"Yes, but—"

"Go on."

"Nothing."

"All right," Bill Eldon said at length. "Tell you what you do, George. Take a page from your notebook and just tear off a bit here and there until we get it so it just fits that place out of the right front tire."

Quinlan nodded. He took a page from his notebook and bent over the tracks in the moist earth, carefully tearing off little bits of paper until he had the size and shape to suit him. "It's an exact fit, Bill."

"All right," the sheriff said. "You keep it. Now let's drive on to the house. I want you to take a look at that cigarette case."

"We'll obliterate these tracks," Quinlan objected.

"But we'll know the car if we ever run across it on account of that tire," the sheriff drawled. "Come on, George."

Quinlan started to say something, then checked himself.

They drove through the plowed strip of ground to the level field where the car jolted along over the weed-encrusted road, through the big shade trees, to the Higbee house.

The sheriff led the way to the creaking side door which he opened.

The scurrying of rats and mice for shelter was distinctly audible, a pattering of tiny feet beating a tattoo of panic on the floor.

The sheriff paused long enough to lower the angle of the flashlight. "At least one woman, and at least one man," he pointed out. "Sort of zigzagging around."

Bill Eldon shifted the beam of his flashlight. "This way to the kitchen, George."

They entered the kitchen. The beam of the flashlight showed the table with its waxed paper, the lipstick, the cigarette stubs, and the charred groove in the table. The beam of the flashlight illuminated the silver cigarette case, glanced from it in a splash of reflected light on the cobwebbed ceiling.

Quinlan opened the fingerprint outfit he was carrying, carefully gripped the corners of the cigarette case with rubber-tipped tongs, and dusted powder over the silver.

"Hump! That's funny."

"What's the matter?"

"There isn't a print on it."

"Maybe the person who handled it was wearing gloves," the sheriff said. "How about the lipstick?"

Quinlan managed to get two prints from the lipstick that were legible enough to give results.

The sheriff seemed unimpressed to the point of disinterest. His flashlight was exploring the floor. *"One* burnt match," he said. "That's significant."

"I don't get it."

"If you were lighting three cigarettes how many matches would you use?"

Quinlan grinned. "If a good-looking girl was sitting across the table from me I'd use one—wait a minute, I'd use two."

"That's right. But there's only one."

"Then something must have happened to one of the burnt matches. Perhaps a pack rat carried it away."

"Nope," the sheriff drawled. "It ain't that. The way I figure it, the man was a chain smoker. He and the girl sat down here at the table. They had some sandwiches, then they settled down for a smoke. He lit her cigarette and lit his own—one match. After they'd smoked their cigarettes he lit his second one from the stub of the first. The girl only smoked one cigarette. When she'd finished it she took out her lipstick and started to fix up her mouth—and it was then something happened, right at that particular moment."

"How do you fix it as being at that time?"

"Because they jumped up and were startled. The man put his cigarette down on the table and never had a chance to get back to pick it up. It lay there and burned that groove. The woman dropped her lipstick."

"And then?" Quinlan asked.

"And some time after that," the sheriff said, "the girl was found stabbed in a plowed field with no tracks going in either direction, not even her own."

"How long after that?" Quinlan asked.

"That, son," the sheriff said, "is something we've got to find out. By puttin' two and two together, you get an answer, and it don't seem to be the right one."

It began to rain about three in the morning, a fine, misty cold rain. By daylight the tangled grass and weeds of the field were glistening with moisture, and the dark lumps on the ridges of the plowed ground reflected the sullen daylight which filtered through the low bank of clouds.

The bent figures of the sheriff and George Quinlan moved slowly along over the boundary between the grassy field and the freshly plowed earth. With the thoroughgoing patience of veteran trackers they inched their way along, covering every foot of ground.

Daylight was well advanced and the drizzle had stopped when they returned to their point of beginning.

"Well," Quinlan said, "that settles it. No one left this piece of ground after the murder was committed, so the body must have come in from the outside—unless it was dropped from an airplane."

The sheriff straightened. He rolled and lit a cigarette. "I noticed one thing back there in the house, George. You remember where those drapes hang over the door? There's a long braided silk doodad with tassels on it—but there's only one. Shouldn't there be two?"

Quinlan laughed. "Shucks, Bill, the way this place has been left it's lucky there's even one. But there should be two. I've got the same sort of drapes at home."

The sheriff thought for a while. "What do you s'pose frightened those people after they'd just eaten?"

"I'm darned if I know," Quinlan said. "I'm an officer, not a mind reader. It must have been shortly before the murder, and that must have been after dark. Seems strange they'd have been eating sandwiches then. They must have planned to stay all night searching. And speaking of eating, I'm going home, change my wet clothes, and have some breakfast."

"Well, now," the sheriff drawled, "guess *I'll* drop in at a restaurant and—"

"A restaurant!"

"Uh huh. My sister-in-law's stayin' up at my house."

Quinlan laughed. "Come on up with me—no, hang it, if you don't change your wet clothes you'll catch cold. Get up to your house and get into some dry clothes."

The sheriff looked down at his wet trousers, sighed wearily. "Well, I s'pose I've got to."

It was a few minutes before nine when Beryl Quinlan saw Roy Jasper turn the corner and come walking toward the house.

Beryl ran to the door, whipped it open, and dashed down the stairs. Roy saw her coming and flung up his arm in a gesture of greeting. They met at the edge of the sidewalk.

"Roy!"

"Hi, Beryl!"

She gave him her lips in a swift eager kiss, then pulled away.

"Hey," he said, "what's the idea of such a nervous little peck?"

"We may have an audience. Come on, I want to talk with you. When did you leave the fort?"

"Last night—late."

"Been up all night?"

"Just about. Couldn't get a bus until after midnight. Travel sure is heavy these days."

"Where were you when you telephoned me, at the fort?"

"Just outside of the fort, a row of telephone booths there. Why?"

"Oh, just wondering. Let's not go in for a minute. Dad's been out pretty much all night on a case and came home soaking wet, took a hot bath, changed his clothes, and has to go to the office in a minute. The family will engulf you if you go inside. Let's sit out on the porch."

"Suits me," Roy said. "This isn't front-porch weather, though. Been raining here?"

"Just a drizzle. It quit about an hour and a half ago. Let's sit here. How about a cigarette?"

"How about a kiss, baby? We don't have an audience here."

She gave him her lips.

"That's better. What's the matter, honey?"

"Just getting a good look at you. How about the discharge?"

"Don't know yet. Think I may get it."

"And how about my cigarette?"

Roy casually produced a silver cigarette case, snapped the catch with his thumb, opened it, and extended it to Beryl.

"Roy!" she exclaimed.

He glanced up quizzically at the sound of her voice.

"That's the case I gave you for Christmas."

"Sure. What's funny about that?"

"I—I thought perhaps you'd lost it."

His forehead puckered into a puzzled frown. "Now what gave you *that* idea? And do you really want a cigarette?"

"Of course," she said, taking a cigarette.

He took one and lit her cigarette, then his own. He dropped the case back into his pocket, regarding her thoughtfully. "What's the big idea?" he asked.

"I—oh, nothing. Roy, how much did you pay for that telephone call last night?"

He threw back his head and laughed. "I really got even with the telephone company that time," he said. "I let one of the other boys come in and place a call to a nearby town while I was waiting. The rate there is only twenty-five cents. I guess the operator got the calls mixed."

"What happened to the other boy?"

"Don't worry about him," Roy said. "He wouldn't have paid any more than twenty-five cents on *his* call, and they couldn't make him. I got to feeling a little cheap about it afterwards. I hope they don't take it out of the telephone girl's salary, but, honey, you know how it is. I've been stuck so many times when I'd stay in a hotel and put in a call—"

"That wasn't the fault of the telephone company. That was the fault of the girl at the hotel switchboard. She didn't clear the line right away and naturally the telephone company had to charge you for all that extra time."

"Well, he admitted, "I felt cheap about it afterwards, but there was nothing I could do. You see, honey, you were on the line and I didn't want to take time then telling her she'd made a mistake in my favor and having her wait and look up the call. I—"

The door opened. George Quinlan took two or three steps before he caught sight of the couple from the corner of his eye. He whirled almost apprehensively, then laughed nervously and said, "I didn't know you two were out here. Hello, Roy. When did you get in?"

"Just now."

Quinlan came across and shook hands. "Been up all night," he said, "and I'm a little jumpy. Had breakfast?"

"Yes, thanks, had it more than an hour ago."

"There's some coffee on the table. Mrs. Quinlan will be glad to see you."

"We'll be in in a minute," Beryl said, and then smiling at her father said, "Tell Mother, will you?"

That gave the deputy his cue. He said, "I will. See you later, Roy," and went back into the house.

"What's the big case?" Roy asked.

"A murder down at the old Higbee place. I understand she's a girl around my age, blonde, stabbed in the back."

"The old Higbee place?" Jasper asked, frowning.

"Yes. A man named Beckett bought the place and had started to plow. He found the body."

"Beckett?" Roy repeated the name after her as though trying to refresh his recollection. "Oh, yes, Sam Beckett. I know him. What in the world was this girl doing in the old Higbee place?"

"No one knows. They don't seem to have any clue as yet to her identity."

Jasper finished his cigarette. Almost mechanically he opened the cigarette case, took out another, and lit the second cigarette from the end of the first. "Guess that's going to keep your father busy," he said. "How about going in and getting some of that coffee, Beryl?"

Sheriff Bill Eldon propped the *Rockville Morning Register* in front of his coffee cup.

The *Register* had gone to press about two o'clock in the morning, and had relied on large headlines and bold-faced type to obscure the fact that the paper had but few facts concerning the murder.

The editorial attitude of the paper was hostile to the entire County administration and Sheriff Eldon expected no quarter from it. On the other hand, it did a pretty good job of news coverage, although it occasionally slipped some editorial barb into its factual reporting.

Bill Eldon read the account carefully and then slowly reread it in order to give himself that semblance of preoccupation which would curb the conversation of his sister-in-law.

Finally Doris could stand it no longer. She said, "Well, if you ask me, somebody's making an awful fool out of you officers."

The sheriff's silence was a courteous suggestion that no one was asking her.

"Or," Doris went on, "perhaps you're making fools of yourselves."

"Could be," the sheriff admitted laconically.

"Will you kindly tell me, Bill Eldon, how in the name of sense any person can walk over moist, freshly plowed, loamy soil and not leave any footprints?"

"I didn't say it could be done."

"The newspaper says it *has* been done."

"Well, I'm not responsible for what the newspapers say."

"The way they talk about you makes you sound like an old fossil."

"The *Register* is on the opposite side of the political fence."

"Well, the *Gazette* doesn't seem to be putting you up on any pedestal."

"It won't be out until tonight."

"I'm not talking about this case. I'm talking about the way they've been writing you up lately."

"They're friendly."

"Well, you'd better watch out for friends like that."

The sheriff was silent.

"It *does* seem to me," Doris went on exasperatedly, "that if you had more git-up-an'-git you'd command more respect."

The sheriff grinned. "You don't get respect from the opposite political party—not publicly and in print, anyway. If you move along slow and easy, you're an old fossil. If you have git-up-an'-git you're trying to cover your incompetence behind a smokescreen of hysterical activity."

There was a moment of welcome silence while Doris thought this over. "Well," she demanded at length, "who *is* this girl?"

"We don't know."

"What are you doing to find out?"

"We've got a couple of clues we're working on."

"What clues?"

"Cleaning marks on her jacket and skirt, the name of a store sewed inside the jacket."

"A local store?"

"No, one in San Rodolpho."

The sheriff's wife interposed to say quietly, "Bill, you want me to send that suit out to be cleaned and pressed?"

"Please."

"How soon do you want it back?"

"Soon as I can get it."

"You going to get some sleep today?"

"Afraid I'll have to keep going today. I—"

The telephone rang.

The sheriff went to the phone. He heard a woman's voice say, "Long-distance call from San Rodolpho," and then the voice of Everett Gilmer, the chief of police in San Rodolpho. "Hello, Bill. Think I've got your party located. The Acme Cleaners has a record of cleaning the jacket. The girl's name is Elizabeth Dow. Does that mean anything to you?"

"Not a thing. She live there?"

"Apparently. We have an address in an apartment house. She's moved from there, but we're tracing her. The description fits. Want to come down?"

The sheriff hesitated a moment, then said, "Okay, I'll be down. See what you can find out and have it ready for me by the time I get there. I'll stop by the courthouse and pick up some photographs."

The sheriff hung up the telephone and glanced over at the table. Seeing the alert angle at which the head of his sister-in-law was cocked, he said suddenly, "I've got to rush out. I'll be back this evening."

"Where are you going?" Doris demanded so eagerly that the words all ran together into one continuous rattle of sound.

"Out," the sheriff said.

Everett K. Gilmer, chief of police of San Rodolpho, was a big bluff man whose twinkling eyes radiated cordiality to brother officers, but could assume an ominous hardness when scrutinizing prisoners. He said to Bill Eldon, "Well, Sheriff, I've got a line on her. If you've got some photos we might just check with someone who can make an identification."

"Who you got?"

"Woman who runs the apartment house where she had an apartment for a while. When she moved she left a forwarding address. But I thought we'd better check up first with someone who can make an absolute identification. If she's the one I've got quite a lot on her. And I think she's the one."

"Let's go," the sheriff agreed.

They drove to a frame house that had at one time been an example of three-storied prosperity, but with the spread of the business area it had now been turned into an apartment house.

The heavy-set woman who ran the place promptly identified the photographs which Sheriff Eldon produced.

"That's the girl. That's Elizabeth. What's happened to *her*?"

"She was killed."

"How?"

"Stabbed."

"Good heavens! And such a nice girl, too!"

"Any idea who might have done it? Enemies or anything of that sort?"

"No. While she was here she was just as quiet and well-behaved as anyone could ask."

"Know anything about her friends or relatives?"

"No, I don't. I took over the place just before she moved out and—"

"We got some more recent stuff lined up, Bill," Gilmer interposed. "Just wanted to make sure she was the party before I started following the other trails."

"Her mother had died just before she moved out," the apartment manager volunteered, "somewhere in—now, let me see. I think it was somewhere in Colorado. I remember she got a wire saying her mother was very low and she flew out, and then wrote me that her mother had passed away and that she'd stay for the funeral and move to another apartment when she got back, and she sent me two weeks' rent and asked if that would be all right."

"Know where that letter is?"

"I burned it."

"About when was this?"

"Five or six months ago. I can look up the date when she left if you want."

"I already have that," Gilmer said to the sheriff. "It was in August."

"That's right," the woman said. "I think it was August."

Bill Eldon nodded to Gilmer. "Let's go, Everett."

They went to the telegraph office and wired the Denver police to consult statistical records and rush any information concerning a woman by the name of Dow who had died in Colorado within the last few months.

Then Chief Gilmer and Bill Eldon spent a couple of hours plodding along in the dull monotony of routine legwork, tracing Elizabeth Dow from one lodging house to another, finding where she had been employed and locating friends who had known her.

From this scattered pattern of information the sheriff and Gilmer pieced together a mosaic showing a clear picture of a young woman, vivacious, intelligent, alert, a steady, dependable worker, a loyal friend filled with the joy of life, yet respecting herself and commanding the respect of her friends. There had been one or two boy friends, but for the most part she had preferred a group of intimates to the more intimate companionship of boy friends. She had been employed as a cashier in a cafeteria. Her nimble fingers, quick eyes, and winning personality had made for adept efficiency as well as for popularity with customers.

The day before had been her day off, and about ten o'clock she had been seen with a young man who was strange to the girl's set, although he had been seen with her off and on during the past week. The couple had sat for half an hour talking earnestly at a table in the cafeteria. And then Elizabeth Dow had got a cardboard container and put up a lunch—roast beef sandwiches, deviled eggs, crisp lettuce, and pie. Then she and the young man, a tall dark chap in Army uniform, had left the cafeteria. That had been around eleven. Neither one had been seen since.

At this point in the investigation a wire came in from the Denver police:

ELVIRA DOW AGED FIFTY-SIX DIED CORONARY THROMBOSIS AUGUST 23RD, BURIED HERE. FUNERAL ARRANGEMENTS MADE BY DAUGHTER ELIZABETH WHO REGISTERED HOTEL GIVING ADDRESS YOUR CITY.

"Well, Gilmer said, "that's all there is to it. Find the man who was with her and you've got the murderer. You say there was waxed paper on the table in that old house?"

"That's right."

"Find this chap in uniform. That'll be all there is to it."

The sheriff reached for his battered sombrero and put it on. He started for the door, and then paused to regard the chief of police with thought-puckered eyes. "You know, Everett," he said, "it *may* not be that simple. When you've been in office as long as I have you get so you pay more attention to people and less to clues."

Rush Medford, the district attorney, stepped out from his private office to receive George Quinlan.

"Hello, George. I asked you to come up here because I wanted to talk with you—confidentially."

Quinlan glanced significantly at the unlocked door of the reception office, then at the closed door of Medford's private office. Medford, lowering his voice, went on hastily, "I have a man waiting in there, George. I want you to meet him. I want you to give him every bit of help you can. His name's Walworth—Martin Walworth. Ever hear of him?"

Quinlan shook his head.

"Famous all over the state as a criminologist. He—"

"Oh, yes! I've heard of *him*. I place him now."

The district attorney said confidentially, "I'm calling him in,

George, at the suggestion of some very, very influential citizens. They feel that there's a soft spot in the County administration. You know, old Bill prides himself on paying more attention to people's reactions than to material evidence. Some whimsical eccentricity on his part that's going to get us all into trouble one of these days. You know how it is when word gets around that the crowd in the courthouse has been in office too long. There's always a tendency to make a clean sweep. And that takes in *all* of us."

"What do you expect Walworth to do?" Quinlan asked.

The district attorney smiled. "I expect him to solve this mystery very quickly and very competently, demonstrating to the voters of this County the fact that the old hit-or-miss methods of investigating a crime are as obsolete as the horse and buggy. The modern criminologist uses scientific equipment and streamlined efficiency."

"You mean you're going to use him to show up the sheriff?"

"I mean I'm going to use him to solve the mystery."

"The sheriff won't like that," Quinlan said.

"Of course he won't like it. But there's a murder to be solved, and the County has *some* rights. I certainly trust that *you* have no objections."

"No," Quinlan said, "I haven't any objections."

"Come on in," Medford invited and opened the door of his private office.

Martin Walworth was a short-bodied, heavy-featured man with bushy eyebrows and huge spectacles. His round black pupils were pinpoints of perpetual scrutiny in the center of pale, steady eyes. He didn't get up or shake hands when the district attorney performed the introduction.

"No weapon was found?" Walworth asked after a few preliminaries.

"No weapon," Quinlan admitted.

"The autopsy seems to have been handled in rather a careless manner," Walworth said. "However, I'm hopeful of getting a fairly good description of the murder weapon by an investigation which I shall make personally. There were no fingerprints whatever on the cigarette case?"

"None whatever."

The criminologist's eyes were stern with accusation. "Do I understand that the sheriff picked it up?"

Almost mechanically Quinlan moved the few steps necessary to hold the triangular torn bit of paper over the gouged-out place in the tire.

The mud-stained triangle of paper his wife had carefully saved for him was a perfect pattern, just fitting the hole in the tire.

Quinlan straightened, holding the triangle of paper between the thumb and forefinger of his right hand. The hand seemed strange to him.

Once, when he had been arresting a man charged with some minor crime, the prisoner had unexpectedly whirled and delivered a smashing punch to the side of Quinlan's head. The blow had lashed out so fast and hard that not only had Quinlan failed to see it coming, but the smashing impact had, for the moment, robbed him of all memory. And as his senses had begun to struggle for orientation, he had fancied himself in the midst of a strange world wherein surroundings that should have been familiar failed to have any significance whatever.

Now, in the same way, Quinlan's mind was reeling from the impact of his discovery. It seemed only last week that Beryl had been a baby, getting her first tooth—the worry over whooping cough—the starting of school—blossoming into a young woman—and now this.

Gradually Quinlan's mind reasserted itself. There was Martin Walworth waiting at the courthouse with the district attorney for this triangular piece of paper. Walworth would make a life-size photograph. The *Rockville Gazette* would publish it. Everyone in the community from service-station attendants on down would be looking for an automobile with this triangular gouge in the tread of the right front tire.

His first instinctive desire being to protect Beryl, Quinlan thought of changing the tire and putting on the spare. Then he took a deep breath and let his faith in his daughter assert itself. Surely Beryl could have had no part in a murder! It was simply that there were things that needed explaining, and George Quinlan, man of action, had never been one to postpone that which needed doing. Slowly he turned and walked back to the house.

Beryl was crossing the kitchen as the deputy opened the back door. She glanced up and smiled casually. Then she caught his eyes and stopped in her tracks.

"Where's your mother?"

"Upstairs. She's coming down now. Why, Dad?"

"Come to the front room. I want to talk with you. I don't want her to hear."

Silently Beryl followed her father into the living room. George Quinlan indicated a chair, but Beryl didn't sit down. Instead she remained standing, very trim, very erect, and very white.

"Your car," Quinlan said with a gesture of weariness. "Last night, after the murder, did you go to the Higbee place?"

For a long moment she hesitated, and in that moment Quinlan knew the most awful suspense he had ever experienced. If she should lie to him now, it would rip his soul to shreds.

"Yes," she said finally.

"Why?"

"I was . . . The sheriff telephoned. He asked me to look for you."

George Quinlan ceased to be a father. He was now only a representative of the law, his eyes keeping a steady, insistent pressure on his daughter's mind, his questions probing her thoughts. "What did the sheriff tell you?"

"Told me he'd found a cigarette case. He wanted you to take fingerprints."

"Did he ask you to look for me?"

"He asked me where you were—asked me to try and find you."

"And you went to the Higbee place?"

"Yes."

"Looking for me?"

There was a pause, a pause long enough for George Quinlan to be conscious of his perspiring hands, of the hammering of his heart, but his eyes didn't waver.

"No."

"*Why* did you go there?"

"I went . . . Oh, Dad!" Her lips quivered at the edges, and tears swam into her eyes. Then the mouth became firm. She brushed aside the tears and met her father eye to eye. "I went there because I thought it was Roy's cigarette case."

"Was it?"

"I—I thought so."

"Was it?"

"Apparently not."

"What did you do?"

"I took a chamois skin from the car and wiped every single fingerprint off of it."

"Why?"

"Because . . . because he had called me—and, well, he said it was from Fort Bixling, but I think now it was from San Rodolpho, and I . . . Dad, I don't know *why* I did it. Don't ask me why. I can't tell you. All I know is that I thought I had a chance to protect Roy, and all of a sudden it seemed more important to me to do that than anything else on earth. I didn't care if they killed me, I was going to protect him."

A vast weariness settled on George Quinlan. This was the end of the trail so far as he was concerned. He was discredited, finished. "You say it wasn't Roy's cigarette case after all?"

"Dad, I don't know. I can't understand it. Roy was here this morning. I asked him for a cigarette and he acted just as naturally as could be. He reached into his pocket, took out the silver cigarette case and—and afterwards, when he'd gone, I suddenly realized that I hadn't seen the engraving on it. He'd acted so completely offhand about the whole thing that it had put me off my guard. I—"

"Where's Roy now?"

"At the hotel, I guess. He wanted to clean up and get a short sleep. He wants to come out here a little later."

"Say nothing about this to him," Quinlan said. "Say nothing about it to *anyone*."

"Dad—I'm sorry."

Quinlan looked at her as though she were some stranger in the house.

"Will it make much difference?" she asked.

For twenty years George Quinlan had been trying to stand between Beryl and life, trying to protect her, to ward off the blows that Fate might deal, telling little white lies when he thought those might be necessary to reassure her. Now, looking at her, he suddenly realized that the time for this had passed. She was a woman, not a child, and she had become a woman by reason of her own act.

"Will it, Dad? Will it make much difference?"

"Yes, it will," Quinlan said and walked out, letting it go at that.

As he walked past Beryl's automobile the thought occurred to Quinlan once more to change the tire on her car. He shook it off and walked out to where he had left the car. The door swinging open was a grim reminder of the extent of the gap which existed between his life of only a few minutes ago and the maelstrom of events into which he had been swept.

"George, oh, George!"

His wife was calling from the upstairs window.

Quinlan turned. "Yes, dear?"

"You'll be home for dinner tonight?"

It needed only that homely touch to bring him back to realities. His answer was mechanical. "I don't know, dear—yet. I'll telephone."

"Okay, let me know," she called cheerily.

Quinlan got in the car. A new worry had entered his mind, the thought of what this would mean to Martha. A man might have enough resilience and dogged determination to slug his way through to a comeback, but Martha couldn't take it. As the wife of the deputy she enjoyed a certain position in the social life of the community. People liked her for herself, but in addition there was the recognition of the importance of her husband's position.

Quinlan carefully placed the damning triangle of paper in between the leaves of his notebook. It would hold flat there. It—

It was at that moment a thought struck him.

Changing the tire on Beryl's automobile might or might not stave off discovery, but there was one absolutely certain way by which George Quinlan could give his daughter complete immunity.

Hardly realizing the full significance of what he was doing, Quinlan tore another sheet of paper from the notebook. Seemingly without orders from Quinlan's mind, but working mechanically his fingers shaped a new triangle, a triangle not quite so broad at the base and a little more pointed. He had only to walk into the district attorney's office, hand that new triangle to Martin Walworth and walk out—and Beryl's connection with the murder at the Higbee homestead need never be known.

He started the car and drove directly to the courthouse.

The district attorney's secretary was at her desk. "You may go in. They are expecting you," she said.

Quinlan entered the private office. Martin Walworth had moved over to occupy the district attorney's swivel chair. Edward Lyons, publisher of the *Rockville Gazette*, was seated at the other side of the desk, his pencil sprawling extensive notes on folded newsprint that Quinlan could read over Lyons' shoulder.

Printed on top of one of the sheets, apparently to be used as a headline, were the words: SHERIFF'S SLIPSHOD METHODS MAY RESULT IN MURDERER'S ESCAPE, DECLARES CRIMINOLOGIST.

Rush Medford, his face suffused with smiles, was standing behind Walworth, and Bertram Glasco, puffing contentedly on a cigar, was nodding his head as though not only agreeing with something the criminologist had said, but also signifying his continuing agreement with anything the man might be going to say.

John Farnham, sitting erect in a chair to the right of the criminologist, was watching Walworth with fixed intensity. Leave it to Farnham not to approve entirely of anything or anyone, Quinlan thought. Farnham was a typical dour-faced crusader who would never be happy, never satisfied. A one-time cowboy, he still did a little horse trading in addition to his real-estate business, and Quinlan couldn't help thinking that while he was sanctimoniously honest in his real-estate transactions, his reputation as a horse trader was such that the initiated seldom dealt with him. There had been a bay saddle horse that Farnham had sold Beckett a couple of months ago. Quinlan had seen it in the Higbee place. Farnham had said the horse was twelve, but Quinlan would bet a month's salary it was at least—

"Do you have that piece of paper, George?" Medford asked.

Quinlan opened the notebook. There was, he noticed, just the slightest tremor as his fingers took out the triangular piece of paper which he handed to the district attorney, who in turn passed it across to Walworth.

"That the triangle?" Walworth asked Quinlan, and it seemed to Quinlan that the man's eyes were unnecessarily intense in their boring scrutiny.

Quinlan nodded.

Walworth picked up the piece of paper. He turned it over to look at the other side and then said to Lyons, "Now, this is an excellent example of what I've been talking about. This piece of paper represents the outline of a piece of rubber that has been gouged out of a tire. There are no identification marks on the paper—none whatever. In the first place, the tire pattern should have been preserved with a plaster mold. But unsatisfactory as this paper method is, it's rendered doubly so by the fact that there are no identifying marks on it.

"That triangle of paper should have been initialed by the sheriff and the deputy right on the ground so that there wouldn't have been any possible chance of a mistake or—or of substitution. As it is, it's quite possible the defense attorney will rip the case wide open by claiming that anyone could have substituted another piece of paper in place of the original, and that this piece is one that *was* substituted."

Glasco said hastily, "That's all right, Walworth. The sheriff is slipping, but Quinlan here is all right. He's going to be the next sheriff. We don't want to have any criticism of him. Ain't that right, Ed?"

Edward Lyons, scribbling rapidly with his pencil, nodded emphatically.

Walworth almost contemptuously jerked Rush Medford's desk pen out of its well, handed it to Quinlan, and said, "Write your name or initials on the back of this piece of paper so you can identify it in court."

Quinlan leaned over the desk. The tension of his nerves was such that the initials which came jerking from the point of the pen were an angular travesty of his usual handwriting.

"Now then," Walworth said, "we'll print thousands of perfect facsimiles of this slip of paper and put a copy in the hands of every service station in the County. The original, Mr. Medford, will be carefully preserved where it can't be tampered with."

Quinlan said, "You won't want me any more?"

"Better stick around, George," Glasco told him amiably. "This is really good. Mr. Walworth is analyzing the crime, pointing out just where Bill slipped up on—"

"I've got to see a man," Quinlan apologized. "I'd like to stay, but this visit I've got to make is important."

"Go ahead," Medford said somewhat impatiently. "But just don't talk to anybody about the case, and—don't say anything about this."

Quinlan paused only briefly at the desk of the Palace Hotel. "You have a Roy Jasper here," he said. "What room's he in?"

"Two-o-five. But he's out. He checked in, cleaned up, and went right out again."

"You know him?" Quinlan asked.

"Sure. Talked with him. He'd been up all night, needed a bath and a shave. Said he tried to sleep for a couple of hours, but he couldn't make it—had too much on his mind."

Quinlan phoned his house from the lobby. "Beryl," he said when she answered the telephone, "I want to get in touch with Roy."

"Yes, Dad, I know."

"He isn't there?"

"No, Dad."

"If you hear from him, find out where he is and let me know. If he comes there, get a call through to me right away."

Beryl said with dignity, "If he telephones or if I see him, Dad, I'll tell him that you want to get in touch with him right away, and for him to call you."

"That isn't what I said, " Quinlan said angrily.

"Father, you *can't* doubt Roy. You simply can't do it. If I tell him to call you, I know he will."

There was something in his daughter's voice that left Quinlan feeling strangely helpless. He just didn't know how to cope with this grownup daughter, and he couldn't bring himself to threaten her as he would have threatened any other recalcitrant citizen

He heard Beryl hang up at the other end of the line, and he slowly dropped his own receiver into place.

The *Rockville Gazette* created a sensation when it hit the streets at five o'clock that evening. Headlines screamed across the top of the page: CONSULTING CRIMINOLOGIST CALLED IN BY DISTRICT AT-TORNEY MEDFORD TO SOLVE BAFFLING CASE.

Quinlan noticed that Lyons had toned down his headlines on the interview he had had with Walworth so that they now read: SLIPSHOD METHODS OF LAW-ENFORCEMENT OFFICERS GIVE CRIMINALS GREATEST BREAK, SAYS WALWORTH.

Over on the left was a silhouette, a photograph in actual size of the torn triangular piece of paper that Quinlan had given to Walworth. Accompanying the photograph in bold letters was the caption: CAN THIS BE CUT IN TIRE OF KILLER'S CAR? A boxed-in notice in bold-faced type suggested that each reader of the paper cut out this triangle and watch for a car whose right front tire had a gouged-out place in the tread corresponding with the shape of this piece of paper.

Quinlan glanced through the paper; the vague accusation of the article, the unfair tone of the entire account of the crime itself, only added to his worries.

For the fifth time in an hour he called his house.

The promptness with which Beryl answered the phone showed that she was once more sitting by the telephone, waiting.

"Anything from Roy?" the deputy asked.

"No, Dad."

"Let me know if he calls."

"I'll tell him you want to hear from him," she said.

Quinlan hung up. That interchange of comments between father and daughter had not varied substantially since he had begun calling her at frequent intervals asking for a report.

Sheriff Bill Eldon opened the door to find Quinlan nervously pacing the office, chewing a cigar to shreds.

"Hello, George. Anything new at this end?"

"You've seen the paper."

The sheriff nodded. "Sort of a smear, isn't it?"

"They're really going to town."

"You met Walworth?"

"Yes."

"What sort?"

"I imagine he's very able."

"Cordial?"

Quinlan glanced in the direction of the paper.

The sheriff smiled. "To you, I mean."

Quinlan paced the floor for a few turns, then abruptly whirled to face the sheriff. "Bill," he said, "I've got to tell you something."

"Take it easy," Eldon said.

"Bill, I've put you in a spot. I want to—"

"Nothing to apologize for."

"But I want to tell you about this."

"Won't it keep?"

"No."

"We've got that murder case to work on now, George."

"Well, this is—this has something to do with it, only it's personal."

"If it's personal it'll keep."

Quinlan frowned in exasperation.

"I've got some information," the sheriff went on, talking quickly, his characteristic drawl scarcely noticeable now. "Found out quite a bit about the girl. Got her located and identified. She's an Elizabeth Dow from San Rodolpho, working as cashier in a cafeteria there, and her mother was Elvira Dow. That name mean anything to you, George?"

Quinlan shook his head.

"Didn't to me, either," the sheriff said, "until I got to thinking.

Seems to me I remember that name of Dow. It's now a common name. Thought I'd come back to the office and dig through the files of the local papers. You take the *Register*, George, and I'll take the *Gazette,* and we'll see what we can find. Look through the personal-mention columns—just sort of give them a once-over."

"That'll be almost an endless job," Quinlan protested.

"Oh, it won't take us over two or three hours."

"Two or three hours!" Quinlan stormed. "Here you have a red-hot murder case on your hands, with the district attorney bringing in a consulting criminologist, the cards all stacked against you, The *Gazette* just fairly itching to lift your political scalp, and you talk about looking through the personal columns for two or three hours. Good heavens, man, if it's *that* important why don't you hire some girl to run through them instead of wasting your time?"

"Take it easy, George. Take it easy!" the sheriff drawled. "You know the County doesn't give us the money to hire a girl. It expects us to—"

"Bill, there's something I want to tell you."

"Sure, sure," the sheriff said soothingly, "but let's chase down this name first. I seem to remember it, somebody outside—sort of a Red Cross business. No, that ain't it, either. It's a nurse. That's it! Say, George, ring up the hospital. Ask them if they know anything about a nurse by the name of Dow."

Quinlan reluctantly called the hospital and after a few moments relayed the information to the sheriff. "They don't know of anyone."

"Well, now," the sheriff said, "that's too bad. I had a pretty strong hunch that name of Dow was connected with a nurse. Well, I guess we've got to dig through these columns of personal mention. Don't see what else there is to be done."

"We could—"

Abruptly the door opened. A delegation came trooping into the office, Rush Medford in the lead, Martin Walworth, the criminologist, following behind, then John Farnham, his face a mask of austere self-righteousness, with Bertram Glasco bringing up the rear.

"Sheriff," the district attorney said, "I want you to meet Martin Walworth," and then he added reproachfully, "We've been trying to get in touch with you all afternoon."

"I was out of town," the sheriff said to the district attorney, and put out his hand to the criminologist. "How de do, how are you?"

Walworth's handshake was perfunctory.

The district attorney, in the voice of a lawyer making a prepared speech, said, "Sheriff, this murder at the Higbee place is an important case. This County can't afford to let the murderer get away by slipshod methods. At the behest of influential citizens my office has, therefore, called in Martin Walworth, the famous consulting criminologist."

The sheriff said, "Fine. Who's he consulting with?"

Medford flushed. "That's his title. He's a consulting criminologist."

"Then he doesn't consult with anyone?"

"He solves crimes. He advises police officers how to catch criminals."

"That's fine, Rush. I'm always willing to take advice from anyone—or is he supposed to give me advice?"

"He's supposed to solve the crime," Medford said.

"You mean he isn't going to give advice? He's going to just go ahead and solve it all by himself?"

"He's working with me," Medford said.

"To solve the case," Walworth announced calmly, "and I think I am well on the way to solving it."

"Yes?" the sheriff asked, and then added quite casually, "Sit down, boys."

"I take it," Walworth said, disregarding the invitation, "no attempt was ever made to trace that cigarette case which you found."

"What do you mean, to trace it?"

"To find out who owns it."

"Well, now, I don't know just how you'd go about—"

"Exactly," Walworth interrupted. "However, a moment's thought should have convinced you that the distinctive part of that case was the engraving. It was obviously done by some jeweler who had sold the case. It took only a few minutes to call the local jewelers and find that none of them had done it. Then I got in touch with the Los Angeles police and asked them to cover the better-class jewelry stores and ask the engravers there. It took less than two hours for that to yield results."

"Well, now," the sheriff said, his tone indicating his pleased surprise. "What did you find out?"

"The case was sold by Weed, Sisson and Company to a young woman who paid cash for it. She's about nineteen years of age, rather tall, slender, dark hair, very dark eyes, and has an unusual speaking voice, a clear flute-like quality that is definitely noticeable. She weighs about a hundred and fifteen, and wears a pale pink tourmaline ring on the finger of her left hand."

Quinlan cleared his throat.

"Anything else?" the sheriff asked quickly.

"And we've located the car that left that track, the one that drove out of the Higbee place after *you* had gone away and left the place without any guard and without making a search to see if an automobile was parked anywhere in the field."

"Now wait a minute, son," the sheriff said. "You mean the car that drove in and then turned around and drove out?"

"I mean the car that drove *out*," Walworth said. "At least that's all we know. You saw the tracks going out, and that's all you could and did see. If there were tracks going in, the tracks made by the car going out obliterated them."

"Well, now," the sheriff said with something of a drawl, "we can talk about that later. *I* saw tracks going in and out. But you said you'd located the car."

"Well, we've located the license number of the car, and we've wired to find out the owner of the car. The report will come in here."

"Well, well, you might as well sit down, boys," the sheriff said.

They hesitated a moment; then to the tune of scraping chairs they seated themselves into an inquisitorial half circle.

"How did you locate the car?" Quinlan asked, and his voice sounded dry and husky.

"The *Gazette* hadn't been on the street more than twenty minutes," Lyons announced triumphantly, "until a service-station man rang up. He had sold gas to a car and happened to notice that there was a gouge in the right front tire. He spoke to the young woman who was driving it, a brunette about nineteen with a very sweet clear voice. She said she didn't want to do anything about it, but the owner of the service station thought he might write her a follow-up, and see if he couldn't get a repair job out of it, so he jotted down her license number. It—"

The telephone rang sharply.

Walworth said, "That will be the call, I guess," and reached for the phone.

Bill Eldon's shoulder managed to get in the way. "I'm taking my phone calls," he said, and scooped up the telephone. "Sheriff's office," he announced.

But the voice of Central said, "I have a person-to-person call for Mr. Martin Walworth. Is he there?"

So the sheriff surrendered the telephone with what grace he could and watched the criminologist's face as he heard the metallic sounds which emanated from the receiver.

"You're certain?" Walworth asked into the telephone, then snapped, "Spell it."

After that he hung up and turned to face the others.

"You folks know a Beryl M. Quinlan of 1792 Walnut Drive?" he asked, his eyes, hard and accusing, boring into those of George Quinlan.

It was impossible to miss the collective gasp which emanated from the others.

Martin Walworth continued to stare at George Quinlan. "Is she a relative of *yours*?"

John Farnham answered the question. "A daughter," he said.

The brief period of tense silence which followed that statement was again broken by the strident ringing of the telephone.

Sheriff Eldon picked up the receiver, said, "Sheriff's office, Bill Eldon speaking." Then he said, "Wait a minute . . . What's that? . . .Oh, I see . . . All right . . . Wait for about fifteen or twenty minutes, will you? Okay, goodbye."

The sheriff hung up, saying nothing to any of the others.

Walworth's manner was that of a teacher who is demonstrating some problem which to him is entirely simple, but which is puzzling a roomful of pupils. "May I ask," he inquired sarcastically, "whether this Beryl Quinlan is around nineteen, a rather tall dark girl with dark eyes and an unusually clear voice?"

He needed no answer other than the glances which the men gave each other.

"That, gentlemen," Walworth said, "probably disposes of your murder case. It will account for the B on the cigarette case."

Rush Medford took charge at that point. "I think," he announced, "that, under the circumstances, it would be better if the district attorney's office handled this by itself from this point on," and with that he strode toward the door, jerked it open, and stood to one side, waiting for the others to precede him.

They made a self-righteous little procession as they stalked through the door, but Bertram Glasco couldn't help stopping for one final dig at the discomfited deputy. "This," he said, "probably accounts for something that puzzled me in our conversation last night."

And with that he marched out into the corridor, Rush Medford closed the door with a mild slam, and Bill Eldon and George Quinlan were left alone in the sheriff's office.

"Well," Quinlan said, "I guess that does it."

"Does what?"

"Wipes me out," Quinlan said gloomily. "And I guess I've dragged you down along with me, Bill."

"What did Glasco mean when he said something about last night?" Eldon asked.

"They wanted me to run against you."

"What did you tell them?"

"I told them I wouldn't do it as long as you wanted to run."

"Then what?"

"Then they suggested that the next big case that came along I sort of keep in the background and let you run the thing all by yourself and see if you wouldn't bungle on fingerprints or something."

Eldon nodded. "I thought something like that might be in the wind. And that's why Rush Medford called Martin Walworth in as a special investigator."

Quinlan nodded. He felt so utterly dejected that he didn't want to talk. They'd go and get Beryl. Rush Medford would take her to his office, go through the old rigmarole of advising her she didn't need to talk, call in a court reporter to take down what she said—

The sheriff calmly lifted the telephone, dialed a number. Quinlan slumped in his chair, chin on his chest, heard the sheriff's fatherly voice say, "Hello, Beryl? That you? . . .Where's your car? . . .Go down and get in it quick and go out to the Stanwood Auto Camp, rent a cabin under your own name. Be sure you use your own name and give the correct license number of your car. Then look around. You'll find a friend of yours there. Your father and I will be out in a few minutes, but get started *now*."

The sheriff hung up.

"You can't do that, Bill," Quinlan said.

"Why not?"

"That's compounding a felony. You know the district attorney is on his way to question her concerning what happened, and—"

"Well?" the sheriff asked.

"You can't advise her to avoid him."

The sheriff grinned. "I'm asking her to go where *I* can question her."

"But the district attorney wants to take a statement from her."

"And *I* want to take a statement from her. Rush Medford wants to solve this murder case, and *I* want to solve it. Buck up, George. We're going places. Know who telephoned just a minute ago?"

"No," Quinlan said.

"Roy Jasper. He's out at the Stanwood camp. I told him to wait there."

"I don't see where we can do any good," Quinlan said.

Bill Eldon put a sympathetic hand on the deputy's shoulder. "Now, don't get down in the dumps, George. You can't blame Beryl for what she did. My gosh! I didn't even bother to stop her."

"You didn't bother to do *what*?" Quinlan exclaimed.

"To stop her."

"You mean you *knew*—"

"Of course I did," the sheriff said. "I picked up that cigarette case and recognized it right away."

"You recognized it? How?"

The sheriff said, "On your mantelpiece there's a picture of Roy Jasper. He's in uniform, and if you'll remember he's holding this cigarette case out in front of him half open just as though he was offering someone a cigarette. You can see the engraving on the side clearly."

"Why, yes," Quinlan said. "I do remember now. How did you happen to notice that?"

"Oh, I just notice lots of things," the sheriff said. "It's a habit a man gets when he's been fooling around with crime as long as I have. You see, George, I never had a chance to study up on all this fingerprint business, and things of that sort, and because I don't do so good on those things I have to keep up on other stuff. I always felt that you have to know and understand people in order to make a good officer. It's easier for me to understand people than it is to understand all this scientific stuff about whorls and loops. Now, Beryl isn't going to be mixed up in any murder, and you know it."

"She's mixed up in one now," Quinlan said dejectedly.

Bill Eldon shook his head. "I thought that was Roy's cigarette case," he said, "so I went to a phone and instead of telephoning the coroner's office or the *Gazette* and locating you myself, I phoned Beryl and told her about wanting to get hold of you, and about my finding this cigarette case down there, and that I wanted you to fingerprint it. So then I went back where I could watch, and waited to see what happened."

"What did you have in mind?"

"I wanted to see whether Beryl knew where the cigarette case was. I was very careful to tell her that I found it in the Higbee place and describe it to her, but I didn't tell her *where* in the Higbee place I'd found it."

"And what did she do?"

"Did just what I thought she'd do," the sheriff said. "Drove down there."

"You didn't stop her?"

"No. I saw Beryl drive down, stop her car, open the gate, get in, drive up to the Higbee place, and then she had to do quite a bit of looking around before she found what she wanted.

"Then I watched her drive out and close the gate behind her. I really thought she'd taken the cigarette case with her, but she was too smart for that. She'd just wiped the fingerprints off it and left it."

"She had no right to do that," Quinlan said.

"She didn't, for a fact," the sheriff admitted cheerfully, "but I thought it was best to let her play it that way."

"Why?"

"Because then she'd go to Roy Jasper and get him to tell her just exactly what had happened, and he'd tell *her* where he wouldn't tell either you or me. All I had to be certain of was that Beryl hadn't been in the house when the cigarette case had been dropped. She proved that to me when she had to fumble around looking for it. If she'd gone right to the kitchen where the cigarette case had been left, I'd have had to stop her when she drove out and ask her questions. I'd have hated to do it, too, because Beryl's a nice girl."

Quinlan was having difficulty in adjusting himself to these new developments. "Then you knew before I got there what car it was that had the triangular piece out of the right front tire?"

"Sure."

"Then why did you have me go through all that business of tearing out a piece of paper?"

"Well, George," the sheriff said, "I sort of wanted to see what *you'd* do. That's why I gave *you* that triangular piece of paper to keep. I thought perhaps—"

"Don't think for a minute I wasn't tempted," Quinlan interrupted bitterly. "I even went so far as to tear out a substitute piece of paper. But when it came to a showdown I couldn't use it."

"I know," the sheriff said soothingly. "Well, let's go out to the auto camp and see what's up. I'll call my house first."

Sheriff Eldon called his house. Then, when the answer came, his face winced with displeasure. "Hello, Doris," he said. "Where's Merna? Is she there?...I see, Well, take a message for her, will you? Tell her that I want her to start looking through the personal mentions in the back issues of the papers beginning about six or seven months ago and see if she can find some mention of an Elvira Dow. I think she—"

The sheriff was interrupted by a burst of high-pitched staccato noises which came rattling over the wire.

Slowly the look of annoyance on his face faded to a whimsical smile. "All right, Doris," he said, "I guess it's a good thing to have a gossip in the family after all."

He hung up and grinned at Quinlan. "Looks as though we're getting somewhere, George. That was the old Human Encyclopedia, my sister-in-law, who sticks that long nose of hers into more different business of more different people than you'd ever suspect. She was visiting here when old Higbee died, and she eagerly devoured all the scandal about his common-law marriage to his housekeeper, and all the stink that was raised. Elvira Dow was the nurse who lived at the house for about ten days after Marvin Higbee had his stroke. She was with him up until the time of his death."

"Then this girl who was murdered was—"

"Elvira Dow's daughter. Put that together with the fact that people were zigzagging back and forth around the house looking for something, and we begin to get an answer. We—"

The telephone rang again. Eldon answered, listened to a rasping voice, and said, "So what?" After an interval he slammed the receiver back.

Quinlan looked at him questioningly.

"Rush Medford," the sheriff said. "He's down at your place. Your wife told him Beryl got a call a few minutes ago and then jumped in her jalopy and went tearing out."

Quinlan groaned. "And I suppose he suspects me!"

Eldon grinned. "Come on, son. Kinda looks as though we gotta move fast."

The little group in the cabin at the Stanwood Auto Court talked in low voices.

"All right, Roy," the sheriff said, "I think it's your move."

Roy Jasper shifted his position uneasily. "I didn't want Beryl to know about this," he said. "I suppose I was foolish. After all, there was no reason why—it would have meant explaining and—"

"Go ahead," the sheriff said.

"It began last week," Roy said, "when I was in San Rodolpho on official business. I ate in a cafeteria and—well, the cashier was a good-looking blonde, and I got to passing the time of day with her. I told her I was from Rockville and that I certainly hated to be so close to home without going on up to see my friends, and she laughed and wanted to know whether it was friends, plural, or *a* friend, singular, and we got to chatting."

"Then what?"

"Well, then she asked me about whether I knew Marvin Higbee, and I told her he was dead, and she asked a few questions about the place, and I told her something about the lawsuit. Well—"

"Go ahead," the sheriff said.

"Well, I could see this girl kept wanting to talk about Higbee, and finally she told me the story. Her mother nursed Higbee during his last illness, and then in Colorado her mother became critically ill and sent for the daughter. The daughter was there for a couple of days before the mother died, and the mother told her that Higbee had said to her in effect, 'If anything happens and I shouldn't pull through, you've got to do something for me. He'll pay you for it and pay you well—make him pay. I told him he'd have to pay,' but he wouldn't tell her any more than that, just that she'd be paid well for what she was to do.

"Higbee had had a stroke and it had paralyzed one side. Then the day before he died, he had another stroke and knew he wasn't going to make it. The nurse could see that he wanted to tell her something very badly, but there was always someone else in the room. No one trusted anyone else—people were waiting, watching. The housekeeper kept flitting around, and the doctor was there, in and out, and Carlotta, the man's favorite sister, was there almost constantly, and business associates kept hanging around.

"Finally, in desperation, Higbee said to her, talking apparently with great effort, 'Remember, I said you'd have to do something,' and she nodded, and just then Carlotta came and stood by the bed, and Higbee frowned and said with the effort that talking costs a man who has had a stroke, 'The joke is behind the joker,' and that was all.

"Carlotta kept asking, 'What was that? What about a joker?' But he closed his eyes and pretended he couldn't hear her. But the nurse felt certain that it was a message for her, but she never was able to figure it out. Higbee died the next day, and there was, of course, no further necessity for a nurse.

"Well, Elizabeth kept thinking over what her mother had told her, and after her mother's death she began to wonder if it hadn't been related to something in the house, so she started pumping me about the Higbee place, and I told her all I knew. Elizabeth wanted me to go with her and see if we couldn't find something in the house, but of course she swore me to absolute secrecy.

"Well, it was an adventure, and I was there in San Rodolpho on official business. I got off once to come up and see Beryl, but the rest of the time they held me there so I couldn't go anywhere. Then I went back to Fort Bixling, and then I got this furlough and—well, I'd promised Elizabeth that I'd get in touch with her the first chance I had. So I did, and she insisted that I mustn't call anyone, or let anyone know about what we were going to do. She said she'd drive me up in her car, and that after I'd helped her locate what she wanted I could get in touch with my *friends* up here. I think she was just a little bit hurt that I was so eager to—well, you know."

Beryl nodded.

"So when I left Camp Bixling yesterday morning, I took the bus up to San Rodolpho. I'd telephoned her that I was coming. She met me in the cafeteria. We talked for a while, and then we had some lunch put up, got in her car, and drove up to the old Higbee place. It certainly was a mess. I found that a passkey I'd picked up in a hardware store would work the lock on the side door, and we went in and prowled all around the place."

"Find anything?" the sheriff asked.

Roy said, "At the time I didn't think that we had, but now—well, now I don't know."

The sheriff raised his eyebrows, asking a silent question.

"You see," Roy said, "we were sitting down eating lunch—in

fact, we'd finished lunch and I'd had a cigarette, and I think she had—when all of a sudden we heard a car drive up. Well, you know, there'd been so much trouble among the heirs and, after all, we'd really broken into the place—I'd used a passkey—so we jumped up and ran to the window. It was all covered with cobwebs, but I could vaguely see a car and people coming to the house.

"So I grabbed her hand and we ran away from the window and dashed for the side door. We played hide and seek around there for a while until the people walked around the other side of the house, then we ran out and jumped in her car and drove away."

"You saw those people?"

"Yes, after we'd got out of the house. It was Sam Beckett and John Farnham. They didn't see us. Farnham was evidently selling the place to Beckett. Anyway, I let Elizabeth drive me back to San Rodolpho, and I waited until evening and then telephoned Beryl. I didn't want to tell Beryl that I was in San Rodolpho, so I told her I was just leaving Fort Bixling—and well, that's all there was to it. I stuck around there, took the night bus, and came up here.

"Now, Elizabeth must have uncovered some clue to something she didn't want me to know about. After she took me back to San Rodolpho she must have turned around and driven right back up here. She told me she had a bad headache and was going up to her room and go to bed. And by that time I was thinking of Beryl. Elizabeth had been all right to kill a little time with when I was down where I couldn't see Beryl, but once I could get up here I was kicking myself for the time I'd wasted out of my furlough. When a soldier's in a strange town and is lonely, he'll do anything just to talk with some friendly girl.

"Well, that was it. I'd promised her I'd go up to the Higbee place with her and look it over, and I went, and that's all there was to it as far as I know."

"And you left your cigarette case there?" Beryl asked.

"Yes."

"But you had one the next morning when you—"

Roy said, "I felt miserable about that. You see, Beryl, you sent me the cigarette case for Christmas, but I already had one cigarette case, so I used it for a spare. Then after I lost your— well, I intended to go back to the Higbee place and pick up the one with the engraving on it, but the one I showed you this morning was the spare. It was silver, about the same type as the one you gave me except for the engraving, and I held it so you couldn't see that the engraving wasn't on it. I was afraid that I couldn't explain to you about Elizabeth without you getting sore."

"You mustn't feel that way, Roy—ever."

"I know," he said, "now. But I wasn't sure."

A car drew up outside. The sound of excited voices mingled with hurried steps. A perfunctory knock on the door was followed by a turning of the knob and the influx of an excited group.

"*There* they are!" Lyons proclaimed dramatically.

District Attorney Rush Medford demanded angrily, "What's the idea?"

"Idea of what?" the sheriff drawled innocently.

"Spiriting these people away."

The sheriff's eyebrows went up. "We didn't spirit them anywhere. We're questioning them."

"I'm putting this young man under arrest for the murder of Elizabeth Dow."

"Got any evidence?" the sheriff asked.

"All the evidence in the world. That is, we will have as soon as we check some fingerprints. Beryl Quinlan thought she was wiping all the fingerprints off that cigarette case and she did—off the outside. But what everyone overlooked was the fact that at some time when the case had been empty and the owner was filling it with fresh cigarettes, he left his fingerprints on the *inside*, back of the cigarettes.

"Mr. Walworth very shrewdly deduced he'd find fingerprints there and carefully removed the cigarettes, then dusted the interior of the case, and we got some very fine latents. In my official capacity as district attorney of this County, Sheriff, I order you to take this man into custody."

"Suit yourself, but I'm not going to be the one to swear out the complaint," Bill Eldon drawled.

"*I* will swear out the complaint," Martin Walworth said, but then added hastily, "in the event it appears that this young man's fingerprints check with the latents I found on the inside of the cigarette case."

"We'll determine that in short order," the district attorney said.

They drove to the courthouse. Walworth made prints of Roy Jasper's fingertips. There was no concealing his anxiety as Walworth focused a magnifying glass on the latent prints and then

The sheriff seemed unimpressed to the point of disinterest. His flashlight was exploring the floor. "*One* burnt match," he said. "That's significant."

"I don't get it."

"If you were lighting three cigarettes how many matches would you use?"

Quinlan grinned. "If a good-looking girl was sitting across the table from me I'd use one—wait a minute, I'd use two."

"That's right. But there's only one."

"Then something must have happened to one of the burnt matches. Perhaps a pack rat carried it away."

"Nope," the sheriff drawled. "It ain't that. The way I figure it, the man was a chain smoker. He and the girl sat down here at the table. They had some sandwiches, then they settled down for a smoke. He lit her cigarette and lit his own—one match. After they'd smoked their cigarettes he lit his second one from the stub of the first. The girl only smoked one cigarette. When she'd finished it she took out her lipstick and started to fix up her mouth—and it was then something happened, right at that particular moment."

"How do you fix it as being at that time?"

"Because they jumped up and were startled. The man put his cigarette down on the table and never had a chance to get back to pick it up. It lay there and burned that groove. The woman dropped her lipstick."

"And then?" Quinlan asked.

"And some time after that," the sheriff said, "the girl was found stabbed in a plowed field with no tracks going in either direction, not even her own."

"How long after that?" Quinlan asked.

"That, son," the sheriff said, "is something we've got to find out. By puttin' two and two together, you get an answer, and it don't seem to be the right one."

It began to rain about three in the morning, a fine, misty cold rain. By daylight the tangled grass and weeds of the field were glistening with moisture, and the dark lumps on the ridges of the plowed ground reflected the sullen daylight which filtered through the low bank of clouds.

The bent figures of the sheriff and George Quinlan moved slowly along over the boundary between the grassy field and the freshly plowed earth. With the thoroughgoing patience of veteran trackers they inched their way along, covering every foot of ground.

Daylight was well advanced and the drizzle had stopped when they returned to their point of beginning.

"Well," Quinlan said, "that settles it. No one left this piece of ground after the murder was committed, so the body must have come in from the outside—unless it was dropped from an airplane."

The sheriff straightened. He rolled and lit a cigarette. "I noticed one thing back there in the house, George. You remember where those drapes hang over the door? There's a long braided silk doodad with tassels on it—but there's only one. Shouldn't there be two?"

Quinlan laughed. "Shucks, Bill, the way this place has been left it's lucky there's even one. But there should be two. I've got the same sort of drapes at home."

The sheriff thought for a while. "What do you s'pose frightened those people after they'd just eaten?"

"I'm darned if I know," Quinlan said. "I'm an officer, not a mind reader. It must have been shortly before the murder, and that must have been after dark. Seems strange they'd have been eating sandwiches then. They must have planned to stay all night searching. And speaking of eating, I'm going home, change my wet clothes, and have some breakfast."

"Well, now," the sheriff drawled, "guess *I'll* drop in at a restaurant and—"

"A restaurant!"

"Uh huh. My sister-in-law's stayin' up at my house."

Quinlan laughed. "Come on up with me—no, hang it, if you don't change your wet clothes you'll catch cold. Get up to your house and get into some dry clothes."

The sheriff looked down at his wet trousers, sighed wearily. "Well, I s'pose I've got to."

It was a few minutes before nine when Beryl Quinlan saw Roy Jasper turn the corner and come walking toward the house.

Beryl ran to the door, whipped it open, and dashed down the stairs. Roy saw her coming and flung up his arm in a gesture of greeting. They met at the edge of the sidewalk.

"Roy!"

"Hi, Beryl!"

She gave him her lips in a swift eager kiss, then pulled away.

"Hey," he said, "what's the idea of such a nervous little peck?"

"We may have an audience. Come on, I want to talk with you. When did you leave the fort?"

"Last night—late."

"Been up all night?"

"Just about. Couldn't get a bus until after midnight. Travel sure is heavy these days."

"Where were you when you telephoned me, at the fort?"

"Just outside of the fort, a row of telephone booths there. Why?"

"Oh, just wondering. Let's not go in for a minute. Dad's been out pretty much all night on a case and came home soaking wet, took a hot bath, changed his clothes, and has to go to the office in a minute. The family will engulf you if you go inside. Let's sit out on the porch."

"Suits me," Roy said. "This isn't front-porch weather, though. Been raining here?"

"Just a drizzle. It quit about an hour and a half ago. Let's sit here. How about a cigarette?"

"How about a kiss, baby? We don't have an audience here."

She gave him her lips.

"That's better. What's the matter, honey?"

"Just getting a good look at you. How about the discharge?"

"Don't know yet. Think I may get it."

"And how about my cigarette?"

Roy casually produced a silver cigarette case, snapped the catch with his thumb, opened it, and extended it to Beryl.

"Roy!" she exclaimed.

He glanced up quizzically at the sound of her voice.

"That's the case I gave you for Christmas."

"Sure. What's funny about that?"

"I—I thought perhaps you'd lost it."

His forehead puckered into a puzzled frown. "Now what gave you *that* idea? And do you really want a cigarette?"

"Of course," she said, taking a cigarette.

He took one and lit her cigarette, then his own. He dropped the case back into his pocket, regarding her thoughtfully. "What's the big idea?" he asked.

"I—oh, nothing. Roy, how much did you pay for that telephone call last night?"

He threw back his head and laughed. "I really got even with the telephone company that time," he said. "I let one of the other boys come in and place a call to a nearby town while I was waiting. The rate there is only twenty-five cents. I guess the operator got the calls mixed."

"What happened to the other boy?"

"Don't worry about him," Roy said. "He wouldn't have paid any more than twenty-five cents on *his* call, and they couldn't make him. I got to feeling a little cheap about it afterwards. I hope they don't take it out of the telephone girl's salary, but, honey, you know how it is. I've been stuck so many times when I'd stay in a hotel and put in a call—"

"That wasn't the fault of the telephone company. That was the fault of the girl at the hotel switchboard. She didn't clear the line right away and naturally the telephone company had to charge you for all that extra time."

"Well, he admitted, "I felt cheap about it afterwards, but there was nothing I could do. You see, honey, you were on the line and I didn't want to take time then telling her she'd made a mistake in my favor and having her wait and look up the call. I—"

The door opened. George Quinlan took two or three steps before he caught sight of the couple from the corner of his eye. He whirled almost apprehensively, then laughed nervously and said, "I didn't know you two were out here. Hello, Roy. When did you get in?"

"Just now."

Quinlan came across and shook hands. "Been up all night," he said, "and I'm a little jumpy. Had breakfast?"

"Yes, thanks, had it more than an hour ago."

"There's some coffee on the table. Mrs. Quinlan will be glad to see you."

"We'll be in in a minute," Beryl said, and then smiling at her father said, "Tell Mother, will you?"

That gave the deputy his cue. He said, "I will. See you later, Roy," and went back into the house.

"What's the big case?" Roy asked.

"A murder down at the old Higbee place. I understand she's a girl around my age, blonde, stabbed in the back."

"The old Higbee place?" Jasper asked, frowning.

"Yes. A man named Beckett bought the place and had started to plow. He found the body."

"Beckett?" Roy repeated the name after her as though trying to refresh his recollection. "Oh, yes, Sam Beckett. I know him. What in the world was this girl doing in the old Higbee place?"

"No one knows. They don't seem to have any clue as yet to her identity."

Jasper finished his cigarette. Almost mechanically he opened the cigarette case, took out another, and lit the second cigarette from the end of the first. "Guess that's going to keep your father busy," he said. "How about going in and getting some of that coffee, Beryl?"

Sheriff Bill Eldon propped the *Rockville Morning Register* in front of his coffee cup.

The *Register* had gone to press about two o'clock in the morning, and had relied on large headlines and bold-faced type to obscure the fact that the paper had but few facts concerning the murder.

The editorial attitude of the paper was hostile to the entire County administration and Sheriff Eldon expected no quarter from it. On the other hand, it did a pretty good job of news coverage, although it occasionally slipped some editorial barb into its factual reporting.

Bill Eldon read the account carefully and then slowly reread it in order to give himself that semblance of preoccupation which would curb the conversation of his sister-in-law.

Finally Doris could stand it no longer. She said, "Well, if you ask me, somebody's making an awful fool out of you officers."

The sheriff's silence was a courteous suggestion that no one was asking her.

"Or," Doris went on, "perhaps you're making fools of yourselves."

"Could be," the sheriff admitted laconically.

"Will you kindly tell me, Bill Eldon, how in the name of sense any person can walk over moist, freshly plowed, loamy soil and not leave any footprints?"

"I didn't say it could be done."

"The newspaper says it *has* been done."

"Well, I'm not responsible for what the newspapers say."

"The way they talk about you makes you sound like an old fossil."

"The *Register* is on the opposite side of the political fence."

"Well, the *Gazette* doesn't seem to be putting you up on any pedestal."

"It won't be out until tonight."

"I'm not talking about this case. I'm talking about the way they've been writing you up lately."

"They're friendly."

"Well, you'd better watch out for friends like that."

The sheriff was silent.

"It *does* seem to me," Doris went on exasperatedly, "that if you had more git-up-an'-git you'd command more respect."

The sheriff grinned. "You don't get respect from the opposite political party—not publicly and in print, anyway. If you move along slow and easy, you're an old fossil. If you have git-up-an'-git you're trying to cover your incompetence behind a smokescreen of hysterical activity."

There was a moment of welcome silence while Doris thought this over. "Well," she demanded at length, "who *is* this girl?"

"We don't know."

"What are you doing to find out?"

"We've got a couple of clues we're working on."

"What clues?"

"Cleaning marks on her jacket and skirt, the name of a store sewed inside the jacket."

"A local store?"

"No, one in San Rodolpho."

The sheriff's wife interposed to say quietly, "Bill, you want me to send that suit out to be cleaned and pressed?"

"Please."

"How soon do you want it back?"

"Soon as I can get it."

"You going to get some sleep today?"

"Afraid I'll have to keep going today. I—"

The telephone rang.

The sheriff went to the phone. He heard a woman's voice say, "Long-distance call from San Rodolpho," and then the voice of Everett Gilmer, the chief of police in San Rodolpho. "Hello, Bill. Think I've got your party located. The Acme Cleaners has a record of cleaning the jacket. The girl's name is Elizabeth Dow. Does that mean anything to you?"

"Not a thing. She live there?"

"Apparently. We have an address in an apartment house. She's moved from there, but we're tracing her. The description fits. Want to come down?"

The sheriff hesitated a moment, then said, "Okay, I'll be down. See what you can find out and have it ready for me by the time I get there. I'll stop by the courthouse and pick up some photographs."

The sheriff hung up the telephone and glanced over at the table. Seeing the alert angle at which the head of his sister-in-law was cocked, he said suddenly, "I've got to rush out. I'll be back this evening."

"Where are you going?" Doris demanded so eagerly that the words all ran together into one continuous rattle of sound.

"Out," the sheriff said.

Everett K. Gilmer, chief of police of San Rodolpho, was a big bluff man whose twinkling eyes radiated cordiality to brother officers, but could assume an ominous hardness when scrutinizing prisoners. He said to Bill Eldon, "Well, Sheriff, I've got a line on her. If you've got some photos we might just check with someone who can make an identification."

"Who you got?"

"Woman who runs the apartment house where she had an apartment for a while. When she moved she left a forwarding address. But I thought we'd better check up first with someone who can make an absolute identification. If she's the one I've got quite a lot on her. And I think she's the one."

"Let's go," the sheriff agreed.

They drove to a frame house that had at one time been an example of three-storied prosperity, but with the spread of the business area it had now been turned into an apartment house.

The heavy-set woman who ran the place promptly identified the photographs which Sheriff Eldon produced.

"That's the girl. That's Elizabeth. What's happened to *her?*"

"She was killed."

"How?"

"Stabbed."

"Good heavens! And such a nice girl, too!"

"Any idea who might have done it? Enemies or anything of that sort?"

"No. While she was here she was just as quiet and well-behaved as anyone could ask."

"Know anything about her friends or relatives?"

"No, I don't. I took over the place just before she moved out and—"

"We got some more recent stuff lined up, Bill," Gilmer interposed. "Just wanted to make sure she was the party before I started following the other trails."

"Her mother had died just before she moved out," the apartment manager volunteered, "somewhere in—now, let me see. I think it was somewhere in Colorado. I remember she got a wire saying her mother was very low and she flew out, and then wrote me that her mother had passed away and that she'd stay for the funeral and move to another apartment when she got back, and she sent me two weeks' rent and asked if that would be all right."

"Know where that letter is?"

"I burned it."

"About when was this?"

"Five or six months ago. I can look up the date when she left if you want."

"I already have that," Gilmer said to the sheriff. "It was in August."

"That's right," the woman said. "I think it was August."

Bill Eldon nodded to Gilmer. "Let's go, Everett."

They went to the telegraph office and wired the Denver police to consult statistical records and rush any information concerning a woman by the name of Dow who had died in Colorado within the last few months.

Then Chief Gilmer and Bill Eldon spent a couple of hours plodding along in the dull monotony of routine legwork, tracing Elizabeth Dow from one lodging house to another, finding where she had been employed and locating friends who had known her.

From this scattered pattern of information the sheriff and Gilmer pieced together a mosaic showing a clear picture of a young woman, vivacious, intelligent, alert, a steady, dependable worker, a loyal friend filled with the joy of life, yet respecting herself and commanding the respect of her friends. There had been one or two boy friends, but for the most part she had preferred a group of intimates to the more intimate companionship of boy friends. She had been employed as a cashier in a cafeteria. Her nimble fingers, quick eyes, and winning personality had made for adept efficiency as well as for popularity with customers. The day before had been her day off, and about ten o'clock she had been seen with a young man who was strange to the girl's set, although he had been seen with her off and on during the past week. The couple had sat for half an hour talking earnestly at a table in the cafeteria. And then Elizabeth Dow had got a cardboard container and put up a lunch—roast beef sandwiches, deviled eggs, crisp lettuce, and pie. Then she and the young man, a tall dark chap in Army uniform, had left the cafeteria. That had been around eleven. Neither one had been seen since.

At this point in the investigation a wire came in from the Denver police:

ELVIRA DOW AGED FIFTY-SIX DIED CORONARY THROMBOSIS AUGUST 23RD, BURIED HERE. FUNERAL ARRANGEMENTS MADE BY DAUGHTER ELIZABETH WHO REGISTERED HOTEL GIVING ADDRESS YOUR CITY.

"Well, Gilmer said, "that's all there is to it. Find the man who was with her and you've got the murderer. You say there was waxed paper on the table in that old house?"

"That's right."

"Find this chap in uniform. That'll be all there is to it."

The sheriff reached for his battered sombrero and put it on. He started for the door, and then paused to regard the chief of police with thought-puckered eyes. "You know, Everett," he said, "it *may* not be that simple. When you've been in office as long as I have you get so you pay more attention to people and less to clues."

Rush Medford, the district attorney, stepped out from his private office to receive George Quinlan.

"Hello, George. I asked you to come up here because I wanted to talk with you—confidentially."

Quinlan glanced significantly at the unlocked door of the reception office, then at the closed door of Medford's private office. Medford, lowering his voice, went on hastily, "I have a man waiting in there, George. I want you to meet him. I want you to give him every bit of help you can. His name's Walworth—Martin Walworth. Ever hear of him?"

Quinlan shook his head.

"Famous all over the state as a criminologist. He—"

"Oh, yes! I've heard of *him*. I place him now."

The district attorney said confidentially, "I'm calling him in,

George, at the suggestion of some very, very influential citizens. They feel that there's a soft spot in the County administration. You know, old Bill prides himself on paying more attention to people's reactions than to material evidence. Some whimsical eccentricity on his part that's going to get us all into trouble one of these days. You know how it is when word gets around that the crowd in the courthouse has been in office too long. There's always a tendency to make a clean sweep. And that takes in *all* of us."

"What do you expect Walworth to do?" Quinlan asked.

The district attorney smiled. "I expect him to solve this mystery very quickly and very competently, demonstrating to the voters of this County the fact that the old hit-or-miss methods of investigating a crime are as obsolete as the horse and buggy. The modern criminologist uses scientific equipment and streamlined efficiency."

"You mean you're going to use him to show up the sheriff?"

"I mean I'm going to use him to solve the mystery."

"The sheriff won't like that," Quinlan said.

"Of course he won't like it. But there's a murder to be solved, and the County has *some* rights. I certainly trust that *you* have no objections."

"No," Quinlan said, "I haven't any objections."

"Come on in," Medford invited and opened the door of his private office.

Martin Walworth was a short-bodied, heavy-featured man with bushy eyebrows and huge spectacles. His round black pupils were pinpoints of perpetual scrutiny in the center of pale, steady eyes. He didn't get up or shake hands when the district attorney performed the introduction.

"No weapon was found?" Walworth asked after a few preliminaries.

"No weapon," Quinlan admitted.

"The autopsy seems to have been handled in rather a careless manner," Walworth said. "However, I'm hopeful of getting a fairly good description of the murder weapon by an investigation which I shall make personally. There were no fingerprints whatever on the cigarette case?"

"None whatever."

The criminologist's eyes were stern with accusation. "Do I understand that the sheriff picked it up?"

"He said he picked it up."

"But there were *no* fingerprints?"

"None."

"Not latents that were smudged?"

"No. There were none."

Walworth grunted. "Then someone wiped it," he said, "wiped it clean—*after* the sheriff picked it up."

"Looked as though it might have been wiped with something like a chamois skin, polished as smooth and slick as a whistle," Quinlan admitted.

"*After* the sheriff picked it up."

Quinlan nodded. "I guess it has to be that way."

"But you didn't say so," the district attorney accused, "not until after Walworth pointed it out."

"I didn't volunteer any suggestions. The fact speaks for itself," Quinlan said.

Walworth grunted, "And there were *no* tracks in the soft soil?"

"No tracks."

"That, manifestly, is impossible."

"You can see the photographs—"

"Photographs, bah! They are taken with a synchronized flash. That makes the picture flat as a pancake. The lighting should have been scientifically controlled."

Quinlan said nothing.

"Obviously," Walworth went on, "the fact in itself is impossible. Therefore someone is lying It may be this Beckett."

"It may be," Quinlan admitted.

The district attorney interposed hastily, "Here in the country where a good many people know each other and—well, you have to be a little careful, you know, Mr. Walworth. Political consideration as well as a person's integrity—"

"I understand," Walworth said. "Is there any other evidence?"

Quinlan told him about the car which had driven into the field after the tractor had made its last trip out.

Walworth digested that information with the profound expression of a deep thinker. "This piece that was gouged out of the right front tire," he said, "you say you used a piece of paper to get the outline of that?"

"Yes."

"Where is that paper?"

Almost involuntarily, Quinlan's hand dropped to his pocket.

Then he remembered. The triangular piece of paper had been in the pocket of the wet suit he had taken off to have sent to the cleaner. Because the paper had no weight, no bulk, he had overlooked it. To confess his negligence in this was unthinkable. He tried to keep his voice casual.

"I have it at home."

Walworth's comment was short and to the point.

"Get it," he said, and then added disgustedly, "What a slipshod way of identifying a tire!"

Quinlan parked his car in front of his house and because he intended to start back for the courthouse almost at once, left the door open.

He walked across the sidewalk, turned to the right on the smaller walk which skirted the house, and went around to the back.

He entered quietly and climbed the stairs to his room. He wondered if his wife had made a careful search of his pockets in preparing the wet suit for the cleaners. If she hadn't, could he get hold of the suit before the bit of paper was ruined?

Quinlan's pulse gave an involuntary reaction to the relief he felt as he looked at the place on the top of his dresser which was reserved for his personal belongings. Every minute since his talk with the criminologist had been a thought-tortured nightmare of apprehension that the piece of paper might have been irrevocably lost. But there it was, lying on the dresser, a mud-soiled triangular slip of paper, silent tribute to the thorough-going loyalty of a steadfast helpmeet.

Quinlan picked up the paper, turned, and walked quietly back down the stairs.

From the living room he heard Beryl's clear voice, remarkable for its low-pitched carrying power, saying into the telephone, "Will you *please* give me the long-distance rate to San Rodolpho—after seven o'clock at night, please . . . Twenty-five cents for three minutes? . . .Thank you, Operator, *very* much."

Quinlan left the house by the back door. He noticed that his daughter's car was parked in front of the garage—a jalopy she had picked up herself a couple of years ago.

She should sell that car, the deputy thought, looking at it without quite seeing it. Then a sudden discovery jarred George Quinlan's mind into a new line of activity. He stood regarding a triangular nick in the right front tire, his eyes locked in a stare of incredulous dismay.

Almost mechanically Quinlan moved the few steps necessary to hold the triangular torn bit of paper over the gouged-out place in the tire.

The mud-stained triangle of paper his wife had carefully saved for him was a perfect pattern, just fitting the hole in the tire.

Quinlan straightened, holding the triangle of paper between the thumb and forefinger of his right hand. The hand seemed strange to him.

Once, when he had been arresting a man charged with some minor crime, the prisoner had unexpectedly whirled and delivered a smashing punch to the side of Quinlan's head. The blow had lashed out so fast and hard that not only had Quinlan failed to see it coming, but the smashing impact had, for the moment, robbed him of all memory. And as his senses had begun to struggle for orientation, he had fancied himself in the midst of a strange world wherein surroundings that should have been familiar failed to have any significance whatever.

Now, in the same way, Quinlan's mind was reeling from the impact of his discovery. It seemed only last week that Beryl had been a baby, getting her first tooth—the worry over whooping cough—the starting of school—blossoming into a young woman—and now this.

Gradually Quinlan's mind reasserted itself. There was Martin Walworth waiting at the courthouse with the district attorney for this triangular piece of paper. Walworth would make a life-size photograph. The *Rockville Gazette* would publish it. Everyone in the community from service-station attendants on down would be looking for an automobile with this triangular gouge in the tread of the right front tire.

His first instinctive desire being to protect Beryl, Quinlan thought of changing the tire and putting on the spare. Then he took a deep breath and let his faith in his daughter assert itself. Surely Beryl could have had no part in a murder! It was simply that there were things that needed explaining, and George Quinlan, man of action, had never been one to postpone that which needed doing. Slowly he turned and walked back to the house.

Beryl was crossing the kitchen as the deputy opened the back door. She glanced up and smiled casually. Then she caught his eyes and stopped in her tracks.

"Where's your mother?"

"Upstairs. She's coming down now. Why, Dad?"

"Come to the front room. I want to talk with you. I don't want her to hear."

Silently Beryl followed her father into the living room. George Quinlan indicated a chair, but Beryl didn't sit down. Instead she remained standing, very trim, very erect, and very white.

"Your car," Quinlan said with a gesture of weariness. "Last night, after the murder, did you go to the Higbee place?"

For a long moment she hesitated, and in that moment Quinlan knew the most awful suspense he had ever experienced. If she should lie to him now, it would rip his soul to shreds.

"Yes," she said finally.

"Why?"

"I was . . . The sheriff telephoned. He asked me to look for you."

George Quinlan ceased to be a father. He was now only a representative of the law, his eyes keeping a steady, insistent pressure on his daughter's mind, his questions probing her thoughts. "What did the sheriff tell you?"

"Told me he'd found a cigarette case. He wanted you to take fingerprints."

"Did he ask you to look for me?"

"He asked me where you were—asked me to try and find you."

"And you went to the Higbee place?"

"Yes."

"Looking for me?"

There was a pause, a pause long enough for George Quinlan to be conscious of his perspiring hands, of the hammering of his heart, but his eyes didn't waver.

"No."

"*Why* did you go there?"

"I went . . . Oh, Dad!" Her lips quivered at the edges, and tears swam into her eyes. Then the mouth became firm. She brushed aside the tears and met her father eye to eye. "I went there because I thought it was Roy's cigarette case."

"Was it?"

"I—I thought so."

"Was it?"

"Apparently not."

"What did you do?"

"I took a chamois skin from the car and wiped every single fingerprint off of it."

"Why?"

"Because . . . because he had called me—and, well, he said it was from Fort Bixling, but I think now it was from San Rodolpho, and I . . . Dad, I don't know *why* I did it. Don't ask me why. I can't tell you. All I know is that I thought I had a chance to protect Roy, and all of a sudden it seemed more important to me to do that than anything else on earth. I didn't care if they killed me, I was going to protect him."

A vast weariness settled on George Quinlan. This was the end of the trail so far as he was concerned. He was discredited, finished. "You say it wasn't Roy's cigarette case after all?"

"Dad, I don't know. I can't understand it. Roy was here this morning. I asked him for a cigarette and he acted just as naturally as could be. He reached into his pocket, took out the silver cigarette case and—and afterwards, when he'd gone, I suddenly realized that I hadn't seen the engraving on it. He'd acted so completely offhand about the whole thing that it had put me off my guard. I—"

"Where's Roy now?"

"At the hotel, I guess. He wanted to clean up and get a short sleep. He wants to come out here a little later."

"Say nothing about this to him," Quinlan said. "Say nothing about it to *anyone.*"

"Dad—I'm sorry."

Quinlan looked at her as though she were some stranger in the house.

"Will it make much difference?" she asked.

For twenty years George Quinlan had been trying to stand between Beryl and life, trying to protect her, to ward off the blows that Fate might deal, telling little white lies when he thought those might be necessary to reassure her. Now, looking at her, he suddenly realized that the time for this had passed. She was a woman, not a child, and she had become a woman by reason of her own act.

"Will it, Dad? Will it make much difference?"

"Yes, it will," Quinlan said and walked out, letting it go at that.

As he walked past Beryl's automobile the thought occurred to Quinlan once more to change the tire on her car. He shook it off and walked out to where he had left the car. The door swinging open was a grim reminder of the extent of the gap which existed between his life of only a few minutes ago and the maelstrom of events into which he had been swept.

"George, oh, George!"

His wife was calling from the upstairs window.

Quinlan turned. "Yes, dear?"

"You'll be home for dinner tonight?"

It needed only that homely touch to bring him back to realities. His answer was mechanical. "I don't know, dear—yet. I'll telephone."

"Okay, let me know," she called cheerily.

Quinlan got in the car. A new worry had entered his mind, the thought of what this would mean to Martha. A man might have enough resilience and dogged determination to slug his way through to a comeback, but Martha couldn't take it. As the wife of the deputy she enjoyed a certain position in the social life of the community. People liked her for herself, but in addition there was the recognition of the importance of her husband's position.

Quinlan carefully placed the damning triangle of paper in between the leaves of his notebook. It would hold flat there. It—

It was at that moment a thought struck him.

Changing the tire on Beryl's automobile might or might not stave off discovery, but there was one absolutely certain way by which George Quinlan could give his daughter complete immunity.

Hardly realizing the full significance of what he was doing, Quinlan tore another sheet of paper from the notebook. Seemingly without orders from Quinlan's mind, but working mechanically his fingers shaped a new triangle, a triangle not quite so broad at the base and a little more pointed. He had only to walk into the district attorney's office, hand that new triangle to Martin Walworth and walk out—and Beryl's connection with the murder at the Higbee homestead need never be known.

He started the car and drove directly to the courthouse.

The district attorney's secretary was at her desk. "You may go in. They are expecting you," she said.

Quinlan entered the private office. Martin Walworth had moved over to occupy the district attorney's swivel chair. Edward Lyons, publisher of the *Rockville Gazette*, was seated at the other side of the desk, his pencil sprawling extensive notes on folded newsprint that Quinlan could read over Lyons' shoulder.

Printed on top of one of the sheets, apparently to be used as a headline, were the words: SHERIFF'S SLIPSHOD METHODS MAY RESULT IN MURDERER'S ESCAPE, DECLARES CRIMINOLOGIST.

Rush Medford, his face suffused with smiles, was standing behind Walworth, and Bertram Glasco, puffing contentedly on a cigar, was nodding his head as though not only agreeing with something the criminologist had said, but also signifying his continuing agreement with anything the man might be going to say.

John Farnham, sitting erect in a chair to the right of the criminologist, was watching Walworth with fixed intensity. Leave it to Farnham not to approve entirely of anything or anyone, Quinlan thought. Farnham was a typical dour-faced crusader who would never be happy, never satisfied. A one-time cowboy, he still did a little horse trading in addition to his real-estate business, and Quinlan couldn't help thinking that while he was sanctimoniously honest in his real-estate transactions, his reputation as a horse trader was such that the initiated seldom dealt with him. There had been a bay saddle horse that Farnham had sold Beckett a couple of months ago. Quinlan had seen it in the Higbee place. Farnham had said the horse was twelve, but Quinlan would bet a month's salary it was at least—

"Do you have that piece of paper, George?" Medford asked.

Quinlan opened the notebook. There was, he noticed, just the slightest tremor as his fingers took out the triangular piece of paper which he handed to the district attorney, who in turn passed it across to Walworth.

"That the triangle?" Walworth asked Quinlan, and it seemed to Quinlan that the man's eyes were unnecessarily intense in their boring scrutiny.

Quinlan nodded.

Walworth picked up the piece of paper. He turned it over to look at the other side and then said to Lyons, "Now, this is an excellent example of what I've been talking about. This piece of paper represents the outline of a piece of rubber that has been gouged out of a tire. There are no identification marks on the paper—none whatever. In the first place, the tire pattern should have been preserved with a plaster mold. But unsatisfactory as this paper method is, it's rendered doubly so by the fact that there are no identifying marks on it.

"That triangle of paper should have been initialed by the sheriff and the deputy right on the ground so that there wouldn't have been any possible chance of a mistake or—or of substitution. As it is, it's quite possible the defense attorney will rip the case wide open by claiming that anyone could have substituted another piece of paper in place of the original, and that this piece is one that *was* substituted."

Glasco said hastily, "That's all right, Walworth. The sheriff is slipping, but Quinlan here is all right. He's going to be the next sheriff. We don't want to have any criticism of him. Ain't that right, Ed?"

Edward Lyons, scribbling rapidly with his pencil, nodded emphatically.

Walworth almost contemptuously jerked Rush Medford's desk pen out of its well, handed it to Quinlan, and said, "Write your name or initials on the back of this piece of paper so you can identify it in court."

Quinlan leaned over the desk. The tension of his nerves was such that the initials which came jerking from the point of the pen were an angular travesty of his usual handwriting.

"Now then," Walworth said, "we'll print thousands of perfect facsimiles of this slip of paper and put a copy in the hands of every service station in the County. The original, Mr. Medford, will be carefully preserved where it can't be tampered with."

Quinlan said, "You won't want me any more?"

"Better stick around, George," Glasco told him amiably. "This is really good. Mr. Walworth is analyzing the crime, pointing out just where Bill slipped up on—"

"I've got to see a man," Quinlan apologized. "I'd like to stay, but this visit I've got to make is important."

"Go ahead," Medford said somewhat impatiently. "But just don't talk to anybody about the case, and—don't say anything about this."

Quinlan paused only briefly at the desk of the Palace Hotel. "You have a Roy Jasper here," he said. "What room's he in?"

"Two-o-five. But he's out. He checked in, cleaned up, and went right out again."

"You know him?" Quinlan asked.

"Sure. Talked with him. He'd been up all night, needed a bath and a shave. Said he tried to sleep for a couple of hours, but he couldn't make it—had too much on his mind."

Quinlan phoned his house from the lobby. "Beryl," he said when she answered the telephone, "I want to get in touch with Roy."

"Yes, Dad, I know."

"He isn't there?"

"No, Dad."

"If you hear from him, find out where he is and let me know. If he comes there, get a call through to me right away."

Beryl said with dignity, "If he telephones or if I see him, Dad, I'll tell him that you want to get in touch with him right away, and for him to call you."

"That isn't what I said, " Quinlan said angrily.

"Father, you *can't* doubt Roy. You simply can't do it. If I tell him to call you, I know he will."

There was something in his daughter's voice that left Quinlan feeling strangely helpless. He just didn't know how to cope with this grownup daughter, and he couldn't bring himself to threaten her as he would have threatened any other recalcitrant citizen

He heard Beryl hang up at the other end of the line, and he slowly dropped his own receiver into place.

The *Rockville Gazette* created a sensation when it hit the streets at five o'clock that evening. Headlines screamed across the top of the page: CONSULTING CRIMINOLOGIST CALLED IN BY DISTRICT AT-TORNEY MEDFORD TO SOLVE BAFFLING CASE.

Quinlan noticed that Lyons had toned down his headlines on the interview he had had with Walworth so that they now read: SLIPSHOD METHODS OF LAW-ENFORCEMENT OFFICERS GIVE CRIMINALS GREATEST BREAK, SAYS WALWORTH.

Over on the left was a silhouette, a photograph in actual size of the torn triangular piece of paper that Quinlan had given to Walworth. Accompanying the photograph in bold letters was the caption: CAN THIS BE CUT IN TIRE OF KILLER'S CAR? A boxed-in notice in bold-faced type suggested that each reader of the paper cut out this triangle and watch for a car whose right front tire had a gouged-out place in the tread corresponding with the shape of this piece of paper.

Quinlan glanced through the paper; the vague accusation of the article, the unfair tone of the entire account of the crime itself, only added to his worries.

For the fifth time in an hour he called his house.

The promptness with which Beryl answered the phone showed that she was once more sitting by the telephone, waiting.

"Anything from Roy?" the deputy asked.

"No, Dad."

"Let me know if he calls."

"I'll tell him you want to hear from him," she said.

Quinlan hung up. That interchange of comments between father and daughter had not varied substantially since he had begun calling her at frequent intervals asking for a report.

Sheriff Bill Eldon opened the door to find Quinlan nervously pacing the office, chewing a cigar to shreds.

"Hello, George. Anything new at this end?"

"You've seen the paper."

The sheriff nodded. "Sort of a smear, isn't it?"

"They're really going to town."

"You met Walworth?"

"Yes."

"What sort?"

"I imagine he's very able."

"Cordial?"

Quinlan glanced in the direction of the paper.

The sheriff smiled. "To you, I mean."

Quinlan paced the floor for a few turns, then abruptly whirled to face the sheriff. "Bill," he said, "I've got to tell you something."

"Take it easy," Eldon said.

"Bill, I've put you in a spot. I want to—"

"Nothing to apologize for."

"But I want to tell you about this."

"Won't it keep?"

"No."

"We've got that murder case to work on now, George."

"Well, this is—this has something to do with it, only it's personal."

"If it's personal it'll keep."

Quinlan frowned in exasperation.

"I've got some information," the sheriff went on, talking quickly, his characteristic drawl scarcely noticeable now. "Found out quite a bit about the girl. Got her located and identified. She's an Elizabeth Dow from San Rodolpho, working as cashier in a cafeteria there, and her mother was Elvira Dow. That name mean anything to you, George?"

Quinlan shook his head.

"Didn't to me, either," the sheriff said, "until I got to thinking.

Seems to me I remember that name of Dow. It's now a common name. Thought I'd come back to the office and dig through the files of the local papers. You take the *Register*, George, and I'll take the *Gazette,* and we'll see what we can find. Look through the personal-mention columns—just sort of give them a once-over."

"That'll be almost an endless job," Quinlan protested.

"Oh, it won't take us over two or three hours."

"Two or three hours!" Quinlan stormed. "Here you have a red-hot murder case on your hands, with the district attorney bringing in a consulting criminologist, the cards all stacked against you, The *Gazette* just fairly itching to lift your political scalp, and you talk about looking through the personal columns for two or three hours. Good heavens, man, if it's *that* important why don't you hire some girl to run through them instead of wasting your time?"

"Take it easy, George. Take it easy!" the sheriff drawled. "You know the County doesn't give us the money to hire a girl. It expects us to—"

"Bill, there's something I want to tell you."

"Sure, sure," the sheriff said soothingly, "but let's chase down this name first. I seem to remember it, somebody outside—sort of a Red Cross business. No, that ain't it, either. It's a nurse. That's it! Say, George, ring up the hospital. Ask them if they know anything about a nurse by the name of Dow."

Quinlan reluctantly called the hospital and after a few moments relayed the information to the sheriff. "They don't know of anyone."

"Well, now," the sheriff said, "that's too bad. I had a pretty strong hunch that name of Dow was connected with a nurse. Well, I guess we've got to dig through these columns of personal mention. Don't see what else there is to be done."

"We could—"

Abruptly the door opened. A delegation came trooping into the office, Rush Medford in the lead, Martin Walworth, the criminologist, following behind, then John Farnham, his face a mask of austere self-righteousness, with Bertram Glasco bringing up the rear.

"Sheriff," the district attorney said, "I want you to meet Martin Walworth," and then he added reproachfully, "We've been trying to get in touch with you all afternoon."

"I was out of town," the sheriff said to the district attorney, and put out his hand to the criminologist. "How de do, how are you?" Walworth's handshake was perfunctory.

The district attorney, in the voice of a lawyer making a prepared speech, said, "Sheriff, this murder at the Higbee place is an important case. This County can't afford to let the murderer get away by slipshod methods. At the behest of influential citizens my office has, therefore, called in Martin Walworth, the famous consulting criminologist."

The sheriff said, "Fine. Who's he consulting with?"

Medford flushed. "That's his title. He's a consulting criminologist."

"Then he doesn't consult with anyone?"

"He solves crimes. He advises police officers how to catch criminals."

"That's fine, Rush. I'm always willing to take advice from anyone—or is he supposed to give me advice?"

"He's supposed to solve the crime," Medford said.

"You mean he isn't going to give advice? He's going to just go ahead and solve it all by himself?"

"He's working with me," Medford said.

"To solve the case," Walworth announced calmly, "and I think I am well on the way to solving it."

"Yes?" the sheriff asked, and then added quite casually, "Sit down, boys."

"I take it," Walworth said, disregarding the invitation, "no attempt was ever made to trace that cigarette case which you found."

"What do you mean, to trace it?"

"To find out who owns it."

"Well, now, I don't know just how you'd go about—"

"Exactly," Walworth interrupted. "However, a moment's thought should have convinced you that the distinctive part of that case was the engraving. It was obviously done by some jeweler who had sold the case. It took only a few minutes to call the local jewelers and find that none of them had done it. Then I got in touch with the Los Angeles police and asked them to cover the better-class jewelry stores and ask the engravers there. It took less than two hours for that to yield results."

"Well, now," the sheriff said, his tone indicating his pleased surprise. "What did you find out?"

"The case was sold by Weed, Sisson and Company to a young woman who paid cash for it. She's about nineteen years of age, rather tall, slender, dark hair, very dark eyes, and has an unusual speaking voice, a clear flute-like quality that is definitely noticeable. She weighs about a hundred and fifteen, and wears a pale pink tourmaline ring on the finger of her left hand."

Quinlan cleared his throat.

"Anything else?" the sheriff asked quickly.

"And we've located the car that left that track, the one that drove out of the Higbee place after *you* had gone away and left the place without any guard and without making a search to see if an automobile was parked anywhere in the field."

"Now wait a minute, son," the sheriff said. "You mean the car that drove in and then turned around and drove out?"

"I mean the car that drove *out*," Walworth said. "At least that's all we know. You saw the tracks going out, and that's all you could and did see. If there were tracks going in, the tracks made by the car going out obliterated them."

"Well, now," the sheriff said with something of a drawl, "we can talk about that later. *I* saw tracks going in and out. But you said you'd located the car."

"Well, we've located the license number of the car, and we've wired to find out the owner of the car. The report will come in here."

"Well, well, you might as well sit down, boys," the sheriff said.

They hesitated a moment; then to the tune of scraping chairs they seated themselves into an inquisitorial half circle.

"How did you locate the car?" Quinlan asked, and his voice sounded dry and husky.

"The *Gazette* hadn't been on the street more than twenty minutes," Lyons announced triumphantly, "until a service-station man rang up. He had sold gas to a car and happened to notice that there was a gouge in the right front tire. He spoke to the young woman who was driving it, a brunette about nineteen with a very sweet clear voice. She said she didn't want to do anything about it, but the owner of the service station thought he might write her a follow-up, and see if he couldn't get a repair job out of it, so he jotted down her license number. It—"

The telephone rang sharply.

Walworth said, "That will be the call, I guess," and reached for the phone.

Bill Eldon's shoulder managed to get in the way. "I'm taking my phone calls," he said, and scooped up the telephone. "Sheriff's office," he announced.

But the voice of Central said, "I have a person-to-person call for Mr. Martin Walworth. Is he there?"

So the sheriff surrendered the telephone with what grace he could and watched the criminologist's face as he heard the metallic sounds which emanated from the receiver.

"You're certain?" Walworth asked into the telephone, then snapped, "Spell it."

After that he hung up and turned to face the others.

"You folks know a Beryl M. Quinlan of 1792 Walnut Drive?" he asked, his eyes, hard and accusing, boring into those of George Quinlan.

It was impossible to miss the collective gasp which emanated from the others.

Martin Walworth continued to stare at George Quinlan. "Is she a relative of *yours*?"

John Farnham answered the question. "A daughter," he said.

The brief period of tense silence which followed that statement was again broken by the strident ringing of the telephone.

Sheriff Eldon picked up the receiver, said, "Sheriff's office, Bill Eldon speaking." Then he said, "Wait a minute . . . What's that? . . .Oh, I see . . . All right . . . Wait for about fifteen or twenty minutes, will you? Okay, goodbye."

The sheriff hung up, saying nothing to any of the others.

Walworth's manner was that of a teacher who is demonstrating some problem which to him is entirely simple, but which is puzzling a roomful of pupils. "May I ask," he inquired sarcastically, "whether this Beryl Quinlan is around nineteen, a rather tall dark girl with dark eyes and an unusually clear voice?"

He needed no answer other than the glances which the men gave each other.

"That, gentlemen," Walworth said, "probably disposes of your murder case. It will account for the B on the cigarette case."

Rush Medford took charge at that point. "I think," he announced, "that, under the circumstances, it would be better if the district attorney's office handled this by itself from this point on," and with that he strode toward the door, jerked it open, and stood to one side, waiting for the others to precede him.

They made a self-righteous little procession as they stalked through the door, but Bertram Glasco couldn't help stopping for one final dig at the discomfited deputy. "This," he said, "probably accounts for something that puzzled me in our conversation last night."

And with that he marched out into the corridor, Rush Medford closed the door with a mild slam, and Bill Eldon and George Quinlan were left alone in the sheriff's office.

"Well," Quinlan said, "I guess that does it."

"Does what?"

"Wipes me out," Quinlan said gloomily. "And I guess I've dragged you down along with me, Bill."

"What did Glasco mean when he said something about last night?" Eldon asked.

"They wanted me to run against you."

"What did you tell them?"

"I told them I wouldn't do it as long as you wanted to run."

"Then what?"

"Then they suggested that the next big case that came along I sort of keep in the background and let you run the thing all by yourself and see if you wouldn't bungle on fingerprints or something."

Eldon nodded. "I thought something like that might be in the wind. And that's why Rush Medford called Martin Walworth in as a special investigator."

Quinlan nodded. He felt so utterly dejected that he didn't want to talk. They'd go and get Beryl. Rush Medford would take her to his office, go through the old rigmarole of advising her she didn't need to talk, call in a court reporter to take down what she said—

The sheriff calmly lifted the telephone, dialed a number. Quinlan slumped in his chair, chin on his chest, heard the sheriff's fatherly voice say, "Hello, Beryl? That you?...Where's your car?...Go down and get in it quick and go out to the Stanwood Auto Camp, rent a cabin under your own name. Be sure you use your own name and give the correct license number of your car. Then look around. You'll find a friend of yours there. Your father and I will be out in a few minutes, but get started *now*."

The sheriff hung up.

"You can't do that, Bill," Quinlan said.

"Why not?"

"That's compounding a felony. You know the district attorney is on his way to question her concerning what happened, and—"

"Well?" the sheriff asked.

"You can't advise her to avoid him."

The sheriff grinned. "I'm asking her to go where *I* can question her."

"But the district attorney wants to take a statement from her."

"And *I* want to take a statement from her. Rush Medford wants to solve this murder case, and *I* want to solve it. Buck up, George. We're going places. Know who telephoned just a minute ago?"

"No," Quinlan said.

"Roy Jasper. He's out at the Stanwood camp. I told him to wait there."

"I don't see where we can do any good," Quinlan said.

Bill Eldon put a sympathetic hand on the deputy's shoulder. "Now, don't get down in the dumps, George. You can't blame Beryl for what she did. My gosh! I didn't even bother to stop her."

"You didn't bother to do *what*?" Quinlan exclaimed.

"To stop her."

"You mean you *knew*—"

"Of course I did," the sheriff said. "I picked up that cigarette case and recognized it right away."

"You recognized it? How?"

The sheriff said, "On your mantelpiece there's a picture of Roy Jasper. He's in uniform, and if you'll remember he's holding this cigarette case out in front of him half open just as though he was offering someone a cigarette. You can see the engraving on the side clearly."

"Why, yes," Quinlan said. "I do remember now. How did you happen to notice that?"

"Oh, I just notice lots of things," the sheriff said. "It's a habit a man gets when he's been fooling around with crime as long as I have. You see, George, I never had a chance to study up on all this fingerprint business, and things of that sort, and because I don't do so good on those things I have to keep up on other stuff. I always felt that you have to know and understand people in order to make a good officer. It's easier for me to understand people than it is to understand all this scientific stuff about whorls and loops. Now, Beryl isn't going to be mixed up in any murder, and you know it."

"She's mixed up in one now," Quinlan said dejectedly.

Bill Eldon shook his head. "I thought that was Roy's cigarette case," he said, "so I went to a phone and instead of telephoning the coroner's office or the *Gazette* and locating you myself, I phoned Beryl and told her about wanting to get hold of you, and about my finding this cigarette case down there, and that I wanted you to fingerprint it. So then I went back where I could watch, and waited to see what happened."

"What did you have in mind?"

"I wanted to see whether Beryl knew where the cigarette case was. I was very careful to tell her that I found it in the Higbee place and describe it to her, but I didn't tell her *where* in the Higbee place I'd found it."

"And what did she do?"

"Did just what I thought she'd do," the sheriff said. "Drove down there."

"You didn't stop her?"

"No. I saw Beryl drive down, stop her car, open the gate, get in, drive up to the Higbee place, and then she had to do quite a bit of looking around before she found what she wanted.

"Then I watched her drive out and close the gate behind her. I really thought she'd taken the cigarette case with her, but she was too smart for that. She'd just wiped the fingerprints off it and left it."

"She had no right to do that," Quinlan said.

"She didn't, for a fact," the sheriff admitted cheerfully, "but I thought it was best to let her play it that way."

"Why?"

"Because then she'd go to Roy Jasper and get him to tell her just exactly what had happened, and he'd tell *her* where he wouldn't tell either you or me. All I had to be certain of was that Beryl hadn't been in the house when the cigarette case had been dropped. She proved that to me when she had to fumble around looking for it. If she'd gone right to the kitchen where the cigarette case had been left, I'd have had to stop her when she drove out and ask her questions. I'd have hated to do it, too, because Beryl's a nice girl."

Quinlan was having difficulty in adjusting himself to these new developments. "Then you knew before I got there what car it was that had the triangular piece out of the right front tire?"

"Sure."

"Then why did you have me go through all that business of tearing out a piece of paper?"

"Well, George," the sheriff said, "I sort of wanted to see what *you'd* do. That's why I gave *you* that triangular piece of paper to keep. I thought perhaps—"

"Don't think for a minute I wasn't tempted," Quinlan interrupted bitterly. "I even went so far as to tear out a substitute piece of paper. But when it came to a showdown I couldn't use it."

"I know," the sheriff said soothingly. "Well, let's go out to the auto camp and see what's up. I'll call my house first."

Sheriff Eldon called his house. Then, when the answer came, his face winced with displeasure. "Hello, Doris," he said. "Where's Merna? Is she there?...I see, Well, take a message for her, will you? Tell her that I want her to start looking through the personal mentions in the back issues of the papers beginning about six or seven months ago and see if she can find some mention of an Elvira Dow. I think she—"

The sheriff was interrupted by a burst of high-pitched staccato noises which came rattling over the wire.

Slowly the look of annoyance on his face faded to a whimsical smile. "All right, Doris," he said, "I guess it's a good thing to have a gossip in the family after all."

He hung up and grinned at Quinlan. "Looks as though we're getting somewhere, George. That was the old Human Encyclopedia, my sister-in-law, who sticks that long nose of hers into more different business of more different people than you'd ever suspect. She was visiting here when old Higbee died, and she eagerly devoured all the scandal about his common-law marriage to his housekeeper, and all the stink that was raised. Elvira Dow was the nurse who lived at the house for about ten days after Marvin Higbee had his stroke. She was with him up until the time of his death."

"Then this girl who was murdered was—"

"Elvira Dow's daughter. Put that together with the fact that people were zigzagging back and forth around the house looking for something, and we begin to get an answer. We—"

The telephone rang again. Eldon answered, listened to a rasping voice, and said, "So what?" After an interval he slammed the receiver back.

Quinlan looked at him questioningly.

"Rush Medford," the sheriff said. "He's down at your place. Your wife told him Beryl got a call a few minutes ago and then jumped in her jalopy and went tearing out."

Quinlan groaned. "And I suppose he suspects me!"

Eldon grinned. "Come on, son. Kinda looks as though we gotta move fast."

The little group in the cabin at the Stanwood Auto Court talked in low voices.

"All right, Roy," the sheriff said, "I think it's your move."

Roy Jasper shifted his position uneasily. "I didn't want Beryl to know about this," he said. "I suppose I was foolish. After all, there was no reason why—it would have meant explaining and—"

"Go ahead," the sheriff said.

"It began last week," Roy said, "when I was in San Rodolpho on official business. I ate in a cafeteria and—well, the cashier was a good-looking blonde, and I got to passing the time of day with her. I told her I was from Rockville and that I certainly hated to be so close to home without going on up to see my friends, and she laughed and wanted to know whether it was friends, plural, or a friend, singular, and we got to chatting."

"Then what?"

"Well, then she asked me about whether I knew Marvin Higbee, and I told her he was dead, and she asked a few questions about the place, and I told her something about the lawsuit. Well—"

"Go ahead," the sheriff said.

"Well, I could see this girl kept wanting to talk about Higbee, and finally she told me the story. Her mother nursed Higbee during his last illness, and then in Colorado her mother became critically ill and sent for the daughter. The daughter was there for a couple of days before the mother died, and the mother told her that Higbee had said to her in effect, 'If anything happens and I shouldn't pull through, you've got to do something for me. He'll pay you for it and pay you well—make him pay. I told him he'd have to pay,' but he wouldn't tell her any more than that, just that she'd be paid well for what she was to do.

"Higbee had had a stroke and it had paralyzed one side. Then the day before he died, he had another stroke and knew he wasn't going to make it. The nurse could see that he wanted to tell her something very badly, but there was always someone else in the room. No one trusted anyone else—people were waiting, watching. The housekeeper kept flitting around, and the doctor was there, in and out, and Carlotta, the man's favorite sister, was there almost constantly, and business associates kept hanging around.

"Finally, in desperation, Higbee said to her, talking apparently with great effort, 'Remember, I said you'd have to do something,' and she nodded, and just then Carlotta came and stood by the bed, and Higbee frowned and said with the effort that talking costs a man who has had a stroke, 'The joke is behind the joker,' and that was all.

"Carlotta kept asking, 'What was that? What about a joker?' But he closed his eyes and pretended he couldn't hear her. But the nurse felt certain that it was a message for her, but she never was able to figure it out. Higbee died the next day, and there was, of course, no further necessity for a nurse.

"Well, Elizabeth kept thinking over what her mother had told her, and after her mother's death she began to wonder if it hadn't been related to something in the house, so she started pumping me about the Higbee place, and I told her all I knew. Elizabeth wanted me to go with her and see if we couldn't find something in the house, but of course she swore me to absolute secrecy.

"Well, it was an adventure, and I was there in San Rodolpho on official business. I got off once to come up and see Beryl, but the rest of the time they held me there so I couldn't go anywhere. Then I went back to Fort Bixling, and then I got this furlough and—well, I'd promised Elizabeth that I'd get in touch with her the first chance I had. So I did, and she insisted that I mustn't call anyone, or let anyone know about what we were going to do. She said she'd drive me up in her car, and that after I'd helped her locate what she wanted I could get in touch with my *friends* up here. I think she was just a little bit hurt that I was so eager to—well, you know."

Beryl nodded.

"So when I left Camp Bixling yesterday morning, I took the bus up to San Rodolpho. I'd telephoned her that I was coming. She met me in the cafeteria. We talked for a while, and then we had some lunch put up, got in her car, and drove up to the old Higbee place. It certainly was a mess. I found that a passkey I'd picked up in a hardware store would work the lock on the side door, and we went in and prowled all around the place."

"Find anything?" the sheriff asked.

Roy said, "At the time I didn't think that we had, but now—well, now I don't know."

The sheriff raised his eyebrows, asking a silent question.

"You see," Roy said, "we were sitting down eating lunch—in

fact, we'd finished lunch and I'd had a cigarette, and I think she had—when all of a sudden we heard a car drive up. Well, you know, there'd been so much trouble among the heirs and, after all, we'd really broken into the place—I'd used a passkey—so we jumped up and ran to the window. It was all covered with cobwebs, but I could vaguely see a car and people coming to the house.

"So I grabbed her hand and we ran away from the window and dashed for the side door. We played hide and seek around there for a while until the people walked around the other side of the house, then we ran out and jumped in her car and drove away."

"You saw those people?"

"Yes, after we'd got out of the house. It was Sam Beckett and John Farnham. They didn't see us. Farnham was evidently selling the place to Beckett. Anyway, I let Elizabeth drive me back to San Rodolpho, and I waited until evening and then telephoned Beryl. I didn't want to tell Beryl that I was in San Rodolpho, so I told her I was just leaving Fort Bixling—and well, that's all there was to it. I stuck around there, took the night bus, and came up here.

"Now, Elizabeth must have uncovered some clue to something she didn't want me to know about. After she took me back to San Rodolpho she must have turned around and driven right back up here. She told me she had a bad headache and was going up to her room and go to bed. And by that time I was thinking of Beryl. Elizabeth had been all right to kill a little time with when I was down where I couldn't see Beryl, but once I could get up here I was kicking myself for the time I'd wasted out of my furlough. When a soldier's in a strange town and is lonely, he'll do anything just to talk with some friendly girl.

"Well, that was it. I'd promised her I'd go up to the Higbee place with her and look it over, and I went, and that's all there was to it as far as I know."

"And you left your cigarette case there?" Beryl asked.

"Yes."

"But you had one the next morning when you—"

Roy said, "I felt miserable about that. You see, Beryl, you sent me the cigarette case for Christmas, but I already had one cigarette case, so I used it for a spare. Then after I lost your— well, I intended to go back to the Higbee place and pick up the one with the engraving on it, but the one I showed you this morning was the spare. It was silver, about the same type as the one you gave me except for the engraving, and I held it so you couldn't see that the engraving wasn't on it. I was afraid that I couldn't explain to you about Elizabeth without you getting sore."

"You mustn't feel that way, Roy—ever."

"I know," he said, "now. But I wasn't sure."

A car drew up outside. The sound of excited voices mingled with hurried steps. A perfunctory knock on the door was followed by a turning of the knob and the influx of an excited group.

"*There* they are!" Lyons proclaimed dramatically.

District Attorney Rush Medford demanded angrily, "What's the idea?"

"Idea of what?" the sheriff drawled innocently.

"Spiriting these people away."

The sheriff's eyebrows went up. "We didn't spirit them anywhere. We're questioning them."

"I'm putting this young man under arrest for the murder of Elizabeth Dow."

"Got any evidence?" the sheriff asked.

"All the evidence in the world. That is, we will have as soon as we check some fingerprints. Beryl Quinlan thought she was wiping all the fingerprints off that cigarette case and she did—off the outside. But what everyone overlooked was the fact that at some time when the case had been empty and the owner was filling it with fresh cigarettes, he left his fingerprints on the *inside*, back of the cigarettes.

"Mr. Walworth very shrewdly deduced he'd find fingerprints there and carefully removed the cigarettes, then dusted the interior of the case, and we got some very fine latents. In my official capacity as district attorney of this County, Sheriff, I order you to take this man into custody."

"Suit yourself, but I'm not going to be the one to swear out the complaint," Bill Eldon drawled.

"*I* will swear out the complaint," Martin Walworth said, but then added hastily, "in the event it appears that this young man's fingerprints check with the latents I found on the inside of the cigarette case."

"We'll determine that in short order," the district attorney said.

They drove to the courthouse. Walworth made prints of Roy Jasper's fingertips. There was no concealing his anxiety as Walworth focused a magnifying glass on the latent prints and then

I tried to make Mama comfortable. I catered to her every whim and fancy. I loved her. All the same I had another reason to keep her alive as long as possible. While she breathed I knew I had a place to stay. I was terrified of what would happen to me when Mama died. I had no high school diploma and no experience at outside work and I knew my sisters-in-law wouldn't take me in or let my brothers support me once Mama was gone.

Then Mama drew her last breath with a smile of thanks on her face for what I had done.

Sure enough, Norine and Thelma, my brothers' wives, put their feet down. I was on my own from then on. So that scared feeling of wondering where I could lay my head took over in my mind and never left me.

I had some respite when Mr. Williams, a widower twenty-four years older than me, asked me to marry him. I took my vows seriously. I meant to cherish him and I did. But that house we lived in! Those walls couldn't have been dirtier if they'd been smeared with soot and the plumbing was stubborn as a mule. My left foot stayed sore from having to kick the pipe underneath the kitchen sink to get the water to run through.

Then Mr. Williams got sick and had to give up his shoe repair shop that he ran all by himself. He had a small savings account and a few of those twenty-five-dollar government bonds and drew some disability insurance until the policy ran out in something like six months.

I did everything I could to make him comfortable and keep him cheerful. Though I did all the laundry I gave him clean sheets and clean pajamas every third day and I think it was by my will power alone that I made a begonia bloom in that dark back room Mr. Williams stayed in. I even pestered his two daughters and told them they ought to send their father some get-well cards and they did once or twice. Every now and then when there were a few pennies extra I'd buy cards and scrawl signatures nobody could have read and mailed them to Mr. Williams to make him think some of his former customers were remembering him and wishing him well.

Of course when Mr. Williams died his daughters were johnny-on-the-spot to see that they got their share of the little bit that tumbledown house brought. I didn't begrudge them—I'm not one to argue with human nature.

I hate to think about all those hardships I had after Mr. Williams died. The worst of it was finding somewhere to sleep; it all boiled down to having a place to stay. Because somehow you can manage not to starve. There are garbage cans to dip into—you'd be surprised how wasteful some people are and how much good food they throw away. Or if it was right after the garbage trucks had made their collections and the cans were empty I'd go into a supermarket and pick, say, at the cherries pretending I was selecting some to buy. I didn't slip their best ones into my mouth. I'd take either those so ripe that they should have been thrown away or those that weren't ripe enough and shouldn't have been put out for people to buy. I might snitch a withered cabbage leaf or a few pieces of watercress or a few of those small round tomatoes about the size of hickory nuts—I never can remember their right name. I wouldn't make a pig of myself, just eat enough to ease my hunger. So I managed. As I say, you don't have to starve.

The only work I could get hardly ever paid me anything beyond room and board. I wasn't a practical nurse, though I knew how to take care of sick folks, and the people hiring me would say that since I didn't have the training and qualifications I couldn't expect much. All they really wanted was for someone to spend the night with Aunt Myrtle or Cousin Kate or Mama or Daddy; no actual duties were demanded of me, they said, and they really didn't think my help was worth anything except meals and a place to sleep. The arrangements were pretty makeshift. Half the time I wouldn't have a place to keep my things, not that I had any clothes to speak of, and sometimes I'd sleep on a cot in the hall outside the patient's room or on some sort of contrived bed in the patient's room

I cherished every one of those sick people, just as I had cherished Mama and Mr. Williams. I didn't want them to die. I did everything I knew to let them know I was interested in their welfare—first for their sakes, and then for mine, so I wouldn't have to go out and find another place to stay.

Well, now, I've made out my case for the defense, a term I never thought I'd have to use personally, so now I'll make out the case for the prosecution.

I stole.

I don't like to say it, but I was a thief.

I'm not light-fingered. I didn't want a thing that belonged to anybody else. But there came a time when I felt forced to steal. I had to have some things. My shoes fell apart. I needed some stockings and underclothes. And when I'd ask a son or a daughter or a cousin or a niece for a little money for those necessities they acted as if I was trying to blackmail them. They reminded me that I wasn't qualified as a practical nurse, that I might even get into trouble with the authorities if they found I was palming myself off as a practical nurse—which I wasn't and they knew it. Anyway, they said that their terms were only bed and board.

So I began to take things—small things that had been pushed into the backs of drawers or stored high on shelves in boxes— things that hadn't been used or worn for years and probably would never be used again. I made my biggest haul at Mrs. Bick's where there was an attic full of trunks stuffed with clothes and doodads from the twenties all the way back to the nineties— uniforms, ostrich fans, Spanish shawls, beaded bags. I sneaked out a few of these at a time and every so often sold them to a place called Way Out, Hippie Clothiers.

I tried to work out the exact amount I got for selling something. Not, I know, that you can make up for theft. But, say, I got a dollar for a feather boa belonging to Mrs. Bick: well, then I'd come back and work at a job that the cleaning woman kept putting off, like waxing the hall upstairs or polishing the andirons or getting the linen closet in order.

All the same I *was* stealing—not eveywhere I stayed, not even in most places, but when I had to I stole. I admit it.

But I didn't steal that silver box.

I was as innocent as a baby where that box was concerned. So when that policeman came toward me grabbing at the box I stepped aside, and maybe I even gave him the push that sent him to his death. He had no business acting like that when that box was mine, whatever Mrs. Crowe's niece argued.

Fifty thousand nieces couldn't have made it not mine.

Anyway, the policeman was dead and though I hadn't wanted him dead I certainly hadn't wished him well. And then I got to thinking: well, I didn't steal Mrs. Crowe's box but I had stolen other things and it was the mills of God grinding exceeding fine, as I once heard a preacher say, and I was being made to pay for the transgressions that had caught up with me.

Surely I can make a little more sense out of what happened than that, though I never was exactly clear in my own mind about everything that happened.

Mrs. Crowe was the most appreciative person I ever worked for. She was bedridden and could barely move. I don't think the registered nurse on daytime duty considered it part of her job to massage Mrs. Crowe. So at night I would massage her, and that pleased and soothed her. She thanked me for every small thing I did—when I fluffed her pillow, when I'd put a few drops of perfume on her earlobes, when I'd straighten the wrinkled bedcovers.

I had a little joke. I'd pretend I could tell fortunes and I'd take Mrs. Crowe's hand and tell her she was going to have a wonderful day but she must beware of a handsome blond stranger—or some such foolishness that would make her laugh. She didn't sleep well and it seemed to give her pleasure to talk to me most of the night about her childhood or her dead husband.

She kept getting weaker and weaker and two nights before she died she said she wished she could do something for me but that when she became an invalid she had signed over everything to her niece. Anyway, Mrs. Crowe hoped I'd take her silver box. I thanked her. It pleased me that she liked me well enough to give me the box. I didn't have any real use for it. It would have made a nice trinket box, but I didn't have any trinkets. The box seemed to be Mrs. Crowe's fondest possession. She kept it on the table beside her and her eyes lighted up every time she looked at it. She might have been a little girl first seeing a brand-new baby doll early on a Christmas morning.

So when Mrs. Crowe died and the niece on whom I set eyes for the first time dismissed me, I gathered up what little I had and took the box and left. I didn't go to Mrs. Crowe's funeral. The paper said it was private and I wasn't invited. Anyway, I wouldn't have had anything suitable to wear.

I still had a few dollars left over from those things I'd sold to the hippie place called Way Out, so I paid a week's rent for a room that was the worst I'd ever stayed in.

It was freezing cold and no heat came up to the third floor where I was. In that room with falling plaster and buckling floorboards and darting roaches, I sat wearing every stitch I owned, with a sleazy blanket and a faded quilt draped around me waiting for the heat to rise, when in swept Mrs. Crowe's niece in a fur coat and a fur hat and shiny leather boots up to her knees. Her face was beet-red from anger when she started telling me that she had traced me through a private detective and I was to give her back the heirloom I had stolen.

Her statement made me forget the precious little bit I knew of the English language. I couldn't say a word, and she kept on screaming that if I returned the box immediately no criminal charge would be made against me. Then I got back my voice and I said that box was mine and that Mrs. Crowe had wanted me to have it, and she asked if I had any proof or if there were any witnesses to the gift, and I told her that when I was given a present I said thank you, that I didn't ask for proof and witnesses, and that nothing could make me part with Mrs. Crowe's box.

The niece stood there breathing hard, in and out, almost counting her breaths like somebody doing an exercise.

"You'll see," she yelled, and then she left.

The room was colder than ever and my teeth chattered.

Not long afterward I heard heavy steps clumping up the stairway. I realized that the niece had carried out her threat and that the police were after me.

I was panic-stricken. I chased around the room like a rat with a cat after it. Then I thought that if the police searched my room and couldn't find the box it might give me time to decide what to do. I grabbed the box out of the top dresser drawer and scurried down the back hall. I snatched the back door open. I think what I intended to do was run down the back steps and hide the box somewhere, underneath a bush or maybe in a garbage can.

Those back steps were steep and rose almost straight up for three stories and they were flimsy and covered with ice.

I started down. My right foot slipped. The handrail saved me. I clung to it with one hand and to the silver box with the other hand and picked and chose my way across the patches of ice.

When I was midway I heard my name shrieked. I looked around to see a big man leaping down the steps after me. I never saw such anger on a person's face. Then he was directly behind me and reached out to snatch the box.

I swerved to escape his grasp and he cursed me. Maybe I pushed him. I'm not sure—not really.

Anyway, he slipped and fell down and down and down, and then after all that falling he was absolutely still. The bottom step was beneath his head like a pillow and the rest of his body was spreadeagled on the brick walk.

Then almost like a pet that wants to follow its master, the silver box jumped from my hand and bounced down the steps to land beside the man's left ear.

My brain was numb. I felt paralyzed. Then I screamed.

Tenants from that house and the houses next door and across the alley pushed windows open and flung doors open to see what the commotion was about, and then some of them began to run toward the back yard. The policeman who was the dead man's partner—I guess you'd call him that—ordered them to keep away.

After a while more police came and they took the dead man's body and drove me to the station where I was locked up.

From the very beginning I didn't take to that young lawyer they assigned to me. There wasn't anything exactly that I could put my finger on. I just felt uneasy with him. His last name was Stanton. He had a first name of course, but he didn't tell me what it was; he said he wanted me to call him Bat like all his friends did.

He was always smiling and reassuring me when there wasn't anything to smile or be reassured about, and he ought to have known it all along instead of filling me with false hope.

All I could think was that I was thankful Mama and Papa and Mr. Williams were dead and that my shame wouldn't bring shame on them.

"It's going to be all right," the lawyer kept saying right up to the end, and then he claimed to be indignant when I was found guilty of resisting arrest and of manslaughter and theft or robbery—there was the biggest hullabaloo as to whether I was guilty of theft or robbery. Not that I was guilty of either, at least in this particular instance, but no one would believe me.

You would have thought it was the lawyer being sentenced instead of me, the way he carried on. He called it a terrible miscarriage of justice and said we might as well be back in the eighteenth century when they hanged children.

Well, that was an exaggeration, if ever there was one; nobody was being hung and nobody was a child. That policeman had died and I had had a part in it. Maybe I had pushed him. I couldn't be sure. In my heart I really hadn't meant him any harm. I was just scared. But he was dead all the same. And as far as stealing went, I hadn't stolen the box but I had stolen other things.

And then it happened. It was a miracle. All my life I'd dreamed of a nice room of my own, a comfortable place to stay. And that's exactly what I got.

The room was on the small side but it had everything I needed in it, even a wash basin with hot and cold running water, and the walls were freshly painted, and they let me choose whether I wanted a wing chair with a chintz slipcover or a modern Danish armchair. I even got to decide what color bedspread I preferred. The window looked out on a beautiful lawn edged with shrubbery, and the matron said I'd be allowed to go to the greenhouse and select some pot plants to keep in my room. The next day I picked out a white gloxinia and some russet chrysanthemums.

I didn't mind the bars at the windows at all. Why, this day and age some of the finest mansions have barred windows to keep burglars out.

The meals—I simply couldn't believe there was such delicious food in the world. The woman who supervised their preparation had embezzled the funds of one of the largest catering companies in the state after working herself up from cook to treasurer.

The other inmates were very friendly and most of them had led the most interesting lives. Some of the ladies occasionally used words that you usually see written only on fences or printed on sidewalks before the cement dries, but when they were scolded they apologized. Every now and then somebody would get angry with someone and there would be a little scratching or hair pulling, but it never got too bad. There was a choir—I can't sing but I love music—and they gave a concert every Tuesday morning at chapel, and Thursday night was movie night. There wasn't any admission charge. All you did was go in and sit down anywhere you pleased.

We all had a special job and I was assigned to the infirmary. The doctor and nurse both complimented me. The doctor said that I should have gone into professional nursing, that I gave confidence to the patients and helped them get well. I don't know about that but I've had years of practice with sick people and I like to help anybody who feels bad.

I was so happy that sometimes I couldn't sleep at night. I'd get up and click on the light and look at the furniture and the walls. It was hard to believe I had such a pleasant place to stay. I'd remember supper that night, how I'd gone back to the steam table for a second helping of asparagus with lemon and herb sauce, and I compared my plenty with those terrible times when I had slunk into supermarkets and nibbled overripe fruit and raw vegetables to ease my hunger.

Then one day here came that lawyer, not even at regular visiting hours, bouncing around congratulating me that my appeal had been upheld, or whatever the term was, and that I was as free as a bird to leave right that minute.

He told the matron she could send my belongings later and he dragged me out where TV cameras and reporters were waiting.

As soon as the cameras began whirring and the photographers began to aim, the lawyer kissed me on the cheek and pinned a flower on me. He made a speech saying that a terrible miscarriage of justice had been rectified. He had located people who testified that Mrs. Crowe had given me the box—she had told the gardener and the cleaning woman. They hadn't wanted to testify because they didn't want to get mixed up with the police, but the lawyer had persuaded them in the cause of justice and humanity to come forward and make statements.

The lawyer had also looked into the personnel record of the dead policeman and had learned that he had been judged emotionally unfit for his job, and the psychiatrist had warned the Chief of Police that something awful might happen either to the man himself or to a suspect unless he was relieved of his duties.

All the time the lawyer was talking into the microphones he had latched onto me like I was a three-year-old that might run away, and I just stood and stared. Then when he had finished his speech about me the reporters told him that like his grandfather and his uncle he was sure to end up as governor of the state.

At that the lawyer gave a big grin in front of the camera and waved goodbye and pushed me into his car.

I was terrified. The nice place I'd found to stay in wasn't mine any longer. My old nightmare was back—wondering how I could manage to eat and how much stealing I'd have to do to live from one day to the next.

The cameras and reporters had followed us.

A photographer asked me to turn down the car window beside me, and I overheard two men way in the back of the crowd talking. My ears are sharp. Papa always said I could hear thunder three states away. Above the congratulations and bubbly talk around me I heard one of those men in back say, "This is a bit too much, don't you think? Our Bat is showing himself the champion of the Senior Citizen now. He's already copped the teeny-boppers and the under-thirties, using methods that ought to have disbarred him. He should have made the gardener and cleaning woman testify at the beginning, and from the first he should have checked into the policeman's history. There ought never to have been a case at all, much less a conviction. But Bat wouldn't have got any publicity that way. He had to do it in his own devious, spectacular fashion." The other man just kept nodding and saying after every sentence, "You're damned right."

Then we drove off and I didn't dare look behind me because I was so heartbroken over what I was leaving.

The lawyer took me to his office. He said he hoped I wouldn't mind a little excitement for the next few days. He had mapped out some public appearances for me. The next morning I was to be on an early television show. There was nothing to be worried about. He would be right beside me to help me just as he had helped me throughout my trouble. All that I had to say on the TV program was that I owed my freedom to him.

I guess I looked startled or bewildered because he hurried on to say that I hadn't been able to pay him a fee but that now I was able to pay him back—not in money but in letting the public know about how he was the champion of the underdog.

I said I had been told that the court furnished lawyers free of charge to people who couldn't pay, and he said that was right, but his point was that I could repay him now by telling people all that he had done for me. Then he said the main thing was to talk over our next appearance on TV. He wanted to coach me in what I was going to say, but first he would go into his partner's office and tell him to take all the incoming calls and handle the rest of his appointments.

When the door closed after him I thought that he was right. I did owe my freedom to him. He was to blame for it. The smart aleck. The upstart. Who asked him to butt in and snatch me out of my pretty room and the work I loved and all that delicious food?

It was the first time in my life I knew what it meant to despise someone. I hated him.

Before, when I was convicted of manslaughter, there was a lot of talk about malice aforethought and premeditated crime.

There wouldn't be any argument this time.

I hadn't wanted any harm to come to that policeman. But I did mean harm to come to this lawyer.

I grabbed up a letter opener from his desk and ran my finger along the blade and felt how sharp it was. I waited behind the door and when he walked through I gathered all my strength and stabbed him. Again and again and again.

Now I'm back where I want to be—in a nice place to stay.

Phyllis Bentley

Miss Phipps Exercises Her Métier

Remember Phyllis Bentley's story titled "Miss Phipps and the Nest of Illusion," in the August 1969 issue of Ellery Queen's Mystery Magazine? You'll recall that in the editorial preface your Editor innocently confessed to not knowing the meaning of the word "dogsbodies." Well! You would not believe how many readers wrote in to enlighten us, some refusing to believe that EQ could be so ignorant (thank you, but, alas, our ignorance was genuine).

One reader of EQMM who answered the unintentioned challenge was the creator of Miss Phipps herself. Here is her definition of dogsbodies: "Just for your amusement," Phyllis Bentley wrote, "let me elucidate the term 'dogsbodies.' A dogsbody is, in any sphere, a trusted reliable subordinate who performs all the tiresome, essential, minor, non-prestige-producing tasks. He (or often she) checks railway timetables, gets rid of pesters, lays on coffee, tracks down missing persons who have wandered off, and in general eases the path of those whose work is more important to the task in hand. The slang term 'dogsbody' is usually employed by dogsbodies themselves, in humorous self-deprecation."

At the end of her letter Phyllis Bentley had news of her spinster-novelist-sleuth: "Dear Miss Phipps is stranded at the moment on a Shetland island. A lovely scene for murder . . ."

Here is Miss Phipps's adventure on a remote, lonely, Viking-haunted, storm-tossed Shetland isle—and a strange adventure it is—with only a hint of dogsbodies . . . (No, we are not questioning any words this time, thank you!)

Detective: MISS MARIAN PHIPPS

All of a sudden Miss Marian Phipps felt lonely.

This was rather strange, for up to that moment she had been enjoying the peace of this remote Shetland isle. After the repeated discussions, the divergent human wishes, and the frequent telephonings of the morning, the present silence—the sheer absence of human voices—was restful in the extreme. The island was small, but large enough to offer considerable grassy slopes, and over the steepest of these her four companions on the excursion were now climbing rapidly.

The dark cliffs rose to fine and jagged heights; the northern sea was a rich dark blue with white surf fringes; the sun shone; the sea birds—gulls, gannets, oyster-catchers, shags, terns, puffins, what-have-you (Miss Phipps was not too well up in birds)—clamored a good deal, to be sure, as they swooped about the sky; but their various modes of flight were beautiful to watch, and their resonant tones were a pleasant change from the motor horns and airplane engines which formed her usual sound track.

The rest of the party had wanted to see the remains of the old Viking settlement for which they had indeed come to the island, but these lay on the far side of the steep hill. Miss Phipps, surveying its gradient, and perhaps, in spite of her real affection for them, a little tired of Inspector Tarrant and his wife after a fortnight's holiday together—and certainly tired of Professor Morison and *his* wife after a mere few hours—decided to remain idly in the vicinity of the tiny harbor and landing stage. A neighboring bay, gained by climbing a much slighter slope, was as far as Miss Phipps was prepared to walk.

If she felt a little less than her usual warmth toward the Tarrants this afternoon it was not, she admitted at once, their fault but just part of the usual exasperation of things in general, which so often refused to fit, to go right. Today was the last one of their stay in Shetland, and though they had seen several fine Viking remains, everyone at their hotel in the main port had assured them that those on Fersa were the finest, grimmest, most complete in existence. But to reach Fersa one had to proceed to a village on the mainland coast and there rent a boat. "Just telephone the village post office," urged their hotel acquaintances. "They keep a motor vessel for hire."

They telephoned. In fact, they seemed to spend the whole morning at the telephone. Sometimes Inspector Tarrant telephoned, sometimes his wife Mary did, sometimes Miss Phipps. All without

result. At first a young man's voice had replied, saying crossly
that the sea was too high, and besides, he hadn't the time. Then
the wind calmed a little, so they telephoned again. This time a
young woman's voice replied. Her voice had sobs in it, and cried
out that she couldn't "fash" with them now.

After an hour's wait they telephoned again—and then again.
The receiver was lifted and replaced, only a kind of moan being
heard in the brief interim. Miss Phipps urged the Tarrants to give
up Fersa and decide on some other excursion. Although disappointed as to Vikings, the Tarrants would probably have accepted
her advice if it had not been for the Morisons, who now appeared
to be seized by Fersa and telephone.

Professor Morison was one of those long, concave, balding
academics devoted to abstruse subjects; he had a sallow complexion and sad brown eyes—the type whom Miss Phipps respected
but regarded as supremely dreary. His wife, short, plump,
fairhaired, bossy, appeared soft-hearted, but in defense of her
husband she took on the consistency of marble. When the Tarrant
party left the hotel to accompany some fellow guests to the ship
about to leave the port harbor for Scotland, Mrs. Morison was
again at the telephone in the hall.

"Her husband's away—her husband's out with the boat," she
reported over her shoulder to the Professor. When the Tarrant
party returned for lunch she was still telephoning.

Meanwhile, Miss Phipps had had a poignant experience. Indeed
it was to the poignancy of this experience that she attributed her
present sudden attack of loneliness; the usual well-adjusted balance of her feelings had been upset, leaving her open to alarms.
(For was she, in fact, feeling "lonely" now, or was she, in reality,
for some inexplicable cause merely feeling nervous? She was uncertain.)

The poignant experience was simply the sight of a face peering
out from the lower deck of the ship bound for Scotland. A young
man's face, dark and handsome, but fixed with such a look of
agony that Miss Phipps hoped never to see the like again. As
Miss Phipps was a novelist, suitable explanations of other people's
feelings were naturally apt to rush into her mind.

Poor lad! she thought with genuine pity. Going away from
home for the first time, I expect. The heart beholds the islands. A
difficult place to leave. Mountains and sea. Poor boy.

On entering the lobby of the hotel she found Mrs. Morison

again at the end of the telephone cord, and addressing her husband.

"She says her father-in-law will take us," she cried in triumph. With a sudden change of tone she added, "It'll cost enough."

"Er-hrrumph," said Professor Morison, concaving (Miss Phipps thought) almost more than before.

"Shall we go, James?" pressed Mrs. Morison.

"Er-hrrumph."

"Would you allow our party of three to join you?" said Miss Phipps, springing cheerfully into the breach. "That would lessen the—"

"Er-hrrumph!" said Professor Morison, straightening a little, hopefully.

Mrs. Morison looked eager but still doubtful.

"We have a hired car at our disposal," Miss Phipps added as bait.

Mrs. Morison beamed.

"A happy suggestion," she said. "I'm *sure* my husband will approve."

While she clinched the arrangement on the telephone, Miss Phipps flew off to tell the Tarrants of her achievement. It was not well received.

"Fancy spending an afternoon with that old stick!" growled the Inspector.

"Er-hrrumph!" said Mary peevishly.

"Very well, tell them you've changed your mind and don't want to go," said Miss Phipps, vexed.

"Of course we'll go," said Inspector Tarrant with decision.

"Er-hrrumph," said Mary in a kinder tone.

After lunch they drove down to the village, which was almost too tiny to be called a village, consisting chiefly of a post office, above which a home-painted board announced MACKAY. Near a tiny stone landing stage, just across the road from this building, tossed a small boat with an outboard motor, the boat attached to a red buoy. It tossed a good deal; looking out to sea Miss Phipps observed with interest that the waves were also tossing a good deal and were topped by quite a few whitecaps.

Professor Morison, carrying a pair of binoculars, a camera, and a notebook, with two textbooks protruding from his pockets, walked to the end of the little jetty and began to examine such birds as flew into view. Bill Tarrant, looking a little more cheer-

ful, followed him, and Mrs. Morison trotted after them on her fat
little ankles. Mary and Miss Phipps entered the post office and
began to choose picture postcards. Mary, hearing the approach of
a distant car, tapped sharply with a coin on the counter.

A most beautiful creature entered. A young woman, not yet 20,
Miss Phipps thought; of dazzlingly smooth and unblemished complexion, with pale golden hair twined and piled about her head in
thick lustrous swaths. She wore a thin white dress, so short that
if another inch were subtracted it would almost be a belt, and so
tightly modeled as to show every line of her lovely body except an
inch or two hinted at by a few tiny scraps of lace.

She turned her head and Miss Phipps started; her beauty was
marred by a heavy bruise on one temple, imperfectly concealed by
a good deal of crude makeup, and her large pale blue eyes were
red from crying. A wedding ring, and an engagement ring with a
single no doubt much-prized pearl, decked the hand with which
she pointed out, competently enough, the various categories of
postcards and their prices. Her accent had none of the island lilt
that Miss Phipps liked so much, and it seemed tinged with
Cockney.

"What's come into ye, Zelda?" boomed an angry voice.

The post office door was thrust open vehemently, sounding its
little bell, and in strode a solid grizzled figure wearing one of the
patterned knit garments native to the island.

"Hae ye no sense, woman? Why can't Eric take the boat across?
Dragging me all this way from ma sheep."

"Eric isn't here, Mr. Mackay," said Zelda timidly.

"Whaur's Magnus then?"

"He left."

"Did they go off together, then? Whaur did they go?"

"I don't know," moaned Zelda, almost weeping.

"Women!" exclaimed Mackay. "Sons!"

"I thought you wouldn't want to miss the chance of a boatload
of passengers."

"How many are ye, then?" barked Mackay, fixing Miss Phipps
with an angry glare.

"Five."

"It'll cost ye two pun ten."

"Very well," said Miss Phipps shortly. "You'll give us enough
time on the island to visit the broch?"

Mackay gave a prolonged growl in which might be distinguished the vowels composing an assenting "aye" or "yaas."

"Ye may nae like the sea," he said with what struck Miss Phipps as rather sinister enjoyment. "It's a wee high. Come awa' wi' ye, then."

As they followed Mackay Senior out of the post office and down the little stone pier, Mary and Miss Phipps exchanged glances indicating their unfavorable impressions of the dour boatman. Mary's raised eyebrows brought also a familiar accusation against Miss Phipps.

"I'm irritated by the way you find *a story* in everything," Mary had said not once but several times to Miss Phipps. "It seems an insult to reality."

But Miss Phipps could not help it—it was by now an inveterate habit, and usually she replied cheerfully to these accusations; and this time, as Mary suspected, Miss Phipps had been swept irresistibly into her dearly loved profession. She had begun her imaginings the moment she set eyes on Zelda and the bruise on the girl's temple. The lad with the agonized face was Zelda's husband; they had quarreled; he had struck her, then in shame and fury had left the island. And now this fierce old Mackay had come to confirm her imaginings.

Oh, yes, reflected Miss Phipps, surveying the strong aquiline features, the solid body and crisp graying hair, his older face is strongly akin to the face of the anguished lad on the ship; Zelda had said on the telephone that her father-in-law would ferry the party across to Fersa; the anguished lad is therefore this man's son and this girl's husband.

"Why will people make each other so unhappy?" murmured Miss Phipps. Eric, a good Norse name. As for Magnus, she could not fit him in; perhaps only a minor character in her burgeoning plot.

The Tarrants and Mrs. Morison stood the rough sea well; Miss Phipps enjoyed it, tossing her white curls to the breeze; the Professor turned a curious pea-green and was watched anxiously by his wife, but he yielded no further to queasiness. They landed on the island in a tiny bay, arranged a time for re-embarkation, and then the two married couples strode vigorously up the long green slope. Mr. Mackay vanished round a cliff in his chugging boat, and Miss Phipps wandered about.

It was then that Miss Phipps began to feel lonely. After all, she was apparently left by herself on a small island in the far North

Sea, surrounded by a far from calm ocean. Nothing human was visible. The remains of an old cottage—empty windows, broken chimney, vacant doorway—served only to make the absence of life more obvious. The birds soared by uncaring—almost, one might think, contemptuous. Even a sheep's company would have been acceptable. But there was no sheep.

She could no longer hear the chugging of Mr. Mackay's engine. Suppose they had all gone off and left her! It was an uneasy thought. Yes, she did feel uneasy. I'll go back to the landing stage, thought Miss Phipps. She turned; and bobbing in the waters of the bay beneath her feet she saw a gray head.

"It's a seal!" exclaimed Miss Phipps, delighted. For though on Shetland they had seen the towering brochs (like huge buckets turned upside down), eider ducks, underground funeral chambers, Vikings' descendants (at a gala) agreeably rigged out as Vikings, Shetland ponies with correct shortage of height and length of mane and tail, sheep with half their fleece hanging off their backs, jumpers of many patterns knitted from this silky wool, lochs, mountains, peat hags, seas in every mood, fishing fleets— indeed, almost everything they had expected and hoped to see in Shetland—their view of seals had been singularly scanty. To return to England without having seen some of these massive northern sea mammals would, Miss Phipps believed, diminish their prestige and credibility as Shetland tourists.

"A seal!" she repeated with delight. "I wonder if it lives in the rocks of this bay? Where do seals have their lairs, if any?"

Scanning the rocks which edged the little bay, all thought was suddenly struck from her mind. For beside a low seaweed-covered ledge of rock lay Mr. Mackay's boat, its painter wound round a protruding buttress, and on the ledge knelt Mr. Mackay himself, and he was actually—yes, actually—wringing his hands and bowing back and forth as if in uncontrollable sorrow.

Miss Phipps stared—at first amazed, then in horror. For what was it, lying amid the seaweed, urgently lapped by long waves, over which Mr. Mackay showed so much grief? He raised his face to the sky; tears coursed down his leathery cheeks. Wasn't the object over which he grieved the outstretched corpse of a young man in fisherman's jersey, a young man with dark curly hair, the image of the young man with the anguished face on the boat, and sufficiently like Mackay Senior to confirm the relationship?

"Brothers!" she exclaimed. "It must be Magnus!"

Yes, now the story was complete—in Miss Phipps's bubbling mind. The dead boy was the younger brother; he had been paying attention to the older son's beautiful wife; the older son had caught him at it, taken him off in the boat to Fersa, tipped his body over a cliff, expecting the tides to carry off the corpse; but a hand or foot had caught in a niche of the rock and the body still lay there awaiting discovery.

But heavens, what was old Mackay doing now? He pulled at a foot, released it, then heaving the body on its side, pushed it into the waters of the bay. It rolled, paused, drifted, was sucked below a nose of rock, was freed by a stronger wave, then edged its way slowly toward the open sea.

Mackay looked up; Miss Phipps quickly hid behind a rock. A pebble shot from beneath her foot. She hoped he had not heard it or seen her; but she could not feel comfortably sure, for he stood still and gazed round the bay, even shading his eyes with his hand to give himself clearer vision.

There were only two possible courses of action, thought Miss Phipps: go down and confront him, or slip away unseen. With immense relief she perceived that the cliffs were too precipitous here for an elderly lady to descend with reasonable safety, not to mention ease. For a moment which seemed an hour, Mackay gazed and Miss Phipps crouched, peering sideways round her concealing rock. Then at last the old man gave up his search, stepped down into his boat, released the painter and chugged away.

The moment he was out of sight beyond the cliff Miss Phipps flew. She climbed up the rocks behind her with no care for knees or hands, rushed up the green slope, ran down the rough path, and was sitting on a grassy knoll with her hands clasped round her knees, breathing hard but gazing serenely out to sea when Mackay in his boat came round the nose of the cliff and approached the rocks. Miss Phipps gave him a friendly wave.

"Have ye seen all the isle ye fancy?"

Miss Phipps found this inquiry a trifle sinister. Was he trying to discover if she had visited the bay which held the body?

"Enough," she replied in an off-hand but, she hoped, reassuring tone.

Mackay gave one of those northern snorts whose meaning can only be discovered by its context. He climbed out of his boat, tied it up to the iron ring provided for the purpose, and approached her.

He suspects me; I must admit, reflected Miss Phipps, that I'm afraid.

She looked with longing at the massive hillside beyond which her companions were presumably still engrossed in Viking remains.

"Wad it please ye to come round in the boat wi' me to fetch the others awa'?" suggested Mackay, obviously noting the direction of her glance.

Not on your life, thought Miss Phipps. There was a gleam in his eye which she found most disturbing. If she went out alone in the boat with him, she was sure there would be another body lost off this island. But how to put him off?

"Is there a landing stage there?" she said aloud, with an obvious note of doubt.

"There's a slab of concrete amid the rocks."

"We should probably miss them, wouldn't we?"

"We could always turn back."

"We could," began Miss Phipps, "but is it wise to take the risk of missing them?"

Mackay gave another island snort and extended his hand. Miss Phipps—unhappily, but not able to think of further delaying tactics—took it and rose. She gave a last despairing glance toward the hillside, and there, oh, joy, came her rescuers. Just over the brow appeared Professor Morison and Inspector Tarrant.

"There they are!" she exclaimed gratefully. "Bill! Professor Morison! Cooee!"

Deep in conversation they took not the slightest notice of her appeals. She waved, she cried out, she almost screamed, but Inspector Tarrant remained bent toward the Professor, who continually talked and pointed. Obviously he was deep in his favorite subject of ornithology.

"These birdwatchers," said Miss Phipps with irritation.

"Aweel, you can get in the boat and sit," urged Mackay.

"I'll wait for them here," said Miss Phipps, reminding herself how many a slip there could be between boat and rock. That iron ring too—a nasty thing to strike one's head against. She withdrew her hand. "I'll wait for them here," she repeated.

"As ye please," said Mackay.

He withdrew to his boat, but with true Norse economy did not start the engine.

At long, long last the Viking-fans reached Miss Phipps. Professor Morison, his sad eyes beaming, was now talking about the varying coloration of puffins.

"You might have acknowledged my greetings," snapped Miss Phipps, peevish.

"I'm sorry, but we didn't hear you," said Bill Tarrant mildly.

After a further long wait Mary and Mrs. Morison arrived talking about fashions. They all got into the boat without incident, Miss Phipps taking care to descend with, and sit between, her two female companions.

The sea was rougher than before. Professor Morison's shade of green was now a darkling olive. Waves slapped overboard, and Miss Phipps, normally a lover of stormy seas, began to wish that they were safely ashore—really this tossing gave too many opportunities for an "accident." Mackay was capable of drowning the whole lot of them to save his son, she reflected.

"Hae ye bairns?" inquired Mackay suddenly.

It seemed the Morisons had none; the Tarrants admitted their two.

"And you?" said Bill politely.

"I have two sons, Eric and Magnus," said Mackay, glancing at Miss Phipps. "But they're footloose. Shetland's too small for them. They're both intending to be awa' to London."

"What will they do there?" asked Professor Morison. "No mountains, no sea, no birds."

"Zelda will like it. Eric's wife. Her at the post office. She's London-born," said Mackay, with a certain bitterness. "She came to the island on a holiday cruise."

"Oh, look, there's a seal!" cried Mary Tarrant enthusiastically.

Glancing up, Miss Phipps found Mackay's eyes fixed fiercely on her. Of course—there was a seal at the entrance of the murder bay, she thought; if he learns I saw it he'll think I saw other things in that bay too. All this passed through her mind in a flash. As if she had never seen a seal in her life and would not recognize a seal if she saw one, she cried out cheerfully, "Where?"—and conscientiously scanned the horizon.

It was a good lie—accepted, Miss Phipps noted with great relief, where acceptance was most needed.

Two mornings later, with Scottish soil safely beneath their feet and Shetland lying far behind them in the northern waves, Miss Phipps began to argue with her conscience as to whether she should tell Inspector Tarrant of her Fersa adventure. It seemed, on the one hand, her duty as a citizen to do so. But on the other hand, she thought of old broken-hearted Mackay, of that silly lovely Zelda, of the anguished Eric . . .

"They will have enough misery as it is," she murmured, "and it won't do Magnus any good."

After a few moments she smiled. "Besides, I don't *know* anything—I don't *really* know. After all, it was only an exercise of my métier!"

It was one of the rare occasions on which Miss Phipps the professional novelist triumphed over Miss Phipps the amateur criminologist.

Joe Gores

File #6: Beyond the Shadow

*Here is one of the most unusual Christmas Eve detective stories
we have ever read . . . In the letter accompanying the original
manuscript, the author, Joe Gores, short-story Edgar winner of
1969, wrote: "I tried to write this story on three levels. First,
simply as a File Series story about the repossession of a car;
second, as a new kind of procedural detective story; and third,
as a 'challenge to the reader' (with a bow to E.Q.) in which the
final twist, the revelation that explains all, comes in the last
three words of the story."*

*We'll say no more now—but please take the author's chal-
lenge seriously. It will add immeasurably to your reading enjoyment . . . Happy holiday!*

Detectives: DANIEL KEARNY ASSOCIATES

Christmas Eve in San Francisco: bright decorations under al-
ternating rain and mist. Despite the weather, the fancy shops
ringing Union Square had been jammed with last-minute buyers,
and the Santa Claus at Geary and Stockton had long since found
a sheltered doorway from which to contemplate his imminent un-
employment. Out on Golden Gate Avenue the high-shouldered
charcoal Victorian which housed Daniel Kearny Associates was
unusually dark and silent. Kearny had sent the office staff home
at 2:30; soon after, Kathy Onoda, the Japanese office manager,
had departed.

Sometime after 9:00, Giselle Marc stuck her shining blonde
head through the open sliding door of Kearny's cubbyhole in the
DKA basement.

"You need me for anything more, Dan?"

Kearny looked up in surprise. "I thought I sent you girls home."

"Year-end stuff I wanted a head start on," she said lightly.
Giselle was 26, tall and lithe, with a Master's degree in history

and all the brains that aren't supposed to go with her sort of looks. That year she had no one special to go home to. "What about you?"

"I've been looking for a handle in that Bannock file for Golden Gate Trust. There's a police A.P.B. out on Myra, the older girl, and since she's probably driving the Lincoln that we're supposed to repossess—"

"An A.P.B.! Why?"

"The younger sister, Ruth, was found today over in Contra Costa County. Shot. Dead. She'd been there for several days."

"And the police think Myra did it?" asked Giselle.

Kearny shrugged. Just then he looked his 44 hard driving years. Too many all-night searches for deadbeats, embezzlers, or missing relatives; too many repossessions after non-stop investigations; too many bourbons straight from too many hotel-room bottles with other men as hard as himself.

"The police want to talk to her, anyway. Some of the places we've had to look for those girls, I wouldn't be surprised at *anything* that either one of them did. The Haight, upper Grant, the commune out on Sutter Street—how can people live like that, Giselle?"

"Different strokes for different folks, Dan'l." She added thoughtfully, "That's the second death in this case in a week."

"I don't follow."

"Irma Carroll. The client's wife."

"She was a suicide," objected Kearny. "Of course, for all we know, so was Ruth Bannock. Anyway, we've got to get that car before the police impound it. That would mean the ninety-day dealer recourse would expire, and the bank would have to eat the car."

He flipped the Bannock file a foot in the air so that it fell on the desk and slewed out papers like a fanned deck of cards. "The bank's deadline is Monday. That gives us only three days to come up with the car."

He shook a cigarette from his pack as he listened to Giselle's retreating heels, lit up, and then waved a hand to dispel the smoke from his tired eyes. A rough week. Rough year, actually, with the state snuffling around on license renewal because of this and that, and the constant unsuccessful search for a bigger office. There was that old brick laundry down on 11th Street for sale, but their asking price . . .

Ought to get home to Mama and the kids. Instead he leaned back in the swivel chair with his hands locked behind his head to stare at the ceiling in silence. The smoke of his cigarette drifted almost hypnotically upward.

Silence. Unusual at DKA. Usually field men were coming in and going out. Phones were ringing, intercom was buzzing. Giselle or Kathy or Jane Goldson, the Limey wench whose accent lent a bit of class to the switchboard, calling down from upstairs with a hot one. O'Bannon in to bang the desk about the latest cuts in his expense account . . .

The Bannock Lincoln. Damned odd case. Stewart Carroll, the auto zone man at Golden Gate Trust, had waited three months before even assigning the car to DKA. That had been last Monday, the 21st. The same night Carroll's wife committed suicide. And now one of the free-wheeling Bannock girls was dead, murdered maybe, in a state park on a mountain in the East Bay. One in the temple, the latest news broadcast had said.

Doubtful that the sister, Myra, had pulled the trigger; if he was looking for a head-roller in the case he'd pick that slick friend of theirs, that real-estate man down on Montgomery Street. Raymond Edwards. Now there was a guy capable of doing anything to . . .

The sound of the front door closing jerked Kearny's eyes from the sound-proofed ceiling. He could see a man's shadow cast thick and heavy down the garage. It might have belonged to Trinidad Morales, but he'd fired Morales last summer.

The man who appeared in the office doorway *was* built like Morales, short and broad and overweight, with a sleepy, pleasantly tough face. Maybe a couple of years younger than Kearny. Durable-looking. Giselle must have forgotten to set the outside lock.

"You're looking hard for that Bannock Lincoln."

"Any of your business?" asked Kearny almost pleasantly. Not a process server: he would have been advancing with a toothy grin as he reached for the papers to slap on the desk.

"Could be." He sat down unbidden on the other side of the desk. "I'm a cop. Private tin, like you. We were hired by old man Bannock to find the daughters, same day you were hired by Golden Gate Trust to find the car."

Kearny lit another cigarette. Neither Heslip nor Ballard had cut this one's sign, which meant he had to be damned smooth.

"The police found one of the girls," Kearny said.

"Yeah. Ruth. I was over in Contra Costa County when she turned up. Just got back. Clearing in the woods up on Mount Diablo, beside the ashes of a little fire." He paused. "Pretty odd, Stewart Carroll letting that car get right up to the deadline before assigning it out."

"He probably figured old man Bannock would make the payments even though he wasn't on the contract." Then Kearny added, his square hard face watchful, "You have anything that says who you are?"

The stocky man grunted and dug out a business card. Kearny had never heard of the agency. There were a lot of them he'd never heard of, mostly one-man shops with impressive-sounding names like this one.

"Well, that's interesting, Mr. Wright," he said. He stood up. "But it *is* Christmas Eve and—"

"Or maybe Carroll had other things on his mind," Wright cut in almost dreamily. "His wife, Irma, for instance. Big fancy house out in Presidio Terrace—even had a fireplace in the bedroom where she killed herself. Ashes in the grate, maybe like she'd burned some papers, pictures, something like that."

Kearny sat down. "A fire like the one where Ruth died?"

The stocky detective gave a short appreciative laugh. "The girls got a pretty hefty allowance—so why were they three months' delinquent on their car payment? And why, the day before they disappeared—last Thursday, a week ago today—did they try to hit the old man up for some very substantial extra loot? Since they didn't get it—"

"You checked the pawnshops." It was the obvious move.

"Yeah. Little joint down on Third and Mission, the guy says that Myra, the older sister, came in and hocked a bunch of jewelry on Friday morning. Same day she and her sister disappeared. She had a cute little blonde with her at the pawnshop."

Kearny stubbed out his cigarette and lit another. The smoke filled the cramped office. Cute little blonde didn't fit the dead Ruth at all.

"Irma Carroll," he said. "You think her husband delayed assigning the Lincoln for repossession because she asked him to. Why?"

"So old man Bannock wouldn't know his daughters had financial woes," beamed the other detective. "We got a positive ident on Irma Carroll from the pawnbroker. Plus she was away from home Friday—the day the sisters disappeared."

"And on Monday she killed herself. When did Ruth die?"

"Friday night, Saturday morning, close as the coroner can tell."

"Mmmm." Kearny smoked silently for a moment. James (Jimmy) Wright—according to the name on his card—had a good breadth of shoulder, good thickness of chest and arm. Physically competent, despite his owl-like appearance. With a damned subtle mind besides. "I wonder how many *other* local women in the past year—"

Wright held up three fingers. "I started out with a list like a small-town phone book—every female suicide and disappearance in San Francisco since January first. Three of them knew the Bannock girls *and* the Carroll woman, and all three needed money *and* burned something before they killed themselves. No telling how many more just burned whatever it was they were buying and then sat tight."

Kearny squinted through his cigarette smoke. He had long since forgotten about spending Christmas Eve with Jeanie and the kids.

"I figure you've got more than just that. Another connection maybe between your three suicides and the Bannock girls and Irma Carroll—" He paused to taste his idea, and liked it. "Raymond Edwards?"

The stock man beamed again.

"Edwards. Yeah. I'd like to get a look at that bird's tax returns. Real-estate office on Montgomery Street—but no clients. Fancy apartment out in the Sunset and spends plenty of money—but doesn't seem to make any. What put you on to him?"

"Two of the hippies at that Sutter Street commune gave us a make on a cat in a Ferrari who was a steady customer for psilocybin—the 'sacred mushrooms' of the Mex Indians. On their description I ran Edwards through DMV in Sacramento and found he holds the pink on a Ferrari. A lot of car for a man with no visible income not to owe any money on. And—no other car."

"I don't see any significance in that," objected Wright.

"You don't sell real estate out of a Ferrari."

The other detective nodded. "Got you. And Edwards made it down to his office exactly twice this week—to pick up his mail. But every night he made it to a house up on Telegraph Hill—each time with a different well-to-do dame."

"But none of them the Bannock girls," said Kearny.

The phone interrupted. That would be Jeanie, he thought as he picked up. But after a moment he extended the receiver to Wright.

"Yeah . . . I see." He nodded and his eyes glistened. "Are you sure it was Myra? In this fog . . . that close, huh?" He listened some more. "Through the cellar window? Good. Yes. No. Kearny and I'll go in—what?" Another pause. "I don't give a damn about that, we need someone outside to tail her if she comes out before we do."

He hung up, turned to Kearny.

"Myra just went into the Telegraph Hill place through a cellar window. She's still in there. You heavy?"

"Not for years." You wore a gun, you sometimes used it. "And what makes you so sure I'll go along with you?"

The stocky detective grinned. "Find Myra, we find the Lincoln, right? *Before* the cops. You get your car, I get somebody who ain't shy to back my play. I'd have a hell of a time scraping up another of my own men on Christmas Eve."

Kearny unlocked the filing cabinet and from its middle drawer took out a Luger and a full clip. A German officer had fired it at him outside Aumetz in 1944, when the 106th Panzer SS had broken through to 90th Division HQ.

He dropped it into his right-hand topcoat pocket, stuck Wright's card in his left. He had another question but it could wait.

The fog was thick and wet outside, glistening on the streets and haloing the lights. They walked past Kearny's Ford station wagon, their shoes rapping hollow against the concrete. He felt twenty years old again. From a Van Ness bus they transferred to the California cable, transferred again on Nob Hill where the thick fog made pale blobs of the bright Christmas decorations on the Mark and the Fairmont. A band of caroling youngsters drifted past them, voices fog-muted. Alcatraz bellowed desolately from the black bay like an injured sea beast.

They were the only ones left on the car at the turn-around in the 500 block of Greenwich. Fog shrouded the crowded houses slanting steeply down the hill. Christmas trees brightened many windows, their candles flickering warmly through the steamy glass. The detectives paused in the light from the tavern on Grant and Greenwich.

"Which way?" asked Kearny.

"Up the hill. Then we work around to the Filbert Street steps. My man'll meet us somewhere below Montgomery."

They toiled up the steep brushy side of Telegraph beyond the Greenwich dead end, their shoes slipping in the heavy yellowish loam. Kearny went to one knee and cursed. When they paused at the head of the wooden Filbert Street steps, both men were panting and sweat sheened their faces. The sea-wet wind off the bay swirled fog around them, danced the widely-scattered street lights below.

Just as they started down, the fog eddied to reveal, beyond the shadow of clearly etched foilage, the misty panorama of the bay. Off to the left was grimly lit Alcatraz, and ahead, to the right of dark Yerba Buena Island, the 11:00 o'clock ferry to Oakland, yellow pinpoints moving against the darkness. Then foliage closed in wetly on either side. The Luger was a heavy comfortable weight in Kearny's pocket. He could see only about two yards ahead in the bone-chilling fog. When they crossed Montgomery the air carried the musty tang of fermenting grapes. The old Italians must make plenty of wine up here. There was another, more acrid scent; somewhere an animal bleated.

"They ought to pen up their goats once in a while," chuckled Kearny's companion. "They stink."

More wooden steps in the fog. They paused where a narrow path led off into the grayness.

"Catfish Row," muttered the stocky detective in Kearny's ear. "My man ought to be around some—" He broke off as a short dark shape materialized at their elbow. "Dick?"

"Right."

"She's still inside?"

"Right."

The newcomer pulled out a handkerchief to wipe the fog from his sharp-featured irritable face. Kearny got a vagrant whiff of scent.

"We're going in," breathed the stocky detective. "If the Bannock girl comes out, stick with her."

"Right," said Dick.

They started along an uneven brick path slippery with moss, then began climbing another set of narrow wooden steps which paralleled those on Filbert.

"Your man is talkative," said Kearny drily.

"Canadian," said the other. "A good detective."

"But you don't trust him in this." Kearny then asked the question he hadn't asked back in the office. "Why?"

Wright shrugged irritably. "I've got enough to do without having to watch him." He didn't elaborate.

They stopped and peered through the gloom at a three-storied narrow wooden house that looked egg-yolk yellow in the fog. Dripping bushes flanked it both uphill and down. There was a half basement; the uphill side had not been excavated from the rock. Myra Bannock must have entered by one of the blacked-out windows which flanked the gray basement door.

The two detectives climbed past it to the first-floor level. Here a small porch cantilevered out over the recessed basement. The front door and windows were decorated to echo the high-peaked roof of the house itself.

A big black man answered the bell. The hallway behind him was so dark that his face showed only highlights: brows, cheekbones, nose, lips, a gleam of eyeballs. He was wearing red. Red fez, red silk Nehru jacket over red striped shirt, red harem pants with baggy legs, red shoes with upturned toes.

"*As-salaam aleikum,*" he said.

"Mr. Maxwell, please," said Wright briskly.

The door began to close. The dumpy detective stuck his foot in it and immediately a gong boomed in the back of the house. Kearny's companion sank a fist into the middle of the red shirt as Kearny's shoulder slammed into the door.

The guard was on his hands and knees in the dim hallway, gasping. His eyes rolled up at Kearny's as the detectives stormed by him.

A door slammed up above. They climbed broad circular stairs in the gloom, guns out. Their shoulders in unison splintered a locked door at the head of the stairs. The room was blue-lit, seemingly empty except for incense, thick carpets, and strewn clothing of both sexes. Then they saw three women and a man crowded into a corner, a grotesque frightened jumble, all of them nude.

"Topless *and* bottomless," grunted Kearny.

"But no Myra," said Wright in a disgust that was practical, not moral. "Let's dust."

As they came out of the room, feet pounded down the stairs. They'd been faked out—drawn into the room by the slamming door so that someone who was trapped upstairs by their entrance could get by them. Peering down, Kearny saw Raymond Edwards' head just sliding from view around the stairs' old-fashioned newel post. Edwards. The real-estate promoter who didn't promote real estate.

Kearny went over the banister, landed with a jar that clipped his jaw against his knee, stumbled to his feet, and charged down the hall. He went through an open doorway to meet a black fist traveling very rapidly in the other direction. The doorkeeper.

"Ungh!" Kearny went down, gagging, but managed to wave Wright through the door where Edwards and the black man had just disappeared.

There was a crash within, and furious curses. A gun went off. Once more. Kearny tottered through the doorway, an old man again, to see another door across the room just closing and the stocky detective and the guard locked in a curious dance. The black man had the detective's arms pinned at his side, and the detective was trying to shoot his captor in the foot.

Kearny's Luger, swung in a wide backhand arc, made a thwucking sound against the black's skull. The black shook his head, turned, grabbed Kearny, who dropped the Luger as he was bounced off the far wall. A hand came up under his jaw and shoved. He started to yell at the ceiling. His neck was going to break.

The black shuddered like a ship hitting a reef. Again. Again. Yet again. His hands went away. Wright was standing over the downed man, looking at his gun in a puzzled way.

"I hit him with it four times before he went down. Four times."

"Edwards?" Kearny managed to gasp.

"That way." He shook his head. "Four times."

The door was locked. They broke through after several tries and went downstairs to the empty cellar. But there was another door; the durable detective kicked off the lock. A red glow and a chemical smell emerged.

"Darkroom," said Kearny.

A girl came out stiffly, her eyes wide with shock. It was Myra Bannock. A solid meaty girl in a fawn pants suit with a white ruffled Restoration blouse. Square-toed high heels made her two inches taller than either of them.

"Did you kill him, sister?"

"Y—yes."

Over her shoulder Kearny could see Edwards on the floor with one hand still stretched up into an open squat iron safe. He was dressed in 19th Century splendor: black velvet even to his shirt and shoes. Once in the temple, a contact wound with powder burns. Kearny looked at his watch automatically. They'd been in the house exactly six minutes. *Six minutes?* It seemed like a weekend.

"Why'd you come here tonight?" demanded the other detective.

"Pic-pictures. I wanted—" Her jaw started to tremble.

"What kind of scam was Edwards running?" Kearny wondered.

"Cult stuff, I'm sure," said Wright. "Turning on wealthy young matrons to the Age of Aquarius or something. Getting them up here, doping them up, taking pictures of them doing things they'd pay to keep their parents or husbands from seeing." He turned sharply to the girl. "What kind of pictures?"

"Ter-terrible. Nasty things. We—he would give us 'sacred' wine to drink. It—distorted—able to see beyond . . . beyond the shadow. At the time everything seemed *right*." A long shudder ran through her flesh like the slow roll of an ocean wave.

"You and Ruth both?"

"Yes. Both. Together, even. With my own sister, with Irma—" She drew a ragged breath. "I sneaked in to get the negatives. I found the safe—but it was locked. Then Raymond ran in. I was behind the door." She suddenly giggled, a little girl sound. "He opened the safe and I saw the pictures inside, so I walked up and—and I shot him. Just shot him."

Without warning she started to cry, great racking sobs that twisted her face and aged her. The stocky detective was on his knees at the safe, dragging out a thick sheaf of Kodacolor negatives and a heavy stack of prints.

"Where'd you get the gun?" he asked over his shoulder.

"On Third Street," she got out through her sobs. "We pawned our jewelry to pay for the pictures."

"Same gun your sister was killed with?" asked Kearny.

"Does this have to go on and on?" she demanded suddenly, with an abrupt synthetic calmness. "I killed him. Just take me in—"

"We're private," snapped Wright. "Hired by your father to find you girls. Tell us what happened up on Mount Diablo."

His tone got through and started words again.

"I—we opened the pictures we bought—Friday morning after we pawned the jewelry to pay for them. Just prints. No negatives. We knew then that he planned to ask for more money. Irma was trying to raise it, but Ruth and I decided to just—well, kill ourselves. So we drove up to the mountains to—" Her face was starting to crumple, but the detective held her with his eyes. "To do it. But then I said I wouldn't give him the satisfaction. I would burn the pictures and then come back with the gun. But when I started burning them—when I—"

"Keep going," said Kearny.

"Ruth just grabbed the gun from the glove compartment and ran across the little clearing. I ran after her but she stopped and—and—" She started to cry.

"There's no time for that now!" snarled the stocky detective to her tears. "Let's have it."

"She put the gun against her head and it made such a little noise." Her eyes were puzzled now. "Like a twig breaking. Then she fell down."

"Where have you been since then?" asked Kearny.

"I paid for a Lombard Street motel with a credit card and just stayed there. I wanted to shoot myself but I couldn't. Tonight the radio said they had found Ruth. I knew then that I had to come here and get the negatives, so she wouldn't have died for nothing."

"Just dumb luck she made it here without being spotted by the cops," said Kearny. He swung back to her. "Where did you leave the Lincoln?"

"On Montgomery. In front of Julius's Castle."

"Give me the keys." She did. He said to Wright, "The pawnbroker isn't about to identify the gun, since he sold it to her illegally in the first place. So if the cops find it here beside the body with only Edwards' fingerprints on it—"

The squat detective's eyes narrowed. He paused in his picture shuffling. "Yeah. It'll work. And they'll think Edwards burned whatever was in the safe before he did himself in. Yeah. Hand her over to Dick, tell him to take her back to her old man so his doctor can knock her out before they call in the police. I'll—"

"You'll burn the pictures," said Kearny. "While I watch."

Wright laughed, then handed a slim sheaf of them to Kearny. As Myra had said, they were indescribably nasty—acts performed by people strung out on the mind-altering psilocybin. The things people got themselves into while looking for kicks. It was lucky Edwards was dead or Kearny might have been tempted to do the job himself. He handed the pictures back.

"Burn them," he said harshly. "All of them."

The squat durable detective did. A good man, good when the trouble started. Myra drifted away into the fog with Dick's hand on her arm. The Lincoln was parked by the closed restaurant, as she had said, and the key started it. No cops spotted Kearny getting it back to the DKA garage . . .

Kearny came to with a start, found himself slumped in his chair, his head hanging over the back at an odd angle, the edge of the typing stand digging into him. He groaned. His stomach hurt, his neck was stiff. Must have fallen asleep after getting the Lincoln—

Mists of sleep and dream cleared. He dug strong fingers into the back of his neck. Midnight and after, and he and Jeanie still faced a night of trimming the tree. The kids were at an age when Santa arrived while they slept, so Christmas morning dawned to awe and delight.

He stood up. Damned neck. Sleep and dream. Dream.

Dream.

Dammit! He'd fallen asleep over the Bannock file, with Stewart Carroll's wife's suicide on his mind, and Ruth Bannock's death, and had dreamed the whole crazy thing! Fog. Cable cars. The house on Telegraph Hill.

He rubbed his neck again. So damned vivid; but there was no Greenwich Street cable car. Had there ever been? Catfish Row was now Napier Lane. And the Christmas trees now had, not candles, but strings of electric lights. Goats and the smell of wine were both long gone, fifty years or more, from Telegraph Hill.

He flipped through the big maroon *Polk Cross-Street Directory* to 491 Greenwich. *Mike's Grocery.* In the dream, a tavern. And in the dream, an Oakland ferry: they had stopped running a dozen years before. No Bay Bridge either—it had been built in the 'thirties. As had Treasure Island, also missing from the dream, man-made in 1938, '39, as a home for the San Francisco World's Fair.

All so damned vivid. Usually a dream faded in a few minutes, but this one had remained, sharp and clear.

Kearny started to sit down, frowning, then stood up abruptly and felt his topcoat hanging on the rack. Damp. It should have dried off from the rain he'd ducked through this afternoon. Well, it hadn't, that's all. A better way to check: merely pull open the middle drawer of the filing cabinet to look at the Luger—

The Luger was gone.

Kearny stood quite still with the hairs tingling on the back of his sore neck. Then he slammed the drawer impatiently shut. Hell, it could have been missing for weeks.

But what if the Luger was found in a yellow house on Telegraph Hill, a house with a dead body in the basement and a safe full of ashes? So? The gun had never been registered, and it was tougher to get fingerprints off them than people realized.

Dammit, he thought, stop it. It had been a dream, just a dream. And despite the dream he still had to find the Bannock Lincoln before the deadline. He strode around the desk, slid back the glass door, stuck his head out to look down the garage.

Kearny's face felt suddenly stiff. Bright gleam of chrome and black enamel. Correct license plate. He went out, stiff-legged like a dog getting ready to fight, rapped his knuckles on the sleek streamlined hood. Real. The Bannock Lincoln. How in hell—

Larry Ballard, of course. Larry had been working the case, had spotted the car, repo'd it, dropped it off in the garage without even knowing that Kearny was asleep in his sound-proofed cubbyhole.

But what if Ballard *hadn't* repo'd the car?

Well, then, dammit, Kearny would dummy up some sort of report for the client. They had the car, that was the important thing. And—well, there would be some rational explanation if Larry *hadn't* been the one who'd brought it in.

Kearny left the office, setting the alarms and double-locking the basement door to activate them. He walked slowly down to the Ford station wagon. What did it all add up to? A crazy dream that *couldn't* be true, because it was mixed up with San Francisco of fifty years ago. Certain things seemed to have slopped over from the dream into subsequent reality, but there was a rational explanation for all of them—there must be. He would take that rational explanation, every time. Dan Kearny was not a fanciful man.

He reached for his keys in the topcoat pocket and touched a small oblong of thin cardboard. He looked at it for a long moment, then with an almost compulsive gesture he flipped it into the gutter between his car and the curb. It had probably been in his pocket for a week—people were always handing him business cards. Especially guys in his own racket, guys with little one-man outfits sporting those impressive-sounding names.

Kearny snorted as he got into the station wagon. What was the name on his business card? Oh, yeah. Continental Detective Agency.

Author's Note

I think I have invented a new kind of procedural detective story—what might be termed a "procedural fantasy." While it uses the dream "story-within-a-story" which antedates even William Langland's *The Vision of Pierce Plowman* (1550), it is also a Files Series procedural.

There are numerous clues in the story that suggest it is a dream, beginning with Kearny and Jimmy Wright walking past Kearny's car as if it doesn't exist in the time continuum the two men now inhabit. Some clues—for example, candles on Christmas trees—should be apparent to all readers; others—such as the nonexistent Bay Bridge—would obviusly have more significance to those who are familiar with San Francisco.

Because the story grew out of my personal conviction that San-Francisco-in-the-fog still belongs to Dashiell Hammett, I have inserted quite a few clues pointing to the identity of Jimmy Wright.

First, the plot was frankly adapted from Hammett's masterly Continental Op story, *The Scorched Face*; even DKA's client (Golden Gate Trust) was borrowed from it, as were the first names of other characters.

Next, the detective on stakeout was obviously that old Continental hand, Dick Foley. Besides retaining his first name, I described him essentially as Hammett did in *Red Harvest*. (It was in *Red Harvest*, you'll remember, that Foley suspected the Continental Op of murder and was sent away with the remark, "I've got enough to do without having to watch you.")

As for Jimmy Wright himself, his physical de-

trimly built man on a chestnut mare. The man seemed to be one of the jump judges.

Presently there was some commotion across the field, and they could see that one of the horses had thrown its youthful rider at a water jump. The standby ambulance started toward the scene and the other riders were held at their starting point. The man on the chestnut mare watched for a time through his binoculars, then cantered over to Nick's car.

"Looks like rain," he said, smiling. "Enjoying the show?"

"We were until now." Nick motioned across the field. "Is the rider badly hurt?"

"No, no! Just had the wind knocked out of her. It's Lynn Peters, one of our new members. I'm afraid she's not up to water jumps yet." He seemed to remember that he hadn't introduced himself. "I'm Frader Kincaid, master of the hunt here. You folks coming to the open house afterwards?"

"We're not members," Nick told him.

"Don't worry about that—it's open to all. The big house at the top of the hill. I'll be looking for you."

When Kincaid had ridden away, Gloria tugged on Nick's sleeve. "I'd love to go for a little while, Nicky."

He sighed, seeing there was no way out. "We'll stop by."

When Nick and Gloria arrived at the house on the hill two hours later, the party was already in full swing. A light rain had started to fall, but it hadn't dampened any spirits. Middle-aged men and somewhat younger women in riding togs filled two large downstairs rooms, sipping cocktails while they chattered and giggled and generally relaxed. It was not Nick's sort of gathering, but he knew Gloria would enjoy it.

"Glad you could make it," Kincaid greeted them. It was obvious now that the house was his, and the party was his also. "Martinis all right?"

"Fine."

He produced two with a smile and then hooked an arm around the waist of a passing girl. "This is Lynn Peters, who scared us all with her fall this afternoon. Feeling better, Lynn?"

She was young and sandy-haired, with cheeks flushed pink from drink or embarrassment. Her riding breeches and red corduroy vest fitted her well, and she was quick with a smile that included them all. "I'm fine now, Frader. My mount just didn't like the looks of that water hole."

Kincaid smiled benevolently. "Why don't you girls talk it over while I show Mr. Velvet my den? I have a nice collection I'd like to show him."

Nick followéd the tall man through a door at the far end of the room, into a book-lined study that overlooked the valley where the horse trials had been held. "Beautiful country, even on a rainy day," Kincaid commented.

Nick sipped his drink and asked, "How did you happen to know my name?"

"Oh, you noticed that? Once down at the Yacht Club someone pointed you out to me. I recognized you watching the jumps today and thought I might interest you in a business venture."

"My business activities are strictly limited."

Frader Kincaid moved around to the side of the desk, carefully resting his cocktail glass on a used envelope. "You're a professional thief, Mr. Velvet, and that's exactly the sort of venture I have in mind."

Nick's expression didn't change. He simply said, "My fee is quite large—$20,000—and I steal only objects of little or no value."

"I understand all that."

"What is the object you had in mind?"

Kincaid motioned toward the wall between the bookcases where an elaborate oil painting hung. It was an odd subject for a rich man's wall—a prehistoric scene of two dinosaurs locked in deadly combat against a dank swampy landscape. "How much do you know of these things, Mr. Velvet?"

"Nothing I didn't learn from the monster films when I was a kid."

"I publish several lines of paperbound books, and this was the cover painting for a science-fiction novel. I liked the painting, even if the book lost money. Only one thing sells these days." He grinned and chose a book at random from the case beside him. Nick needed only a glance at the bare-bosomed model and the sex-slang title to know the kind of book it was.

"You publish pornography?" he asked Kincaid.

"I publish what the people buy. One year it's dinosaurs, the next it's derrières. Makes not a particle of difference to me."

Nick merely grunted. He was hardly in a position to comment on other men's morals. "What is it you want stolen?"

Kincaid tapped the framed painting with his index finger. "This one is a Tyrannosaurus Rex, the largest flesh-eating creature that ever existed. Its teeth alone were eight inches long, and its total length was something like fifty feet. The Brontosaurus was larger, of course, but it ate only herbs and plants."

"You seem to know a great deal about them."

"It's a hobby of mine." Kincaid smiled with satisfaction. "But to get to the point, Mr. Velvet. You are familiar with the Museum of Ancient History in upper Manhattan?"

"Of course."

"They have a fine complete skeleton of a Tyrannosaurus Rex there. I want you to steal its tail."

Nick Velvet simply stared at him, letting the words sink in. He had received some strange assignments in his career, but never anything like stealing the tail from a museum's dinosaur skeleton. "Not the whole thing? Just the tail?"

"Just the tail. The last few bones of the tail, to be exact."

"All right. How soon do you need it?"

"Before the end of the week. I do believe it was fate that brought you here today, just when I needed you." He walked a few steps to a small wall safe and returned with a packet of money. "This much in advance. The rest when you deliver the tail."

They shook hands and Nick pocketed the money. Then he left the room in search of Gloria. When he found her she was looking unhappy. "I never thought you were coming back, Nicky!"

"Didn't you enjoy your chat with Lynn Peters?"

"Not really. She doesn't actually know too much about jumping." Gloria put down her glass. "Maybe we should go now, Nicky. They really aren't our sort of people."

"No," he agreed. "I don't think they are."

On Monday morning Nick drove down to New York. He left the Major Deegan Expressway at 155th Street and crossed the Harlem River into Manhattan's northern limits. From there it was only a five-minute drive to the Museum of Ancient History, a big rambling red-brick monstrosity that reminded him of the Smithsonian on a bad day. The parking lot was nearly deserted this early, and he pulled up near the front entrance.

Inside, the place was all that its exterior promised—high ceilings with dusty skylights, marble floors, an air of mustiness that seemed to filter right through his clothes. It was everything a museum of the 1920's should have been, and if it was still that way nearly a half century later, one could only sigh with regret and remember those earlier, grander days.

Nick made his way through the Egyptian Room and the Etruscan Wing, coming at last to the Hall of Great Reptiles. And there it was, in all its baroque splendor—Tyrannosaurus Rex, towering 25 feet into the air and stretching back nearly 50 feet from head to tail. There was something sad and oddly dated about the hundreds of polished bones wired together as a memorial to this creature of long ago. After the indignities of the zoo, would modern animals be subjected to such extravagances, too? He'd read somewhere that only 600 tigers remained in the world, and he wondered if some future generation might be forced to view the skeleton of a Bengal as he now viewed this blanched relic.

He walked the full length of the great beast and paused to examine the jointed tail section. There was certainly nothing remarkable about the dozens of small bones that made up the tail. He bent closer across the rope barrier for a better look, but there was nothing to explain his assignment. He'd hardly expected a jeweled tail, for example; yet there must be some reason for the proposed theft.

Almost at once a uniformed guard appeared and called out, "Not too close there, mister. Them things are delicate!"

"Sorry. Just wanted a good look. Know where these bones came from?"

The guard moved closer, friendly now. "Out west somewhere. It tells on the sign. In most of these skeletons we have to use some fake bones. It's impossible to find one of these things complete."

Nick nodded and turned away, not wanting to show too much interest. "It sure was big," he said by way of conclusion, and drifted back to the Etruscan Wing.

He might have passed directly through to the Egyptian Room if he hadn't recognized a familiar face bent over one of the glass display cases. It was that of Lynn Peters, the girl he'd met at Kincaid's house. Her flushed cheeks and sandy hair were unmistakable, even if she was not wearing her riding costume.

"Hello there," he said. "I believe we met yesterday after the horse trials."

She turned, the fresh young smile coming naturally to her face. "Oh, it's Mr. Velvet, isn't it? I had a nice chat with your wife last evening."

"Gloria's just a friend," he corrected her amiably. "But what brings you here? I don't see a single horse in the whole place. Not a live one, anyway."

"They're having a special exhibit of antique jewelry, including some pieces from ancient Egypt." She led him to a nearby case filled with what looked to him like beaded trinkets. "That necklace of gold and jasper and amethyst is from the twelfth dynasty—two thousand years B.C.! Can you imagine?"

She seemed genuinely excited by the necklace, and Nick had to pretend a mild interest. Almost at once he noticed another guard, watching them from a high balcony that ran around the room. "This place is alive with guards, isn't it? Don't they trust anyone?"

Lynn Peters brushed the long hair from her eyes. "They've had some trouble—a number of robberies during the past couple of years. The latest one, a few months gack, was the last straw, I guess. Someone stole the famous Pliny diamond, one of several brought from India to Rome about the year 60 A.D., and described by Pliny in his writings."

Nick grunted, vaguely remembering having read something about the robbery in the papers. "I don't know much Roman history, but I always thought Pliny was a politician of some sort."

"Pliny the Younger was, but his father was a naturalist. He wrote a thirty-seven-volume *Natural History*, which still survives. The diamond that bears his name is a really fabulous stone, almost priceless. Though of course it doesn't have the brilliancy of modern gems."

"Why is that?"

"The art of lapidary wasn't fully developed until the middle years of the Eighteenth Century—around 1746, to be exact. Before that, very little was known about the faceting of diamonds to give them the sparkle and brilliance we know today."

"You speak like a true authority."

She smiled at the compliment. "I'm studying to be a lapidarist. I work at the diamond exchange on West Forty-seventh Street."

"An unusual occupation for a young lady."

The grin turned impish. "Did you think I spent my life falling off horses?"

"Hardly." He was watching the guard on the balcony. "Just what happened to this Pliny diamond?"

"It was stolen from one of these showcases, just as other jewelry had been earlier. An alarm sounded when the glass was broken, of course, but by the time the guards got here there was no sign of the thief. Each of the thefts happened during the daytime hours, which is why they now have a guard assigned to every room. At night they have an elaborate alarm system, and two guard dogs patrol the place." She chuckled at the thought. "I always imagine the dogs carrying off the dinosaur bones and burying them somewhere."

"That stolen diamond would be difficult to dispose of."

"Not if it was cut up and refaceted. Pieces of a necklace from a similar robbery turned up with a fence in Boston. Museum robberies have been quite a problem around New York ever since the Star of India was stolen from the Museum of Natural History back in 1964."

Nick nodded. The watching guard made him nervous, and he didn't know how far their voices might carry in this high-ceilinged room. "Look," he decided suddenly, "I have to be going. Can I drop you anywhere?"

She shook her head. "This is part of my homework."

"Is this Egyptian stuff valuable, too?"

Lynn shrugged. "Depends on what you mean by valuable. To a collector it would be priceless, though it's not the sort of thing a fence would care to handle."

He nodded and started for the door. "I'll see you around. Don't fall off any more horses!"

Each time Nick Velvet was handed an assignment like this he reminded himself of the Clouded Tiger affair, some years back. In that one he'd been hired to steal a tiger from a zoo and it turned out to be only a means of drawing attention from the real crime being committed at the same time. The same trick had been tried with Nick on other occasions too, but he was usually able to see through the ruse and bow out in time. He didn't like being played for a patsy, and he had a suspicion that Frader Kincaid was trying to do just that.

No man, Nick felt, not even a dinosaur enthusiast, could have any use for the bones from a Tyrannosaurus tail. It seemed much more likely that Kincaid was connected with the museum thefts, and that he was using Nick simply to get by the added security precautions so he could enter the museum behind him and pull off another jewel robbery.

It made sense, in a way, and it might even explain why Lynn Peters had been at the museum. She might be working with Kincaid, watching Nick to see when he would pull the job. She might even be the lapidarist who cut up the gems for Kincaid after the robberies.

Thinking about it, Nick turned his car north and headed toward Kincaid's big house on the hill. He wanted another chat with the man before he undertook the theft of the dinosaur's tail.

When he reached it in mid-afternoon the big house was quiet. It was possible that Kincaid was in the city, but the elaborate study had indicated he did much of his work at home.

Nick was in luck. Kincaid himself answered the door on the second ring. "Well, Mr. Velvet! Don't tell me you're bringing the tail to me already!"

"No, not quite."

"Well, come in for a drink, anyway. I was just dictating some business correspondence on my machine, but I always welcome a little break. This big place gets lonely."

"That was quite a party last evening. We enjoyed it."

"My pleasure! Who would have thought that fate would bring you to me at the very moment I needed your services?" He led Nick into the study and opened a well-stocked liquor cabinet. "Is Scotch satisfactory?"

"Fine."

"What brings you here? Are there any complications?"

"Somewhat. The number of guards at the museum has been increased considerably since a recent string of thefts."

"That should present no problem to a man of your skill, Mr. Velvet."

"It doesn't, really." He accepted the drink and took a sip. It was good Scotch. Expensive. "But as you know, I never steal things of value, like cash or jewelry. Nor do I allow myself to be used as a decoy for such thefts."

Kincaid smiled indulgently. "But, Mr. Velvet, by the very nature of your chosen calling you invite people to take advantage of you. After all, what truly valueless object would be worth your fee of $20,000, even to an eccentric like myself.?"

"Then you admit you haven't told me the whole truth?"

"What other explanation could there be?"

"Some jewels have already been stolen from that museum, and more are on exhibit now. You could be using me only to provide access or diversion while your own gang carried out the real theft."

"Gang, gang! Mr. Velvet, I'm a businessman, a publisher. I don't have any gang!"

"Then why do you really want the dinosaur's tail?"

Kincaid sighed and put down his drink. "Come with me, Mr. Velvet. I'm going to show you something very few people have ever seen."

Nick followed him across the study to a small door that might have led to a closet. Surprisingly, it opened to reveal a narrow staircase to the basement. In that moment, descending toward the unknown, Nick's first thought was of a velvet-lined chamber where Kincaid might act out the orgies of his pornographic books. Then he remembered a story he'd read as a boy—about a man who bred giant ants, and he wondered if some living creature from the distant past might be awaiting him in Frader Kincaid's basement.

The first thing he saw as Kincaid snapped on the lights did nothing to relieve his mind. Nick had paused only inches from the gaping jaws of a dinosaur's skull. He jerked back quickly and looked around. The entire basement workroom was filled with bones—skulls, ribs, shinbones, jawbones. They hung from the ceiling and they littered the rows of shelves that circled the room.

"What in hell is this?" Nick asked.

Frader Kincaid smiled at his reaction. "My hobby, my avocation. I told you last evening of my great interest in prehistoric creatures. Here I find a way to enjoy that interest and even make a little money out of it." He took down one of the jawbones and handed it to Nick. "This particular one is carved from wood and, as you see, highly polished. But I have others of molded plastic and even of bone. Bones made out of bone!"

"You *make* these? But what for?"

"I sell them to museums. A complete skeleton of a prehistoric reptile or mammal is very hard to come by. Many museums, especially the smaller ones, often possess only a few bones from a Mammoth or a Brontosaurus. They want to reconstruct a complete skeleton, and the only way to do it is to use a number of artificial bones. That's where I come in."

"Amazing," was all Nick could say.

"I can furnish a single bone or a dozen. Generally I go right to the museum and work on the skeleton myself, fitting the missing bones in place. They close off the room, and I do my work."

"Are there many New York museums that do this sort of thing?"

"All of them use reproductions in one form or another. I suppose the largest must be the giant blue whale at the American Museum of Natural History. Many people viewing it believe that it's stuffed, but actually it's a complete reproduction, carefully formed in every detail. I don't work on anything that complex, though. I stick to bones."

"And you need the tail of the Tyrannosaurus to serve as a model?"

"Of course! I must have it, and soon."

Nick Velvet sighed and avoided the gaping jaws. "All right," he said at last. "I'll steal it for you."

"I'd be most grateful," Kincaid said with a smile, and led the way upstairs.

Nick spent Tuesday morning checking out one more point, just to ease his mind. The Egyptian jewelry on display at the museum had little market value. It was not to be compared with the Pliny diamond and other stolen pieces. Nick now felt certain that he'd been wrong in suspecting another jewel robbery.

When the museum closed its doors at six o'clock, Nick was still inside. He'd already decided that the theft must take place after hours, despite the alarm system and the dogs. The daytime guards in all the rooms were obstacles he could not safely overcome. A quick test had shown him that they were quite professional and not the sort to be diverted by fire-crackers or an escaped mouse. Besides, Nick estimated he would need at least two or three minutes to cut through the wires that held the tail bones in place. So it had to be at night.

When the guard in the Egyptian Room turned away for an instant at the sound of the closing buzzer, Nick had simply stepped into one of the large upright sarcophagi against one wall and pulled the lid almost shut. The guard passed once, glancing around, but apparently assumed that Nick had left by the other exit. He flicked off the light switch and Nick was alone in his own dark tomb. The sarcophagus was far from comfortable, being a bit shorter than Nick's six feet, but he knew he would have to remain inside for at least an hour.

Through the crack in the lid he watched the dusky remains of daylight filter through the overhead skylight until the Egyptian

Room settled into total darkness. Then at last it was night, and he slipped from his cramped hiding place to move silently through the darkened halls. It was easy to spot the electric eye alarms in each doorway, and just as easy to avoid them by bending very low. They would have trapped only the most amateur of thieves. He entered the Etruscan Wing and crossed the marble floor toward the Hall of Great Reptiles. So far, all was well.

Then he froze, hearing a guard's voice far off, echoing through the lonely building. It was answered by the barking of a dog. Nick listened and moved a bit faster.

Avoiding the electric eye at the entrance to the Hall of Great Reptiles, he made his way toward the enormous white skeleton in the center of the room. He took a moment to shine his narrow-beam flashlight at the walls, but there was nothing except the tall dusty display cases filled with fossils and petrified footprints from ages ago. He wondered why he'd done that and then realized there was something wrong. It was—what?—a feeling that he was not alone here?

He tensed his body, but no sound came. Then he allowed the flashlight to return to its target on the dinosaur's bony tail. He went under the rope and clamped the flashlight to his left wrist, leaving both hands free. As he had assumed, the individual bones were strongly wired together, but a few quick snips with his wire cutters should free them.

The ominous feeling came again, and this time he knew that someone else was in the room. He raised his left arm slightly, until the flashlight beam targeted a black-clad figure crouched like a cat some ten feet in front of him. Despite the black knit cap that covered her sandy hair, he had no trouble recognizing Lynn Peters.

"What in hell are you doing here?" he whispered harshly.

"The same thing as you," she said with a grin, sliding closer across the polished floor. "You hid somewhere after the place closed, so I did the same thing."

"But—you mean you've been following me?"

"Of course. You're the famous thief Nick Velvet, aren't you?"

"Where did you hide?" he asked, ignoring her question.

"In the Ladies' Room. The male guards never think to check it. I had this black outfit on under my raincoat, just in case. You're after the jewelry, aren't you?"

He shifted the light from her face and brought out his wire cutters. "No, I think that's your game. If you really knew anything about me, you'd know I don't steal anything valuable."

"But you're working for Kincaid," she insisted.

"I have what I want right here." He snipped away at the wires, carefully disengaging about fifteen inches of the tail section. The bones felt zero-cold in his hands.

Then suddenly they heard voices nearby, and the barking of a dog. "Come on," Nick snapped. "We've got to get out of here."

"What are you doing with those bones?"

"Stealing them." He grabbed her arm.

"But the jewelry—"

"No time for your jewels now. If those guard dogs catch our scent we're in trouble—big trouble."

He led her back through the Etruscan Wing, grasping her wrist with one hand and the dinosaur's tail with the other. The voices seemed farther off, and for a moment he relaxed, certain they were going to make it.

"Duck under here," he warned. It's an electric eye."

She ducked, but not low enough. Instantly a clanging alarm bell shattered the silence. "Damn!"

"I'm sorry."

He tugged her and broke into a run. "A fine burglar you'd make!"

"I never pretended to be one."

"Then what in hell are you doing here?"

There were shouts and running footsteps now, and up ahead the lights were going on. "Nick, I'm scared!" she cried as the barking of the dogs sounded closer.

"You should be. Right now I'm scared myself."

They had reached the main hall of the museum, and the front exit was only a hundred feet away. But already they could see the guards converging. Someone spotted them, shouted to the others.

"Run!" Nick told her.

Their running footsteps echoed on the polished marble as they retreated toward the Egyptian Room. He remembered the mummy cases, but knew the dogs would sniff them out in a minute.

"There's no way out, Nick."

Ahead, appearing suddenly like some hound of hell, a large German shepherd blocked their path. Nick reversed direction, dragging Lynn with him.

"I—I can't—"

The dog started after them, so close they could hear its panting as it ran. "I know just how Sir Henry Baskerville must have felt," Nick gasped.

"We can't make it," Lynn moaned.

Nick slid to a sudden stop and pulled a handful of capsules from his pocket. The dog was only twenty feet away, coming fast, as Nick hurled the capsules to the floor, breaking them.

"What's that?" Lynn asked.

The dog slowed its charge, turning its nose to the floor. "Come on! That'll only divert him for a minute or two."

"But what—?"

"It's a chemical that looks like blood and has a strong meat scent. Fishermen use it to attract good catches. I thought it might distract the dogs for a minute if I got into a jam."

The German shepherd had paused, sniffing, but already it was losing interest in this new odor. It turned again toward them. "Now what, Nick? I can't run any more."

"There they are!" a guard shouted from the corridor ahead of them.

Nick sighed and braced himself. "Through the window. It's our only chance."

"The window!"

"We're on the first floor. It's no worse than falling off a horse."

Ten minutes later, bruised, cut, and out of breath, they sat in the front seat of Nick's car as he pursued a winding route through upper Manhattan.

"Do you always cut things that close?" she asked him.

He tried a relaxed smile, and it didn't feel bad at all. There was a glass cut along one cheek, but it wasn't deep. "Not usually. I hadn't counted on your being there. What about your car?"

"I parked it a few blocks away, just in case. But they'll find my raincoat in the Ladies' Room."

"Any identification in it?"

"No." She grinned at a sudden thought. "My, won't they be surprised when they discover the only thing missing is the dinosaur's tail!"

"Sorry you didn't have time for the jewels."

"Look, Nick—Mr. Velvet—I was only there because you were. I thought Kincaid hired you to steal that jewelry."

He took one hand from the steering wheel to rub a bruise on his arm. "But why would you care anyway, unless you were after the jewelry yourself?"

"Those things aren't worth much in the open market, but the diamonds that were already stolen are worth a fortune. There's a $5,000 reward for the Pliny diamond alone, and I mean to collect it."

"You mean you're—?"

She nodded. "Not a lapidarist at all, but an insurance investigator. Sorry to disappoint you."

"But what about the horses and the jumping?"

"I joined the group recently, to get close to Kincaid. I'm not much of a horsewoman—that's why I fell on Sunday. You see, Kincaid was doing some work at the museum the same day the Pliny diamond was stolen. The insurance companies are suspicious of him."

"He makes bones," Nick explained. "For dinosaurs. That's what he was doing at the museum."

"Maybe that's just a cover."

Nick ran his fingers over the length of tail bone at his side. "We'll find out soon enough. We're going to Kincaid's place."

The lights were still burning when they reached the house on the hill, and Kincaid greeted them at the door. He couldn't quite mask his surprise, though, at seeing Lynn. "Well, hello. I thought you two barely knew each other."

We've gotten friendly," Lynn explained. "We've been through a lot together."

But Kincaid's eyes were on the length of wired bone that Nick carried in his left hand. "You did it! You stole the Tyrannosaurus tail!"

"I did it," Nick agreed.

"Splendid, splendid! This calls for a drink while I get you the rest of your money."

Nick accepted the bundle of bills and stuffed it into his pocket without counting. By now he was used to payments in cash, and it felt like the right amount. "I should tell you that Miss Peters here is an insurance investigator. If you're wise, you won't carry out your scheme to recover the Pliny diamond."

Kincaid's face went white. "What are you talking about?"

Nick saw that Lynn was listening intently, so he hurried on. "You do work for the museum. Surely they would have allowed you to take a plaster cast of the tail bones for your models. No, Mr. Kincaid, you didn't pay me $20,000 because you wanted to have the tail, but rather because you wanted the museum *not* to have it. I asked myself what they'd do without this tail segment, and the answer was obvious. They'd hire you to replace it with a reproduction."

Kincaid lowered his eyes. "You're right. I needed the work."

"Enough to pay me $20,000 so you could get a job worth maybe a few hundred? I think not. But you were working in the museum on the day the Pliny diamond was stolen. And that started me thinking. You said yourself that when you fitted an artificial bone they usually closed off that room of the museum while you did your work. That means, at least for a brief period, the guard would probably be removed—or he wouldn't be watching you too closely. The jewelry at the museum now isn't worth your trouble, but suppose the Pliny never left the building. Suppose you simply broke the display case, removed the Pliny and hid it somewhere. Somewhere, say, in the Hall of Great Reptiles."

"That's crazy!"

"Is it? You couldn't risk carrying it out of the building on your person with alarm bells ringing all around, but you could hide and return for it later—a week or a month later, if necessary. But what happened after the Pliny diamond was stolen? The museum tightened its security by placing a guard in every room. The Pliny was still there, safer now than ever, except that the museum didn't know it."

"Of course!" Lynn Peters breathed at his side. "That would explain everything."

Nick nodded. "It would certainly explain why you were so pleased to see me on Sunday, Kincaid. You knew I couldn't be hired to steal the diamond for you, but if I could steal part of the dinosaur, the museum would ask you to come down and fix it. Alone in that room you could retrieve the Pliny from its hiding place."

"You'll never convince anyone of that story, Velvet."

"I've convinced Miss Peters already, and I'm sure she'll be able to convince the museum officials. You were growing nervous and wanted me to steal the tail soon, which means the hiding place isn't too safe. I think a search of the room will turn it up quickly."

Kincaid bit his lip and looked from one to the other. "I have money. I'll pay you both well."

"I already have my pay from you," Nick said.

"A deal?"

"That's up to Miss Peters now. But if you tell us exactly where the Pliny is, I think she'd allow you enough time to catch a morning flight to South America."

"South—"

"They must read dirty books down there, too. You could start a whole new life."

Kincaid made a sudden motion toward the desk, but Nick stopped him. "No guns, please. Nothing like that."

"Where's the Pliny?" Lynn demanded.

He stared at the carpeted floor for a long moment before he answered. Then he said, so softly that they could hardly hear, "On top of one of those tall display cases along the wall. I just threw it up there. The cases are so dusty I knew they were rarely cleaned or even examined."

They left him in his house on the hill, and as they drove away Lynn asked, "Is your work always this much fun?"

"Sometimes. When there's somebody like you along."

"What are you thinking about right now?"

He turned to her and grinned. "You know, in a sense that damned dinosaur had a jeweled tail after all."

Gerald Kersh

The Scar

This is one of the treasure-trove of manuscripts found in the late Gerald Kersh's effects. So far as could be checked, these newly discovered stories had never been published anywhere in the world. We are deeply grateful to Mrs. Kersh for sending the manuscripts to us for first publication in Ellery Queen's Mystery Magazine—so that Gerald Kersh's inimitable stories can keep coming to you at intervals, so that Gerald can, through his work, be with us a long time . . .

Here is Gerald Kersh spinning one of his fascinating yarns—puckish, captivating, irresistible . . .

W ragg was one of those little people whom Nature seems to have designed in order to convince us that things might be worse—a tiny, fleshless, wispy man more than 60 years old, and dressed in a suit of vivid checks which had belonged to someone at least 70 pounds heavier than himself. The shoulders of the jacket reached three or four inches down each arm, and when he waved his hands the sleeves flapped like the wings of some ragged, fantastic bat. In place of a shirt he usually wore a sky-blue polo jersey darned on the breast with red rug-wool. His trousers were so long that he was able to strap them under a pair of ordinary black-cotton socks, and his feet were encased in bizarre light-gray shoes decorated with little blue hearts—survivals of the Brighter Clothes for Men craze of the twenties.

It was easy to tell by his face that he had some connection with the stage. He had that pasty, leathery complexion which you may see in innumerable men who lounge at the doors of the theatrical agents' offices in Charing Cross Road: the small fry of the old music halls, and the comedians who used to bawl mildewed jokes and tuneless songs for 40 years between Morecambe and Margate, never earning more than the barest of livings. You could see, in the face of little Wragg, the spoilage of half a century of drafty dressing rooms and the stuffiness and hot-white gaslights of grimy little theaters; the ravages of many long fasts broken only by evil theatrical boarding-house cookery.

You could perceive, in Wragg's interminable, rambling monologues and the nervous hurry with which he forced the words out, the habit of desperate impromptu in the teeth of hostile audiences. His vocal cords which had strained against the hissing of multitudes seemed to have turned to frayed string: in order to force any sound out of them, he had to exert his entire body. Yet he never stopped talking, in an ingratiating tone, while his toothless mouth remained fixed in the mirthless grin of the half-starved "pro" whom the manager sternly orders to "look cheerful."

He picked up a livelihood at the time by tearing paper patterns in front of theater queues, but he was not strong enough in the fingers and his patterns usually shook out into shapelessness. But this, in Wragg, had a humorous result: just as one expects the unsophisticated guest, in the film, to drink out of his fingerbowl, so one expected little Wragg to bungle his paper tearing. Nobody laughed at Wragg's patter, but everybody laughed at Wragg.

He occupied a room next to mine. Like more of Busto's rooming-house tenants, he did not stay long; he came and went, dragging with him down his dreary road a battered cardboard attaché case with a string handle and a disgusting old violin, black with dirt and white with resin, passionately clasped under his right arm. I got to know him through this instrument.

He insisted on playing the opening bars of *The Blue Danube* on it over and over and over again one night when I was trying to go to sleep. I protested. He shouted, "All you people know is the pub and the pawnshop—not good music!" I went into his room to argue the point and saw him sitting up in bed and torturing the screeching strings with a milk bottle, which he was using instead of a bow.

"See that?" he said. "There's only one man in the world who could do that, apart from myself, and that was Dan Gregory. He could play a Russian dance on the violin and turn a somersault at the same time. Kreisler plays a couple of straight tunes and gets thousands for it. Dan Gregory gets nothing—and he could play the violin with a matchstick. But they don't appreciate art in this country. Pub and pawnshop, that's all they know.

"Look at me! You've heard of Monty Wragg? Monty Wragg,

Versatile Comedian—that's me. I used to do a double turn—
Wragg and Bone—a scream, I don't mind telling you. And they
were real names. My partner's name was Agatha Bone. A great
girl! You can talk about your Greta Garbos—that girl Agatha had
talent. You don't get girls like that now. She chucked a great
theatrical career when we were at the Heysham Palace of Variety
to go into domestic service—she was a good cook too. Listen to
me, laddie: that girl could cook, she could do trick cycling stunts,
she could sing, she could dance, she could play the cornet, she
could do elocution—everything. What can Greta Garbo do? Now
ask yourself, is there any justice?"

It was impossible to stop him. His tongue rattled on like
clockwork for at least 30 minutes until he stopped to cough. I took
that opportunity of saying, "Well, I won't be able to get to sleep
after this. Come into my room and have a cup of tea."

He bounded out of bed and put on his clownish trousers. As I
put on my kettle on the gas ring and took a pork pie out of a
paper bag, he watched me with hungry eyes. His mouth watered.
He gulped once or twice, and then began again, "Nice of you. Not
many people would think of it. All they know is pub and
pawnshop. No hospitality—that's a thing of the past in this country.

"Now when I was in Ostende it was 'Monsieur' this and 'Monsieur' that, and 'Do you find your bed comfortable, Monsieur
Wragg?' But here? 'Ger! Ger!'—that's all they can say. Some
people look down on foreigners, but not me. We're all brothers. I
know some people in Ramsgate, and they had a little boy thirteen
years old who did all the scrubbing while his mother carried on
all day with fellas. Now . . . "

He took a mouthful of pie and swallowed it hastily. "No," he
said, "they got no manners here. Savages, that's what they are.
Once, when I was at the Olympia Hackney, a fella threw a
gingerbeer bottle at me. Missed me by inches. And just look at
this—"

He lowered his head, pulled aside his soiled white hair, uncov-
ering a frightful scar which divided the top of his head. The bone
underneath must have been dented at least half an inch.

I said, "I'm interested in scars. How did you get that one?"

"I'll tell you, if you like. That scar's got a history."

"Where did you get it? The war?"

"War? No, not this one. The war? Ha, that was nothing! No, I got this one up in Yorkshire. I was unconscious two weeks with it, as true as I'm sitting here. All my brains came out, almost. P'raps that's why I'm crazy now—ha, ha, ha! Somebody done it with a butcher's cleaver."

"Fight?"

"No—attempted murder."

"Over a woman?"

"How did you guess? You'd hardly believe it, but I used to be much sought after by women. You can take it from me—good looks and big chests don't carry no weight with women. Charm, that's what counts—personality and brains. I could talk to 'em. You'd hardly believe it, but I could talk any woman off her feet in those days. They used to fall in love with me, head over heels. I could have had my pick of them."

"But you never married?"

"No. I nearly did, once or twice. Once I was within a few days of going to the altar, but—"

"But you were going to tell me about that scar."

"—oh, yes! I was coming to that. Once I start talking I run on and on and get right away from the subject. Oh yes . . . Well, I was up in Yorkshire, in a little town called Hudford. See! A proper little North Country town where the people don't know a thing. You know, a population of about forty thousand, and hardly one of them had been to London in his life. I ask you!

"Well, that was over twenty years ago, and I don't mind telling you I was somebody in those days. Three or four pounds a week on the average was nothing to me. I was in partnership with a fella called Walters, and we were putting over the famous Wragg and Walters act—pretty hot stuff; it brought the house down—a real bit of class.

"Well, as it happened, the manager of the Hudford Hippodrome kicked the bucket, and as they wanted somebody with brains and personality they made me a firm offer to take over the management; which I did.

"I got a very nice front room over a butcher's shop, with full board and laundry, for a pound a week, and settled in. I was somebody. Everybody used to point me out when I crossed the Circus, and all the millhands and yokels used to say, 'Good day to you, Mr. Wragg.' And I don't mind telling you, every blessed girl in the town fell for me like a ton of bricks. I was over forty—you wouldn't think I was over sixty now, would you?—and something to look at. I used to go to church every Sunday for the sake of appearances, and I got known.

"Well, among the girls who fell in love with me was one called Mary Curtis. She used to come along to church with her sister, a girl called Agnes, and I don't mind telling you she couldn't take her eyes off me. They were both very nice girls, twins, about thirty-eight or thirty-nine years old, and although they looked pretty much alike, I never saw a pair of twins with such different characters. You know what I mean: you usually find that twin sisters think and dress similar, but these two were as different as chalk from cheese.

"Mary was my type, a lovely girl; big-built, nice shape, light wavy hair, nice eyes, and full of life—bubbling over with it. She liked a bit of color in her dress. The way she got herself up was quite stylish for a little town: blues and pinks, and silks and satins, a nice enameled watch, hats that were something to *look* at. One of 'em had half a Bird of Paradise on it, and you don't get things like that for twopence-halfpenny. She liked a song and a dance, too, and wasn't keen on church and all that kind of thing—in fact, she only used to go to see me there.

"But the other one, Agnes—Gor bless me soul!—how different she was! She could have made something of herself, but she preferred to look like a blooming schoolteacher. Hair parted in the middle, and dragged right back into a bun as big as that teapot; black dress, black gloves, black jet beads, black velvet band round her neck; and never a smile on her face. A proper misery, I tell you.

"Well, I got to know Mary through her coming to the Hippodrome. I did a turn myself, and she used to take a one-and-sixpenny seat in the front row of the stalls, just to get a good look at me. She inspired me, I don't mind telling you.

"You don't get girls like that nowadays. All they know is Lipsticks and Picture Palaces—no reality about 'em. Nothing like that about Mary. She had intelligence—she wouldn't have given a 'thank you' for your Clark Gables and your Joe E. Browns. She knew what was what: she appreciated genuine *talent*.

"Well, we started going about a bit together, and I began to call at the house for tea. I don't mind telling you, I brought a bit of life into that house. I showed those girls a thing or two. I talked to 'em. I entertained 'em till you would have thought their eyes would pop out. And I even got a laugh out of Agnes. Yes, I even made Agnes smile, and you would have needed a blooming burglar's jimmy to bend up the corners of her mouth.

"Well, after a time Agnes took to me more and more until she even started coming to the Hippodrome every Monday evening, and the whole town started talking about it. You know what they are in these small towns—they've got nothing better to do than talk, talk, talk. But I could see with half an eye that Agnes had also fallen in love with me. It's all very nice, having all these young women fall in love with you, but Agnes wasn't my type. It was Mary for me, not blooming black beads and religion.

"But you know what women are—they can't help falling in love, and they can't fall in love without getting jealous. So the result was that Agnes and Mary, who'd got on together perfectly well up to then, they started bickering. I could see the coolness springing up between them until it made me uncomfortable to be with the two of 'em together. It sort of damped me down. There were silences. I'm not used to silences—I like a bit of intelligent conversation. Then, when one day me and Mary announced to Agnes that we were going to get properly engaged, Agnes gets up from the table, bursts into tears, and slams out of the room.

"Yes—" said Wragg, with a grin of pride, fishing in his hip pocket—"they used to lose their heads over me something terrible. This was me, then." He handed me a faded photograph.

I looked at it with interest, half expecting to see some Casanova of the early twentieth century, some Maurice Costello or Francis X. Bushman. Instead, I saw an ordinary, grinning, straw-hatted "professional," somewhat the worse for wear, and apparently not quite sober; skinny, with a silly-looking grin, striking an attitude with a whangee cane against a cardboard column supporting a flowerpot.

"Very nice," I said. "Go on."

"Ah, yes . . . After that they quarreled in real earnest. I never saw anything like it—they just wouldn't have anything more to do with one another. Before I'd come into their lives they used to go everywhere together, except that Mary used to go to the theater oftener than Agnes, and Agnes used to go to church more regular than Mary. But now—Gor bless my soul!—they were dead enemies. They avoided each other.

"Mary stopped going to church because she wouldn't share the same pew with Agnes. I had to keep it up, for the sake of my reputation in the town, and I used to see Agnes, with her nose in the prayer book, never even looking in my direction. And whenever I went to the house to tea, Agnes would keep out of sight. She wouldn't sit at the same table with us alone.

"Well, that suited me down to the ground. But all this enmity upset Mary a good deal; she wanted to get away from it. She said to me one day, she said, 'Let's hurry up and get married, and get away from it all. Let's get married quickly'—those very words. I didn't mind a bit. I was forty, and it was time I settled down. And Mary was a nice girl—bright, cheerful, nice-looking, a good housekeeper, and two hundred a year in her own right. Her old man had been a master builder. He built the Town Hall and the Library. Pots of money. She was a lovely girl. Her and Agnes had a matter of eight or nine quid a week between them. Mary had a nice bit in the bank too. You don't get girls like that nowadays. No reality about 'em.

"All right. 'Marry you?' I says. 'Only name the day.' 'Now,' she says. So I starts getting ready. We made arrangements. She insisted on paying the preliminaries. She handed me twenty-five quid in golden sovereigns. I got myself a lovely new black cutaway suit for four guineas—you got a better suit for four guineas then than you get for ten now—and I had the banns put up. And believe me or believe me not, laddie, they were read out, and the wedding was booked to come on the following Tuesday week. Yes, I come as near to it as that!"

"And why didn't you?" I asked.

"I'm coming to that. It was all on account of Agnes. On the Tuesday after the banns had been read for the third time, Agnes had to go to the Women's Guild. It was about seven o'clock in the evening. I was busy at the Hippodrome, and Mary was at home. See? Well, Agnes leaves the house, and just as she steps into the road, along comes some blasted lunatic at the double with a handcart and knocks her down and breaks her ankle.

"Well, they picks her up and takes her to her door, and she starts struggling and screaming: 'I won't! I won't be taken home! I won't! I won't!' But they puts that down to her being delirious on account of shock, and gets the door open, and takes her in, and calls for Mary. But Mary isn't there. They looks upstairs, they looks downstairs, they sends to the theater to see if she's there, and then they looks in the cellar—and there they finds her. She'd been dead for five weeks."

"No!" I said.

"I'm telling you," said Wragg, "five weeks! Her sister had poisoned her with arsenic and put her down in the cellar, and then put on her clothes and impersonated her. I would have married her without knowing the difference. Agnes, with her hair fluffed up, and bright clothes, and a smile on her face, looked as like her sister as two peas in a pod."

"Good God! And what happened to Agnes?"

"Oh, she died soon after they took her to prison. Took poison. Murder and suicide—that's what a woman'll do for love . . . And do you know what? I'm damned if I know now whether it was Mary who murdered Agnes or Agnes who murdered Mary. *She* said nothing. Nobody knew. And I've often wondered . . . "

"How terrible!"

"Terrible is right. If only it could have been discovered a week later!"

"What difference would that have made?"

"What difference! I would have come into eight or nine quid a week *and* the house—romance is very nice indeed, but you can't eat romance, you can't drink romance, and romance won't keep you warm in the winter. Now eight or nine quid a week—"

"But where does the scar come in?"

"What scar?"

"The one on your head."

"Oh—well, now! The way I ramble on! I was going to tell you about that in the first place, but once I get talking I sort of run on and on . . . The scar, you say? Now, that's a different story altogether—something really extra-ordinary. One of these days I'll tell you about that scar—really extra-ordinary!"

"Q"

Q. Patrick (Patrick Quentin)

The "Laughing Man" Murders

*A sure-fire 'tec theme: multiple murder, set in San Francisco,
and the desperate hunt for a mysterious avenger known only as
the "Laughing Man"—and the most difficult case that Inspector
Martin Field ever had to face . . .*

*This short novel, complete in this anthology, will remind you
of the detective stories of "The Golden Age"—with its twisting,
turning plot, full of ingenious touches, with every clue planted
(but beware!), and always, to the very end, with one more surprise jumping out of the author's bag of tricks . . .*

Detective: INSPECTOR MARTIN FIELD

The old woman's voice on the telephone was almost incoherent
with terror: ". . . and he laughed, I say! When he shot my son
he was laughing all the time. A terrible, mad laugh."

In the August heat of the squad room, Inspector Martin Field,
who had planned on taking the afternoon off to go sailing with his
nephew, scribbled notes: *Homicide. Victim: Sylvester Twing, 14
Jubilee Street. Reported by mother. 3:15 P.M.*

"Then you saw the murderer, Mrs. Twing?"

"No, no! I can't see anything. I'm blind. And I'm all alone.
Hurry! He may come back again to kill me—the laughing man."

The Laughing Man! Mrs. Twing was the first to use that phrase
which, in a few hours, was to sweep across San Francisco like the
Great Fire . . .

She opened the door to them; tiny, terrified, and insubstantial
as a ghost. The house was a ghost too—an improbable survival
from the 1910s, crammed between two warehouses in a neighborhood which had long since succumbed to industrial expansion
sprawling up from the Bay.

Mrs. Twing was wearing a nightgown and a woolen bed jacket.

Her feet were bare like a child's, in grotesque contrast to the old seamed face with its blank eyes. She stretched quivering hands toward Martin Field and the homicide squad crowding in behind him.

"My son," she moaned. "Oh, my son, my son."

They found the body in a large living room cluttered with ponderous Victorian furniture. Thick red draperies cut the summer sunlight to a dim pink radiance. Sylvester Twing was lying in a corner under two murky pictures of fruit in baskets. On a clawlegged table beside him sat a plump stuffed Pekingese under a glass bell; it was eerily alive-looking with its blue-button eyes.

The police doctor had dropped to his knees by the body. Martin Field, the youngest and most thorough Inspector on the San Francisco police force, looked down at the victim. Sylvester Twing had been shot in the heart. He was about fifty-five, with a dry, unfriendly face, thinning hair, and, even in death, a certain air of self-righteousness. The blood didn't show much. It had seeped into the formal blue serge of his suit.

"Okay, boys, take it from here," Martin said. "I'll take care of the old lady."

He found Mrs. Twing, near collapse, in the hall. He carried her up the gloomy stairs to her bedroom. He was as big as she was small. In his arms she looked like a forlorn and faded doll.

"The laughing man," she was whimpering. "Oh, that terrible laughing man!"

He put her down on the bed. She was still much too frightened to make any sense. But gradually, as he coaxed a little calm into her, bits of information came out.

The house had belonged to a Miss Van Loon, a once-wealthy old spinster. Mrs. Twing and her son, who were English, had worked there as cook and butler for twenty-five years. Even after Mrs. Twing went blind, Miss Van Loon had kept her on. And a few months ago, when the owner died, it was found she had willed the house to Sylvester.

"Her people came from Holland," Mrs. Twing said. "She had no family. No friends. Just Sylvester and me. We were always good to her. We've never done anyone any harm. Why, oh, why should that dreadful man—?"

"You've got to tell me what happened, Mrs. Twing, if you want me to help you."

"I'll try. It was like a nightmare. But I'll try."

She had been in bed that afternoon. She was almost always in bed now because of her heart. About three o'clock she had heard a car drive up to the rear of the house and her son go to answer the back doorbell.

There had already been a visitor that morning around nine thirty. A man. She didn't know who it had been. Her son never told her things and she didn't pry. But people very seldom came to the house. When the second visitor arrived she was curious. She sat up in bed and listened.

"I heard their footsteps, the two of them, going through the hall to the living room. I couldn't hear their voices, not from my bedroom. But then, after a minute or two, I heard the laugh." She gave a sob. "Oh, I can't tell you what it was like. Long and loud and—and sort of cackling. It was mad. It was a madman's laugh."

She twisted around on the bed toward him. "I was terrified. But I was terrified for Sylvester, too. I made myself get up and go out in the passage. I reached the head of the stairs, and the laugh came again—booming, rolling around the house. My heart was pounding. I thought I was going to have an attack. Then the laughter stopped and I heard him speak. It was as clear as if I'd been down there in the room with them. He said—" She broke off.

"Yes, Mrs. Twing. What did he say?"

In a slow, awed whisper she breathed, "He said, 'You must have known I'd be back sooner or later. This time I've come to get you all, Sylvester—you, Bernard, George, and Ramona.' "

"Bernard, George, and Ramona. Who are they?"

"I don't know. I've never heard of any of them. But that's what he said. And then—then he started to laugh again, and there was a shot."

Her hand fluttered to her mouth. "Oh, if you knew what it is like to be blind, to be in darkness, not to be able to see! I stood there. I don't know how long. I couldn't move. Then I heard the footsteps. They were coming out of the living room toward the stairs, toward me. And he saw me. I know he saw me, because he laughed.

"It was different from the other laugh. A soft, horrible little chuckling. And I ran. I ran back to my room. I locked the door. And the footsteps came nearer and nearer. They stopped at my door. He shook the handle. He shook and shook it. Then he laughed again, and he went away down the passage. I heard him banging and slamming in all the other rooms. He even went to the attic. Then at last he came downstairs again. I heard the back door shut and the car drive away. I—"

The horror story dissolved into sobs.

Gently Martin Field said, "Bernard, George, and Ramona. You're sure you don't know anyone by those names?"

"No. I told you."

"And you haven't any idea what all this could be about?"

"No, no. Unless—unless it was Evangeline."

"Evangeline?"

"My granddaughter. Her mother died when she was a baby. Sylvester and I tried to bring her up right. So did Miss Van Loon. She loved her just like her own daughter. But Evangeline was always bad. Willful, disobedient, thinking she could sing that cheap jazz music, sneaking off to night clubs. And then—"

Mrs. Twing's voice had changed. It had become prim and self-righteous. Like her son's voice? Martin wondered. "Two years ago Miss Van Loon found her, right here in this house, with a man. There was a terrible scene. Miss Van Loon and Sylvester told her to leave and never come back. And they were right, of course. They were strict, both of them, but they were always right. But Evangeline was mean. Maybe she did it. Maybe she sent that terrible man in revenge. Oh, that laugh, that dreadful laugh!"

She had forgotten Martin now, caught up in a new surge of remembered terror. There was a lot more to ask, but it could wait. Quietly he slipped out of the room.

Mrs. Twing had said that this fantastic, laughing murderer had gone "slamming and banging" into all the other rooms. He made a tour of inspection. In every bedroom the covers and sheets had been ripped from the heavy, mahogany beds. In one room there were no sheets at all. In another, they had been torn into ribbons and scattered around on the faded plush carpet.

He stood, looking at the havoc, awed as one always is by the evidence of madness.

One of the detectives came in. "Telephone, Mart. Headquarters." He whistled. "Boy, what's this—a maniac?"

"That's right," said Martin grimly. "A maniac. Looks like this is the worst case we've ever had."

He took the telephone call downstairs. It was the sour voice of the sergeant at the switchboard. "Seems this is Homicide Day, Mart. Another report just come in. Newlands Gallery on Powell. The owner's been shot. Guy by the name of Bernard Olin."

"Did you say Bernard?"

"Yeah. Bernard Olin."

Martin felt a chill run up his spine. "I'll handle it. Send a couple of boys over there right away. I've got to leave this squad here."

"Sure, Mart. Anything else?"

"Yes. Check all asylums, mental homes, for an escaped lunatic."

You must have known I'd be back sooner or later. This time I've come to get you all, Sylvester—you, Bernard, George, and Ramona.

Sylvester, Bernard—

He took Dr. Casey with him, leaving one of the detectives in charge, with instructions to search for tire tracks at the back of the house, and to find some neighbor or friend to take care of Mrs. Twing. It was only when he passed his own apartment on the way to Powell Street that he remembered his sailing date with his nephew. His old black sedan was parked outside the house. That meant Rickie was still waiting for him.

Rickie was younger than Martin. His parents, Martin's brother and his wife, had been killed in an automobile accident. From then on Martin had raised and educated him. Since Rickie's return from Korea a couple of months ago Martin knew he had been fussing over his nephew like a hen with one chicken. He was ashamed of himself, but he couldn't change. Rickie was the only person he'd ever found time to love.

He swung the police car to the curb and climbed to the apartment. Rickie was in the attic-studio which Martin had kept for him during his two-year army stretch. He was at his typewriter, revising his article on ghost mining towns which had kept him stubbornly occupied since his return from a recent camping trip in Nevada.

"Hi, Mart. What happened? Get tangled with a corpse?"

"Two of them," Martin explained. It was his admitted and dearest wish to get Rickie interested in police work. The boy was crazy about his writing now, but free-lancing could be tough, and Martin had hopes that he would win his nephew over in the end. "How about coming along? Maybe you could write something on police procedure."

"More propaganda, eh?" Rickie's blunt, boyish face broke into a grin. "Okay. I'll come along. But don't think you've got me into uniform yet."

When they reached the new office building on Powell Street, a

Reporters started to press around Martin. He gave them a full report. He knew that it would place him under the heaviest press fire of his career. But the more publicity the Laughing Man got, the better the chance to stall any other killings.

He left the reporters dashing off for telephones, and swung the car, after Hilton's, up the great hump of Nob Hill. As they reached its peak and plunged down the other side, the glimpse of the Bay, calm and blue ahead of them, tied up absurdly in his mind with Anne Lyle's suntanned skin and soft yellow hair. He and she were together in his star-boat. The sail was flapping in a lazy summer breeze . . .

What's the matter with me? he thought disgustedly.

Anne's apartment was on the top floor of a little white mission house which looked over the Yacht Harbor. Rickie carried Lorna Williams into Anne's bedroom. Then he joined Martin, Anne, and Robert Hilton in the living room.

Martin was questioning Anne Lyle. It wasn't helping. Three months ago, she explained, she had separated from her husband, Renshaw Lyle. Martin had heard of him. He was one of the best-known society philanthropists in San Francisco, head of many charity committees, a director of the Art Museum and of the Opera.

Anne had had a little money of her own and, because she was asking no alimony in the pending divorce, she needed to earn her living. She had always been interested in modern art. When she had heard from Hilton and Lorna that Olin was looking for a partner with some capital, she had jumped at the deal. But she knew practically nothing about Olin's personal life except that he was a notoriously honest, able, and respected dealer.

Robert Hilton had nothing useful to offer. Nor had Lorna when Martin interviewed her again for a few minutes in the bedroom. Olin, she said, had come into the office around eleven that morning. He had seemed perfectly normal. He had dictated a few routine letters, which she had mailed as she went out to lunch.

When she got back Olin had gone out to eat, himself. He'd returned about three, and at around three thirty had sent her out for the frames. There'd been no visitors to the gallery that day, because it had been closed to the public in preparation for a new show.

The telephone by the bed started to ring. Martin picked it up. It was the detective from the Newlands Gallery.

"No one seems to have seen the guy, Mart, but it's pretty hopeless. Thousands of people go in and out of this building every day. The elevator captain did talk with Olin, though, when Olin was going out to lunch. He says Olin seemed in an extra good humor and kidded with him. He had a letter in his hand. He mailed it while he was talking to the captain."

Martin cupped the receiver. "Miss Williams, you're sure you mailed *all* the letters that Olin dictated?"

"Quite sure."

So there was another letter—one, presumably, that Olin had written when Lorna was out to lunch. It was something. Not much, though.

"Okay," he said into the phone. "Keep trying. "I'll be back later, but I've got to take in the Twing house first."

As he started for the door Robert Hilton came in. "I'm leaving, Lorna. How do you feel?"

"I'm okay. But I thought you and Anne had a dinner date."

Hilton scowled. "She won't go. Says she's going to stay with you."

Martin eased past him into the living room. Anne Lyle was sitting with Rickie by the window. They were talking casually, but, watching them, Martin felt a sudden, quite inexplicable jealousy.

"Come on, Rickie." The words came out before he could stop them. "This is not a taffy-pull. There's a job to be done."

He drove furiously back to the Twing house. Rickie, at his side, seemed unaware of his change of mood.

"That Mrs. Lyle—she's a good-looking girl."

"Girls!" exploded Martin. "Don't you ever think about anything but girls?"

His nephew glanced at him with affectionate astonishment. "Hey, what's the matter with you?"

"Matter! With a lunatic on my hands, with two corpses, two more to come—and not a single clue! And all you can think about is a blonde—" Sudden shame overcame him. He grinned at Rickie sheepishly. "Sorry, boy."

Rickie patted his arm. "That's okay. Policemen have a right to be temperamental. Just wait till I'm a traffic cop. I'll have all Market Street in a frenzy."

Martin was mollified. "You really think you'll come in?"

"Don't worry. If this is a typical policeman's day, you'll get me yet."

There were three other cars parked with the police car outside the forlorn old house on Jubilee Street. Martin hurried with Rickie into the hall. The detective he had left in charge was talking harriedly to a group of reporters. He left them and went with Martin and Rickie into the dining room.

"Hey, Mart, is it on the level what those newspaper boys are saying—that these two killings tie together?"

"They tie together, all right."

"A laughing maniac running amok! Boy, are we going to take a beating if we don't clean this up quick." The detective looked awed. "Nothing much here. I searched the alley in back, but it's paved. No sign of any tracks. No neighbors. No one to have seen anything. Only thing I found in the house was this." He tilted a cigarette butt out of an envelope. "The old lady says Twing was death on smoking and drinking. I found it in a vase in the living room."

Martin took the butt. Printed across its tip was the word MARLEY'S. Olin smoked Marley's cigarettes. Mrs. Twing had said there'd been a visitor at nine thirty. A man. Olin hadn't shown up at the gallery until eleven. It looked as if at last he had a link.

Olin must have come here. To warn Twing of their great danger? Possibly. But the elevator captain said Olin had been in an extra good humor at lunchtime.

A thin, solemn man in a seersucker suit came in. The detective said, "This is Mr. Danvers from the Tyson Gallery. I asked him over to check the contents of the house to make sure there's nothing valuable."

Martin nodded. "Where's Mrs. Twing?"

"Upstairs, packing. I raked up some dame, a Mrs. Ross, who works here as a laundress. She's come to take the old lady over to her place for the night."

Out in the hall the reporters besieged Martin. He eased them into the street and shut the door; then he sent Rickie with the art expert into the living room and hurried upstairs to Mrs. Twing's bedroom.

Mrs. Twing was fully dressed. Mrs. Ross, the laundress, was with her, putting a few things into a small suitcase. Mrs. Twing's groping hands had picked up a photograph from the table beside the bed. The moment Martin entered, she said, "So it's you, Inspector."

"How did you know it was me?"

"You can always recognize footsteps when you're blind."

Mrs. Twing was very different from the terrified little rag doll he had last seen. With most of her composure recovered, she looked alert and forbidding, much more like the kind of old woman who could stand by without lifting a finger while her son and Miss Van Loon threw her only granddaughter out of the house.

Martin glanced at the photograph in her hand. It showed an angular, tight-lipped old lady, sitting in the living room downstairs, beneath two pictures of shadowy interiors, with the stuffed Pekingese under its glass bell beside her.

"This is Miss Van Loon?"

Mrs. Twing stroked the frame respectfully. "It's all I have to remember her by. I always keep her picture."

"What about Evangeline's?"

The old lady's mouth tightened.

Mrs. Ross spun around. "Tell him, Mrs. Twing! Tell the Inspector what I told you." But she didn't wait for Mrs. Twing to speak. "Evangeline's mixed up in all this," she said. "I know it. I saw her!"

"You saw her?"

Mrs. Ross nodded vigorously. "Yesterday. I was bringing the laundry. Just Mr. Twing's shirts and things. I don't do the heavy work. Real early, it was. Around nine in the morning. I turned into Jubilee Street, and there was this girl hurrying down the steps from the house, with Mr. Twing standing there, watching her go."

"What did she look like?"

"She was wearing a white dress and a scarf over her head. That's about all I could tell. She ducked real quick in the other direction and around the corner. But I saw her."

Martin said to Mrs. Twing, "Did your son tell you a girl was here yesterday?"

"Sylvester never told me things unless there was a reason."

"And you didn't hear anything—voices, footsteps?"

"I guess maybe I was asleep."

"But I saw her," insisted Mrs. Ross. "And I said right out to Mr. Twing, 'So you've had a visitor.' He just looked at me and didn't say anything. He was always terrible close-mouthed. But he was acting kind of different. I never met Evangeline. She'd gone when I started to work here. But it's obvious it was her. Evangeline

THE "LAUGHING MAN" MURDERS

came back, trying to get money from Mr. Twing now he'd inherited the house and all. He wouldn't have anything to do with her, so she sent that man, that terrible laughing man—"

Martin cut in, "I'll need a photograph of Evangeline, Mrs. Twing. Have you got one?"

The old lady hesitated, and then gave a grudging shrug. "There's one in the bureau. Middle drawer. It's an old one."

Martin found the photograph. It was on its face at the bottom of the drawer. It showed a pretty, cheerful, brash-looking girl of around nineteen in a sloppy-joe sweater. Martin held it out to Mrs. Ross. "Is this the girl you saw?"

She looked at the picture intently. "Well, as I say, I didn't get a good look at her. It was mostly the white dress I noticed." Then she added indignantly, "But of course it was Evangeline! Who else could it be?"

Martin was silent. Could Mrs. Ross be right? Could all this link up through Evangeline? Sylvester had thrown his daughter out because of some man. What if the man was unbalanced? What if Evangeline had been wronged, too, either actually or in her lover's imagination, by Bernard Olin, by the unknown George, and the unknown Ramona? Could the lover, crazed with hatred, have launched an insane campaign of revenge?

"How old is Evangeline now, Mrs. Twing?"

"Twenty-three this August."

"And the man who got her in trouble—who was he?"

"I don't know anything about him. One of the men from those dreadful night clubs, I expect." Mrs. Twing's voice was icy. "I told you, Sylvester always kept unpleasant things from me. Sylvester took care of it all." Her lips started to tremble. "Sylvester was always so considerate, so good to his old mother. And now—" She began to whimper. "Oh, what's going to become of me now? I'm all alone."

"Did your son leave a will?"

"No, no. He never dreamed he'd die before me."

In that case, the property would go to his daughter, Evangeline. Maybe, when she heard about it, the girl would show up. Maybe.

As he left the room Mrs. Ross was comforting the old lady. "There now, Mrs. Twing, don't you worry so. Somehow it'll work out."

Martin picked up Rickie downstairs and they drove to headquarters. The art expert's report on the contents of the living room had been emphatic. The furniture and pictures were from the worst period of Victorian decoration, mixed with a lot of fake European antiques which had obviously been foisted on Miss Van Loon by unscrupulous dealers.

Martin stayed at headquarters for half an hour, leaving Evangeline's photograph for release to the press and turning in a preliminary report on both murders. He drove, then, with Rickie back to the Newlands Gallery.

The boys there had unearthed nothing new. He called Anne Lyle and asked her if she had ever heard of an Evangeline Twing in Olin's life. She hadn't. Neither had Lorna. But the sound of Anne's voice brought him that same, unwanted excitement.

He was tired, he told himself, and scared by a case that was getting hopelessly out of control. That's why he was developing this obsession about a girl he didn't know.

Back in the apartment, he insisted on cooking dinner. Since Rickie's return he had got into the habit anyway. It made a kind of family mood, something he'd never had since he was a kid. That night he hoped it would help him to relax. But it didn't.

I'm going to get you all, Sylvester—you, Bernard, George and Ramona.

After dinner he went back to headquarters. He called Anne Lyle again, asking for a list of Olin's friends and acquaintances and every George he had known. She and Lorna gave him about twenty names.

He started calling them. Some of them, at first, thought it was a gag. None of them had heard of the Twings, or any Ramona, or any significant George.

Around midnight there were still a few names on the list, but it was too late to call any more. Martin went out and bought a paper. It was all there, screaming across the front page:

THE LAUGHING MAN, MAD MURDERER, KILLS TWO . . . MORE VICTIMS TO COME . . . WHO IS GEORGE? WHO IS RAMONA?

Evangeline Twing's picture was there, too, gazing cheerfully and rather vacantly out from under the headlines.

"Inspector Field," the story read, "has the toughest job of his career on his hands. At the moment he is baffled . . . "

Inspector Field was baffled, all right. And this had to be the case he'd picked to get Rickie interested in a police career!

When he got back to the apartment Rickie was asleep. Martin went to bed, too.

He awoke next morning at seven thirty. Rickie ˅
He didn't wake him. He drank some coffee and walk
ters. Most of the newsstands were already open.
Man, George, Ramona, Evangeline Twing glare
every headline. One had demanded:
WHEN WILL THE LAUGHING MAN STRIKE AGAIN?

At headquarters it was even worse than he had expected. All
night, reports had been pouring in. Panic-stricken women had
heard mad laughter below their windows, on fire escapes, outside
their bedroom doors. Dozens of people from all over the city had
seen men with gaunt faces and staring eyes. Some had been
sneaking down alleys; some had been hovering around street corners; some had been slipping out of obscure bars.

Every George and Ramona in San Francisco, it seemed, had
been calling in, too, shaken by the memory of some guilty episode
in their pasts, certain they were the next victims and pleading for
police protection.

The idea of the Laughing Man had inflamed the city's imagination, and hysteria, sprouting like an army of weeds, was choking
any chance for genuine information. Martin, grimly fighting his
own anxiety, waded through the reports still deluging in.

There was no lead to Evangeline Twing.

None of the Laughing Man tip-offs made any sense. None of the
Georges and Ramonas, chattering on the phone, seemed to have
any connection with the case.

Martin started to help with the calls himself. There was a terrified Mexican woman, whose name was Ramona, gabbling unin-
telligibly in Spanish. There was a call from a man who had just
seen the Laughing Man on the Oakland Ferry. Another call came
a minute later from a woman who had just seen him in Golden
Gate Park.

"Yes, lady . . . Okay . . . We'll check it, lady."

He slammed down the receiver. It shrilled again. It was a woman's voice, high with excitement. "I'm reporting the Laughing
Man! He's been here. He's just driven away in a car. I heard the
laugh. And it wasn't only me. The doorman heard it. A lot of us
heard it!"

Skeptically, Martin asked the address.

"1400 Larchmont. Russian Hill. He must have been to one of
the apartments. We didn't see him. We just heard the laugh as he
drove away. We—"

Martin's shoulder was tapped. He glanced up. A detective, unshaven and haggard from lack of sleep, was standing behind him. "Another one, Mart."

"Murder?"

"Yeah. Just came in on my phone."

"Take this." Martin tossed him his receiver and ran to the other phone. "Inspector Field."

A man's voice said, "Come at once to 1400 Larchmont. There's been a murder."

"1400 Larchmont?"

"Yes. It's Renshaw Lyle. I just found him, shot in bed. I'm Joseph Crummit, his secretary. Some people in the building heard laughter. I think it was the Laughing Man."

"Okay, we'll be there."

Martin dropped the receiver. Automatically he glanced at his watch. 9:18. He thought he'd been prepared for anything. But he felt as if he had been slugged. Renshaw Lyle! Anne Lyle's husband! Not a George or a Ramona.

The detective who had taken over his call hurried to his side. "Lady at an apartment house on Larchmont said a lot of them heard the Laughing Man, Mart. Looks like it's on the level."

"It's on the level, all right."

Dr. Casey wasn't in the building. Martin had a call put through for him to join him on Russian Hill, grabbed three exhausted detectives, and ran down to a police car.

As he sped through the busy morning streets, it seemed to him that he could feel morbid excitement and terror emanating from the crowded sidewalks. It was infecting him, too. Anne Lyle's husband! This thing was completely out of control now, spreading like a plague . . .

The apartment house at 1400 Larchmont was small and discreetly luxurious. A group of agitated men and women were milling in the lobby. They clustered around Martin, all talking at once.

"I heard the laugh . . . out in the street . . . as the car drove away . . . That laugh! Just to hear it made your flesh creep."

A dark, very neat young man with sensitive, almost delicate features pushed through to Martin. With him was an old doorman. The young man said, "I'm Joseph Crummit. The doorman saw Mr. Lyle this morning. You may want him, too."

"Okay." Martin turned to two of the detectives. "Get all these people's stories and bring them up to me."

With the others he hurried into the self-service elevator. Joseph Crummit explained that Renshaw Lyle had flown to Chicago four days ago for a charity drive. He had planned to be away a week and had given his houseboy a vacation. He had left instructions with Crummit to come in every morning to feed his two Siamese cats and take care of the mail.

"I came today at 9:15, as usual. I didn't expect Mr. Lyle to be there. I found him—in the bed."

Martin listened in a mood of mounting frustration. Even the secretary hadn't expected Renshaw Lyle back in San Francisco. But the Laughing Man had known. How? Or had he just blundered in, intent on his mad revenge?

"Mr. Lyle came back because he'd got through his work in Chicago early. He told me." The old doorman's voice broke in, breathy with self-importance. "I was in the lobby when he come in this morning. Around eight. He said he'd slept bad on the plane and was going to spend the morning resting in bed. He asked me to bring up the mail as soon as it came. Around eight thirty I took it up. He opened the door in his pajamas. He was perfectly okay—just like usual. I asked if he wanted anything else. He said no. So I went down cellar to fix the hot-water heater that was on the blink, and then, around nine, that's when I heard the Laughing Man. Up in the street. That laugh! Crazy."

The elevator reached the penthouse. Joseph Crummit opened a door with a key. He led them through an enormous living room into a bedroom with a sweeping view of the Bay. In a canopied four-poster bed, with a newspaper, letters, and empty envelopes scattered over the wrinkled sheets, lay a man in pajamas.

He was about forty, with an ascetic, aristocratic face. Blood had stained the front of his pajama jacket from a bullet wound just above the heart.

Squatting on the window sill, watching the body from bored, impassive blue eyes, were two Siamese cats.

"This is just as I found him." Joseph Crummit was hovering. "I didn't touch anything. I called you at once."

Martin picked up one of the empty envelopes from the bed. It was addressed to Mr. G. Renshaw Lyle. He said to Crummit, "What was Lyle's first name?"

"It was George."

Martin felt close to despair. *George* Renshaw Lyle! There, from the beginning, had been the Laughing Man's George.

Anger merged with his sense of defeat. Why in heaven's name hadn't Anne Lyle told him her own husband's name was George? He told the detective, "Call Mrs. Lyle. Tell her to come over right away."

He looked back at the body. Renshaw Lyle had been killed in bed. It was obvious that, if he'd had to get up to answer the door, he'd never have gone back to bed to let himself be shot. The Laughing Man must have broken in.

He went to the window. The cats jumped grudgingly off the sill. There was a sheer drop of six floors to the street. He investigated the apartment. The kitchen door was bolted on the inside. The door to the fire stairs was outside by the elevator. There was no possible entry except through the front door.

He said to the doorman, "You're sure Lyle closed the front door after he'd taken the mail from you?"

"Sure I'm sure. I saw him."

Then it had to be a key. The Laughing Man with a key! How could an avenging maniac from the past have a key to this apartment? Unless . . .

Martin went back into the bedroom, where Dr. Casey, who had just arrived, was bending over the body. Renshaw Lyle's keys were lying in a little heap of change on the highboy. Martin turned to Joseph Crummit. "Apart from Lyle, who had keys to this place?"

"The houseboy had a set. But he gave them to me when he went on vacation. There's no one else—except Mrs. Lyle."

"Mrs. Lyle?"

The young man's eyes became faintly malicious. "Mr. Lyle was divorcing her, you know. When she left, three months ago, she took her keys with her. I wrote to her, asking for them back, but—"

"I thought Mrs. Lyle was divorcing Mr. Lyle."

"Oh, that's the official story." Joseph Crummit shrugged. "Maybe it's indiscreet of me, but there was a question of Robert Hilton."

"The artist?"

"That's right."

Anne Lyle had a key. Anne Lyle, who had denied all knowledge of the Laughing Man. Anne Lyle, who was being divorced.

Disturbed by his own new thoughts, Martin picked up the scattered letters from the bed. There were four of them: a letter from the president of a musical society, a report from the Art Museum, a financial statement on a cancer drive, and a communication from a welfare headquarters in Washington.

He glanced at Crummit. "A busy man like Lyle would have more mail than this in four days."

"That's only today's. I've been taking care of it every day. The rest is all in the library on his desk."

"You were here yesterday?"

"I was. All morning. I'm an art historian and I'm preparing a book on Dutch painting. Mr. Lyle has a wonderful reference library. It's easier for me to do my work here."

"Did anything unusual happen yesterday morning?"

"Nothing out of the way. There were a couple of phone calls."

"What phone calls?"

"They were all business. Except one. A man called and wanted to speak to Mr. Lyle. I told him he was in Chicago for the week. He didn't leave a name."

"What time was this?"

"About eleven o'clock."

Martin turned to the doorman. "Do you remember how many letters you brought up today?"

The old man nodded. "I counted 'em. Five and a financial paper."

"Five? You're sure?"

"Sure."

Five letters delivered and only four on the bed. Martin searched the bedroom. He didn't find the fifth letter.

He had Joseph Crummit check the pile of earlier mail on the desk in the library. The young man was certain that no letter had been added. So the fifth letter had disappeared. The Laughing Man must have taken it.

Martin's mind jumped back. Yesterday Olin had mailed a letter which he hadn't shown to Lorna Williams. Had Olin been the man who had called Lyle and hadn't left his name? Had the missing letter been written by Olin—to warn Renshaw Lyle, as perhaps he had gone to warn Sylvester Twing?

There was a ring at the front door. The detective went to answer it, and Martin heard Anne Lyle's voice. He turned, to see her coming into the living room. She was wearing white again and, in the morning sunlight slanting through the window, she seemed to him dazzling.

As she hurried toward them his new, unformed suspicion spilled out as anger. "Why didn't you tell me your husband's name was George?"

"If only I'd thought! We always called him Rennie. No one in the world ever called him George. And then you were only interested in friends of Bernard's. Rennie never knew Bernard. He hated modern art. He was only interested in Old Masters. He and Bernard never even met—" She broke off. "Is it the Laughing Man?"

"It's the Laughing Man, all right," Joseph Crummit cut in.

"But what could Rennie have had to do with all—all that horror, Inspector? He was the kindest, the most civilized man in the world. And he never knew the Twings; he never knew anyone called Ramona. I'm sure of it." She glanced at Crummit. "Did he, Joe?"

"Not to my knowledge."

Martin took her into the bedroom. Dr. Casey was still there. The cats were lying sprawled on the rug at his feet.

Anne stood at the end of the bed, her face drawn with grief and bewilderment. "Poor Rennie."

Martin said, "I understand you've got a key to his apartment, Mrs. Lyle."

"A key?" She turned. "Oh, yes, I think I have. When I left I always meant to mail it back, but I forgot."

"Where is it?"

"Home. At my apartment."

"Who else had a key?"

"Only Rennie and the houseboy. Joe never had one . . . Why do you want to know?"

"Your husband's murderer let himself in with a key." Martin avoided looking at her. "I think we'd better go to your place and make sure your key's still there."

He told the detective to take a full report from Crummit. "I'll be back later. Call me at Mrs. Lyle's if you need me."

As he and Anne Lyle went toward the door one of the detectives from downstairs hurried in.

"We've checked all the Laughing Man stories, Mart. They all saw the same thing, but it isn't worth a plug nickel. No one saw him or even heard him in the building. It was outside in the car. They heard the crazy laugh, and some ran to the window. They saw a car drive away. One of them says it was a navy-blue coupé, someone says it was a black sedan, someone else swears it was a dark-green job. Same old routine. Anyway, he drove away in a car."

Martin took Anne down to the lobby. The reporters had arrived. When they saw him, they swarmed around him.

"So he got George, Inspector, right under your nose . . . Sylvester, Bernard, George . . . Three down, one to go . . . Inspector, what's the odds on Ramona now?"

He pushed through them to the police car. Hysteria would mount. Bitter attacks on police inefficiency—his inefficiency—would flock in. To Martin, who had nothing in his life but his work, this feeling of personal failure was almost unbearable.

As he swung the car down Hyde Street, he was maddeningly conscious of Anne sitting close beside him in the front seat. He fostered his anger against her. "Yesterday you told me you were divorcing your husband."

"That's right."

"Why?"

She flashed him a quick, faintly surprised look. "That's fairly easy to answer. I wasn't in love with him. I never really had been."

"Then why did you marry him?"

"Oh, I thought I was then. That was three years ago. I was very young. Both my parents had died and left me a little money. I was studying painting here and I met Rennie at the Museum. I guess I was lonely and overwhelmed by the fact that someone so important could be so kind and—so obviously in love with me."

She paused. "I did a good job of kidding myself. It took a long time before I realized I was just letting myself be loved, grabbing everything, and giving nothing. It was hopelessly one-sided, and Rennie deserved something better. One day I had it out with him. It made him unhappy. I don't think he ever really understood. He thought there must be someone else."

"And there wasn't?"

"No. I don't seem to be very good at falling in love."

"What about Hilton?"

"For heaven's sake, no!"

"He's in love with you."

She shrugged. "That's just his romantic schedule for the summer. Robert makes a hobby of falling in love. Oh, I'm fond of him. I think he's a good painter. But there's absolutely nothing—"

She broke off. "Why do you want to know?"

"Joseph Crummit told me your husband was divorcing you because you'd been having an affair with Hilton."

Martin had expected, half hoped, that she would be indignant or at least embarrassed. She merely looked resigned.

"Joe probably believes it. He's a distant cousin of Rennie's, you know. His only living relative, in fact. He's immensely family-proud. He never thought I was up to the Lyle level."

"Your husband was very rich. Who inherits?"

"I don't really know. Some of his charities, I expect."

"Not you?"

She flushed slightly. "If I do, I certainly won't accept anything."

"Why not?"

"When you've given someone nothing, you don't accept things from him." She turned suddenly to look at him. "You understand that."

"Why me?"

"Because you'd be the same way yourself. You're not someone who would take anything on false pretenses."

That remark, so unexpectedly intimate, threw him off his guard. He turned the car into Jefferson Street. As they passed the Yacht Harbor he saw his own star-boat bobbing placidly among the other moored craft. The sight of it brought the fantasies of the day before crowding back. He and Anne, out together in the Bay with the tang of the salt air and the wide blue sky.

In spite of himself, an improbable elation took possession of him . . .

Robert Hilton opened the apartment door for them. His handsome face was taut and anxious.

"Anne, baby, I called to ask Lorna how she was. She told me about Rennie. I came right over." He added urgently, "Is it the same guy that killed Bernard? The Laughing Man?"

Anne gave a weary little nod. "Inspector, do you want me to bring you the key? It's in the bedroom."

"I'll come with you."

He went with Anne into the bedroom. Lorna Williams, looking pinched and pale, was lying in bed.

"Anne, is it true?"

"I'm afraid it is."

"Oh, Anne, I'm so sorry. But Mr. Olin never knew Rennie. I'm sure of it. He told me so when you bought the partnership. It's all just—crazy."

Anne had opened the lid of a little leather jewel case on a dresser. She turned suddenly. "The key isn't here!"

Martin took a quick step forward. "You're sure that's where you left it?"

"Quite sure . . . Lorna, you never saw my key to Rennie's apartment, did you?"

"No. I'd even forgotten you had one."

Here it was at last: a definite link between these people and the Laughing Man, a definite justification for suspicion. Anne Lyle's key!

The implications were terrifying. If the Laughing Man knew enough to search for a key in Anne Lyle's apartment, then he wasn't just a vague, shadowy figure from the past. He was at least an acquaintance, someone who was an intimate enough part of Anne Lyle's life to be—what? A clever murderer hiding behind madness? With an accomplice?

Martin thought suddenly of the girl in the white dress whom the laundress had seen leaving the house on Jubilee Street. A white dress. Anne's white dress?

The telephone by the bed rang. Lorna picked it up, and handed it to Martin. "For you."

The call was from the detective at Renshaw Lyle's apartment. "Mart, headquarters just called. They want you. They've got a lead on Evangeline Twing."

"Send one of the boys over here." Martin dropped the receiver and glanced at Anne. "Turn this place inside out. Make sure the key isn't here. There's a detective coming around. Give him a full statement."

Anne's face was distraught. "But I don't understand. How could the Laughing Man—?"

"That's something I'd like to know, too, Mrs. Lyle," Martin said grimly. "But some other time. Right now I've got to get out of here."

Martin drove recklessly back to headquarters. In his office he found Rickie. The sight of his nephew made Martin feel even more ashamed and conscious of failure. But Rickie's affectionate smile was encouraging.

"Hi, Mart. Why didn't you tell your eagle-eyed aide that the whole town was apart? When I woke up, I called here and they told me about Lyle. I've been waiting over an hour to report for duty."

A policeman came in with a tall, hard-boiled redhead. "This is Miss Amory, Mart. She called about Evangeline Twing. We had her come right over."

Miss Amory studied the two men appraisingly. "Which is the Inspector?"

"I am," said Martin.

"The girl in that newspaper picture. Evangeline Twing. She's sure lived since that shot was taken, but it's the same girl, okay. Never can fool me on a face. She was in the show with me about a month ago at a strictly unclassy joint, name of The Gold Mandarin. She was a torch singer. Did a Mexican act that was about as Mexican as Limburger. Used a different name, though."

She grinned. "And this is the part that's going to slay you, Mister. The name she wore—and it was about the only thing she did wear—at the club was Ramona. Ramona Gonzales."

Evangeline—Ramona. Yes, it was all fitting together. "Where's The Gold Mandarin, Miss Amory?"

"In one of the alleys off Columbus Avenue. Bentley."

Martin turned to Rickie. "Come on."

They drove through the crowded, gaudy streets of Chinatown. To Martin the miasmic infection of the Laughing Man seemed to lurk even here among the impassive Oriental faces, the shoddy trinket stores, and the fluttering banners with their hieroglyphic inscriptions.

But for the first time he was a jump ahead of his adversary. Ramona and Evangeline were the same person. He had been right from the beginning in deciding that the whole mad massacre had its roots in the Twing family. But not, as he had thought, with Evangeline as the Laughing Man's partner.

Evangeline was another intended victim. And a victim who, with any luck in the world, would be able to reveal the whole mystery—if he could save her in time.

The Gold Mandarin, tucked away in its dim little alley, was closed. Martin's banging on the door brought a wizened old Chinese who took them into a dark bar with its tables stacked untidily in a corner. A suspicious, unshaven proprietor appeared, wrapped in a grimy bathrobe.

"Ramona Gonzales? Phony Mexican? Sure. But she don't work here no more."

"Where can we find her?"

"Don't ask me." The proprietor shouted, "Shirley!" He explained to Martin. "Shirley hires the acts."

A tough, middle-aged blonde with her hair in curlers came in through a rear door.

"Shirley—the cops," the proprietor said. "They're looking for Ramona Gonzales. Remember? Phony Mexican tomato?"

"Mexican, Chinese, from Mars, they're all alike to me. But I got their addresses in the book." The blonde went behind the bar, fumbled, and produced a dogeared black notebook. "How long ago, Mister?"

"About a month."

Her magenta fingernails flicked the leaves. "Yeah. Ramona Gonzales. Fillmore." She gave the number.

Within ten minutes Martin and Rickie were at the house on Fillmore Street. It was a gabled monstrosity, converted into a rooming house and well on the road to decay. Children were playing and screaming outside the drab front door. A fat landlady in a stained apron waddled out from the shadowy depths of the hall.

"Ramona Gonzales? Top floor rear."

"Is she in?"

The landlady shrugged. "I should know. I got more important things on my mind."

With Rickie following close behind him, Martin turned and hurried up the moldy, peeling stairs. From one of the rooms came the sound of shrill, quarreling voices. A girl in a peacock-blue bathrobe, with a towel slung over her shoulder, was shuffling down a passage toward an open bathroom. She glanced at them shrewdly.

"Ramona Gonzales?" asked Martin.

The girl jerked upward with her thumb. "But she's not there. I went up yesterday to bum a pair of stockings. Went up again today. The door's locked."

Martin nodded to Rickie. They started running up the stairs. They reached the top floor. Martin banged on the rear door. There was no answer. He banged again. With a feeling close to despair, he rammed his shoulder against the door's frail woodwork. On a second try, he forced it open.

He stepped into the room, with Rickie close behind. Instantly he saw what he had been dreading to see. A girl was slumped across the old iron bed. Her feet dangled limply over the edge of the bed.

He crossed to her. She might have been Evangeline Twing. She might have been anyone. You couldn't tell any more, because her face was purple and bloated from the pressure of fingers which had throttled her.

"Dead!"

Dimly Martin heard Rickie's startled exclamation through the pain of utter defeat.

Sylvester, Bernard, George, and Ramona. The dreadful murderous pattern had worked itself out. All four of them were dead, and he hadn't been able to do a thing to stop it.

He forced himself to think, automatically, like a machine. Ramona had obviously been dead for some time. Just a glance at her told that. The girl downstairs said the door had been locked yesterday. So Evangeline Twing had been murdered—when? Yesterday? The same day as her father and Bernard Olin?

"Wait here, Rickie. I'm going to talk to the landlady."

As he hurried down the stairs, lodgers started to come out of their rooms. They must have heard him break down the door. They followed him. When he found the landlady in the kitchen, there were three girls, an old man, and a little boy crowding in behind him.

The news of Ramona's death brought an excited babble. But it soon became apparent to Martin that there was no help here in this disorganized household, where people came and went oblivious of one another's activities.

No one had seen the Laughing Man.

No one had the slightest knowledge of Evangeline Twing's personal life.

The only tip-off came from the girl in the peacock-blue bathrobe. "Go see Maisie Roland. She was Ramona's girl friend. Snazzy apartment over on California."

Martin called headquarters, ordered a squad to come at once, then ran upstairs to Rickie. "Stay here until the boys come, Rickie. Don't let any of the mob in. See you later."

He drove to Maisie Roland's address and found her in. She was a tiny, expensive blonde, in an apartment which obviously cost more than she could be expected to afford. She offered Martin a drink and, when he refused, mixed one for herself. She curled up in the corner of a couch.

"Ramona murdered! But how terrible." She arched her eyebrows in dainty dismay. "Of course, she was no real friend of mine. But

I was sorry for her. I'm a night club artiste myself. I was on a
show with her and—well—I felt the poor girl needed a few refined
contacts."

"Did you know her real name was Evangeline Twing?"

"No, but I knew it wasn't Ramona. She was always talking
about her father. She was very bitter about him. He was so
stingy, so stuffy, so harsh. There was an old lady, too, Miss Van
Something-or-other. They'd thrown her out of the house."

"Do you know why?"

Miss Roland delicately fingered the pearls at her throat. "It was
some man. She was bitter about him too. He'd let her down as
well. Whenever anything went wrong, Ramona always blamed the
man. If it hadn't been for that hell, she said, she'd be sitting
pretty today. And not only that . . . "

"Yes?" Martin encouraged.

"Well, I mean, there were times when she got real grand and
mysterious, and she'd say, 'To think of me, a phony señorita singing for peanuts—and I might have been rich.' And once, when
she'd had a couple of drinks here, she said, 'That old dame was
real stuck on me. I was to get the old Van Something-or-other
heirlooms. She told me privately. It was all set. And then, just because that heel had to get fresh right there in the house, and the
old lady found us, out I went without a nickel. And after that,
after I'd lost my chance, he left me flat.' . . . It was something like
that. I didn't pay much attention. Those show girls! They've all
got their hard-luck stories."

Evangeline might have been rich! She had been all set to get
the Van Loon heirlooms. Heirlooms! And her love had left her
flat—after she'd "lost her chance." After Miss Van Loon had cut
her out of her will?

So her love had known about the heirlooms. There was a man
who had known there was something of great value in the Van
Loon house; something about which the cautious old Miss Van
Loon might have kept quiet, so that even Sylvester Twing had
never guessed its true value!

Martin felt the stirring of excitement. The art expert had found
nothing but junk in the old house on Jubilee Street. But if there
had been something valuable, the Laughing Man would certainly
have stolen it when he had killed Sylvester.

The Van Loon heirlooms! Jewels, maybe? Or pictures? Olin was
an art dealer. Lyle had been a director of the Art Museum.

Yes, pictures. That's what the Laughing Man could have been after.

The Laughing Man! The *so-called* Laughing Man. For, if it had all happened that way, Martin's earlier suspicions were justified. This murderer was no maniac.

He said urgently, "Miss Roland, what was the name of this man who let Ramona down?"

Maisie Roland pouted her pretty mouth in a rueful grimace. "Mercy, I can't remember. Ramona was always using it. Was it John, Dick, Bob, Bill? One of those common names." She got up and crossed toward him. "You poor policeman! Why don't you have a little drink and relax?"

Paintings! Yes, that's what it must be.

Martin rose abruptly. "Sorry, Miss Roland. Some other time."

He drove to headquarters, picked up the key to the Twing house, and hurried on to Jubilee Street. The moment he stepped into the dim, pink radiance of the Twing living room, his eye fell on the stuffed Pekingese under its glass bell and the two pictures behind it.

As he crossed to the pictures he felt the excitement pounding in him. They were dark, old still lifes of fruit in baskets, the same pictures that had been hanging there when Sylvester Twing's body had been slumped beneath them. But . . .

His memory sped back to the photograph of old Miss Van Loon, which he had seen in Mrs. Twing's hand. It had been taken in this very corner of the living room. He was sure of that. The Pekingese had been sitting on exactly the same table.

But in Miss Van Loon's photograph the two pictures on the wall behind had not been of fruit in baskets; they had been interiors of rooms.

He took one picture off the wall, and then the other. His excitement soared to triumph. Behind each picture was a lighter square where the old red wallpaper had not become darkened by dirt. But the light squares were not as big as these pictures. Until recently, therefore, two smaller paintings must have been hanging there. The still lifes had been put up in their place.

By the Laughing Man, of course. The Laughing Man had stolen the original two when he had murdered Sylvester Twing.

With a sudden flash of insight Martin thought of the ripped and scattered sheets. The sheets from one bed had been missing. Like Mrs. Twing, he had taken it for granted that the Laughing Man

from nowhere with a suspiciously casual offer, and to have called an art expert for an official assessment of the pictures' worth?

Bernard Olin, as a well-known dealer, was an obvious choice. So he had called Olin, and Olin had gone to his house. Olin, who was an honest man, had told Sylvester of the pictures' immense value. And—yes, of course. Olin had gone back to the gallery and called Lyle as a director of the museum, the most logical place to buy the pictures from Twing. He had called, and Joseph Crummit had told him Lyle was out of town. So he had written the letter, instead.

There it was, Sylvester was linked now with Olin, with George, and, of course, with Ramona, too. They were no longer mere names connected at random in a madman's threat. They were the four people who had stood between Evangeline's lover and the Vermeers.

The plan to plunder Sylvester Twing had turned, by necessity, into a multiple murder. And the accomplice? The girl in the white dress?

He had reached headquarters. He hurried out of the car and up to the squad room. As he crossed to his office, one of the detectives yelled to him, "Telephone, Mart. Urgent."

Martin picked up the receiver. It was Anne Lyle's voice, and it was trembling with anxiety. "Inspector! Thank heaven you're there. Something terrible has happened. It's Lorna."

"Lorna?"

"About an hour ago a man called me at home. He said he was one of the lawyers for my husband's estate, and that he had to see me at once. He gave me an address, 'way out on Bernal Heights. I came out here, but there's no such address. I'd written it down, but I'd left the paper at home. I thought I might have made a mistake, so I called Lorna. When she answered the phone she was almost incoherent with fear. 'Thank heaven it's you,' she said. 'Call the Inspector. I can't go on any longer. I know. I've known everything all along, and now he's going to—' Then there was a scream and a shot, and a terrible mad laugh."

Anne gave a sob. "It's the Laughing Man! My call was just a blind to get me out of the apartment. Hurry! I'll be there as soon as I can, but hurry!"

Martin dropped the receiver, feeling shocked, and furiously angry with himself. Lorna Williams was now on the list of corpses. Of course. Why not? When Lorna Williams had obviously been the Laughing Man's assistant—the girl in the white dress who had been drawn in as a partner, only to end up as another victim.

With merciless clarity he thought back to the frames of the Vermeers in the photograph. They were heavy and gilded and decorated with bunches of grapes. So had been the frames in Olin's office, which Lorna claimed Olin had sent her out to collect. From the beginning the frames had been hidden in the most logical place for frames to be—in an art gallery.

It was clear as daylight now. But now was too late. What good were his theoretical triumphs, when they dragged so hopelessly behind the event? He stumbled, while the Laughing Man killed . . .

The Laughing Man . . . As Martin sped recklessly, but already resigned to disaster, toward Anne Lyle's apartment, the phrase echoed jeeringly in his mind. The Laughing Man. Anne Lyle had heard him laugh. All of San Francisco was babbling about the Laughing Man—the horror that stalked by night and day.

But the Laughing Man did not exist. The Laughing Man was merely a fantastic puppet, fabricated by a brilliant and terrifyingly sane murderer; a puppet built up by fooling a terrified old blind woman and intimidating an accomplice.

It was all quite clear. The ruse had been essential to the murderer, for if the true motive of the Vermeers had ever come out, the pictures would have become notorious and quite impossible to sell.

Everything, for the murderer, had hinged on keeping the existence of the Vermeers a secret. And what better screen than to invent an insane murderer from the past, returned to kill the four people who had wronged him; four people whose names could be announced to the police in such a way that they could be identified only *after* their deaths? Mad laughter and torn sheets to scare Mrs. Twing; a phony physical description from Lorna Williams, who had been knocked unconscious for veracity's sake; a single mad laugh from a car.

That had been all that was necessary. Just a few touches, and the newspapers, the public, had filled in the rest of the portrait.

Martin's anger had turned now to a cold hatred against this killer who had so completely outsmarted him.

He drew the car up outside the house on Jefferson Street. He went up to Anne's apartment. Even before he broke down the door he was prepared for what he saw: the crumpled body of Lorna Williams lying on the floor by the telephone.

And now, beyond his hatred, he felt a bitter, cynical calm. Okay. She was dead. At least, she'd deserved it more than the others. But the murderer had defeated him again.

He called headquarters, wearily conscious of his own humiliating position. "Another corpse. Come and get it if there's room in the morgue."

He looked down again at Lorna Williams, his mind ticking relentlessly on. When she'd tried to buy the pictures from Sylvester Twing she might have thought she had succeeded, but not for long. Next morning she would have known the plot had misfired when Olin came into the gallery with his triumphant news of the Vermeer discovery. Probably Olin had dictated to her his letter reporting the news to Lyle, but he had foiled her by mailing it himself.

Martin could visualize the scene with Lorna alone in the gallery, calling her "partner," warning him that the plan must stop. Twing and Olin knew of the existence of the pictures. Lyle would know as soon as he came back from Chicago and read Olin's letter. And there was always Evangeline Twing, who had known all along.

There were four people now who knew, or would soon know. It would be hopeless to go on.

But her partner hadn't thought it was hopeless. One million dollars was a prize too big to lose. With prodigious daring, he had switched from petty dishonesty to mass murder.

First, of course, he had killed Evangeline, the most dangerous of the four, because she knew about the pictures and also believed he was the only other person who was aware of their existence. Then he had killed Sylvester, created the Laughing Man in Mrs. Twing's panic-stricken mind, and stolen the pictures. After that he had driven straight to Olin's gallery and killed the dealer.

Martin could imagine Lorna Williams' terrifying dilemma. She was now a murderer's accomplice, whether she wanted to be or not. It was far too late to pull out. So she had had to go along with him, memorizing what he wanted her to say about the Laughing Man, and letting herself be knocked unconscious. And later she had had to keep silent, even though Renshaw Lyle was killed.

Martin saw now that, although Renshaw Lyle, as George, had

been added as a precaution, he need not have died. If he had stayed in Chicago as planned, the murderer could have collected Olin's letter at the apartment and destroyed it before Lyle's return. But, by coming back unexpectedly and reading his mail, Lyle had signed his own death warrant.

Martin dropped to his knees by Lorna Williams' body. Faint pity stirred behind his hard veneer of bitterness. Why had she done it? What had happened to make an ordinary, decent girl get tangled with a murderer?

There was a sound behind him. He got up quickly, turned to see Anne Lyle in the bedroom doorway. She gave a little wrenching sob and swayed.

Martin ran to her, putting his arms around her to steady her.

"She's dead. And it's all my fault! If I hadn't left her—" Anne whispered.

"You'd have been dead, too."

As he held her in his arms, Martin found himself pouring out the whole story to her. It was strange the way he was feeling. The bitterness was still there and the professional alertness, but, merged with them was an odd sensation of peacefulness, as if one thing had ended and another was beginning.

"You knew her, Mrs. Lyle. How could she have got caught up in a thing like this?"

"I—I think I know. I told you she'd had to give up her apartment. There was trouble. She'd always been a crazy gambler. She took her vacation in Reno, and she met a man who had a system for roulette. They won enormously, and then they lost. Then they started to borrow, and went on and on until they were hopelessly in debt. She left her apartment because she was afraid—afraid the gamblers might catch up with her."

There it was, the motive, the desperate need for quick money.

"Who was the man?"

"I don't know. She never said."

It was obvious now. Lorna's gambling partner had been her partner in murder. He was also Evangeline's lover, Miss Roland's "John, Dick, Bob, or Bill—one of those common names."

But the task of finding Evangeline's lover seemed hopeless. He might be any man in the United States. Then Martin remembered the key. The Laughing Man could only be someone who had a key to Lyle's apartment.

Joseph Crummit had had a key and, as an art-historian working on a book about Dutch painting, he would have been the first to realize the Vermeers' value. Joseph—Joe. A common name.

And Robert Hilton! As a constant visitor at Anne's apartment he could easily have stolen her key. Robert Hilton was an artist, too. Robert—Bob . . .

A detective, two policemen, and Dr. Casey had arrived. Martin directed them into the bedroom. The Laughing Man, then, must be either Hilton or Crummit.

But in the whole intricate chain of killings, no shred of a clue had been left behind that would stand up in a court of law. Unless he could find the Vermeers in the possession of one of them, how could he possibly—?

The idea came to him with sudden swiftness, as an image rose in his mind of Mrs. Twing turning her sightless eyes on him as he walked into her bedroom.

So it's you, Inspector.

How did you know it was me?

You can always recognize footsteps when you're blind.

Footsteps! The peak of the old woman's terror had been the footsteps of the Laughing Man—the footsteps coming out of the living room, coming up the stairs toward her.

He turned to Anne. "You know Hilton's and Crummit's telephone numbers, don't you?"

"Yes. Why?"

Swiftly he outlined his plan to her. As she gave him the numbers, the phone rang. He picked up the receiver.

A man's voice, edged with excitement, said, "Is Mrs. Lyle there? Joseph Crummit speaking."

Martin handed Anne the phone.

"Yes, Joe . . . Oh, has it? . . .No, I can't right now. I'm with the Inspector. I have to go to his apartment . . . You do? . . .Hold on a minute."

She cupped the receiver. "It's Joe. Something to do with Rennie's will. Joe inherits a lot if I sign a waiver. It's just come in. He wants to take it over to your place so I can sign it right away. Shall I say yes?"

Martin nodded.

She spoke on the phone, then dropped the receiver. "He's coming."

Martin called Robert Hilton and told him, also, to come to his apartment. With Anne and one of the policemen, he drove to the

Rosses'. They found old Mrs. Twing rocking on the porch.

"Mrs. Twing, if you heard the Laughing Man's footsteps again, do you think you could recognize them?"

"Of course I could. Anywhere."

They drove her to Martin's apartment. Martin took her and the policeman up to Rickie's attic. It made an ideal trap, because a tall flight of bare stairs led to it from the apartment below. Martin stationed Anne downstairs.

"When they come, send them both up to me."

He settled the old lady in a chair by the desk and the policeman near the door. He sat down, himself, on Rickie's bed near its head.

Now that the climax was coming, his nervous energy was burning out. He would win; he knew he would win. But it seemed to him that his victory was already tarnished beyond repair. Five people killed—who might have been saved . . .

He sat there, doggedly fighting his inner battle, glancing every now and then at Mrs. Twing who, perched in her chair, looked as grim as Fate.

Below them, the front-door buzzer sounded. Martin tensed, mechanically twisting the edge of the sheet in his fingers. He could hear Anne's voice faintly, and another voice. Then footsteps were audible on the stairs.

Martin's eyes were riveted on the old woman's face. "Listen, Mrs. Twing."

The footsteps came closer. The policeman by the door was moistening his lips. But Martin could see no change on the old woman's face.

"Mrs. Twing, are they the same?"

The old lady shook her head. "No," she said. "No. That isn't the Laughing Man."

As she spoke, Robert Hilton came into the room. "Inspector, you wanted to see me?"

"Not any more." Martin nodded to a chair. "Just sit and wait."

The buzzer downstairs sounded again; there were the muffled voices, and then the footsteps coming up the stairs. The old lady leaned forward a little. Martin watched her, waiting for the moment which, surely, would bring everything to an end. The footsteps were almost at the door . . . The old lady shook her head again.

"No," she said. "No, that isn't him."

"You're sure?"

"I'm absolutely sure."

The door opened, and Joseph Crummit, clutching a brief case, hurried in. "Mrs. Lyle sent me up, Inspector. What is it you want to ask me?"

Martin looked at him in total defeat. So much for the trap, which was to have redeemed him from humiliating failure. It was terrible at this late stage to have no plan any more, not even an idea.

"Mr. Crummit—" he began.

He broke off because footsteps were sounding once more on the stairs. They were coming swiftly upward and, in the same instant, Martin's eyes were caught by a sharp movement from Mrs. Twing.

She had sat up erect in her chair. Her blind eyes stared fixedly.

Slowly there spread over her face an expression of wonder and dark, remembered terror.

"That's him!" Her voice was shrill as a bird's. "He's coming. Those are the footsteps. That's him—that's the Laughing Man!"

The door was flung open. With a cheerful smile on his face Rickie strode into the room.

For one moment, when all of time seemed suspended, Martin sat looking at his nephew. Then, as horror began to dawn on him, he dropped his gaze to his hands. He was still twisting the edge of the sheet. Dimly he was conscious of numbers inked onto the wrinkled linen: 37711.

The numbers were even more terrible to him than his nephew's smiling face. 37711—the Twing laundry mark, the mark on the sheets which had concealed the Vermeers.

He faced it, because it had been his training for so many years to face what had to be faced. Of course. Now it was pitifully obvious.

Robert Hilton was not the only person who could have stolen the key from Anne's bedroom. It was Rickie who had carried Lorna Williams into the bedroom; Rickie, who under cover of his interest in police work, had engineered that opportunity to get the key from Lorna . . .

"John, Dick, Bob, Bill—one of those common names." Dick—Rickie. Rickie, who had always had girls on his mind; Rickie, who had been Evangeline's lover, and had been told about the Vermeers two years ago before his stint in Korea; Rickie, who had been on a camping trip to Nevada—a "camping" trip which had ended up with Lorna Williams, a system for roulette in Reno, and a desperate need for quick cash.

As the chill bit deeper into him, he realized that he, himself, had been indirectly responsible for Lorna's death. Before he left for the museum, he had told Rickie about his discovery of the Vermeers. Rickie had known, then, that the truth was out and would tie up with the frames in the gallery. He had killed Lorna before police questioning would inevitably have made her confess.

Rickie's casual voice penetrated the darkness of his thoughts. "Hey, Mart, what is this—a party?"

Martin got up. His legs felt dead, as if he were standing on two tree stumps. He couldn't look at Rickie. He looked instead at the policeman by the door. "Okay, Fred. Handcuff him."

He saw the startled policeman move forward. He turned his back, then. His thoughts were still scraping at him like knives. Rickie hadn't even bothered to destroy the telltale sheets. He had been as sure of himself as that. There he had been, in the very heart of the police security zone. Who ever, in a million years, would have searched Inspector Field's apartment?

Then, if the sheets were here, the Vermeers . . . Like a zombie, Martin moved to the clothes closet.

Two pictures were propped against the wall behind the hanging suits. He pulled them out. He threw the Vermeers down on the floor. $1,000,000 worth of evidence.

He turned to Rickie. It needed all his strength but he managed it. He stood looking at the only human being he had loved. His nephew was handcuffed to the policeman, but he was still as unruffled as ever. Somewhere, in Martin, the love, which hadn't yet had time to die, felt a reluctant admiration.

In a voice that was almost a whisper he said, "How much did you owe those gamblers in Reno, Rickie?"

"More than a hundred thousand." His nephew made a jaunty little gesture with his hand. "Seems like I didn't get away with it, Mart. But—okay. It was a sporting chance."

A sporting chance! Killing five people—a sporting chance. Martin's incongruous admiration had gone now. He felt only contempt and a growing sense of horror that he could have lived so long with someone and have known him so little.

"Okay, Fred," he said to the policeman. "Take him away."

The machinery of the law was lumbering forward now. Martin's role was played out. He stood, looking down, forcing himself not to listen . . . One day, maybe, he would feel alive again.

A hand touched his arm. He heard a voice, soft, sympathetic. "I know how you must be feeling. I'm sorry."

He glanced up dully. Anne Lyle was watching him. "You did what you had to do," she said.

"Mrs. Lyle!"

A voice behind them made them both turn. Joseph Crummit was hovering with a sheaf of papers in his hand. "I hate to bother you. But if only you could sign the waiver now—"

Anne looked at Martin. "Shall I sign?"

He knew she was trying to distract him, to force him out of his bitter introspection. Beneath the pain there moved a faint, warm sense of gratitude.

"Sign," he said. "Remember what you said? You don't accept things on false pretenses."

Anne Lyle signed the paper with a pen eagerly held out to her by Joseph Crummit.

"Thank you, Mrs. Lyle." Crummit hurried out of the room.

Martin and Anne were alone. For a moment they stood looking at each other. Then, in a small, uncertain voice, Anne said, "Remember something else I said yesterday? I said I wasn't very good at falling in love. Maybe—maybe I was wrong."

Her hand moved toward him. He reached out and took it in his. Yes, one day he'd feel alive again. Already, incredibly, he was sure of it, because the sunny fantasies of the day before were stealing back.

He and Anne in the star-boat, in the Bay, with the sail flapping lazily in the breeze and the tang of salt in the air . . .

"Q"

James Holding

Library Fuzz

*Meet Hal Johnson, a new type of detective—at least, a new type
in the pages of Ellery Queen's Mystery Magazine. Hal Johnson
is library fuzz—he calls himself a "sissy" kind of cop, but he's
definitely a cop. What Johnson does is "chase down stolen and
overdue books for the public library." Would you believe that in
one year a library cop can collect as much as $40,000 in fines
and in the value of recovered books? Granted, most of a library
cop's special kind of skiptracing is "routine and unexciting"—
but every once in a while there is a "Hatfield thing" . . .*

Detective: HAL JOHNSON

It was on the north side in a shabby neighborhood six blocks off
the interstate highway—one of those yellow-brick apartment
houses that 60 years of grime and weather had turned to a dirty
taupe.

The rank of mailboxes inside told me that Hatfield's apartment
was Number 35, on the third floor. I walked up. The stairway was
littered with candy wrappers, empty beer cans, and a lot of
caked-on dirt. It smelled pretty ripe, too.

On the third landing I went over to the door of Apartment 35
and put a finger on the buzzer. I could hear it ring inside the
apartment, too loud. I looked down and saw that the door was
open half an inch, unlatched, the lock twisted out of shape.

I waited for somebody to answer my ring, but nobody did. So I
put an eye to the door crack and looked inside. All I got was a
narrow view of a tiny foyer with two doors leading off it, both
doors closed. I rang the bell again in case Hatfield hadn't heard it
the first time. Still nothing happened.

The uneasiness that had driven me all the way out here from
the public library was more than uneasiness now. My stomach
was churning gently, the way it does when I'm hung over—or
scared.

I pushed the door wide-open and said in a tentive voice, "Hello! Anybody home? Mr. Hatfield?"

No answer. I looked at my watch and noted that the time was 9:32. Then I did what I shouldn't have done. I opened the right-hand door that led off Hatfield's foyer into a small poorly furnished living room, and there was Hatfield in front of me.

At least, I assumed it was Hatfield. I'd never met him, so I couldn't be sure. This was a slight balding man with a fringe of gray hair. He was dressed in a neat but shiny blue suit with narrow lapels. I knew the suit's lapels were narrow because one of them was visible to me from where I stood in the doorway. The other was crushed under Hatfield's body which lay sprawled on its side on the threadbare carpet just inside the living-room door.

I sucked in my breath and held it until my stomach settled down a little. Then I stepped around Hatfield's outflung arms to get a better look at him.

There wasn't any blood that I could see. Looked as though he'd fallen while coming into the living room from the foyer. Maybe a heart attack had hit him at just that instant, I thought. It was a possibility. But not a very good one. For when I knelt beside Hatfield and felt for a pulse in his neck, I saw that the left side of his head, the side pressed against the carpet, had been caved in by a massive blow. There was blood, after all, but not much.

I stood up, feeling sick, and looked around the living room. I noticed that the toe of one of Hatfield's black loafers was snagged in a hole in the worn carpet and that a heavy fumed-oak table was perfectly positioned along the left wall of the room to have caught Hatfield's head squarely on its corner as he tripped and fell forward into the room. A quick queasy look at the corner of the table showed me more blood.

Under the edge of the table on the floor, where they must have fallen when Hatfield threw out his arms to catch himself, was a copy of yesterday's evening newspaper and a book from the public library. I could read the title of the book. *The Sound of Singing.*

I thought about that for a moment or two and decided I was pretty much out of my depth here. So I called the police. Which, even to me, seemed a rather odd thing to do—because I'm a cop myself.

A "sissy kind" of a cop, it's true, but definitely a cop. And it isn't a bad job. For one thing, I don't have to carry a gun. My arrests are usually made without much fuss and never with any violence. I get a fair salary if you consider ten thousand a year a fair salary. And nobody calls me a pig, even though I am fuzz.

Library fuzz. What I do is chase down stolen and overdue books for the public library. Most of my work is routine and unexciting—but every once in a while I run into something that adds pepper to an otherwise bland diet.

Like this Hatfield thing. The day before I found Hatfield's body had started off for me like any other Monday. I had a list of names and addresses to call on. Understand, the library sends out notices to book borrowers when their books are overdue; but some people are deadbeats, some are book lovers, and some are so absent-minded that they ignore the notices and hang onto the books. It's these hard-core overdues that I call on—to get the books back for the library and collect the fines owing on them.

Yesterday the first name on my list was Mrs. William Conway at an address on Sanford Street. I parked my car in the driveway of the small Cape Cod house that had the name "Conway" on its mailbox and went up to the front door and rang the bell.

The woman who answered the door wasn't the maid, because she was dressed in a sexy nightie with a lacy robe of some sort thrown over it, and she gave me a warm, spontaneous, friendly smile before she even knew who I was. She was medium-tall in her pink bedroom slippers and had very dark hair, caught back in a ponytail by a blue ribbon, and china-blue eyes that looked almost startling under her dark eyebrows. I also noticed that she was exceptionally well put together.

What a nice way to start the day, I thought to myself. I said, "Are you Mrs. Conway?"

"Yes," she said, giving me a straight untroubled look with those blue eyes.

"I'm from the public library. I've come about those overdue books you have." I showed her my identification card.

"Oh, my goodness!" she said, and her look of inquiry turned to one of stricken guilt. "Oh, yes. Come in, won't you, Mr. Johnson? I'm really embarrassed about those books. I know I should have returned them a long time ago—I got the notices, of course. But honestly, I've been so busy!" She stepped back in mild confusion and I went into her house.

It turned out to be as unpretentious as it had looked from outside. In fact, the furnishings displayed an almost spectacular lack of taste. Well, nobody is perfect, I reminded myself. I could easily forgive Mrs. Conway's manifest ignorance of decorating principles, since she was so very decorative herself.

She switched off a color TV set that was muttering in one corner of the living room and motioned me to a chair. "Won't you sit down?" she said tentatively. She wasn't sure just how she ought to treat a library cop.

I said politely, "No, thanks. If you'll just give me your overdue books and the fines you owe, I'll be on my way."

She made a little rush for a coffee table across the room, the hem of her robe swishing after her. "I have the books right here." She scooped up a pile of books from the table. "I have them all ready to bring back to the library, you see?"

While I checked the book titles against my list I asked, "Why didn't you bring them back, Mrs. Conway?"

"My sister's been in the hospital," she explained, "and I've been spending every free minute with her. I just sort of forgot about my library books. I'm sorry."

"No harm done." I told her how much the fines amounted to and she made another little rush, this time for her purse which hung by its strap from the back of a Windsor chair. "The books seem to be all here," I went on, "except one."

"Oh, is one missing? Which one?"

"The Sound of Singing."

"That was a wonderful story!" Mrs. Conway said enthusiastically. "Did you read it?" She sent her blue eyes around the room, searching for the missing book.

"No. But everybody seems to like it. Maybe your husband or one of the kids took it to read," I suggested.

She gave a trill of laughter. "I haven't any children, and my husband"—she gestured toward a photograph of him on her desk, a dapper, youngish-looking man with a mustache and not much chin—"is far too busy practicing law to find time to read light novels." She paused then, plainly puzzled.

I said gently, "How about having a look in the other rooms, Mrs. Conway?"

"Of course." She counted out the money for her fines and then went rushing away up the carpeted stairs to the second floor. I watched her all the way up. It was a pleasure to look at her.

In a minute she reappeared with the missing book clutched against her chest. "Ralph *did* take it!" she said breathlessly. "Imagine! He must have started to read it last night while I was out. It was on his bedside table under the telephone."

"Good," I said. I took the book by its covers, pages down, and shook it—standard procedure to see if anything had been left between the pages by the borrower. You'd be surprised at what some people use to mark their places.

"I'm terribly sorry to have caused so much trouble," Mrs. Conway said. And I knew she meant it.

I had no excuse to linger, so I took the books under my arm, said goodbye, and left, fixing Mrs. Conway's lovely face in my memory alongside certain other pretty pictures I keep there to cheer me up on my low days.

I ticked off the last name on my list about one o'clock. By that time the back seat of my car was full of overdue books and my back pocket full of money for the library. Those few-cents-a-day book fines add up to a tidy sum when you put them all together, you know that? Would you believe that last year, all by myself, I collected $40,000 in fines and in the value of recovered books?

I went back to the library to turn in my day's pickings and to grab a quick lunch at the library cafeteria. About two o'clock the telephone in my closet-sized office rang and when I answered, the switchboard girl told me there was a lady in the lobby who was asking to see me.

That surprised me. I don't get many lady visitors at the office. And the lady herself surprised me, too. She turned out to be my blue-eyed brunette of the morning. Mrs. William Conway—but a Mrs. Conway who looked as though she'd been hit in the face by a truck since I'd seen her last.

There was a bruise as big as a half dollar on one cheek, a deep scratch on her forehead; an ugly knotted lump interrupted the smooth line of her jaw on the left side; and the flesh around one of her startling blue eyes was puffed and faintly discolored. Although she had evidently been at pains to disguise these marks with heavy make-up, they still showed. Plainly.

I suppose she saw from my expression that I'd noticed her bruises because as she sat down in my only office chair, she dropped her eyes and flushed and said with a crooked smile, "Do I look *that* bad, Mr. Johnson?" It was a singularly beguiling gambit. Actually, battered face and all, I thought she looked just as attractive now in a lemon-colored pants suit as she had in her nightie and robe that morning.

I said, "You look fine, Mrs. Conway."

She tried to sound indignant. "I fell down our stupid stairs! Can you imagine that? Just after you left. I finished making the beds and was coming down for coffee when—zap!—head over heels clear to the bottom!"

"Bad luck," I said sympathetically, reflecting that a fall down her thickly carpeted stairs would be most unlikely to result in injuries like hers. But it was none of my business.

She said, "What I came about, Mr. Johnson, was to see if I could get back *The Sound of Singing* you took this morning. My husband was furious when he came home for lunch and found I'd given it back to you."

"No problem there. We must have a dozen copies of that book in—"

She interrupted me. "Oh, but I was hoping to get the same copy I had before. You see, my husband says he left a check in it— quite a big one from a client."

"Oh. Then I must have missed it when I shook out the book this morning."

She nodded. "You must have. Ralph is sure he left it there." Mrs. Conway put a fingertip to the lump on her jaw and then hastily dropped her hand into her lap when she saw me watching her.

"Well," I said, "I've already turned the book back to the shelves, Mrs. Conway, but if we're lucky it'll still be in. Let me check." I picked up my phone and asked for the librarian on the checkout desk.

Consulting my morning list of overdue book numbers, now all safely returned to circulation, I said, "Liz, have you checked out number 15208, *The Sound of Singing*, to anybody in the last hour?"

"I've checked out that title but I don't know if it was that copy. Just a second," Liz said. After half a minute she said, "Yes, here it is, Hal. It went out half an hour ago on card number PC28382."

I made a note on my desk pad of that card number, repeating the digits out loud as I did so. Then, thanking Liz, I hung up and told Mrs. Conway, "I'm sorry, your copy's gone out again."

"Oh, dammit anyway!" said Mrs. Conway passionately. I gathered this was pretty strong talk for her because she blushed again and threw me a distressed look before continuing, "*Everything* seems to be going wrong for me today!" She paused. "What

was that number you just took down, Mr. Johnson? Does that tell
who's got the book now?"

"It tells *me*," I answered. "But for a lot of reasons we're not allowed to tell *you*. It's the card number of the person who borrowed
the book."

"Oh, dear," she said, chewing miserably on her lower lip, "then
that's *more* bad luck, isn't it?"

I was tempted to break the library's rigid rule and give her the
name and address she wanted. However, there were a couple of
things besides the rule that made me restrain my chivalrous impulse. Such as no check dropping out of *The Sound of Singing* this
morning when I shook the book. And such as Mrs. Conway's
bruises, which looked to me more like the work of fists than of
carpeted stairs.

So I said, "I'll be glad to telephone whoever has the book now
and ask him about your husband's check. Or her. If the check *is*
in the book, they'll probably be glad to mail it to you."

"Oh, would you, Mr. Johnson? That would be wonderful!" Her
eyes lit up at once.

I called the library's main desk where they issue cards and keep
the register of card holders' names and addresses. "This is Hal
Johnson," I said. "Look up the holder of card number PC28382 for
me, will you, Kathy?"

I waited until she gave me a name—George Hatfield—and an
address on the north side, then hung up, found Hatfield's telephone number in the directory, and dialed it on an outside line,
feeling a little self-conscious under the anxious scrutiny of Mrs.
Conway's beautiful bruised blue eyes.

Nobody answered the Hatfield phone.

Mrs. Conway sighed when I shook my head. "I'll try again in an
hour or so. Probably not home yet. And when I get him I'll ask
him to mail the check to you. I have your address. Okay?"

She stood up and gave me a forlorn nod. "I guess that's the best
I can do. I'll tell Ralph you're trying to get his check back, anyhow. Thanks very much." She was still chewing on her lower lip
when she left.

Later in the afternoon she called me to tell me that her husband Ralph had found his missing check in a drawer at home.
There was vast relief in her voice when she told me. I wasn't relieved so much as angry—because it seemed likely to me that my
beautiful Mrs. Conway had been slapped around pretty savagely

by that little jerk in her photograph for a mistake she hadn't made.

Anyway, I forgot about *The Sound of Singing* and spent the rest of the afternoon shopping for a new set of belted tires for my old car.

Next morning, a few minutes before 9:00, I stopped by the library to turn in my expense voucher for the new tires and pick up my list of overdues for the day's calls. As I passed the main desk, Kathy, who was just settling down for her day's work, said, "Hi, Hal. Stop a minute and let me see if it shows."

I paused by the desk. "See if what shows?"

"Senility."

"Of course it shows, child. I'm almost forty. Why this sudden interest?"

"Only the onset of senility can account for *you* forgetting something," Kathy said. "The man with the famous memory."

I was mystified. "What did I forget?"

"The name and address of card holder PC28382, that's what. You called me to look it up for you not long after lunch yesterday, remember?"

"Sure. So what makes you think I forgot it?"

"You said you had when you called me again at four thirty for the same information."

I stared at her. "Me?"

She nodded. "You."

"I didn't call you at four thirty."

"Somebody did. And said he was you."

"Did it sound like my voice?"

"Certainly. An ordinary, uninteresting man's voice. Just like yours." She grinned at me.

"Thanks. Somebody playing a joke, maybe. It wasn't me."

While I was turning in my voucher and picking up my list of overdues I kept thinking about Kathy's second telephone call. The more I thought about it, the more it bothered me.

So I decided to make my first call of the day on George Hatfield . . .

Well, I didn't touch anything in Hatfield's apartment until the law showed up in the persons of a uniformed patrolman and an old friend of mine, Lieutenant Randall of Homicide. I'd worked with him when I was in the detective bureau a few years back.

Randall looked at the setup in Hatfield's living room and growled at me, "Why me, Hal? All you need is an ambulance on this one. The guy's had a fatal accident, that's all."

So I told him about Mrs. Conway and her husband and *The Sound of Singing* and the mysterious telephone call to Kathy at the library. When I finished he jerked his head toward the library book lying under Hatfield's table and said, "Is that it?"

"I haven't looked yet. I was waiting for you."

"Look now," Randall said.

It was book number 15208, all right—unmistakably the one I'd collected yesterday from Mrs. Conway. Its identification number appeared big and clear in both the usual places—on the front flyleaf and on the margin of page 101. "This is it. No mistake," I said.

"If Hatfield's killing is connected with this book, as you seem to think," Randall said reasonably enough, "there's got to be something about the book to tell us why."

I said, "Maybe there was. Before the back flyleaf was torn out."

"Be damned!" said Randall, squinting where I was pointing. "Torn out is right. Something written on the flyleaf that this Conway wanted kept private maybe?"

"Could be."

"Thought you said you looked through this book yesterday. You'd have seen any writing."

"I didn't look through it. I shook it out, that's all."

"Why would a guy write anything private or incriminating on the blank back page of a library book, for God's sake?"

"His wife found the book under the telephone in their bedroom. He could have been taking down notes during a telephone conversation."

"In a library book?"

"Why not? If it was the only blank paper he had handy when he got the telephone call?"

"So his wife gave the book back to you before he'd had a chance to erase his notes. Is that what you're suggesting?"

"Or transcribe them, yes. Or memorize them."

Lieutenant Randall looked out Hatfield's grimy window for a moment. Then he said abruptly, "I'm impounding this library book for a few days, Hal, so our lab boys can take a look at it. Okay?"

"Okay."

Randall glanced pointedly toward the door. "Thanks for calling us," he said. "Be seeing you."

I stepped carefully around Hatfield's sprawled body. "Right."

"I'll be in touch if we find anything," Randall said.

Much to my surprise he phoned me at the library just about quitting time the next day. "Did you ever see this Mr. Conway?" he asked. "Could you identify him?"

"I never saw him in the flesh. I saw a photo of him on his wife's desk."

"That's good enough. Meet me at the Encore Bar at Stanhope and Cotton in twenty minutes, can you?"

"Sure," I said. "Why?"

"Tell you when I see you."

He was waiting for me in a rear booth. There were only half a dozen customers in the place. I sat down facing him and he said, without preamble, "Conway *did* write something on the back flyleaf of your library book. Or somebody did, anyhow. Because we found traces of crushed paper fibers on the page *under* the back flyleaf. Not good enough traces to be read except for one notation at the top, which was probably written first on the back flyleaf when the pencil point was sharper and thus made a deeper groove on the page underneath. Are you with me?"

"Yes. What did it say?"

Randall got a slip of paper from his pocket and showed it to me. It contained one line, scribbled by Randall:

Transo 3212/5/13 Mi
Encore Harper 6/12

I studied it silently for a minute. Randall said, faintly smug, "Does that mean anything to you?"

"Sure," I said, deadpan. "Somebody named Harper off Transoceanic Airlines flight 3212 out of Miami on May 13th—that's today—is supposed to meet somebody in this bar at twelve minutes after six."

"A lucky guess," Randall said, crestfallen. "The *Encore* and *Transo* gave it to you, of course. But it took us half an hour to figure the meaning and check it out."

"Check it out?"

"There really *is* a Transoceanic flight 3212 out of Miami

today—and there really is somebody aboard named Harper, too. A Miss Genevieve Harper, stewardess."

"Oh," I said, "and of course there *is* an Encore Bar—could even be a couple of them in town."

"Only one that Harper can get to through rush-hour traffic within twenty minutes after she hits the airport," the lieutenant said triumphantly. "She's scheduled in at 5:52."

I glanced at my watch. It was 5:30. "You have time to check whether Conway had any phone calls Sunday night?"

"Not yet. Didn't even have time to find out what Conway looks like. That's why you're here." He grinned. "What's your guess about why they're meeting here?"

I gave it some thought. "Drugs," I said at last, "since the flight seems to be out of Miami. Most of the heroin processed in France comes to the United States via South America and Miami, right?"

Randall nodded. "We figure Conway for a distributor at this end. Sunday night he got a phone call from somebody in South America or Miami, telling him when and where to take delivery of a shipment. That's what he wrote on the flyleaf of your library book. So no wonder he was frantic when his wife gave his list of dates and places to a library cop."

I suddenly felt tired. I called over to the bartender and ordered a dry martini. I said to Randall, "So Hatfield's accident could have been murder?"

"Sure. We think it went like this: Mrs. Conway gave you the book, got knocked around by her husband when she told him what she'd done, then on hubby's orders came to you to recover the book for him. When she couldn't do that, or even get the name of the subsequent borrower, her husband did the best he could with the information she *did* get—the borrower's library card number and how you matched it up with his name and address. Conway got the name the same way you did—by phoning what's-her-name at your main desk."

"Kathy," I said.

"Yeah. Conway must have gone right out to Hatfield's when he learned his identity, prepared to do anything necessary to get that book back—or his list on the flyleaf, anyway. Conway broke the lock on Hatfield's apartment and was inside looking for the book when Hatfield must have walked in on him."

"And Conway hid behind the door and clobbered Hatfield when he walked in?"

"Yeah. Probably with a blackjack. And probably, in his panic, hit him too hard. So he faked it to look like an accident. Then he tore the back flyleaf out of your book thinking nobody would ever notice it was missing."

"You forgot something," I said.

"What?"

"He made his wife call me off by telling me he'd found his lost check."

"I didn't forget it," Randall grinned.

I said, "Of course you can't prove any of this."

"Not yet. But give us time. We get him on a narcotics charge and hold him tighter than hell while we work up the murder case."

"*If* it's Conway," I said, looking at my watch, "who shows up here in twenty-two minutes."

"He'll show." Randall was confident. "Likely get here a little early, even."

And he did, At 5:56 the original of Mrs. Conway's photograph walked in the door of the Encore Bar. Dapper, young-looking, not much chin under a mustache that drooped around the corners of his mouth.

He sat down in the booth nearest the door and ordered a Scotch-and-soda.

Randall threw me a questioning look and I nodded vigorously. Then we talked about baseball until, at 6:14, a bouncy little blonde dish came tripping into the Encore and went straight to Conway's booth, saying loud enough for everybody in the joint to hear, "Well, hello, darling! I'm so thirsty I could drink *water!*" She looked very pert in her uniform and she had a flight bag over her shoulder. She sat down beside Conway with her back to us.

Randall got up, went to the bar entrance, and opened the door. He stepped out into the vestibule and casually waved one arm over his head, as though he were tossing a cigarette butt away. Then he came back in and leaned against the bar until three young huskies appeared in the doorway. Randall pointed one finger at Conway's booth and the three newcomers stepped over there, boxing in Conway and Miss Harper.

It was all done very quietly and smoothly. No voices raised, no violence. One of the narcotics men took charge of Harper's shoulder bag. The other two took charge of Conway and Harper.

When they'd gone, Randall ordered himself a bourbon and carried it back to our booth and sat down. "That's it, Hal," he said with satisfaction. "Harper had two one-pound boxes of bath powder in her flight bag. Pure heroin. This is going to look very good—*very* good—on my record."

I took a sip of my martini and said nothing.

Randall went on, "You're sure Conway's wife has nothing to do with the smuggling? That she doesn't suspect what her hubby is up to?"

I thought about Mrs. Conway's friendliness, so charming and unstudied. I remembered how the animation and pride I'd seen in her eyes yesterday morning had been replaced by distress and bewilderment in the afternoon. And I said to Lieutenant Randall, "I'd stake my job on it."

He nodded. "We'll have to dig into it, of course. But I'm inclined to think you're right. So somebody ought to tell her why her husband won't be home for dinner tonight, Hal." He paused for a long moment. "Any volunteers?"

I looked up from my martini into Randall's unblinking stare. "Thanks, Lieutenant," I said. "I'm on my way."

Michael Gilbert

Mouse in a Trap

The legal firm of Messrs. Lamplough, Fairchild and Brett found itself enmeshed in a little real-estate deal involving two of its valued clients. And the final resolution of the problem was—how do lawyers say it?—"entirely without prejudice"...

When two people fall out and decide to seek legal advice over their dispute it may seem surprising to you that they should both go to the same firm of solicitors. It is only superficially surprising. For, if both of them have used the same firm for a long time, neither may see any reason why he should go elsewhere to oblige the other party. After all, they can always consult different partners. And anyway, in a small country town, there may only *be* one good firm. This explains why the offices of Messrs. Lamplough, Fairchild and Brett recently received visits, on successive mornings, both from Mr. Snuggs and Sir Charles Pellat.

These offices occupy an early Georgian building in the little Square behind the Cornmarket. The brass plate is so worn with age and elbow grease that the names on it are almost illegible. No one living can remember Mr. Lamplough. There is a portrait of him in the waiting room which exhibits a crop of benevolent muttonchop whiskers. If you look very closely you can see the rat-trap mouth behind them.

Mr. Cyprian Fairchild, the senior partner, is the grandson of the original Fairchild, and is himself approaching the age of retirement. Older clients value his advice. They realize that he may not be entirely *au fait* with the complexities of modern legislation, but they look on him as an old friend and a man of the world. The younger generation of lawyers in the office, headed by the junior partner, Mr. Roger Brett, privately consider him an old fuddy-duddy.

Mr. Snuggs parked his brand-new Three Litre Austin across the

backs of two smaller cars, neatly blocking their exit, entered the
office with the deliberate tread which befitted an independent
tradesman and a man of property, and was shown up to the
second-floor room of young Mr. Brett.

"It's the roof, at the front," said Mr. Snuggs. "Not the new bit
over the back extension. That's perfect and will be for another
fifty years."

"It should be," said Mr. Brett, "seeing what it cost your landlord
to put it up."

"He can afford it," said Mr. Snuggs. "No. It's the front bit. Two
tiles off in the gale last week, and Alfred and Henry ran a ladder
up yesterday and stripped off a few more tiles. We found just
what we expected. Wet rot."

Mr. Brett said, "Tchk tchk," and made a note. He reflected that
it was the fourth such discovery that Mr. Snuggs and his sons had
made in the past few years. The others had been dry rot, rising
damp, and wood-worm. All had been rectified at considerable expense, by their long-suffering landlord, Sir Charles Pellat.

"Did you mention it to Sir Charles?"

"I did."

"I don't suppose he was pleased."

"He was upset," said Mr. Snuggs complacently. "But I told him,
it's your property. You've got to keep it in repair. Roof and main
timbers. That's what the lease says, isn't it?"

"That's roughly correct. Of course, he did build on that rear extension for you three years ago. That was an improvement. He
didn't *have* to do that."

"He was improving his own property. It'll come back to him
when we go. He may not get it himself—he's an old man. But it'll
come back to his family, won't it?"

"That's roughly correct."

"Then he's just investing his own money in his own property."

"That's certainly one way of looking at it," said Mr. Brett. "Did
he agree to make the repairs?"

"What he said was, seeing as me and my two boys were all
builders, why didn't we do it ourselves. Well, I wasn't falling for
that! I said, we don't mix business with pleasure, Sir Charles.
We'd rather get an outside firm to do it, then we'd know the job
would be done properly. I suggested Palmer's."

Mr. Brett made another note. He knew that Palmer's were the
most expensive builders in the district. He didn't think that Sir

Charles would be very pleased. He fancied he would be seeing him quite soon.

This prediction was promptly fulfilled. At eleven o'clock on the following morning an aged Rolls-Royce pulled into the Square and parked across the backs of three smaller cars.

Sir Charles was tall and thin. He still retained, in his walk and his talk, a ghost of the cavalry subaltern he had been in the first World War. He refused a seat, and stood beside the fine bow-window of Mr. Cyprian Fairchild's ground-floor office.

"It's that damned fellow Snuggs," he said.

"At it again, is he?"

"He never stops. Why the devil I ever let him have the lodge I don't know!"

"When your lodgekeeper left, you had to let it to someone."

"Should have chosen an old lady. A nice old lady. Not a bounder like Snuggs."

"You couldn't tell."

"Might have known. Fellow's a builder. Bound to be a crook. They all are."

"That's a bit sweeping," said Mr. Fairchild. "There are honest builders. You happen to have struck a bad 'un, that's all. What does he want now?"

"He wants a new front roof. Cost five hundred pounds. Got th estimate here."

"How much did you pay for that back extension?"

"Fifteen hundred. That was three years ago. Cost more now. And that's on top of what I paid for rebuilding the whole chimney and putting in new casement windows downstairs. To say nothing of regular annual repairs. I calculated the other day"—Sir Charles fished a scrap of paper out of his waistcoat pocket—"that lodge has cost me the thick end of five thousand pounds since the Snuggses went in."

"I suppose it's an investment," said Mr. Fairchild gloomily.

"Investment! Who for? Me? I've got no heir, apart from my sister Lucretia, and she's got all the money she wants. And anyway, what sort of investment is it, for God's sake? The place must be the best fitted-out cottage in England by now. Worth eight thousand pounds at least. If I had that money invested I'd get— never was much good at sums."

"At six per cent you'd get get four hundred and eighty pounds a year."

"And the rent I get is thirty-five shillings a week. How much is that a year?"

"Just over ninety pounds."

"Well, there you are," said Sir Charles. He glowered out of the window at a lady driver who was trying with little success to back her car out past his Rolls-Royce.

"The trouble is," said Mr. Fairchild, "that *if* you want to sell the Manor House, and I gather you've more or less made up your mind—"

"Got to. Can't keep it up. Barn of a place. Far too big."

"The park's leased to an agricultural tenant. So the rent of that is regulated. And the lodge is the only cottage left. If you'd been able to give vacant possession of that, it would have been a great attraction. I wonder if we could buy the Snuggses out."

"They wouldn't leave," said Sir Charles. He was staring gloomily out of the window. The woman driver had abandoned the attempt and started blowing her horn. Sir Charles ignored her. He swung round suddenly and said, "Do you suppose he'd do a swap?"

Mr. Fairchild gaped at him.

"Do a *what?*" he said.

"A swap. An exchange. I'll take the lodge. He can have the Manor House. *And* the park."

"He can't mean it," said young Mr. Brett.

"He's quite serious. He reckons he'd be much better off in the lodge. He'll be able to save his income instead of spending it trying to keep up the Manor. And he'll be much warmer in winter."

"But what will the Snugges *do* with the Manor House?"

"They're builders, aren't they? Plenty of scope for them."

"It's mad," said Mr. Brett. "But all the same—"

"Squire Snuggs," said Mr. Fairchild with a chuckle. "Think how he'll enjoy that. There are one or two details. Sir Charles would like to keep the shooting. And there's one particularly nice walk, up the beech avenue to that summerhouse—a gazebo is the correct name for it, I believe—he'd like to keep a right of way up to that. I'll leave the conveyancing details to you, my boy. It shouldn't take very long to fix up."

It took a month to fix up. And Mr. Snuggs seemed happy with the exchange for nearly a year. At the end of that time he called by appointment to see Mr. Brett, and brought his two sons with him, solid youths who sat on the edges of their chairs holding

their hats in their hands. Mr. Snuggs did most of the talking.
"It's like this," he said, "I want to put things back to what they was before."
"You mean you want to re-exchange the properties?"
"That's right. I want to put it back like it was." His two sons nodded their somber approval.
"But why?"
"Because it won't work. First, we get no money out of it. What that farmer chap pays us goes on *his* improvements, and anything that's left goes on rates. Do you know how much the rates are on the Manor?"
"*I* know," said Mr. Brett, "and so do you. Because I told you when you bought it."
"Well, you may have told me, but I didn't take it in. Then there's the repairs. All right, we do them ourselves. But it's bloody hard work—" His two sons nodded emphatically. It was clear to Mr. Brett that most of the hard work was done by them. "*And* it means we can't take on much outside work, so we've got no money coming in. And last but not least, there's the lodge."
"Ah," said Mr. Brett. "The lodge. Yes?"
"Twice already this year he's been at us for money. First it was all the gutters wanted re-doing. Three hundred pounds that cost us. I offered to do it myself."
"What did he say to that?"
"He said he didn't like to see us mixing business with pleasure. He'd get Palmer's to do it."
"Aren't they apt to be a bit expensive?"
"Expensive! They build their houses with bricks of gold. Then there was the drains. *We* never found anything wrong with the drains, did we?"
Alfred and Henry shook their heads in unison.
"There was a surveyor's report. I remember."
"Oh, yes. He got a surveyor's report all right. Six hundred pounds that cost us. And what are we getting for it? I'll tell you." Mr. Snuggs thumped the table with a large mahogany fist. "Ninety pounds a year, and everyone laughing at us. Why, we can't hardly get in our own gate for the bloody great cars round *his* front door. *And* he's bought himself a new Aston-Martin."

"It's true," said Sir Charles to Mr. Fairchild, "that I do seem to have become a lot more popular since I moved. In the old days no one seemed keen on coming to dinner with me. I couldn't blame them really. When I had guests we used to eat in the big dining room—the one my grandparents used when they had a royal visitation. It's got three outside walls, and the central heating system at the Manor is so old-fashioned that although it used a ton of coke a week the pipes never got more than lukewarm. I remember once when I had old Colonel Featherstonehaugh to dinner he took a sip of his burgundy—rather a nice Corton, incidentally—and said, his teeth chattering at the time, 'You know, Charles, the only w-w-way you could get this w-w-wine down to room temperature would be to put a l-l-lump of ice in it.' " Sir Charles laughed heartily, and Mr. Fairchild laughed with him.

"So you're better off now?"

"Oh, we're very snug now. The gas-fired central heating keeps the cottage as warm as toast. Of course, I had to pay for the boiler, but I stung my landlord for all the builders' work involved. And what's more, now that I don't need the cellar for coal, I've got most of my wine into it. I wonder, would you care to come up next week and try the Clos de Vougeot? It's settled nicely."

"I'd love to," said Mr. Fairchild.

Pride, plus a determination not to be proved wrong, enabled Mr. Snuggs to stick it out for another twelve months. Then his Austin, two years old now and in sad need of a re-spray, crept into the little Square behind the Cornmarket. Mr. Snuggs looked almost as battered as his car. He said to Mr. Brett, "It's no good. It's killing me. Something's got to be done."

"It's got worse, has it?"

"Worse? If it goes on for another six months I'll be bankrupt. And every time I go out of my own front gate I can see that old devil. He sits in his front window all the time, grinning at me. Except when he takes a stroll up to the summerhouse, and sits there grinning at all of us. We've got to stop it."

Mr. Brett nearly said, "There's no law against grinning," and then realized that with Mr. Snuggs in his present frame of mind this might cost him a client. He said, "It's not going to be easy."

"Couldn't we raise his rent?"

"It's a controlled rent. I remember explaining it to you when—"

"Yes, yes," said Mr. Snuggs testily. "You've no call to remind me about that. But I recollect there was something about rates."

"The taxable value."

"If it goes up above a certain figure you can get him out. That's right, isn't it?"

"That's roughly correct."

"It's a lovely little cottage. In a beautiful state of repair. Modern drainage. Central heating."

"I seem to remember," said Mr. Brett, "that my partner, Mr. Fairchild, argued all those points most persuasively in front of the rating authority, but between us we succeeded in defeating him."

Mr. Snuggs said, "Tchah," and then, "You're a lawyer, aren't you? Why don't you suggest something instead of just sitting there making remarks?"

"Sir Charles is pretty old. I heard he hasn't been well lately."

"I believe that's right," said Mr. Snuggs, looking more cheerful. "His sister's come to look after him. And I saw the doctor's car up there two days ago. Why?"

"A protected tenancy is a personal thing. Not something he can leave to his family—"

"You mean, if he popped off I'd get the cottage back?"

"That's roughly correct."

It was on a Monday morning in January, sharp with the first frost of the new year, that Mr. Fairchild came into Mr. Brett's room with the news.

"It happened sometime last night," he said. "The old boy must have gone for his usual walk up to the gazebo and had a stroke."

"A fatal stroke?"

"Dr. Shuttleworth says no. It probably paralyzed him. By a damnable piece of bad luck his sister was out on one of her do-gooding committees and didn't get home till quite late. She assumed he'd already gone to bed. It wasn't until she went to call him this morning that the alarm was sounded. They searched the grounds and found him."

"Then he died of exposure, sometime during the night?"

"Probably quite quickly, Dr. Shuttleworth says. After a stroke his vitality would be very low."

"Poor old chap," said Mr. Brett.

Mr. Snuggs, who called on the following day, expressed somewhat different sentiments.

"We've all got to go sometime," he said, concealing any grief he may have felt. "I expect it was as good a way as any. Doctors nowadays keep old people living far too long. If it's right he was paralyzed, he wouldn't have enjoyed life, would he? A misery to himself and everyone else."

"I suppose that's right," said Mr. Brett.

"Person I feel most sorry for is that sister of his. She'll have to find somewhere to live. She gave up her own house, you know, when she came to look after him, in the summer. Something wrong?"

"In the summer?" croaked Mr. Brett.

"That's right. Have I said something I shouldn't?"

"Do you—do you happen to remember exactly when?"

"As a matter of fact, I do. It was on Midsummer Day. Look here, Brett, what's all this about?"

"And she's been living at the lodge ever since?"

"That's right. He needed a bit of looking after at the end."

"And if she came on Midsummer Day she's been there more than six months."

"So what?"

Mr. Brett was thumbing feverishly through the stout olive-green book on his desk.

"It's one of the earlier Rent Acts," he said. "The Act of 1920. Section Twelve. That's right. Subsection One. I'd entirely over-looked the possibility—yes, yes."

"Stop all this monkey talk," said Mr. Snuggs, his face a bright red, "and explain."

Mr. Brett explained.

"You mean," said Mr. Snuggs, when he had finally taken it in, "that because she's a relative, and because she's lived there more than six months, I can't turn *her* out either."

"That's roughly correct."

A gleam of hope appeared in Mr. Snuggs's watery eyes. "Perhaps she don't know about this old Act," he said.

"It's a possibility. But when I saw her coming out of Mr. Fairchild's room this morning I remember thinking she looked remarkably cheerful."

"Perhaps if I offered her something—"

"You could try," said Mr. Brett.

Mr. Snuggs tried that afternoon. He found Miss Lucretia Pellat in the small but nicely furnished front room of the lodge, pouring tea from a heavy old silver pot. He refused the offer of a cup for himself and opened his proposal.

Miss Pellat shook her head.

"I wouldn't dream of moving," she said. "It's a dear little house. Full of memories of the happy times my dear brother had here. He *was* happy, you know."

"I daresay he was," said Mr. Snuggs morosely.

"He kept his health to the last. When providence delivered that final stroke I could not help thinking that it was a perfect ending. Provided—" and on the word Miss Pellat leaned forward so sharply that her earrings tinkled—"provided that it killed him."

"Well, it did," said Mr. Snuggs.

"That's not true. It was the night in the open that killed him. If I had summoned help and had him carried back to the house—taken to a hospital or nursing home—and injected with drugs, no doubt he could have been saved. And saved for what? A pitiful, half-paralyzed old age. Like a mouse, caught by its back legs in a trap. I knew my brother too well to think he'd have wanted that."

Mr. Snuggs had got his breath back by now. He said, "Do you mean to say you were with him when it happened and you just left him there to die?"

"Death by exposure is quick and not too uncomfortable. If you read the diaries of the great Polar explorers you will find that it comes with a feeling of warmth and relaxation."

Mr. Snuggs stared at her, horrified. "But," he said, "you're his sister! How could you do it? Walk off like that and leave him!"

"I didn't walk straight off," said Miss Pellat, and her voice sounded a clear warning.

"You didn't, eh?"

"Because, when I'd only got as far as the edge of the wood, I heard a car coming. Your car, Mr. Snuggs."

Mr. Snuggs stared at her, hypnotized.

"And I saw you get out and walk over and look at my brother. And I saw *you* walk away again."

There was a long, long silence. At last Mr. Snuggs said, in a croaking voice, "I deny it."

"Of course you do. And everything I told you is entirely—what do the lawyers say?—without prejudice. Such a curious expression. No, no, I am sure we can keep each other's little secret, Mr. Snuggs."

As he rose heavily to his feet she added, "By the way, I fear I shall have to ask you to do something about the bath. I really need a new one. And while you're at it you might let me have a new sink as well—"

Patricia Highsmith

The   Nature   of   the   Thing

Strictly speaking, Patricia Highsmith's unusual story is not in EQMM's field. And yet—even strictly speaking—why isn't it? Surely it contains mystery—in the "purest" sense imaginable. And if you accept Patricia Highsmith's premise (and you will—her ability to create "willing suspension of disbelief" is remarkable, uncanny), then this story is not only a mystery, it is also a crime story.

But we admit that most readers will consider "The Nature of the Thing" a fantasy-mystery. All right, we will not argue the point further. But Patricia Highsmith writes fantasy-mystery so hauntingly, so compellingly, that we confess we can't resist her offbeat tales. We hope you too can't resist them.

And this one will haunt you. . .Are people becoming square?—in both meanings of the word, "straight" and "slang." Think about it. Think about all its implications. . .

Eleanor had been sewing nearly all day—sewing after dinner, too—and it was now almost midnight. She looked away from her machine, sideways toward the hall door, and saw something about two feet high, something grayish black, which after a second or two moved and was lost from view in the hall. Eleanor rubbed her eyes. Her eyes smarted, and it was delicious to rub them. But since she was sure she had not really seen something, she did not get up from her chair to go and investigate. She forgot about it.

She stood up about five minutes later, after tidying her sewing table, putting away her scissors, and folding the yellow dress whose side seams she had just let out. The dress was ready for Mrs. Burns tomorrow. Always letting out, Eleanor thought, never taking in. People seemed to grow sideways, not upward any more, and she smiled at this fuzzy little thought. She was tired, but she

had had a good day. She gave her cat Bessie a saucer of milk
—rather creamy milk, because Bessie liked the best of
everything—then heated some milk for herself and took it in a
mug up to bed.

The second time she saw it, however, she was not tired, and the
sun was shining brightly. This time she was sitting in the
armchair, putting a zipper in a skirt, and as she knotted her
thread, she happened to glance at the door that went into what
she called the side room, a room off the living room at the front of
the house. She saw a squarish figure about two feet high, an ugly
little thing that at first suggested an upended sandbag. It took a
moment before she perceived a large square head, thick feet in
heavy shoes, and incredibly short arms with big hands that
dangled.

Eleanor was half out of her chair, her slender body rigid.

The thing didn't move. But it was looking at her.

Get it out of the house, she thought at once. Shoo it out the
door. What *was* it? The face was vaguely human. Eyes looked at
her from under hair that was combed forward over the forehead.
Had the children put some horrid toy in the house to frighten
her? The Rolands next door had four children, the oldest eight.
Children's toys these days—you never knew what to expect!

Then the thing moved, advanced slowly into the living room,
and Eleanor stepped quickly behind the armchair.

"Get out! Get away!" she said in a voice shrill with panic.

"Um-m," came the reply, soft and deep.

Had she really heard anything? Now it looked up from the
floor—where it had stared while entering the room—to her face.
The look at her seemed direct, yet was somehow vague and unfo-
cused. The creature went on, toward the electric heater, where it
stopped and held out its hands casually to the warmth. It was
masculine, Eleanor thought; its legs—if those stumpy things could
be called legs—were in trousers. Again the creature took a
sidelong look at her, a little shyly, yet as if defying her to get it
out of the room.

The cat, curled on a pillow in a chair, lifted her head and
yawned, and the movement caught Eleanor's eye. She waited for
Bessie to see the thing, straight ahead of her and only four feet
away; but Bessie put her head down again in a position for sleeping. Now that was curious!

Eleanor retreated quickly to the kitchen, opened the back door and went out, leaving the door wide-open. She went around to the front door and opened that wide, too. Give the thing a chance to get out! Eleanor stayed on her front walk, ready to run to the road if the creature emerged.

The thing came to the front door and said in a deep voice, the words more a rumble than articulated, "I'm not going to harm you, so why don't you come back in? It's your house." And there was the hint of a shrug in the chunky shoulders.

"I'd like you to get out please!" Eleanor said.

"Um-m." He turned away, back into the living room.

Eleanor thought of going for Mr. Roland next door; he was a practical man who probably had a gun in the house, since he was a captain in the Air Force. Then she remembered that the Rolands had gone off before lunch and that their house was empty. Eleanor gathered her courage and advanced toward the front door.

She didn't see him in the living room. She even looked behind the armchair. She went cautiously toward the side room. He was not in there, either. She looked quite thoroughly.

She stood in the hall and called up the stairs, really called to all the house, "If you're still in this house I wish you would leave!"

Behind her a voice said, "I'm still here."

Eleanor turned and saw him standing in the living room.

"I won't do you any harm. But I can disappear if you prefer. Like this."

She thought she saw a set of bared teeth, as if he were making an effort. As she stared, the creature became a paler gray, and more fuzzy at the edges. And after ten seconds there was nothing. *Nothing!* Was she losing her mind? She must tell Dr. Campbell, she thought. First thing tomorrow morning, she would go to his office and tell him honestly what had happened—what she thought had happened.

The rest of the day, and the evening, passed without incident. Mrs. Burns came for her dress and brought a coat to be shortened. Eleanor watched a television program, then went to bed at half-past ten. She had thought she would be frightened—going to bed and turning all the lights out; but she wasn't. And before she had time to worry about whether she could get to sleep or not, she had fallen asleep.

But when she woke up he was the second thing she saw, the

first thing being her cat, who had slept at the foot of the bed for warmth.

Bessie stretched, yawned, and miaouwed simultaneously, demanding breakfast. And hardly two yards away, there he stood, staring at her. Eleanor's promise of immediate breakfast to Bessie was cut short by her seeing him.

"I could use some breakfast myself," he said. Was there a faint smile on that square face? "Nothing much. A piece of bread will do."

Now Eleanor found her teeth tight together, found herself wordless. She got out of bed on the other side from him, quickly pulled on her old flannel robe, and went down the stairs. In the kitchen she comforted herself with the usual routine—she put the kettle on, fed Bessie while the kettle was heating, cut some bread. But she was waiting for the thing to appear in the kitchen doorway, and as she was slicing the bread he did appear. Trembling, Eleanor held a piece of bread toward him.

"If I give you this, would you go away?" she asked.

The monstrous hand reached out and up and took the bread. "Not necessarily," rumbled the bass voice. "I don't need to eat, you know. I thought I'd keep you company, that's all."

Eleanor was not sure, really not sure she had heard it. She was imagining telling Dr. Campbell all this, imagining the point at which Dr. Campbell would cut her short—politely, of course, because he was a nice man—and prescribe some kind of sedative.

Bessie finished her breakfast and walked so close by the creature that her fur must have brushed his leg; but the cat showed no sign of feeling or seeing anything. That was proof enough that he didn't exist, Eleanor thought.

A strange rumbling "Um-m-m" came from him. He was laughing! "Not everyone—or everything—can see me," he said to Eleanor. "In fact, very few people can see me." He had eaten the bread, apparently.

Eleanor steeled herself to carry on with her breakfast. She cut another piece of bread, got out the butter and jam, scalded the teapot. It was ten to 8:00. By 9:00 she'd be in Dr. Campbell's office.

"Maybe there's something I can do for you today," he said. He had not moved from where he stood. "Odd jobs. I'm strong." The last word was like a nasal burr, like the horn of a large and distant ship.

At first Eleanor thought of the rusty old lawn roller in her barn. She'd rung up Field's, the secondhand dealer, to come and take it away, but they were late as usual, two weeks late. "I have a roller out in the barn. After breakfast you can take it to the edge of the road and leave it there, if you will." That would be further proof, Eleanor thought, proof that he wasn't real. The roller must weigh two or three hundred pounds.

He walked, in a slow, rolling gait, out of the kitchen and into the sitting room. He made no sound.

Eleanor ate her breakfast at the scrubbed wooden table in the kitchen, where she often preferred to eat instead of in the dining room. She propped a booklet on sewing tips in front of her, and after a few moments she was able to concentrate on it.

At 8:30, dressed now, Eleanor went out to the barn behind her house. She had not looked for him in the house—didn't know where he was, in fact; but somehow it did not surprise her to find him beside her when she reached the barn door.

"It's in the back corner. I'll show you." She removed the padlock which had not been entirely closed.

He understood at once, rubbed his big yellowish hands together, and took a grip on the wooden handle of the roller He pulled it toward him with apparently the greatest ease, then began to push it from behind, rolling it. But using the handle was easier, so he took the handle again, and in a few minutes the roller was at the edge of the road.

Billy, the boy who delivered the morning papers, was cycling along the road just then.

Eleanor tensed, thinking Billy would cry out at the sight of him; but the boy only said shyly, "Morning, Mrs. Heathcote," and pedaled on.

"Good morning, Billy," Eleanor called after the boy.

"Anything else?" he asked.

"I can't think of anything, thank you," Eleanor replied rather breathlessly.

"It won't do you any good to speak to your doctor about me," he said.

They were both walking back toward the house, up the carelessly flagstoned path that divided Eleanor's front garden.

"He won't be able to see me, and he'll just give you useless pills," he continued.

What made you think I was going to a doctor? Eleanor wanted

to ask. But she knew. He could read her mind. Is he some part of myself? she asked herself, with a flash of intuition which went no further than the question. If no one *else* can see him—

"I am myself," he said, smiling at her over one shoulder. He was leading the way into the house. "Just me." And he laughed.

Eleanor did not go to see Dr. Campbell. She decided to try to ignore him, to go about her usual affairs. Her affairs that morning consisted in walking a quarter of a mile to the butcher's for some liver for Bessie and half a chicken for herself, and of buying several articles at Mr. White's, the grocer. But Eleanor was thinking of telling all this to Vance—Mrs. Florence Vansittart—who was her best friend in town. Vance and she had tea together, at one or the other's house, at least once a week—usually once every five days, in fact; so Eleanor phoned Vance as soon as she got home.

The creature was not in sight at that time.

Vance agreed to come over at 4:00. "How *are* you, dear?" Vance asked as she always did.

"All right, thanks," Eleanor replied, more heartily than usual. "And you?. . .I'll make some blueberry muffins if I get my work done in time."

That afternoon, though he had kept out of sight since the morning, he lumbered silently into the room just as Eleanor and Vance were starting on their second cup of tea, and just as Eleanor was drawing breath for the first statement, the introductory statement, of her strange story. She had been thinking that the roller at the edge of the road—she must ring Field's again first thing in the morning—would be proof that what she said was not an hallucination.

"What's the matter, Eleanor?" asked Vance, sitting up a little. She was a woman of Eleanor's age, about 55, one of the many widows in town; but unlike Eleanor, Vance had never worked at anything—she had been left enough money. And Vance looked to her right, at the side-room door, where Eleanor had been looking. Eleanor took her eyes away from the creature who was now standing inside the door.

"Nothing," Eleanor said. Vance didn't see him, she thought. Vance *can't* see him.

"She can't see me," the creature rumbled to Eleanor.

"Swallow something the wrong way?" Vance asked, chuckling, helping herself to another blueberry muffin.

The creature was staring at the muffins, but came no closer.

"You know, Eleanor—" Vance chewed "—if you're still charging only two dollars for putting a hem up, I think you need your head examined. People around here, all of them could afford to give you twice as much. It's criminal the way you cheat yourself."

Vance meant, Eleanor thought, that it was high time she had her house painted, or recovered the armchair, which she could do herself if she had the time. "It's not easy to mention raising prices, and the people who come to me are used to mine by now."

"Other people manage to mention price-raising pretty easily," Vance said as Eleanor had known she would. "I hear of a new higher price every day!"

The creature took a muffin. For a few seconds the muffin must have been visible in mid-air to Vance, even if she didn't see him. But suddenly the muffin was gone, chewed by the massive jaw.

"You look a bit absent today, my dear," Vance said. "Something worrying you?" Vance looked at her attentively, waiting for a confidence—such as another tooth extraction that Eleanor felt doomed to, or news that her brother George in Canada, who had never made a go of anything, was once more failing in business.

Eleanor braced herself and said, "I've had a visitor for the last two days. He's standing right here by the table." She nodded her head in his direction.

The creature was looking at Eleanor.

Vance looked where Eleanor had nodded. "What do you mean?"

"You can't see him?. . .He's quite friendly," Eleanor added. "It's a creature two feet high. He's right there. He just took a muffin! I know you don't believe me," she rushed on, "but he moved the roller this morning from the barn to the edge of the road. You saw it at the edge of the road, didn't you? You *said* something about it."

Vance tipped her head to one side, looking in a puzzled way at Eleanor. "You mean the handyman. Old Gufford?"

"No, he's—" But at this moment the creature was walking out of the room, so Vance couldn't possibly see him, and before he disappeared into the side room he gave Eleanor a look and pushed his great hands flat downward in the air, as if to say, "Give it up," or "Don't talk."

"I mean what I said," Eleanor pursued, determined to share her experience, determined also to get some sympathy, even some protection. "I'm not joking, Vance. It's a little—creature—two feet high, and he talks to me." Her voice had sunk to a whisper. She glanced at the side-room doorway, which was empty. "You think I'm seeing things, but I'm not, I swear it!"

Vance still looked puzzled, but quite in control of herself, and she even assumed a superior attitude. "How long have you—been seeing him, my dear?" she asked.

"I saw him first two nights ago," Eleanor said, still in a whisper. "Then yesterday quite plainly, in broad daylight. He has a deep voice."

"If he just took a muffin, where is he now?" Vance asked, getting up. "Why can't I see him?"

"He went into the side room. All right, come along."

Eleanor was suddenly aware that she didn't know his name, didn't know how to address him. She and Vance looked into an apparently empty room, empty of anything alive except some plants on the window sill. Eleanor looked behind the sofa. "Well—he has the faculty of disappearing."

Vance smiled, again in a superior way. "Eleanor, your eyes are getting worse. Are you using your glasses? That constant sewing—"

"I don't need them for sewing. Only for distance. Matter of fact, I did put them on when I looked at him yesterday across the room." She was wearing her eyeglasses now.

Vance frowned slightly. "My dear, are you afraid of him?. . .It looks like it. Stay with me tonight. Come home with me now, if you like. I can come back with Hester and look the house over thoroughly." Hester was her cleaning woman.

"Oh, I'm sure you wouldn't see him. And I'm not afraid. He's rather friendly. But I *did* want you to believe me."

"How can I believe you if I don't see him?"

"I don't know." Eleanor thought of describing him more accurately. But would that convince Vance, or anybody? "I think I could take a photograph of him. I don't think he'd mind," Eleanor said.

"A good idea! You've got a camera?"

"No. Well, I have, an old one of John's, but—"

"I'll bring mine. This afternoon. Now I'm going to finish my tea."

Vance brought the camera just before 6:00. "Good luck, Eleanor. This should be interesting!" Vance said as she left.

Eleanor could tell that Vance had not believed a single word of what she had told her. The camera said "5" on its indicator. There were eight more pictures on the roll, Vance had said. Eleanor thought two would be enough.

"I don't photograph," his deep voice said on her left, and Eleanor saw him standing in the doorway of the side room. "But I'll pose for you. Um-m-m." It was the deep laugh.

Eleanor felt only a mild start of surprise, or of fear. The sun was still shining. "Would you sit in a chair in the front garden?"

"Certainly," the creature said, and he was clearly amused.

Eleanor picked up the straight chair which she usually sat on when she worked, but he took it from her and went out the front door with it. He set the chair in the garden, careful not to tread on flowers. Then with a little boost he got himself onto the seat and folded his short arms.

The sunlight fell full on his face. Vance had showed Eleanor how to work the camera. It was a simple one compared to John's. She took the picture at the prescribed six-foot distance. Then she saw Old Gufford, the neighborhood handyman, going by in his little truck, staring at her. They did not usually greet each other, and they did not now, but Eleanor could imagine how odd he must think she was to be taking a picture of an ordinary empty chair in the garden. But she had seen him clearly in the finder. There was no doubt at all about that.

"Could I take one more of you standing next to the chair?" she asked.

"Um-m." That was not a laugh, but a sound of assent. He slid off the chair and stood beside it, one hand resting on the chair's back.

This was splendid, Eleanor thought, because it showed his height compared with that of the chair.

Click!

"Thank you."

"They won't turn out," he remarked, and took the chair back into the house.

"If you'd like another muffin," Eleanor said, wanting to be polite and thinking also he might have resented her asking him to be photographed, "they're in the kitchen."

"I know. I don't need to eat. I just took one to see if your friend would notice. She didn't. Not many do."

Eleanor thought again of the muffin in mid-air for a few seconds—it must have been—but she said nothing. "I—I don't know what to call you. Have you got a name?"

A fuzzy, rather general expression of amusement came over his square face. "Lots of names. No particular name. No one speaks to me, so there's no need of a name."

"I speak to you," Eleanor said.

He was standing by the stove now, not as high, not nearly as high as the gas burners. His skin looked dry, yellowish, and his face somehow sad. She felt sorry for him.

"Where have you been living?"

He laughed. "Um-m-m. I live anywhere, everywhere. It doesn't matter."

She wanted to ask some questions, such as, "Do you feel the cold?" but she did not want to be personal, or seem to be prying. "It occurred to me you might like a bed," she said more brightly. "You could sleep on the couch in the side room. I mean, with a blanket."

Again a laugh. "I don't need to sleep. But it's a kind thought. You're very kind."

His eyes moved to the door as Bessie walked in, making for her tablecloth of newspaper on which stood her bowl of water and her unfinished bowl of creamy milk. His eyes followed the cat.

Eleanor felt a sudden apprehension. It was probably because Bessie had not seen him. That was certainly disturbing, when she could see him so well that even the wrinkles in his face were quite visible. He was clothed in strange material, gray-black, neither shiny nor dull.

"You must be lonely since your husband died," he said. "But I admit you do well. Considering he didn't leave you much."

Eleanor blushed. She could feel it. John hadn't been a big earner, certainly. But he was a decent man, a good husband—yes, he had been that. And their only child, a daughter, had been killed in a snow avalanche in Austria when she was twenty. Eleanor never thought of Penny. She had set herself never to think of Penny. She was disturbed, and felt awkward, because she thought of her now. And she hoped the creature would not mention Penny. Her death was one of life's tragedies. But other families had similar tragedies—only-sons killed in useless wars.

"Now you have your cat," he said, as if he read her thoughts.

"Yes," Eleanor said, glad to change the subject. "Bessie is ten. She's had fifty-seven kittens. But three—no, four years ago, I finally had her doctored. She's a dear companion."

Eleanor slipped away and got a big gray blanket, an army-surplus blanket, from a closet and folded it in half on the couch in the side room. He stood watching her. She put a pillow under the top part of the blanket. "That's a little cosier," she said.

"Thank you," came the deep voice.

In the next few days he cut the high grass around the barn with a scythe and moved a huge rock that had always annoyed Eleanor, embedded as it was in the middle of a grassy square in front of the barn. It was August, but quite cool. They cleared out the attic, and he carried the heaviest things downstairs and to the edge of the road to be picked up by Field's. Some of these things were sold a few days later at auction, and fetched nearly $30.

Eleanor still felt a slight tenseness when he was present, a fear that she might annoy him in some way; and yet in another way, she was growing used to him. He certainly liked to be helpful. At night he obligingly got onto his couch bed, and she wanted to tuck him in, to bring him some cookies and a glass of milk; but he ate and drank next to nothing, and then, as he said, only to keep her company. Eleanor could never understand where all his strength came from.

Vance rang up one day and said she had the pictures. Before Eleanor could ask about them, Vance had hung up. Vance was coming over at once.

"You took a picture of a chair, dear! Does he look like a chair?" Vance asked, laughing. She handed Eleanor the photographs.

There were twelve photographs in the batch, but Eleanor looked only at the top two, which showed him seated in the straight chair and standing next to it. "Why, there he *is!*" she said triumphantly.

Vance hastily, but with a frown, looked at the two pictures again, then smiled broadly. "Are you implying there's something wrong with *my* eyes? It's only a chair, darling—an empty chair!"

Eleanor knew that Vance, speaking for herself, was right. Vance couldn't see him. For a moment Eleanor couldn't say anything.

"I told you what would happen. Um-m-m."

Eleanor knew he was behind her, in the doorway of the side room, though she did not turn to look at him.

"All right. Perhaps it's my eyes," Eleanor said. "But I *do* see him there!" She couldn't give up. Should she tell Vance about his Herculean feats in the attic? Could she have got a big heavy chest of drawers down the stairs by herself?

Vance stayed for a cup of tea. They talked of other things —everything to Eleanor was now "other" and a bit uninteresting and unimportant compared with him. Then Vance left, saying, "Promise me you'll go to Dr. Nimms next week. I'll drive you, if you don't want to drive. Maybe you shouldn't drive if your eyes are acting funny."

Eleanor had a car, but she seldom used it. She didn't care for driving. "Thanks, Vance, I'll go on my own." She meant it at that moment, but when Vance had gone, Eleanor knew she would not go to the eye doctor.

He sat with her while she ate dinner. She now felt defensive and protective about him. She no longer wanted to share him with anyone.

"You shouldn't have bothered with those photographs," he said. "You see, what I told you is true. Whatever I say is true."

And yet he didn't look brilliant or even especially intelligent, Eleanor reflected.

He tore a piece of bread rather savagely in half and stuffed one half into his mouth. "You're one of the very few people who can see me. Maybe only a dozen people in the whole world can see me. Maybe less than that. Why should the others see me?" he continued, and shrugged his chunky shoulders. "They're just like me."

"What do you mean?" she asked.

He sighed. "Ugly." Then he laughed softly and deeply. "I am not nice. Not nice at all."

She was too confused to answer for a moment. A polite answer seemed absurd. She was trying to think what he really meant.

"You enjoyed taking care of your mother, didn't you? You didn't mind it," he said, as if he were being polite himself and filling in an awkward silence.

"No, of course not. I loved her," Eleanor said readily. How could he know? Her father had died when she was 18, and she hadn't been able to finish college because of a shortage of money. Then her mother had become bedridden, but she had lived on for ten years. Her treatment had taken all the money Eleanor had been able to earn as a secretary, and a little more besides, so that everything of value they had possessed had finally been sold. Eleanor had married at 29, and gone with John to live in Boston. Oh, the gone and lovely days! John had been so kind, so understanding of the fact that she had been exhausted, in need of human company—or rather, the company of people her own age. Penny had been born when she was thirty.

"Yes, John was a good man, but not so good as you," he said and sighed. "Um-m."

Now Eleanor laughed spontaneously. It was a relief from her thoughts. "How can one be good—or bad? Aren't we all a mixture? You're certainly not all bad."

This seemed to annoy him. "Don't tell me what I am."

Rebuffed, Eleanor said nothing more. She cleared the table.

She put him to bed, thanked him for his work in the garden that day—gouging up a thousand dandelions was no easy task. She was glad of his company in the house, even glad that no one else could see him. He was a funny doll that belonged to her. He made her feel odd, different, yet somehow special and privileged. She tried to put these thoughts from her mind, lest he disapprove of them, because he was looking, vaguely as usual, at her, with a resentment or a reproach. "Can I get you anything?" she asked.

"No," he answered shortly.

The next morning she found Bessie in the middle of the kitchen floor with her neck wrung. Her head sat in the strangest way on her neck, facing backward. Eleanor seized the corpse impulsively and pressed the cat to her breast. The head lolled. She knew he had done it. But why?

"Yes, I did it," his deep voice said.

She looked at the doorway, but did not see him. "How could you? Why did you do it?" Eleanor began to weep. The cat was not warm any longer, but she was not stiff.

"It's my nature." He did not laugh, but there was a smile in his voice. "You hate me now. You wonder if I'll be going. Yes, I'll be going." His voice was fading as he walked through the living room, but still she could not see him. "To prove it I'll slam the front door, but I don't need to use the door to get out." She heard the door slam.

She was looking at the front door. The door had not moved.

Eleanor buried Bessie in the back yard near the barn, and the pitchfork was heavy in her hands, and the earth heavier in her spade. She had waited until late afternoon, as if hoping that by some miracle Bessie might come alive again. But the cat's body had grown rigid. Eleanor wept again. . .

She declined Vance's next invitation to tea, and finally Vance came to see her, unexpectedly. Eleanor was sewing. She had quite a bit of work to do, but she was depressed and lonely, not knowing what she wanted, and there was no person she especially wanted to see. She realized that she missed him, that strange creature. And she knew he would never come back.

Vance was disappointed because Eleanor had not gone to see Dr. Nimms. She told Eleanor that she was neglecting herself. Eleanor did not enjoy seeing her old friend. Vance also remarked that Eleanor had lost weight.

"That—little monster isn't annoying you still, is he? Or is he?" Vance asked.

"He's gone," Eleanor said, and managed a smile, though what the smile meant she didn't know.

"How's Bessie?"

"Bessie—was killed by a car a couple of weeks ago."

"Oh, Eleanor! I'm sorry. Why didn't you—you should've *told* me! What bad luck! You'd better get another kitty. That's always the best thing to do. You're so fond of cats."

Eleanor shook her head a little.

"I'm going to find out where there's some nice kittens. The Carters' Siamese might've had another batch." Vance smiled. "They're always nice, half-Siamese. Really!"

That evening Eleanor ate no supper. She wandered through the empty-feeling rooms of her house, thinking not only of him, but of her lonely years here, and of the happier years here when John had been alive. He had tried to work in Millersville, ten miles away, but the job hadn't lasted. Or rather, the company hadn't lasted. That had been poor John's luck. No use thinking about it now, about what might have been if John had ever had a business of his own.

But now she thought more of when *he* had been here, the funny little fellow who had turned against her. She wished he were back. She felt he would not do such a horrid thing again, if she spoke to him the right way. He had become annoyed when she had said he was not entirely bad. But she knew he would not come back, not ever.

She worked until midnight. More letting out. More hems taken up. People were becoming square, she thought, but the thought did not make her smile any more. She looked at his photographs again, half expecting not to see him—like Vance; but he was still there, just as clear as he had been before. That was some comfort to her—but pictures were so flat and lifeless.

The house had never seemed so silent. Her plants were doing beautifully. Not long ago she had repotted most of them. Yet Eleanor sensed a negativity when she looked at them. It was very curious—a happy sight like blossoming plants causing sadness. She longed for something, and did not know what it was. That was strange also, this unidentifiable hunger, this loneliness that was worse and more profound than it was after John had died. . .

Tom Roland phoned one evening at 9:00 P.M. His wife was ill and he had to go at once to an "alert" at the Air Base. Could she come over and sit with his wife? He'd be home before midnight.

Eleanor went over at once, taking a bowl of fresh strawberries sprinkled with powdered sugar. Mary Roland was not seriously ill—it was a 24-hour virus attack of some kind; but she was grateful for the strawberries. The bowl was put on the bedtable. It was a pretty color to look at, though Mary could not eat anything.

Eleanor heard herself chatting as she always did, though in an odd way she felt she was not present with Mary, not even in the Rolands' house. It wasn't a "miles away" feeling, but a feeling it was not taking place. It was not even as real as a dream.

Eleanor went home at midnight, after Tom returned. Somehow she knew she was going to die that night. It was a calm and destined sensation. She might have died, she thought, if she had merely gone to bed and fallen asleep. But she wished to make sure of it, so she took a single-edge razor blade from her shelf of paints in the kitchen closet—the blade was rusty and dull, but no matter—and cut her two wrists at the basin in the bathroom.

The blood ran and ran, and she washed it down with running cold water, still mindful, she thought with slight amusement, of conserving the hot water in the tank. Finally, she could see that the streams were lessening. She took her bathtowel and wrapped it around both her wrists, winding her hands as if she were coiling wool. She was feeling weak, and she wanted to lie down and not soil the mattress, if possible.

The blood did not come through the towel before she lay down on her bed. Then she closed her eyes and did not know if the blood came through or not. It really did not matter, she supposed. Nor did the finished and unfinished skirts and dresses downstairs. People would come and claim them.

Eleanor thought of him, small and strong, strange and yet so plain and simple. He had never told her his name. She realized that she loved him.

Cornell Woolrich

Only One Grain More

Another highly charged, emotionally packed, suspense-filled detective novelet by Cornell Woolrich . . .

At one point Inspector Burke thought: "Why, there was no difficulty about this case, it was a pushover." But Inspector Burke was never more wrong. The beautiful Princess—was she guilty or innocent? "The scales remained evenly balanced and counterbalanced, to the last hair's-breadth milligram. Only one grain more had fallen on one side . . ."

Detective: INSPECTOR BURKE

He sent his card in to me. We don't get much of that down at Headquarters. Any, you might say. They're either dragged in, or, if they come of their own accord, they just say who they are by word of mouth. What was on it made me raise my brows.

Arnoldo, Prince of Iveria

With a crown over it. We don't get much of *that* either, down at Headquarters. I was so impressed I even talked it over with Crawley, who happened to be in the room at the time, before I did anything about having him shown in. Sort of trying to get my bearings.

"What the hell do you suppose a blueblood like this could want? And he comes to us instead of sending for us to come to him!"

"I suppose the family rubies have been stolen," Crawley snickered.

"In the first place, is he a real prince or a phony?"

"There is a party by that name," Crawley told me. "I've seen it in the papers once or twice. Wait a minute, I can check, so we'll be that much ahead."

He seemed to know how to go about it; I wouldn't have myself.

265

He called *Who's Who*, and also some very swank club, and managed to find out what we wanted, without letting on we were the police. "Get a description while you're at it," I said over his shoulder.

When he got through he said, "The genuine article is about twenty-nine, nearly six feet tall, lean, and light-haired; looks more English than Latin."

The cop who had brought in the card nodded vigorously and said, "That's who's waiting out there right now."

"All right, then we don't have to worry about phonies," I said, relieved.

"Here's a thumbnail sketch of the rest of it," Crawley said. "His own country don't exist any more, it was annexed by another country. He's married to an American girl, the former Marilyn Reid. Scads of dough. Her grandfather first invented chocolate bars with peanuts in 'em. They live out at Eastport."

"That ought to do. I hate to have to ask a lot of fool questions with a guy like this. Better not keep him waiting any more, O'Dare."

I was almost stage-frightened by this time. I straightened the knot of my tie, polished the toe of my shoe against the opposite trouser leg, sat down and arranged a lot of papers in front of me, like I was up to my ears in work. "How does this look?" I asked Crawley nervously.

"Phony as hell—to me," he grinned. "But he won't know the difference."

The cop held the door open and there was one of those breathless waits, like in a play on the stage. He came in on a cane. For a minute I thought it was just swank, but then I could see he seemed to need it. A little shaky on his legs.

I didn't know how to address him, so I didn't. Just nodded.

Maybe he didn't know how to address me either, because he nodded back. He said, "Do you mind if I sit down? I'm not—very strong."

Crawley slid a chair up, and I said, "Sorry we kept you waiting—"

"I don't mind. You see, I had to come to you myself. If I'd sent for you it would have defeated the purpose—for which I've come to you."

I said, "What can we do for you, your highness?"

He shook his head. "There are no highnesses here. I am taking out my first papers next month. But of course I won't live to become a full-fledged citizen—"

I looked at Crawley and he looked at me.

Iveria had taken out a hammered-gold cigarette case with a sapphire clasp. I thought, to smoke, but he didn't open it, just passed it to me. "I may not be able to prevent it coming out that I stopped in here. In which case I shall say that I came in to report the loss of this case. So suppose you keep it in the meantime, as an excuse. Let us say some honest person found it and turned it in. You are holding it for me. That will explain my visit here. Is that all right with you?"

I could have told him that I was a Homicide man, not the Lost and Found Department, but I didn't. "If you want it that way, yes," I said uncertainly. Again Crawley and I exchanged a look.

"Now, as to what I have actually come here about"—he looked from one to the other of us—"I am sorry, but I don't intend to speak about it before more than one person. I want this held confidential between myself and just one detective or police official. Until the time comes for this one official to act upon what I have told him today. Then let the whole world know. I will be gone by then, anyway. Now—can that be arranged?"

I didn't answer him right away.

He went on, "It is very painful; it is very personal; it is so subtle it will require a man of acute perception and great tact."

I said, "Well, would you care to tell Crawley here? He's very perceptive and tactful."

He took just one look at him, then he turned back to me. "You have just shown yourself to be the more tactful of the two, by the very fact that you recommended him. You are the man I would like to tell this to, if I may."

"I'm at your disposal," I said.

Crawley took it in good part. He said, "See you later," and eased out.

"And now—"

"Inspector Burke."

"And now, Inspector Burke ... " He opened his fluffy llama wool coat, took a thick manila envelope soldered with sealing wax out of its inner pocket. "This is an affidavit, duly notarized, which merely restates what I am about to tell you. It will bear more weight later than a verbal accusation, particularly after I am no longer alive. You will put it away, please, until the time comes for you to use it. Write your own name on it; show it to no one."

I scrawled *Burke, in re Iveria* across it, went over and put it in the safe, along with the cigarette case. Then I came back and waited for him to begin.

He made a steeple of his hands. "Now it is a very simple matter. Stated in its simplest form—which, however, does not do it justice—it is merely this: I am about to be killed by my wife. But without me you will not be able to prove that she did such a thing."

"I won't have to prove it, I'll prevent it—" I started to say.

He flexed his hand at me almost indifferently. "No, neither you nor I will be able to prevent it. It will surely happen. Nothing will be able to prevent it. For it is coming in such a small way. So, for all practical purposes, let us say I am already dead."

"We don't go along in things like that here—" I started to say, but again he overrode me.

"But it is not right that she should do such a thing and remain unpunished, isn't it so? Or at least enjoy the fruits of her crime, enjoy peace of mind afterwards—with *him.* That is why I have come to you ahead of time. Even so, you will have a difficult time proving it. Without me, you would never even be able to establish it *was* a murder."

I just sat there eying him unblinkingly. Whatever else I was, I wasn't bored. He had the gift of holding you spellbound. Once the desk phone rang and I switched the call into another room without even trying to find out what it was.

"Here is the background, so you will understand the thing fully," he went on. "You must realize that it is difficult for me to speak of these things to another man. But for present purposes you are not a man, you are a police official—"

I considered that a dubious compliment at best, but I let it go.

"—so, I will hold nothing back. I am descended from a branch of the ruling house of what was formerly Iveria. I therefore bear in my veins both the assets and the liabilities of royalty." He smiled ruefully when he said that, I noticed.

"I met my wife, the former Marilyn Reid, three years ago in St. Moritz and we were married there. She was supposedly enormously wealthy; both parents dead, sole heiress to the Reid peanut-bar fortune. I have seen American papers which thought it was one of those usual fortune-hunting matches, and didn't hesitate to say so. I gave her the title, for what it was worth, she gave me the use of her money. As a matter of fact, it was quite the other way around. I was the wealthier by far, even at the time of our marriage.

"On the other hand, through bad management and her own extravagance, the enormous estate that had come down to Marilyn from her grandfather was already badly depleted at the time I first met her, and since then has dwindled away to nothing. Naturally, that isn't commonly known. Even if it were, it wouldn't be believed.

"The point is, I did not marry Marilyn for her money. When you see her face you won't have to be told why I did: she was the most beautiful girl in Europe, and she still is the most beautiful in America today. Try to keep in mind—when the time comes—that she murdered me. It won't be easy to do so.

"The rest is rather shabby. I will hurry over it as quickly as I can. I am ill; she married only a shadow of a man. But when a thing is once mine, I keep it. If she wanted freedom only for herself, I would give it to her. But she wants it for this—this automobile speed-racer.

"In Cannes we met this 'Streak' Harrison. She'd always had a mania for breakneck driving herself, so that gave him a good head start. What is there about boxers, airplane pilots, racers, that makes women lose their heads? After we'd been back six months and he had 'casually' turned up over here himself, she asked me for her freedom. I said no.

"She was tied hand and foot, the decision rested with me, and it has brought murder into her heart. She could not buy me off—*I* had the fortune, and she no longer had a dime of her own by that time. She could not get a divorce, because divorce is not recognized in Iveria, and my entire estate is there. Nor could she have it annulled on the grounds of my hereditary disability. I took pains to warn her of that before our marriage, and there are documents in existence to prove that. She went into the marriage with her eyes open.

"I am the last of my line. As my widow—but only as my widow—she would be sole inheritor under Iverian law.

"Now we come to my imminent murder. My affliction is hemophilia, the disease of kings. You know what that is." I did, but he went on to illustrate, anyway. "Once the blood begins to flow, there is no checking it. There is imminent death about me all day long. Things which to you are simply an 'Ouch!' and a suck at the finger, to me can mean death. For instance, I am sitting here in this office with you. There is a nail on the underpart of this chair. I touch it—so—and accidentally make a little puncture on the pad of my finger. Within a few hours, if they can't find a way of stopping it, I am done for."

"Don't do that again, will you?" I said, white-faced. I knew that chair, and there *was* a nail under it; Crawley had torn his pants on it once.

He smiled; he saw that he'd got his point across.

"But are you sure she contemplates actual murder, Iveria?"

"If I weren't, do you think I would be here?"

"Let me ask you something. Is she a stupid woman, your wife?"

"She is one of the most keen-witted, diabolically clever women who ever lived."

"Then why should she risk murder? Granting that she wants to be rid of you, wants to marry this Harrison and at the same time enjoy your ancestral fortune, all she needs is a little patience. As you yourself said a few minutes ago, you bear imminent death with you all day long. All she has to do is sit back and wait—"

"You forget something. I have lived with this blood curse all my life. I know how to guard against it, take care of myself. If you or anyone else were suddenly afflicted with it, you would probably do something that would cause your death within the first twenty-four hours; you wouldn't be used to taking precautions against it. That is the difference between us. I avoid angles and sharp-edged or pointed things. I have my hair singed instead of clipped, my nails sandpapered instead of filed. I don't dance on waxed floors or walk about my bedroom barefoot, and so on.

"My father lived to fifty, my grandfather to sixty-four, and both had it. I have lived twenty-nine years with it. What is to prevent my living another twenty-nine? Another thing: she knows that so far, until now, she stands to inherit automatically, under Iverian law, in case of my death. She cannot be sure that tomorrow I will not give away my entire estate to charity or deed it to the state, a privilege which is mine while I am still alive."

That did put a different slant on it; he was winning me over. But I still had to be sure. "In this setup you have outlined," I said, speaking slowly, "there is invitation enough to murder. But what actual proof have you that she intends doing it?"

"I thought you would ask that, as a police official," he smiled wryly. "I cannot give you phonograph records on which she says at the top of her voice 'I will kill him!' I can only give you little things which show the way the wind blows. Tiny, trifling things. Each one in itself meaning nothing. But added to one another over a period of time, meaning—murder. That is why I said I wanted to tell this to someone who was acutely perceptive, who does not need a brick wall to fall on his head before he senses something.

"Well, at random, here are some of these trifling things—and I am leaving out as many as I am recalling. When this Streak first came back here from Europe he seemed very anxious to enjoy my company. He kept asking me to go out driving in his car with them. Since they loved each other, I couldn't understand why he should be concerned with my being present. I unexpectedly agreed one day, simply to find out what it was about. At once a sort of tension came over the two of them. She gave some lame excuse at the last moment, to get out of going with us; apparently it was not part of their plan for her to endanger herself.

"I figured the route he would take, stepped back in the house a moment just as we were ready to leave, and phoned ahead to a gas-station attendant Marilyn and I both knew. When we reached there he was to tell Streak there'd been a call for him—from a lady—and he was to wait there until she called back. He'd think it was Marilyn of course.

"The mechanic flagged us and Streak fell for it. While he was in the office waiting, I said to the attendant, 'Check this car and find out what's the matter with it.' And I got out and stood clear while he was doing it.

"He went over it quickly but expertly, and when he got through he said, 'It's in fine condition, I can't find anything wrong with it.' Then he took his cloth and, from long habit, began polishing the windshield. It fell through the frame and shattered all over the front seat where I'd been until then. The little clamps that held it to the frame had all been unnoticeably loosened, so that any unusual pressure or impact—he would have braked abruptly somewhere along the way, or grazed a tree or a wall or another car—just enough to give it that little shaking out.

"He would have been with me, of course. Maybe he would have even been more hurt than I was. But he could afford a few bloody nicks and gashes. I couldn't. I went back to our place on foot and left him there in the office still waiting for that nonexistent call. I didn't say a word to her, simply said I was not used to being kept waiting at the roadside by anyone. They couldn't tell if I knew or didn't know.

"But that ended his participation, gave him cold feet. He never came around again. I've never seen him since. I know he's lurking there unseen in the background, waiting for her to do the job and give him the all-clear signal. He may be reckless on the speedway, but he has no stomach for murder.

"All the remaining attempts have come from her. More trivial even than that, as befits the feminine genius. So subtle that—how shall I repeat them to you and make them sound like anything?"

"Let me be the judge," I murmured.

"The other night she attempted to embrace me, wound both arms about my neck. A caress, surely? But the gesture was false, had no meaning any more between us, so I quickly warded it off in the nick of time—for that reason alone. What death lurked in that innocent sign of affection?

"Then I noticed a heavy bracelet that didn't seem to close properly on her wrist. Its catch was defective, stuck up like a microscopic spur, needed flattening. What could it do to anyone else but graze them, inflict a tiny scratch? 'Ouch!' 'Oh, I'm sorry, dear, I'll kiss it away.' 'Forget it.' But to me it would have brought death. Strange that only on the night she was wearing that particular ornament did she try to hug me tightly around the neck. The night before, and the night after, she didn't come near me."

He stopped and looked at me. "More?"

"A little more. I'll tell you when to stop."

"In a hundred ways she has tried to draw the single drop of blood from me that will eventually bring death in its wake. She brought a cat into the house, a pedigreed Persian. Yet I happen to know that she hates animals herself. Why a cat, then? I soon found out." He shrugged. "You know the feline propensity for stalking, and finally clawing at anything moving? I sat reading one night before the fire, with the cat there, and finally dozed off, as she must have hoped I would. I opened my eyes just in time to find the cat crouched at my feet, tail lashing, about to spring.

"My arm was hanging limp over the side of the chair. The cat's claws would have raked it in a half dozen places. A loose piece of string was traveling up my arm, drawn from behind the chair. Luckily there was a cushion behind me. I just had time enough to swing it out in front of me, use it as a buffer. The cat struck it, gashed it to ribbons.

"When I stood up and turned, she was behind me, holding the other end of the string she had used to bait the cat. What could I say? 'You tried to kill me just then'? All she seemed to be doing was playing with the cat. Yet I knew she had tried; I knew she must have kept flinging out that piece of string again and again until it trailed across my arm as she wanted it to.

"Whom could I tell such a thing to—and expect to be believed? What bodyguard, what detective, can protect me against such methods?"

He was right about that. I could have sent someone back with him to protect him against a gun, a knife, poison. Not against a woman playing with a cat or twining her arms about his neck. "Why don't you leave her, then? Why don't you get out while there is still time? Why stay and wait for it to happen?"

"We Iverias don't give up the things we prize that easily."

That left me kind of at a loss. Here was a man who knew he was going to be murdered, yet wouldn't lift his little finger to prevent it. "Any more?"

"What is the use of going ahead? I have either convinced you by the few examples I have given or there is no hope of my ever convincing you."

"And now just what is it you want me to do?"

"Nothing. When it happens—maybe tomorrow, maybe next week—I will call you, while I still have the strength left, and say, 'This is it.' But even if I fail to, be sure that it is 'it.' You will read in the papers, within a day or two after that, that the Prince of Iveria died from hemophilia. Some slight mishap in the home. A pin had been left in his freshly laundered shirt.

"There isn't a living soul in the whole world, physician or layman, who will believe such a thing *could* have been murder. But you will know better, Inspector Burke, you will know better after what I have told you today.

"Take my affidavit out of your safe, go up there, and arrest her. Force the issue through, so that she has to stand trial for it. Probably she will not be convicted. That doesn't matter. The thing will be brought out into the open, aired before the whole world. His name will be dragged into it. Convicted or acquitted, I will have succeeded in what I set out to do. *She cannot marry him* or go near him, after I am gone, without branding herself a murderess in the eyes of the world."

"So that's it," I said softly.

"That's it. He can't have her and she can't have him. Unless they are willing to go through a living hell, become outcasts, end by hating each other. In which case they have lost each other anyway. I am the Prince of Iveria. What once belongs to me I give up to no other man."

He'd said his say and had no more to say. He stood up and stretched out his hand to me.

"Goodbye, Inspector Burke. We shall probably not see each other again. Your job is to punish murder. See that you don't fail. You'll do what I've asked you to?"

What could I do? Go up there and arrest her to prevent it? On what charge? Wearing a bracelet with a catch that needed repairing? Playing with a pet cat in the same room he happened to be in? True, he was almost seeking the thing instead of trying to ward it off. But I couldn't compel him to move out of his own home if he didn't want to. If murder was committed, even though he made no move to avoid it, even though he met it halfway, that didn't make it any the less murder.

He kept looking at me, waiting for my answer.

I nodded gloomily at last, almost against my will. "I'll do whatever the situation calls for."

He turned and went slowly out through the doorway with the aid of his cane, stiffly erect, just leaning a little sideways. I never saw him alive again.

It came quicker than I'd expected. Too quickly for me to be able to do anything to prevent it. I'd intended paying a visit up there in person, trying to introduce myself into the establishment in some way, to see if I could size up the situation at first hand, form my own conclusions. He hadn't given me any *physical* evidence, remember, that she was attempting to murder him. All right, granting that he couldn't give me physical evidence—the very nature of the setup forbade it—he still hadn't convinced me one hundred percent. My own eyes and ears would have helped.

But before I had a chance it was already too late—the thing was over.

The second day after his visit, at nine in the morning, just after I'd got in to Headquarters, I was hailed. "Inspector Burke, you're wanted on the phone."

I picked it up and a woman's voice, cool and crisp, said, "Inspector Burke, this is the Cedars of Lebanon Hospital at Eastport. We have a patient here, the Prince of Iveria, who would like to speak to you."

I waited, squeezing the life out of the thing. There were vague preparatory sounds at the other end. He must have been very weak already. I could hardly hear him at first. Just a raspy breathing sound, like dry leaves rustling in the wind. They must have been holding him up. I said, "I can't hear you!"

Then he got words through. Four of them. "Burke? This is it."

I said, "Hello! Hello!" He'd hung up.

I called right back. I couldn't get him again. Just got the hospital switchboard. They wouldn't clear the call. The patient was in no condition to speak further to anyone, they told me. He was—dying.

"You've got to put me through to him again! He was just on the line, so how can an extra thirty seconds hurt?"

Another wait. The hospital operator came back again. "The patient says there is nothing further to be said." *Click.*

If ever a man embraced death willingly, you might even say exultantly, it was he.

I grabbed my hat, grabbed a cab, and went straight to the hospital. Again the switchboard operator blocked me. She plugged in, plugged out. "Sorry, no one can go up. The Prince of Iveria is in a coma—no longer conscious. I'm afraid there's not much hope left."

That cooled me off. If he couldn't talk there wasn't much use in my going up. I said, "I'll wait," and hung around in the lobby for the next two hours, having her ring up at intervals to find out. There was always a chance he might rally. What I wanted to hear from him was: *had* she done it or hadn't she? True, the implication of 'This is it' was she had; he'd warned me that was all he was going to say when the time came, but I had to have more than that.

Probably the only material witness there would ever be against her was slipping through my fingers. I didn't have a nail left intact on my ten fingers, the marble flooring on my side of the reception foyer was swimming with cigarette butts, by the time the two hours were up. I must have driven the poor switchboard girl half crazy.

Twice, while I was waiting, I saw rather husky-looking individuals step out of the elevator. They were both too hale-looking to be hospital cases themselves. One was counting over a small wad of bills, the second hitching at his sleeve, as though his arm were tender. Without knowing for sure, I had a good hunch they were donors who had been called in for blood transfusions.

The operator tried his floor once more, but he was still unconscious, so it looked as though it hadn't helped. Even my badge wouldn't have got me up—this was a hospital, after all—but I didn't want to use it, in any event.

At ten to two that afternoon the elevator door opened and *she* came out—alone. I saw her for the first time. I knew it must be she. He'd said she was the most beautiful girl in Europe or America. He needn't have left out Asia or Africa. She was the most beautiful human being I'd ever seen anywhere in my life. The sort of a face that goes with wings and a halo.

She was all in black, but not the black of mourning—yet—the black of fashion. She wasn't crying, just looking down at the floor as if she had a lot to think about. So at least she was no hypocrite; I gave her that much.

As she moved through the foyer the nurse at the switchboard followed her with her eyes, a pair of question marks in them that couldn't be ignored. She—Iveria's wife—felt their insistence finally, looked over at her, nodded with a sort of calm sadness. About the same degree of melancholy that would go with the withering of a pet plant in one's garden.

So he'd died.

I didn't accost her, didn't do anything about it right then. She wasn't some fly-by-night roadhouse hostess that you grab while the grabbing's good; she would always be where I could reach her. The patrimony of the House of Iveria, immovably fixed in the ground, in mines, farms, forests, castles, would see to that. If she'd done it, there was plenty of time. If she hadn't there was even more time than plenty.

She went out through the revolving door to a car waiting for her. Nobody else was in it but the driver. It skimmed away like a bolt of satin being unrolled along the asphalt.

The switchboard operator turned to me and whispered unnecessarily, "He's dead."

It was up to me now, I was on my own. All I had was the valueless memory of a conversation, and an almost equally valueless affidavit, deposed before the event itself. And my own eyes and ears and good judgment, for whatever they were worth.

There had been a pyramidal hierarchy of medical experience in attendance on him, as was to be expected, but I didn't bother with the lower strata. I took a short cut straight to the apex and singled out the topmost man. I did it right then and there, as soon as I'd seen her leave the hospital.

His name was Drake, and he'd treated everyone prominent who'd ever had it, which meant he got about one patient every five years. And could live nicely on it, at that, to give you a rough idea.

I found him in a small pleasant lounge reserved for the doctors on the hospital staff—it was a private institution—on the same floor where Iveria had just died, but well insulated from the hospital activities around it. He was having a glass of champagne-and-bitters and smoking a Turkish cigarette, to help him forget the long-drawn-out death scene he'd just attended.

I didn't make the mistake of thinking this was heartlessness. I could tell it wasn't, just by looking at him. He had a sensitive face, and his hands were a little shaky. The loss of the patient had affected him, either professionally or personally, or both.

He thought I was a reporter at first, and wasn't having any. "Please don't bother me right now. They'll give you all the necessary details at the information desk." Then when he understood I was police, he still couldn't understand why there should be any police interest in the case. Which didn't surprise me. Whatever the thing was, I had expected it to look natural. Iveria had warned me it would—so natural I might never be able to break it down.

I didn't give him an inkling of what my real purpose was. "This isn't police interest in the usual sense," I glibly explained. "His highness took me into his confidence shortly before this happened, asked me to have certain personal matters carried out for him in case of his death. That's my only interest."

That cleared away the obstructions. "Wait a minute; is your name Burke?" He put down his champagne glass.

"That's right."

"He left a message for you. He revived for a moment or two, shortly before the end, whispered something to us. The nurse jotted it down." He handed me a penciled scrap of paper. "I don't know whether we got it right or not, it was very hard to hear him—"

It said: *Burke. Don't fail me. This is a job for you.*

Which was a covert way of saying *murder*. "Yes, you got it

right," I assented gloomily, and put it in my pocket. "Was his wife present when he whispered this?"

"Not in the room itself, in the outside room."

"Did she see it afterwards?"

"No. He muttered something that sounded like 'Nobody but him,' so we took that to mean he didn't want anyone but you to see it."

"That's right, he didn't."

"Sit down. Have some?" I shook my head. "Swell fellow, wasn't he? Practically doomed from the beginning, though. They always are with that. I tried transfusions, and I even tried this new cobra-venom treatment. Minute doses, of course. Very efficacious in some cases. Couldn't stop the flow this time, though. You see, that's the worst part of the hellish thing. It's progressive. Each time they're less able to resist than the time before. He was too weak by this time to pull through—"

He'd been under a strain, and he was going to work it off in garrulousness, if I didn't stop him; so I stopped him. I wasn't interested in the medical aspects of the case, anyway. There was only one thing I wanted. "What brought it on this time?"

"The lesions were all over his forehead and scalp. An unfortunate chain of trivialities led to an accident. They occupied adjoining bedrooms, you know. The communicating door was faced with a large mirror panel. There was a reading chair in Iveria's room with a large, bulky hassock to go with it, on which he habitually rested his feet. There was a bedside light, which should have cast enough light to avoid what happened.

"At any rate, he said he was awakened from a sound sleep by his wife's voice crying out a name; evidently she was being troubled by a bad dream. There was such terror in her voice, however, that he could not be sure it was just that, and not possibly an intruder. He seized a small revolver he habitually kept under his pillow, pulled the chain of the bedside light. It refused to go on; the bulb had evidently burned itself out since the last time it had been in use. The switch controlling the main overhead lights was at the opposite side of the room.

"He therefore jumped up without any lights, made for the mirror-door by his sense of direction alone, gun in hand. The reading chair and hassock should have been offside. The chair still was; the hassock had become misplaced and was directly in his path. It tripped him. There was not enough space between it and the mirror-faced door to give the length of his body clearance. His forehead struck the mirror, shattered it.

"It would have been a serious accident for anyone—but not a fatal accident. None of the numerous little gashes was deep enough to require stitches. But he and his wife both knew what it meant to him and they didn't waste any time. She telephoned me in Montreal, where I was attending a medical convention, and I chartered a plane and flew right back. But I doubt that I could have saved him even if I had been right in the same room with him when it happened. I had them remove him to the hospital and summon donors before I even started down. I gave him the first transfusion ten minutes after I arrived, but he failed to rally, continued sinking steadily."

I wasn't interested in the rest, only in what the original "mishap," the starting point, had been. I thanked him and left. This was going to be a tricky thing to sift to the bottom of. Acutely perceptive? You needed to be a magnetized divining rod to know what to do!

I opened the safe and I read over his affidavit before I went to tackle her. The affidavit didn't bring anything new to the case, simply restated what he had said to me that day in the office, only at greater length and in more detail. The incident of the loosened windshield was there, the cat incident, and several others that he hadn't told me at the time.

" . . . I, therefore, in view of the above, solemnly accuse my wife, Marilyn Reid d'Iveria, of having at various times sought to cause my death, by means of the affliction known to her to be visited upon me, and of continuing to seek to do so at the time this deposition is taken, and charge the authorities and all concerned that in case of my death occurring at any time hereafter during her continued presence in my house and proximity to me, to apprehend and detain the said Marilyn Reid d'Iveria with a view to inquiring into and ascertaining her responsibility and guilt for the aforesaid death, and of bringing just punishment upon her.

Arnoldo Amadeo
Manfredo d'Iveria"

With that final postscript tacked on, it was going to be damned effective. Enough to arrest her on, book her for suspicion of murder, and hold her for trial. What went on after that, in the courtroom, was none of my business.

I put it in my pocket and left to interview the party of the second part—the murderess.

He'd been buried in the morning—privately—and I got out there about five that same afternoon. There was no question of an arrest yet, not on this first visit anyway, so I didn't bother looking up the locals, even though I was out of jurisdiction here. She could slam the door in my face if she wanted. She wouldn't, if she was smart. It wouldn't help her case any.

It was a much smaller place than I'd expected it to be. White stucco or sandstone or something. I'm not up on those things. I turned into the driveway on foot. It was dusk by now, and a couple of the ground-floor windows on the side were lighted; the rest of the house was blacked out.

There was a high-powered knee-high foreign sports car outside the entrance. It wasn't the one she had driven away from the hospital in. It looked like the kind of job that would belong to a professional auto racer—if he could afford it. I whistled soundlessly and thought: Already? It was almost too good to be true. Maybe this case wasn't going to be such a tough baby to crack after all. One sure thing, she was writing herself up a bad press, if things ever got as far as a jury, by doing this sort of thing. They should have at least let Iveria cool off before they got together.

It was probably the sight of the car that kept me from ringing for admittance right away, that sent me on a little cursory scouting expedition around to the side where those lighted windows were. She'd probably be sitting there all in black trying to look sorrowful, with him holding her hand trying to look consoling, and each one of them knowing the other was a liar.

When I got in line with them, I moved in close enough to come into focus. Just close enough, no closer. Then I stood stock-still there on the lawn. I couldn't believe what I saw.

It was her all right. She was dancing around the room in there, without a partner. The way you do when you're overjoyed, can't contain yourself. Arms stratched out wide in a gesture of release, waltzing, or at least swaying around. She was in a light tan dress, and it billowed out all around her as she went.

He was sitting there, watching her. I got my first look at him. He was dark-haired and broad-shouldered; that was about all I could tell from out where I was. I couldn't see much to him, just something to hang a Stetson on. Iveria's words came back to me. "What is there about boxers, plane pilots, auto racers, that makes women lose their heads?" He was holding his head cocked at a slight angle, with an air of proud ownership, as if to say, "Isn't she lovely? Isn't she cute?" To which my own commentary would have been, "She's the cutest little murderess I've seen in ages."

If this was how she was the afternoon of the day he'd been buried, I couldn't help wondering what she would be like a week—or a month—afterward. Why, there was no difficulty about this case, it was a pushover. I was only sorry I hadn't brought out a warrant with me, made arrangements with the Eastport locals, and got it over with then and there. Whether the crime could ever be proved or not was beside the point. She was begging for arrest if anyone ever was, just on grounds of public decency.

I strode around to the front and rang. Peremptorily. A maid opened the door. I said, "I want to see the Princess, or whatever she calls herself."

She'd received her orders ahead of time. "She's not at home to anyone."

I felt like saying, "No, except to Barney Oldfield, Jr., in there." Instead I elbowed her aside without another word and walked down the hall to where they were. The open doorway of the room cut an orange notch across the corridor, and I turned right at it.

She'd just finished her solo dancing. She'd come to a stop before him, but her filmy tan skirt was still swinging around. She was leaning her face down toward him, a hand resting on either arm of his chair. Their lips were only inches apart, and in another minute—

I just stood there taking it in. Did I say she was beautiful? Double it in spades, and you're still short-suited. I couldn't understand why nature should go to town so over one face, and let the others all go hang.

She became aware of me, shot up and back like something released from a bowstring. He reared his head and turned and looked at me, round the back of his chair. She said, "Who are you?" with a sort of unintentional matter-of-factness that came from not raising her voice high enough to suit the situation.

"Sorry to intrude," I said. "I've come out here to see you. You're d'Iveria's widow, I believe?" I eyed the tan dress meaningfully.

"Yes, but people don't just walk in here . . . " She made a gesture toward some service button or other.

"That won't do any good." I said. "I came here to have a talk with you, and I'm having it."

The Harrison fellow got up at this point, ready to take part in the matter. He was taller than I'd thought. He must have had a hard time tucking away those legs in a racing car. He was just a kid, really. I mean, a kid of about twenty-seven. He was pretty clean-cut looking, too, for a—well, call it home wrecker or whatever you want. I was surprised. He looked like he drank milk with his meals, and when he wanted to paint the town red went to a movie with a bag of salted peanuts in his pocket.

He started toward me, biting off something about, "You'll have the talk when she's ready, and not before."

Suddenly something made her change her mind. Some second look at me, or, more likely, some unspoken thought in her own mind. She wanted the talk right away; it couldn't come fast enough. But without him; she didn't want him to have any part in it.

Her arm shot out, barring his way. "Don't, Streak," she said. "I think I know what this is about. You go now, will you? Call me later." And then to me, almost pleadingly: "It's me you want to speak to, isn't it? Not the two of us. It's all right if—if he goes now, isn't it?"

"Yourself'll do nicely," I said ominously.

Harrison, who wasn't very alert at grasping nuances (a sign of honesty, they say), couldn't get off anything better than, "Well, but—"

She went into high gear, edging and propelling him toward the door. She kept throwing me appealing looks, as if begging me to keep quiet just a minute longer until she could get him out of the way. At least, that was the way I translated them; I couldn't be sure. Meanwhile she was almost crowding him out into the hall, saying disconnectedly: "You go now. I know what this is. It's all right, it's nothing. Call me later. About ten?"

The only way I could figure it was, either she wanted to hang on to his good opinion of her as long as she could, or she wanted to keep him in the clear, and, ostrich-like, thought that by getting him out of here that would do it . . . or thought she could handle me better if he wasn't around to cramp her style. One thing was plain: she already knew what was coming. And if she wasn't guilty, how the hell could she have known? Why should such an idea even enter her head?

I let him go. It made the issue more clear-cut to deal with her alone. He hadn't been in the picture at all since the windshield incident, according to d'Iveria's own affidavit. I could always get him later, anyway.

The last thing I heard her say, when she got him as far as the front door, was: "Get home all right. Don't drive too fast, Streak. I'm always so worried about those intersections along the way." That was sure love, to be able to think of such a thing at such a time. Well, I suppose even murderesses love someone.

She didn't come right back to the room. She called, "I'll be right with you, officer," and then ran up the stairs before I could get out there and stop her. By the time I did, she was already making the return trip down again. She hadn't been up there long enough to do any damage. She was holding a small black folder in her hand. I couldn't quite make out what it was, except that it was no weapon of any sort.

We went back into the room where they had been originally. She was breathing rapidly from the energy she'd used just now in maneuvering him and then running up and down the stairs—or maybe it was from some other cause entirely. People's breathing quickens from fear, too.

She began with beautiful directness. "I know what you're going to say. I wanted to get him out of here before you said it. He would have come to blows with you, and got in trouble. I can handle it more tactfully. You're going to say I killed Arnold, aren't you? You're the police, aren't you? Only a detective would crash into a room the way you did just now. I suppose you looked through the windows first and saw me dancing, because I was happy he was gone. Well, if you didn't, that's what I was doing just before you got here, so now you know, anyway. May I see your credentials?"

I showed her my badge.

"I knew he was going to do this to me," she said. "Yes, I'm not wearing black. Yes, I'm glad he's gone; like a prisoner when his term is up." She had opened the little black folder while she was speaking, torn out a light-blue pad. She was writing something on it. "Do you mind giving me your name?" she said, without looking up.

"The name is Nothing-doing-on-that-stuff." I hitched the light-blue pad out from under the midget gold fountain pen she had point-down on it, so that the last zero—there were three after the '1'—streaked off in a long diagonal inkline across the face of it. "Keep it up," I said. "You're saving some lawyer lots of hard work." I put it in my pocket; the blank check had Iveria's name printed on top, so it was almost as incriminating as if she'd signed it.

"Then there's nothing I can do or say that will—avert this thing, this thing he wanted to happen to me?"

"Not along those lines. What you can do and say, for the present, is sit down quietly and answer a question or two about your husband's death. Would you mind giving me the exact circumstances, in your own words?"

She calmed herself with a visible effort, sat down, lit a cigarette, and then forgot to smoke it. "I was asleep—"

"Do you recall having an unpleasant dream that caused you to cry out?"

She smiled. "One often doesn't, even if one did. The unpleasant dream, in my case, was during my waking hours, you see."

Trying to gain my sympathy, I thought warily. "That has nothing to do with it. Please go on."

"I heard a breakage sound that wakened me, I lit the light, I saw the communicating door move slowly inward and his hand trail after it on the knob. Opened inward, and he kept it locked on his side"—her eyelids dropped—"as if afraid of me at night. I found him attempting to pick himself up, in a welter of glass shards. I saw a gun there on the floor behind him that had spiraled from his hand when he fell. I took it into my room and hid it in my dressing table—"

"Why?"

"We both knew he was doomed. I was afraid that to avoid the pain, the lingering death, he would take a quicker way out."

Which would not look quite so much like an accident? I addressed her silently. "That's the whole sum and substance of the matter?"

"That's the whole sum and substance."

"May I see this room it happened in?"

"Of course."

I followed her up the stairs. "The local authorities have already examined it?"

"The local authorities have already examined it."

I looked at her. Meaning, you didn't have much trouble convincing *them*, did you? She understood the look and dropped her eyes.

The only vestiges remaining of the "accident" were the spokes of emptiness lashed out of the mirror panel, in sun-ray formation.

His head had struck it low; the upper two-thirds were still intact. The reading chair was out of the way, a good two to three yards offside. The hassock now sat directly before it, where it belonged. "Is this the habitual position of this chair?" But I didn't really have to ask her that. The carpet was a soft plush that showed every mark; the chair had stood there a long time; it's four supports had etched deep indentations into the nap. This was a mark against, not for, her. How could a bulky thing like that hassock move three yards away from where it belonged—unaided?

I asked her that; I said I wondered.

"I don't know," she said with an air of resigned hopelessness. "Unless he may have kicked it away from him, in getting up from the chair to go to bed."

I sat down in it, arched my legs to the hassock. I had to try it three times before I could land it all the way out in a line with the mirror-door. And I had stronger leg muscles; he'd had to walk with a cane. Still, he *could* have done it, in a burst of peevishness or boredom.

I looked the bedside light over next. It was just a stick with a bulb screwed in at the top and a shade clamped over that. I pulled the chain; the bulb stayed dark.

"How is it he would not have noticed this bulb was defective before getting into bed?" I wondered aloud for her benefit. "Isn't that what bedside lights are for, to be left on until the last?" The wall switch controlling the overheads was all the way across the room, beside the door leading out to the hall.

"I don't know; maybe he did." She shrugged with that same listless manner as before. "What would he want a new bulb for at that hour, if he was on the point of retiring for the night? He would have had to go downstairs for it himself, the help were all in bed by then. Or perhaps it was still in working order up to the time he turned it off. Bulbs have been known to die between the time they were last used and the next time they are turned on."

I removed the clamped shade. I tested the pear-shaped bulb gingerly. It vibrated slightly beneath my fingertips, I thought. I gave it a turn or two to the right. It responded. There should have been no give there, if it was fastened as tightly into the socket as it would go. Brilliant light suddenly flooded it.

The bulb was in perfectly good condition; it had simply been given a half turn or two to the left, to break the contact.

I looked at her, keeping my hand on it for as long as I could stand the increasing heat. Her eyes dropped long before then.

"You say the communicating mirror-door was kept locked. Was the outside door, to the hall, also kept locked by your husband, do you know?"

"I believe it was," she said lifelessly. "I believe the butler, in whom my husband had the greatest confidence, used a special key to let himself in in the mornings. We were—rather a strange household."

I noticed an old-fashioned bell-pull there by the bed. I reached for it. She stopped me with a quick gesture. "I can give you the answer to what you are about to ask him; it will save time. He forgot his key that night, left it in the outside lock of the door after he had concluded his duties for the night. I noticed it there myself, and returned it to him the next day."

"Then anyone else in the house could—"

She wouldn't let me finish. "Yes, anyone else in the house could have entered my husband's room after he had gone to sleep. To do what? Give a bulb a turn so it wouldn't light? Shift a hassock out of place? Don't you think that would have been a foolish misuse of such an opportunity?"

"No, I don't!" I crackled at her. I couldn't have made it more emphatic if I'd tried. "If a knife had been left sticking in him, or a fine wire tightened around his throat, that would have been *murder*. But he died of an 'accident.' One little mishap leading to another." I drove the point home viciously. "You and I are agreed on that—he died of an 'accident'!" I dropped my voice. "And I'm here to find out who caused it."

She twined and untwined her fingers. "And I cannot defend myself." She shuddered. "It is not that the charge is so hard to prove; it's so hard to disprove. This is what he intended to happen. I saw the smile on his face even when I first found him lying there in the litter of glass. As if to say, 'This time I've got you.' I beg of you to do this much at least. Send for the maid who cleans this room. Don't ask her any questions about the bedside light, just test her. Just—well, let me do it, may I?"

I nodded, more on guard than ever. She yanked the bell-pull a certain number of times, had me replace the lampshade, lit a cigarette, and flicked ashes over the shade.

Within a few minutes a maid appeared—not the same one who had admitted me to the house originally. "Will you dust off the bedside light?" Iveria's wife said casually. "Don't take any extra pains, just do it as you would ordinarily."

The girl took a cloth from her waistband, took a swipe around the stick part. Then she began to swivel the cloth around the shade. She was left-handed; she moved the cloth from right to left. Not only that, but she held the lamp by the stick to steady it, so that the shade was not held fast at all and began to slip unnoticeably round a little under her ministrations. And the wire cleats that gripped the bulb moved with it, of course, turning the bulb a little in its socket.

"That will do." The girl stepped back. Iveria's wife said to me, "Try it now."

I jerked the chain-pull. The bulb failed to light.

She looked at me animatedly, hopefully.

"Very interesting," I said dryly. "You were pretty sure it would happen just that way, though, weren't you?"

I saw the hopefulness ebb out of her face little by little; her former listless resignation came back. "Oh, I see," she said quietly, "I'm supposed to have rehearsed her to do it just that way."

She stood up, smiling wanly. "Will you excuse me for a moment? You'll want to question her alone, I'm sure. And even if she tells you I haven't coached her about this lamp, you won't believe I didn't. There isn't really anything I can do or say. Arnold has won; he won in life, and now he's won in death."

She opened the mirror-door, stepped through to her own room, closed it behind her.

I said to the maid, "Do you always dust off lamps that vigorously?"

She looked undecided for a moment, finally confessed: "Only when someone's around to see. When no one's around . . . " She flicked the edge of her cloth at the lampshade and back to show me.

"Tell Mrs. Iveria I'd like to see her again, if she doesn't mind."

The girl opened the door, went in there after her, closed it again.

I creased my eyes dissatisfiedly to myself. Every new fact that appeared on one side of the ledger brought its corollary on the opposite side. To a chartered accountant it might have been heaven, to a detective it was hell.

I wondered why she was taking so long to come out. I crossed to the mirror-door and threw it open without waiting, even though it led to a lady's room. You couldn't knock on the thing any more without risking bringing the rest of the glass out of its frame.

I didn't see them for a minute; they were over on the side of the room screened by the door, engaged in a breathless, utterly silent, almost motionless hand-to-hand deadlock over a winking little gun—I suppose the one she had taken from him the night of the accident.

I jumped in at them, caught the wrist holding it, turned the skin cruelly round. She dropped it and I caught it in my open palm. The maid stepped back and began to snivel.

I said, "Why didn't you call me, you little fool!"

"I did call you," the maid snuffled.

I pocketed the revolver and said to the girl, "We don't need you any more." And to Iveria's wife, "Come on downstairs." She followed me, white as a ghost.

"Do we go now?" she asked at the foot of the stairs.

"You don't suppose I'm going to leave you behind me out here, after what you just tried to do."

"That was a momentary impulse. It won't happen again. It wouldn't be fair to Streak. It would be giving Arnold his victory too cheaply."

We'd gone back to the room in which I'd first spoken to her.

"Sit down," I said curtly. "Give yourself time to quiet down first."

She looked at me hopelessly. "Is there anything I can do or say that will make you believe me? I had nothing to do with Arnold's death."

I didn't answer—which was answer enough.

"I don't suppose you believe that, do you?" I didn't answer. "You're positive I meant to kill Arnold, aren't you?" I didn't answer. "He saw to it that you would be. He went to you and told you the story, didn't he? Told it *his* way."

I didn't see any point in denying that; it was self-evident by the mere fact of my being there. "Yes, he did."

She let her head slowly droop forward, as if in admission of defeat. But then she raised it again a moment afterward, refusing the admission. "May I have the same privilege? May I tell the story *my* way?"

"You're going to have that privilege anyway, when the time comes."

"But don't you see it'll be too late by then? Don't you see this is a special case? The mere accusation in itself is tantamount to a conviction. One wisp of smoke, and the damage has been done. Streak and I can never live it down again—not if every court in the land finds insufficient evidence to convict us. That's what he wanted, to ruin the two of us—"

"But I'm just a detective. I'm not a judge—"

"But he only told it to you, no one else at the time—"

This did get a rise out of me. "How do you know that?"

"Dr. Drake showed me the dying message he had taken down; it had your name on it—'Burke.' It was addressed to you personally, no one else. It was easy to see he'd made you the sole repository of his confidence—until the time came to shout the charges from the rooftops. The evidence was too nebulous, there was no other way in which to do it."

"Tell it, then," I agreed.

She didn't thank me or brighten up; she seemed to know it would be hopeless ahead of time. She smiled wanly. "I'm sure the external details are going to be the same. He was far too clever to have changed them. He selected and presented each and every one of them so that I cannot deny them—on a witness stand, for instance—unless I perjure myself. It's their inner meaning—or rather the *slant* of the story—that he distorted."

I just sat and waited, noncommittal.

"I met Arnold in St. Moritz and I felt vaguely sorry for him. Pity is a dangerous thing, so often mistaken for love. No one told me what was the matter with him."

Here was the first discrepancy. He'd said she knew ahead of time. And he'd said he had *documents* to prove it.

"He proposed to me by letter, although we were both at the same resort. He used the word 'hemophilia' in one of them, said he knew he had no right to ask me to be his wife. I'm not a medical student—I'd never heard the word before. I thought it was some minor thing, like low blood pressure or anemia. I felt the matter was too confidential to ask anyone; after all, the letter was a declaration of love. I wrote back, using the strange word myself; I said it didn't matter, I thought enough of him to marry him whether he was in good health or poor health.

"By the time I actually found out it was too late. We'd already been married eight months. I stick to my bargains; I didn't welsh. I was married to a ghost. That was all right. But then I met Streak, and—I found out my heart was still single. I went to Arnold and I said, 'Now let me go.' He just smiled. And then I saw I hadn't married any ghost. I'd married a devil.

"You don't know what torture really is, the mental kind. You may have beaten up suspects at times. You don't know what it is to have someone say to you three times a day, 'You wish I was dead, don't you?' Until finally you *do* wish he was dead.

"We didn't want a cheap undercover affair. If that was all we'd wanted it could have been arranged. Streak was born decent, and so was I. He wanted to be my husband, I wanted to be his wife. We were meant for each other, and this ghost was in the way.

"Finally I couldn't stand it any more. I said, 'It would be so easy; why should we go on letting him do this to us?' Streak said, 'Don't talk that way. We don't want to get together by building a bridge over someone's dead body.' Streak's not a murderer. Streak's out of this entirely."

Which didn't prove a thing, except that she loved him.

"They say the female of the species is more deadly than the male. I toyed with the idea. I let it grow on me. Finally it took hold, became decision. Arnold wouldn't give me a chance to change my mind, he kept it at the boiling point.

"Streak came around in his car, to see if he couldn't win Arnold over by having a man-to-man talk with him alone. I knew he didn't have a chance. I knew what a venomous, diseased mind he was up against. *I* was the one loosened the clamps on that windshield, with a little screwdriver, while both were in the house. But it missed fire.

"I tried in one or two other ways. And then suddenly I came back to my senses. I saw what it was I'd been trying to do all those weeks and months. Take away someone's life. Murder. No matter what a fiend he was, no matter how he'd made us suffer, I saw that was no solution. I'd only have it on my conscience forever after. Dead, he would keep me and Streak apart far more effectively than he had when alive.

"It's ironic, isn't it? When I *wanted* to kill him, nothing I tried would work. Then suddenly, after I'd stopped trying, he goes off— like that!"

I said. "D'you realize what you've just been saying? What you've just admitted? That you actually *did* try to murder him several times without succeeding. And now you want me to believe that this last time which finally did succeed, it wasn't you, but an accident!"

"Yes, you've got to—because it's true! I could have denied that I ever had such an idea altogether. But I don't want to mix part truth and part falsehood. What I've told you is *all* truth from beginning to end, and I want you to believe it. I *did* intend killing him, I *did* try; then I changed my mind, gave up the idea, and an accident took his life.

"All right, now you've heard my side of it. If you want me to go with you, I'm ready to go. Only think well what you're doing, because once the damage is done, there's no undoing it."

"Suppose I go back to town now without doing anything—for the present. Say just overnight. What will you do?"

"Wait here—hoping, praying a little, maybe."

"How do I know that?"

"Where can I go? Running away won't help; it'll just fasten guilt on me. It'll just bring on the ignominy *he* wanted Streak and me to suffer. If we were going to run away now, we could have run away while he was still alive."

She was right about that, of course. "Then wait in this house until you hear from me. Consider yourself in the custody of your own conscience. I'm going back to town now, alone. I want to think this whole thing out—by myself, away from here. I can't think clearly when I'm this close to you. You're very beautiful, you know. I'm a human being, I'm capable of making a mistake, and I don't want to make a mistake. As undeniably as you are beautiful, Iveria is just as undeniably dead."

"It's going to be awful," she said, "to have it hang suspended over my head like that. Will it be very long before I know?"

"As soon as I know myself; sometime tomorrow, maybe. Don't leave the house. If the doorbell rings, and you see me standing out there—you'll know I've come to take you back to face a charge of murder. If the telephone rings—that means you're in the clear."

Crawley looked in on me at midnight. "What's the matter, haven't you any home?"

I motioned him on his way. "I'm trying to think something out," I said. "I'm going to sit here if it takes all night."

I had the deposition on the table in front of me, and the cigarette case, and the deathbed note. It all balanced so damnably even, his side and hers. Check and doublecheck. Which was the true story, which the false?

The crux of the matter was that final incident. That was where my dilemma lay. If it was murder, Iveria's death demanded reparation. If it was an accident, then it proved him the devil she claimed him to be, for he himself must certainly have known it to be an accident; yet before he died he deliberately phoned me from the hospital and dictated that deathbed message emphasizing that it was murder.

I reviewed the whole case from start to finish. He had walked in to us at Headquarters and left an affidavit in my hands telling me he expected his wife to kill him, in the guise of a trivial accident; telling me he would say "This is it" when it happened. He'd had a trivial accident, and he'd said "This is it" before he died.

I went out to question her and I found her dancing for joy in the presence of the man she loved. She admitted she had tried to kill Iveria several times in the past. She denied she had tried to kill him this last time. But—*she had tried to bribe me* not to pursue the investigation any further. What was the evidence? A bedside bulb loosened a little in its socket so it wouldn't light, a hassock placed where it didn't belong.

She had left me, as if overwhelmed by this gossamer evidence that was really no evidence at all. She didn't come back. I sent the maid after her. I went in there and found the two of them grappling in desperate silence over a gun she had tried to use on herself. As a guilty person who felt that she had been found out? Or an innocent person who despaired of ever satisfactorily clearing herself? I calmed her down, listened to her side of the story, and finally left to think it over alone, telling her I would let her know my decision by coming back for her (guilty) or telephoning (exonerated).

And here I was.

And I'd finally reached one. Even though the scales remained evenly balanced and counterbalanced, to the last hair's-breadth milligram. Only one grain more had fallen on one side.

In the cold early daylight peering into the office I picked up the phone and asked the sleepy Headquarters operator to get me the number of the Iveria house up there in the country, where she was waiting to know.

I hadn't heard the maid call out from that adjoining room, and I had been fully awake. But *he* claimed he had heard his wife cry out in there, and he was supposedly asleep.

No; he had actually been on his way in there at the time, gun in hand, to take *her* life, when a combination of unexpected little mischances turned the tables on him.

Julian Symons

The   Sensitive   Ears   of   Mr.
Small

"When I become excited, you see, my hearing becomes very—
very acute." Mr. Small had a curious hearing condition—
extraordinary magnification of certain sounds. That was the
curious part of it—not all sounds, only certain sounds. Like
those his wife Lucy made: they grated, bombarded his ears,
jarred his nerves. And like those Marilyn made: they were de-
licious, delightful—they soothed, caressed, excited . . .

Julian Symons' story is a probing and perceptive "study in
crime"—a study in the power of life and death . . .

The kitchen door closed with a slight, yet decisive and delicious promising click. Mr. Small moved smoothly into his
daydream. He got up, went smiling out to the kitchen, discovered
Marilyn there in the act of pulling up her stockings. She gave a
small protesting but delighted gasp as his arms clasped her from
behind. Beneath his hand he heard the soothing sound of fingers
on silk . . .

Crunch. His wife's teeth as they bit into toast destroyed the
dream. Crunch and crunch again, like a series of mortars explod-
ing. It was a relief when she dipped a spoon into the pot for more
marmalade, although the resultant *squelch* was still unpleasant.
But then inevitably came another *crunch*, against which he rus-
tled the morning paper in vain.

The attack quite drowned any sound that Marilyn was making
in the kitchen. He felt himself unable to bear it. This was a very
bad morning. He rose and said he must go. The touch of his lips
on Lucy's cheek was the briefest possible contact. In the car on
the way to the station he said aloud, "It can't go on."

The curious condition of his hearing had existed now for some
four months. It had begun, if he liked to put a time to it, just
after Marilyn came to work for them three mornings a week. It

was as though he felt things through his sense of hearing rather than through his sense of touch; the result was that almost every movement Marilyn made gave him a thrill of pleasure while everything Lucy did, whether it was moving a chair or turning the pages of a magazine, jarred his nerves.

Apart from things done by Marilyn and Lucy his hearing was perfectly normal, which somehow did not make things any better. He tried to explain it to old Dr. Bentham.

"When I become excited, you see, my hearing becomes very—very acute." It did not seem wise to mention Lucy and Marilyn.

Dr. Bentham was old and red-faced. His hand shook a little and his breath smelled of whiskey. He made a cursory examination and said, "Nervous strain. Overworking in the office. The pace we all live at nowadays. Need to slow down a bit. Give you some pills."

The pills had no effect, and within another few days it became clear to Mr. Small that pleasure was associated with Marilyn, pain with Lucy. One was as intense as the other. He began to indulge in daydreams in which the pleasure was accentuated and the pain did not exist . . .

Mr. Small was rather small, although not diminutive. He was 40 years old. Everybody liked him because he was almost always cheerful and placid. His name was Geoffrey, but most people called him Geoff. Friends and acquaintances felt rather sorry for him because Lucy, although a splendid manager and good cook, was inclined to lay down the law about everything and wait for him to agree.

As people said, it was a pity they had no children, although of course they got on terribly well. And at Truwell Hanslit, the firm of manufacturing chemists where Mr. Small was the assistant accountant, he got on terribly well, too, enduring better than anyone else the schoolboy sarcasm of the general manager, Mr. Best. Yes, everybody liked Geoff Small.

On the morning that he had said, "It can't go on," Mr. Small had lunch in the executives' restaurant with Grady, the company's chief analytical chemist. Grady, an ebullient Irishman, liked to talk, and there was no better listener than Geoff Small. As a matter of fact, they'd had lunch together quite often in the past month. While Grady talked, Mr. Small noticed that the ordinary restaurant noises did not bother him at all.

Truwell Hanslit manufactured dozens of different branded preparations, from a new cortisone ointment for rashes to a contraceptive pill that was said to have no side effects of any kind. Grady liked talking about these, but he talked rather more about the power held by analytical chemists in general and the importance of his own work in particular.

"Some of the things we work on and then give up, Geoff, you'd never believe. Talk about the power of life and death! You know what the Home Office analysts say."

"What do they say?" Mr. Small inquired timidly.

"Well, they only whisper it, mind you, but everyone knows there are a hundred different laboratory ways of committing undetected murder."

"Poisons, you mean?"

"Not poisons, Geoff, compounds." Grady jabbed with his fork. "There are half a dozen compounds in the lab at this moment that would send somebody off to sleep for good. Experiments, you know, we shan't manufacture them." He gave a great belly laugh. "Next time you're in the lab—"

It happened that Mr. Small had to go across to the laboratory that very afternoon, on a query which proved to be a mistake in the Accounting Department. Grady was delighted to see him and continue their conversation. At the end they made what was almost a conducted tour of the laboratory in which Grady cast a little light on his companion's ignorance. It had been said that Mr. Small was a good listener, and he did not mention to Grady that long ago he had passed a physics examination which naturally included chemistry. His knowledge was haphazard but genuine.

On the way home that evening Mr. Small made a few purchases at three different drug stores. It would be pointless to say what they were, for each of the substances was harmless in itself. On the way back from the station in the car he repeated, "It can't go on."

Mr. Small had always liked puttering about in the kitchen. He did nothing elaborate, but he baked bread, made teacakes, and always took up a bedtime drink to Lucy. On the evening after his conversation with Grady he pottered about, then took up not only a sleep-inducing drink but one of the little buns he had just made.

Lucy ate it, and burped. A sound like a shot went through Mr. Small's body. "Too much baking powder," she said.

That night she felt ill. Not very ill, but Mr. Small insisted on calling Dr. Bentham. He came, bad-tempered and sleepy, diagnosed injudicious eating, and gave Lucy a sedative.

On the following morning Marilyn arrived to find Mr. Small making breakfast for Lucy, who was still in bed. He explained that she had had a nasty turn.

"Oh ah." She was a blonde girl, whose parents had died a few years back. She had a slightly crooked smile and a way of looking sideways that was conspiratorial and attractively sly. As she took off her coat, standing close to him, there was a rustle like music.

It seemed the moment to turn the daydream into reality, and he put an arm around her. She seemed to move away, but somehow did not. For a moment his lips met hers, then she did move away.

"Now then." She gave that sideways glance. "What would *she* say?"

The tinkle of her charm bracelet rang through his ears, traveled all over his body. He gulped. "Would you come out one night? To, say, a little dinner?"

"What would *she* say?" Marilyn repeated.

Lucy got up later that day and felt much better. When Dr. Bentham came in to look at her on Saturday morning, she said she was quite fit. The doctor had a couple of stiff whiskies and told her to be careful what she ate.

Mr. Small saw the doctor out to his car and said he knew she was still in pain. The doctor said it was gastritis, but if it went on they'd have to do something about it.

On Sunday they had arranged that a couple of neighbors come in to dinner, and Lucy insisted they should not call it off. The Longleys remembered afterward that Geoff had seemed anxious, and had tried to stop Lucy from having a second helping of roast duck. Marilyn had come in to wash up and she was in the kitchen when Geoff, as usual, made the coffee.

At midnight Lucy felt some pains and Mr. Small went downstairs, as he said, to call the doctor. He was distressed about the pains—his chemical knowledge was limited, and he couldn't really be sure about the effects of the white powder that had been the product of his pottering. He had kept it in the kitchen in a small jar labeled *Powder for Wine Making*, which was reasonable enough, because he had previously made parsnip and elderberry wine. Now he locked up the powder in his desk drawer.

He didn't actually call the doctor until half-past one. During that period of an hour and a half he sat in the living room with the door closed and the radio playing so that he could not hear the sounds upstairs.

When Dr. Bentham arrived he was angry, but when he came downstairs he looked grave. The usual unpleasant things were done, but without effect. Mr. Small suggested getting a second medical opinion, but it proved too late for that. The cause of death was stated on the certificate to have been acute gastric inflammation.

Everybody was very sympathetic. Even Best at the office, sarcastic overbearing Best, said he was sorry. Quite a lot of people attended the funeral and several of them came back to the house. Mrs. Longley had arranged a little buffet meal, and Marilyn was there to hand things round.

Mr. Small did not say very much, but his friends said that you could see how he felt. In fact, he hardly heard what was said, because all the time the music of Marilyn's charm bracelet sounded in his ears a message of infinite promise.

After the visitors had gone he could not resist doing what he knew to be unwise. He went out to the kitchen where Marilyn was clearing up and planted a kiss on her neck. It was as soft as roses; in some strange way he did not merely feel the contact but first of all *heard* it. The sound was the most exciting he had ever known.

She half turned but did not disengage herself. "I don't know what you're thinking about," she said. "And her only just buried."

Mr. Small's thoughts were inexpressible. He could only stammer her name. In the end she pushed him away. She said he ought to be ashamed of himself, but that sideways glance seemed to have a different message. Then, enunciating the words carefully, she said she thought it would be better if she did not come in any more. It wouldn't be right.

He could hardly believe what she said. "But I must—I must see you again."

The sound as she put a hand up to her disarranged hair was beautiful. "You'll be moving out anyway. To a flat."

"Oh, I don't think so. I like to have a house. My wife didn't make a will, you know, and she had a little money."

"Did you say something about taking me out to dinner?" As he moved toward her again she said coolly, "No. And I'm not coming in after the end of this week. It wouldn't be right."

She was as good, or as bad, as her word. He took her out, and saw her almost every evening, but she would not come to the house. Mr. Small was no housekeeper, and the place began to look slovenly. That delightful magnification of every sound she made continued, so that in a way it was always a pleasure to be with her; but in another way he knew he was being cheated.

At the end of three weeks they were married by special license, with witnesses brought in from the street. Immediately after the wedding they left for a honeymoon in Venice. There Mr. Small experienced the joys he had contemplated, which proved after all not to be so very joyful. His sensual experiences seemed to be inextricably linked to the extreme sensitivity of his hearing, and after a few days in Marilyn's company her movements and gestures were less vividly heard. By the end of the honeymoon her voice, which was—what else could you call it?—common, had begun to grate on his ears.

When they moved back to the house she got rid of all Lucy's curtains and chair covers and some of the carpets. She said the place needed brightening up. The replacements were in various shades of tangerine and pink, with an occasional essay into burnt gold. Mr. Small had not realized that the colors of furnishings could jar the whole nervous system, but this proved to be the case. He not only *saw* these horrid colors but *heard* them too, and he did not like the sounds.

And yet beyond this he had a deep sense of comfort when he thought about the powder in his desk drawer. Mr. Small had not done many positive things in his life, and it was comforting to feel a kind of power.

He was distressed to find that his popularity had suddenly disappeared. The Longleys came in one evening for drinks, but it was not a success. After they had left, Marilyn said that they were a stuck-up lot round here, why didn't they move? Mr. Small replied that he had no intention of moving.

After all, he had the money—it turned out that Lucy had a nest egg he knew nothing about—and it was a pleasure to dig his toes in. Marilyn shrugged, became sluttish, watched TV all evening, and ate box after box of chocolates. Mr. Small refused to have anybody in to help with the housework, and more often than not it didn't get done.

At the office, too, life was not easy. Grady was still friendly, but Mr. Small rather avoided contact with him, and Best had reverted to type and become his old intolerable self. He was always making references in execrable taste, saying that he hoped Mr. Small got plenty of home comforts, and suggesting that he looked extremely tired mornings.

These remarks were often made in the presence of junior members of the staff who seemed to find them funny, and in the end Mr. Small decided to act. He still did some home cooking and often brought in teacakes for the morning "break." One day he persuaded Best to have a teacake. There were two to choose from, and Best took the one intended for him.

Mr. Small smiled a private smile when he learned that the general manager had gone home after lunch, feeling extremely unwell. He was away the next day and still looked greenish when he returned. Power had been exercised, honor satisfied. The jokes didn't hurt any more.

It was in the following week that Mr. Small, passing through the typing pool, heard a sound that made a shiver of delight pass through his ears and vibrate like a gong in the region of his solar plexus. It recurred, and he identified its source as a new young typist. She was sniffling, and it was the most delicious sniffle he had ever heard.

He took her to lunch in the canteen and learned that her name was Jennifer. The sniffle appeared to be a natural asset, not the result of a cold. Mr. Small felt that he could listen to it forever. He thought of asking her out for the evening, but he decided against it.

He was not shocked or even surprised when, that evening, Marilyn took a chocolate from a box and he heard, with the magnification given by a stethoscope, the rustle of the paper which sounded as though somebody was tearing silk, and the *crunch* of teeth on chocolate which was like a drill attacking rock.

"Why are you looking at me as though I am a freak?" she asked. "What's wrong with me?"

"Nothing," Mr. Small said softly. "There's nothing wrong at all."

"Well, there is something wrong and I'll tell you what." What could her voice be compared to—a file screeching on metal? "There's nothing to do in this damned place! And we never go out now. I'm sick of it."

"I thought perhaps we might go on a holiday."

"A holiday?"

"Perhaps on a cruise."

She stared at him, with that sideways calculating look he had once found so attractive. "It would make a change. But can you get the time off?"

He said he could, although he knew very well he couldn't. He had taken his yearly holiday for their honeymoon and they had been married only six months. It would have been nice if what he thought of as "the event" could take place on a cruise, but it was really not important. Afterward it might be advisable to move from the neighborhood. Perhaps Jennifer would like the idea of a flat?

He unlocked his desk and stared at the powder. He found that he was looking forward to "the event."

He had given up drinking coffee, but a couple of nights after their talk about the cruise he took Marilyn to the cinema and then made coffee for them both. In the night she felt ill, and he suggested getting Dr. Bentham, but she said no. She was so vehement about hating doctors that he did nothing.

After all, it was not necessary for this trial run, as he thought of it. Grady had said that a post-mortem in the case of this compound would reveal nothing but symptoms of unsuspected cardiac trouble; on the other hand, it might be as well if the circumstances did not precisely repeat those in Lucy's case.

The following day something disconcerting happened. Jennifer said she was too busy to come to lunch; but then he passed her as she was going into the canteen with two other girls. After he had gone by he heard their laughter, like the cackle of monkeys. In the past such an incident would have embarrassed him, but now he felt the swell of anger. At some time little Jennifer would have to be taught a lesson; but that could wait.

When he got home Marilyn was on the sofa watching television. She said she felt better and was coy, almost kittenish, as she pulled him down beside her. Soon after their marriage he had bought her a pair of gold bangles, and now he winced as they clattered against each other.

"How about that cruise, Geoff?"

He felt every movement she made—the harsh touch of her thighs, the rub of her dress on the sofa, the shriek of her right-hand index finger as it rubbed his left-hand thumbnail. His ears were assaulted so violently that at first he could not reply. Then he said faintly that it was all settled, they would get the tickets next week.

He unlocked the drawer of his desk and took out the powder. It would have to be tonight.

He took the coffee into the living room. Marilyn continued to be kittenish, saying now that she wanted brown and not white sugar. He fetched it for her. A sense of power and ease flowed through him as she raised the cup to her lips. Now it was a question of waiting, nothing more.

Later he lay in bed with the light out, staring up into the blackness. Marilyn was totally silent, yet with his wonderfully attuned ears he could hear the sibilation of her breath. Who had written something about hearing the press of an ant's foot on grass? He could have heard that, too. He looked at his watch. The time was ten minutes after midnight.

"Are you all right?" he whispered, and the words came back immediately like an echo. "Are you?"

At these two innocuous whispered words he experienced a feeling that could not be identified exactly, a feeling that combined apprehension and discomfort. Her next words were also whispered. "I drank your coffee. You drank mine."

For a few moments the words were meaningless, then he understood them, and at the moment of understanding, the discomfort changed to a pain that gripped his body as though a giant crab had gripped his chest with one claw and his stomach with another. Electric lights struck at his eyes, and Marilyn was spitting at him like some great cat.

"Did you think I was fool enough to let you get rid of me the way you got rid of her?" He gasped something and tried to get out of bed, but his legs seemed made of soft plastic. "I was in the kitchen when you were making coffee that night. Do you think I didn't see what you were doing? *Powder for Wine Making.* You dirty little devil."

The words grated like a rake over gravel. He started to say something. Then the pain came again, and he stopped.

"I thought you'd spend money, not throw it about like a man with no hands. But I've been watching to see if you tried anything." She put on her dressing gown. "There's no will. So I'm your heir."

"Call the doctor." With a supreme effort he managed to swing his legs out of bed. She came and pushed him back.

"Not yet." She looked at her watch. "I reckon you waited more than an hour before you rang old Bentham. I'll make it two. And now I've got to wash up the dinner things. *And* the coffee cups." She held up something bright and shining in her hand. A key. "I don't think you'll be any trouble from the look of you, but better safe than sorry."

As she went out, a lightning stroke of pain—much worse than what he had experienced before—split his body; and at the same moment he heard, like a roll of thunder—terrible, decisive, final—the turning of the key in the lock.

Ellery Queen

Payoff

"Cosa Nostra?" Ellery asked, sitting up.

"No," sighed Inspector Queen, "these operators are about as close to the Cosa Nostra type as the stratosphere to a groundhog. And as hard to reach. It's a real high-class nastiness."

"Tell me more, Dad."

"Well, we were up against a stone wall till evidence turned up that this plush-lined mob has a Board of Directors composed of four men. When I tell you who they are you'll send for the loony wagon."

The Inspector raised his corded hands and began to tick the quartet off. "One: Ever hear of DeWitt Hughes?"

"Certainly I've heard of DeWitt Hughes. Wall Street and banking in the megamillions. You're not seriously suggesting. . . ?"

"I am."

"But DeWitt Hughes? Directing a crime syndicate?"

"As one of four," said his father, shaking his head. "Of whom the second is John T. Ewing."

Ellery gawped. "The oil and mining tycoon?"

"You heard me. And Number Three: Filippo Falcone."

"The construction and trucking king? Dad, is this a rib?"

"I wish I could joke about it," the Inspector said. "And last—you ready, son? Reilly Burke."

"You've got to be kidding," Ellery exclaimed. "Burke, the Great Mouthpiece of our time! Why would a lawyer of Burke's standing and big businessmen like Falcone, Ewing, and Hughes dirty themselves in the rackets?"

The old man shrugged. "Maybe it's so easy for such operators to make big money legit these days that the only kick left is to turn crooked."

"I'd like to help straighten them out," Ellery said grimly. "I take it I fit into your plans some way?"

"Before we move a step I want to know which of those four cuties is top banana, Ellery. Not only would that enable us to move in faster and so cut down on the chances of a tipoff, but my information is that the head man has possession of the main syndicate records. So I'm hoping you can pinpoint him for us."

"Do you have a lead?"

"In a way." Inspector Queen flipped his intercom. "Velie, send in Mrs. Prince."

The ravaged woman Sergeant Velie admitted to the Inspector's office must once have been pretty in a petite, even chic way. But only wreckage was left. She was so nervous that Ellery had to help her into the chair; her arm thrummed like a piano wire.

"Mrs. Prince's husband is an accountant who's serving five to ten for an embezzlement," Inspector Queen said.

"He didn't do it." She had a broken-down voice, too. "He confessed to a crime he didn't commit because it was part of a deal."

"Tell my son what Mr. Prince told you when he was sent up."

"John said that when he got out we'd be set for life," the woman told Ellery. "Meanwhile, every month for over three years now I've received through the mail an unmarked envelope containing $750 in small bills. That's what the children and I have been living on."

"You don't know where the money is coming from?"

"No, and John won't discuss it when I visit him. But he knows, all right! It's part of the deal he made, I'm positive, to make sure he keeps his mouth shut."

"He's being released from Sing Sing on parole tomorrow, Ellery."

"My husband told me not to meet him in Ossining—to wait for him at home," the woman whispered. "Mr. Queen, I'm scared."

"Why?"

"Because of the deal he made, whatever it was. Of the blood money, wherever it comes from, that he's going to be paid off with. I don't want it!" Mrs. Prince cried. "All I want is for us to get away from here, change our name, start all over again somewhere. But John won't listen to me . . ."

"Or to anyone else," said Inspector Queen. "It's a long shot, Ellery, but maybe he'll listen to you. Mrs. Prince says he's always been a fan of yours."

"If you'd only make John see that we can't build a life on that kind of money, Mr. Queen!"

"Nobody, including you, is going to talk Prince out of *that*," the Inspector remarked to his son, when the woman had left, "in spite of what I just said. Not when he's earned the money by sacrificing his good name and over three years of his life."

"Then what's the point, Dad? And what does it have to do with the crime syndicate you're investigating?"

"We've found out," his father answered, "that before Prince was sent up he handled a lot of highly confidential work for Hughes, Ewing, Burke, and Falcone; in fact the embezzlement rap stemmed from a job he did for one of Hughes's banks. He's denied it, but I have good reason to believe Prince was close to the big boys and knows who the head man is. Maybe you can think of a way to trick the information out of him."

"And he's coming home tomorrow?" Ellery looked thoughtful. "All right, Dad. Let's form a reception committee."

At 2:15 p.m. the following day the reception committee turned out to have a noisy and unexpected partner.

The Inspector's men were routinely staked out in various vestibules and tradesmen's entrances in the vicinity of the modest, East Side, corner apartment building where the Princes lived. A taxi turned into the street and pulled up before the building. John Prince got out. The cab drove off, and the emaciated, rather stooped figure of the accountant turned toward the building.

At that instant a nondescript black sedan with muddied license plates careened around the corner and began to chatter and spit fire as it bolted past Prince and up the street and around the corner. Prince fell to the sidewalk, staining it red as he hit.

Squad cars roared futilely off after the vanished murder car as the Queens and Sergeant Velie ran over to the quiet man. They were almost, not quite, too late.

Sergeant Velie took one look and advised, "Better step on it."

"Prince. Prince, listen," Ellery said, stooping over him. "Help us get them. Talk. Can you talk?"

"Four . . . of them," gasped the dying man, looking into Ellery's eyes. "Each one uses . . . a code name . . . of a city."

"Four cities?"

"Boston . . . Philadelphia . . . Berkeley. . . ." The voice guttered like a burned-out candle. Prince made one incredible effort. "And Houston," he said, quite clearly.

"Which one is top man?"

But the accountant's stare glassed over and remained that way.

"Bye-bye, blackbird," announced Sergeant Velie.

"So my hunch was right," muttered Inspector Queen. "He did know. One second—one second more!—and he'd have told us. No, Velie, let her," he said in a gentler tone. "Mrs. Prince, I'm sorry . . ." The old man sounded sorry for a number of things.

The widow stood over her husband's body. "Now you know, John," she said to it. "Now you know how they meant to set you up." And she brushed by the Inspector's proffered arm and went blindly back into the apartment building.

"Well?" the Inspector snapped to his son after a while. "Don't stand there with your mouth hanging open! This code business ought to be your candy; each of the four using the name of a city for identification! What did he say they were again?"

"Boston, Philadelphia, Berkeley, Houston." Ellery was still returning the dead man's stare. Then he turned aside and said, "For the love of heaven, Velie, close his eyes, will you?"

"Well, it doesn't matter. We knew who they are," and the Inspector turned away, too. "The only thing we didn't know—the name of the head man—he didn't get to tell us."

"Oh," said Ellery, "but he did."

CHALLENGE TO THE READER
*Which of the four is head man
in the syndicate? And how
did Ellery know?*

Ellery explained: "If you examine them, there's a connection between the names of the crime directorate and the city code names they chose to cover their identities.

"Take one: Reilly *Burke* and the city of *Berk*eley. Burke—Berk. Identical in sound.

"Or take *Fil*ippo Falcone and *Phil*adelphia. Fil—Phil."

"Oh, come on, Ellery," said Inspector Queen. "Coincidence."

"Then how about DeWitt *Hughes* and *Hous*ton? Hughes—Hous. Two might be a coincidence. Three? No, sir."

"But that leaves John T. Ewing and the code name of Boston. Find me a connection between those two!"

"Ah, that's the missing ingredient," Ellery said, watching the meat wagoneers trundling their poor freight away. "In each city name the corresponding clue was in the first syllable: Berk, Phil, Hous. Try it on Boston."

"Boston. Bos." The Inspector looked doubtful. Then he cried. *"Boss!"*

"Ewing is obviously the head man you're trying to identify," Ellery nodded. "The Boss."

Clayton Rawson

Miracles — All in the Day's Work

*We close this anthology, dedicated to the magicians of mystery,
with a story about the most famous magician-detective in the
genre—Clayton Rawson's The Great Merlini ... Merlini was
going to Jones Beach to have 60 beautiful girls dive into a
swimming pool and then vanish and Inspector Gavigan was
going to Maine on a fishing trip—when an "impossible crime"
stopped them both ...*

Detective: THE GREAT MERLINI

Lieutenant Doran of the Homicide Squad nearly collided
head-on with The Great Merlini in the doorway of the latter's
place of business. Doran was on his way in; the proprietor of the
Magic Shop—slogan: Nothing Is Impossible—was on his way out.

"Where," Doran asked, "are you going?"

"Jones Beach," the magician answered. "I've got to show a man
how to have sixty beautiful girls dive into a swimming pool and
then vanish—underwater."

"I'm glad it's nothing important," Doran said, not believing a
word of it. "You're coming with me."

The Great Merlini shook his head. "If you knew the man I'm
talking about, you wouldn't say that so calmly. He's the producer
of the Marine Theater water show. He is also a boy genius as
temperamental as any six Grand Opera stars, and he has already
blown his top twice this morning because I'm late."

"A boy *genius*? And he thinks you can make sixty girls disappear underwater?"

Merlini grinned. "Nothing hard about that. What he doesn't
know, being a *boy* genius, is that this underwater mass vanishing
act was done three times daily at the old Hippodrome fifty years
ago. The chorus line walked four abreast down a flight of steps

into the big tank and never came up. All I have to do is give him the same gimmick."

"You can give it to him later. My orders are to bring you over to the Chancellor Building fast. Inspector Gavigan, who can blow his top higher than any six boy geniuses, has a job for you that nobody ever did at the Hippodrome. What we got is a murderer who just vanished into thin air—sixty-four stories up!"

The theatrical genius had to wait; Doran's next statement fixed that. "The murder was committed right under the Inspector's nose. He was there when it happened. So now we got the precinct Captain who's carrying the case firing questions at Gavigan—questions he can't answer. Neither of them is enjoying this. And when the Commissioner gets a load of it—and the newspapers . . ." Doran choked. The prospect was too devastating.

Ten minutes later Doran and Merlini entered the sixty-fourth floor offices of the Hi-Fly Rod & Reel Company. The reception room was like a thousand others except that its decor was extremely fishy. On one wall hung a stuffed, mounted, five-foot marlin. This somewhat incredible specimen of the taxidermist's art seemed to have just leaped from the briny deep and now, back arched, mouth open hungrily, and with a mean look in its glassy eyes, was diving with murderous intent down at Gavigan who stood just below. Gavigan's eyes also had a glassy look.

The Inspector faced the reception desk and glared at the young lady who sat there. Rosabelle Polchek, who usually answered to "Rosie" and who was known among the salesmen as "The Dish," wore a tight blue sweater, a platinum-blonde rinse, and a harassed look. Her mascara was smudged and her nose was red.

"I know," Gavigan was saying, "that you want to go home. I know you've had a shock. I know you've answered these questions half a dozen times. But we're going through it again—and again—until it begins to make sense. You opened this office at nine o'clock. Now take it from there."

Rosie blew her nose into a damp handkerchief. "I opened the mail and put the letters Mr. Courtney would want on his desk. I was changing my typewriter ribbon when he came in."

"Time?"

"Nine thirty. And I knew right away that today was going to be a tough one. Instead of 'Hi, Rosie, how's The Dish this morning?' I get 'Phone Joe McCall and tell him to get the hell over here fast. Toledo says that last shipment of reel casings was defective.'"

A dapper young man who sat nervously on a chair in the corner angrily squashed a cigarette in the ashtray beside him, burned his thumb, swore, and said, "Winchester Fishing Supply doesn't manufacture defective—"

Gavigan snapped at him. "Quiet! I'll get to you. Go on, Miss Polchek."

Rosie dabbed at her nose again. "Harry—I mean Mr. Courtney—went into his office and I called Joe. Then a minute or so later this Humphrey Bogart-type character with the dead-pan face and the Panama hat breezed in. Said his name was J. J. Hartman and that Mr. Courtney was expecting him. So I flashed the boss and he said send him in, which I did."

"Now," Gavigan said slowly, "let's get this absolutely straight. He walked through the door there next to your desk and straight into Courtney's office? And you haven't seen him since?"

Rosie nodded. "That's right."

"And you didn't make a trip to the Ladies Room or go out for a coffee break?"

"I was right here every second. Besides, there wasn't time. Two minutes later you walked in."

Gavigan turned to Merlini. "This morning I started on the first vacation I've had in three years. And I had to make the mistake of stopping in here on my way to Grand Central and a train for the Maine woods. Courtney and I get together now and then to talk fish and I've got a nice collection of flies he helped me collect which I never get a chance to use. I should have known better. All a police inspector has to do is get set for a vacation and there's a murder, a gang war, a police department shakeup, or somebody throws a bomb at the mayor." He turned back to Rosie. "Go on."

"Then Joe came in."

"No. Don't skip. I want everything—every little detail. I asked for Courtney and then what?"

"I—I said he had someone with him and asked you to wait. You said you had a train to catch, so—" Rosie blew her nose again.

"So you rang Courtney."

Rosie nodded. "He said he'd be free in a few minutes, and you sat down and—and you know everything else that happened. You were right here all the time."

Gavigan scowled at her. "If I knew everything that happened I wouldn't be here now." He turned to Merlini. "For the next ten minutes I read a copy of *Field and Stream*, and Rosie did a pruning and filing job on her nails. Then McCall here blew in and tried to find out what Courtney was all steamed up about. Rosie said she didn't know, that Courtney was really burned, and advised McCall to sit tight and wait, which he didn't want to do."

"I was in a hurry," McCall said. "I had another appointment at ten—an important one. But I also had to find out what was eating Courtney. I didn't want to lose the account."

"So he sat down," Gavigan continued, "and fidgeted. Rosie finished doing her nails and then phoned a girl friend and they had an important business conference about a movie on last night's Late Show starring Bathsheba and Victor Mature. And just as this started, Courtney also got a phone call. We heard his phone ring twice, then cut off in the middle of the third ring as he picked it up."

Merlini eyed the PBX unit on Rosie's desk. "She took the call and put it through to her boss?"

"No. His call didn't come through the board. Courtney has two phones, the second is an outside line and the call came in on that. Then, after about the second reel of Rosie's movie synopsis, I began to suspect that maybe she had also stayed up to see Richard Barthelmess or Rudolph Valentino on the Late Late Show and I might miss my train. So I stood up and looked impatient."

"Rosie got the idea and cut her call short. I told her I had to go and would see Courtney later. I started for the door. She stopped me. 'I nearly forgot,' she said, and she fished in a desk drawer and came up with a little beauty of a spinning reel."

Gavigan took it from his jacket pocket. "Complete with a hundred yards of a new type nylon line. She said Courtney had asked her to give it to me if I stopped in when she was out. I thanked her and started for the door again . . . "

"And," McCall put in, "I told her I couldn't wait any longer and I started to go out, too."

"And I," Rosie added, "know Mr. Courtney isn't going to like it if Joe leaves, so I ask him to wait and I ring the boss." She flicked a key on her board and a phone rang beyond the closed office door. "He didn't answer, so I tried again." This time Rosie held the key down longer and the phone in the next office rang insistently.

"Still no answer," Gavigan said. "And that's where I made my mistake. I'd be halfway to Boston by now if I had kept going, but I didn't. I came back. And Rosie, who also figured something might be wrong, got up, opened Courtney's door—and screamed."

The Inspector walked to the door, opened it, and told a fingerprint man, a police photographer, and two detectives to wait outside. Then, as Merlini joined him, he said:

"This is what she saw."

There was a window in the opposite wall beyond which lay a magnificent although dizzying view of Manhattan; beside the window was a desk whose top proclaimed that Rosie's boss had been the executive type. It held a desk blotter, the morning mail stacked neatly in its center, six sharpened pencils, an onyx pen set, a framed photograph of Mrs. Courtney, and two telephones.

The businesslike efficiency of the desk top was marred by the fact that Courtney, a fortyish, rather handsome man, still seated in his chair, had fallen forward. His left hand still grasped one of the telephone receivers and his face rested on the blotter. The onyx handle of a paper knife that matched his pen set projected squarely from the center of his back.

Gavigan pointed to the phone in Courtney's hand. "I came in here about five minutes after we heard him answer that phone. During that time, while Courtney was still talking, Panama Harry picked up the knife and let him have it."

"Panama Harry?" Merlini asked.

"Didn't that description Rosie gave mean anything to you?" Doran asked a bit incredulously. "Don't you read the newspapers?"

"I don't always read the crime news," Merlini admitted. "Too often it's not news—just the same old story with a different cast of characters."

"I could do with a lot less of the kind of news Panama Harry makes," Doran growled. "He claims no prison can hold him and he got out of his third one last week. He was one of three cons who engineered a break out of Sing Sing. He's been on all the front pages—with pictures."

"And with every cop in six states looking for him," Gavigan added, "he has the nerve to walk in here and knife Courtney. Either he just doesn't give a damn or he's stir crazy."

"Or," Merlini added, "since he seems to have learned how to vanish as abruptly and completely as a punctured soap bubble he knows he holds all the aces." The magician pointed with his toe at a large lead fishing sinker that lay on the carpet near the desk. "What's this doing here?"

"Courtney used it as a paperweight," Gavigan said. "If he saw Panama Harry pull a knife he may have grabbed for it in self-defense and knocked it off the desk to the floor. But I doubt it. My guess is Courtney was stabbed from behind while he was talking on the phone. Doc Peabody says he died almost instantly."

Merlini walked to a leather-covered sofa along one wall and looked down at the Panama hat that lay there. "Panama's prints are on file, of course. Find any on this that match?"

"Nothing useful. Handling a hat is an automatic action that is almost always done the same way, so all we got was a hopeless mess of superimposed prints."

Merlini surveyed the rest of the room. "Smooth plaster wall and ceiling. Nothing to hide a secret exit. Have you had the carpet up?"

"Would the Chancellor Building architects have put trapdoors in their plans?"

"I doubt it, but Courtney could have made alterations. Did you look?"

"We looked. And . . . "

". . . . didn't find one," Merlini finished. "If you had, you wouldn't have sent Doran to get me." Merlini crossed to the window. "This was unlocked?"

Doran answered. "Who locks a window this far off the ground? And what difference does it make anyway?"

Merlini raised the window, put his head out, and looked down—a sheer drop of sixty-four stories, and no ledges.

Behind him Gavigan said, "Three witnesses, including myself, will testify that no one left this room by the door—the only door. Unless you can come up with something else, it has to be the window."

Merlini pulled his head in. "Then we'll have to come up with something else. I doubt if he had a helicopter waiting outside. This time of day it would be a trifle conspicuous." He eyed the room, frowning. "Panama Harry is in the wrong business. As a vanishing man I could get him night-club bookings for two years solid." He crossed to the desk. "Why are you so sure it was this outside phone, the one Courtney is holding, that you heard ring, Gavigan? How do you know it wasn't the other? Rosie could have rung that from the board."

"Not without three hands, she couldn't. When Courtney's phone rang, she had just started on her nonstop movie synopsis. She had her phone in her left hand and was still waving her right hand to dry the nail polish. After the second ring she swiveled around in her chair looking toward Courtney's door as if wondering why he didn't answer. He elbow-knocked the bottle of nail polish off onto the floor, and she was picking that up when the phone rang again and then cut off as Courtney answered. Then, still talking, she put her polishing equipment away in a desk drawer that contains a wide assortment of bottled beauty preparations, face powder, facial tissues, bobby pins, lipstick, and a couple of paper clips that must be there by mistake. Does that answer your question?"

Merlini, who had found a salesman's sample case on a filing cabinet in one corner of the room, had opened it and was contemplating an assortment of Hi-Fly products. "It does," he said, crossing to the desk and looking down at Courtney's body. "The hand really isn't quicker than the eye. Magicians have been telling audiences that for years to mislead them—to hide the fact that most of their miracles are the result of some form of psychological doublecross. The spectators are led to believe that something had happened which, in fact, did not happen. We seem to be faced with a vanishing man. Suppose we assume there is no such animal and work backwards looking for the twist in logic that misled us."

"He couldn't have left by the window," Gavigan said. "He didn't go out by the door. And he's not here. What's twisted about that?"

"Maybe nothing. But when you add those facts up and conclude that Panama Harry vanished like so much smoke, perhaps your arithmetic is wrong. What if that set of facts has two possible answers and you don't see one because the other is so obvious?"

"You've got another answer?" Doran asked.

"I can think of one," Merlini replied. "The facts you've just listed could also mean that Panama Harry was never in this room at all. What have we got that says he was? The hat? How do we know it isn't Courtney's, or one that some absent-minded visitor left behind? We also have Rosie's testimony. But which is more likely—a vanishing man or a lying witness?"

The Inspector scowled. "We also have Courtney. He's not lying. He's not just pretending to be dead. Somebody here in this room killed him. He didn't do it himself—not with that knife where it is in the middle of his back."

"Oh, it's murder all right," Merlini admitted. "But what if the murderer vanished by leaving earlier—before there were any witnesses to see him go?"

Gavigan thought about that a moment, then said, "You mean that Courtney was already dead when I got here?"

"Why not? At least that's easier to believe than the vanishing man."

"Is it?" Gavigan asked skeptically. "It leaves you with something just as impossible." He pointed to the phone receiver in Courtney's dead hand. "Now you've got a *dead man answering a phone.*"

Merlini grinned. "I know. But that may be an easier miracle to perform than the other. Suppose he should do it again?"

Under his breath Doran groaned. "Now we got a zombie!"

"Do you mean," Gavigan wanted to know, "that you can make Courtney answer a phone now—two hours after Doc Peabody declared him dead?"

"I can try." Merlini pointed to the phone. "Lieutenant, put that receiver back on the cradle and let's see what happens on an incoming call."

Doran simply looked at him. Then the Inspector said, "Okay, Doran, do it."

The Lieutenant moved, rather like a zombie himself. He loosened the dead fingers, removed the phone, and placed it on the cradle. "If you think Doc Peabody is talking through his hat and that Courtney isn't . . . "

"Oh, he's dead all right," Merlini said. "Let's go outside."

He turned and went into the reception room. Gavigan scowled, hesitated, then followed. So did Doran.

Across the room the fingerprint man had laid out his equipment on the magazine table and was now taking Rosie's prints. McCall watched glumly.

Merlini said, "Let's go back a bit. Courtney, still alive, is in his office when the murderer goes in. I'll play the part of the murderer. And you—" he looked at Gavigan and Doran "—both of you stay here and keep your eyes and ears open." Then quickly, before they could object, he moved past them, back into Courtney's office, and closed the door.

Doran took a step forward, but the Inspector stopped him. "He's got something up his sleeve. Or he thinks he has. I want to see it."

"I'm not so sure I do," Doran muttered. "Not if he does what he says he's going to do."

The door opened again a moment later. "I have," Merlini announced, "just killed Courtney. And I leave the office by this door. Unseen because certain witnesses aren't here."

Merlini sat in Rosie's chair behind the receptionist's desk. "Now we skip a bit and I take over Rosie's part." He opened a desk drawer, closed it, opened another, and brought forth a bottle of nail polish which he placed on the desk. "I have just finished doing my nails." He turned to the switchboard and picked up the phone.

"Rosie then phoned a girl friend." He began to dial. "I'll phone my boy-genius producer and tell him I've been detained by a vanishing man. That'll really make him blow his top." Then, into the phone, he said, "Merlini here. Is your boss in? I want to . . . "

He stopped short and looked up at Gavigan who was staring at the closed door to Courtney's office. From beyond it came the sound of a telephone ringing.

Merlini swiveled in his chair. His elbow struck the nail polish bottle, knocking it to the floor.

Inspector Gavigan started forward.

The phone rang a third time—then stopped in mid-ring.

Silence.

"Dead men," Merlini said slowly, "do sometimes answer—"

Gavigan jerked the door open. Close behind him Doran stared over his shoulder.

Courtney's body, as far as they could tell, had not moved. *But the receiver was now back in Courtney's hand!*

Doran turned to Merlini. "Okay," he said, "let's have it. How did you get that receiver off the cradle and into his hand?"

"He put it there," Gavigan said slowly, "while he was in there for a moment with the door closed. And when he pretended to dial the boy genius he actually dialed Courtney's outside phone."

"But," Doran objected, "Courtney's phone wouldn't ring with the receiver off the cradle."

Merlini got to his feet and went through the door. "It would," he said, "if there was something *else* on the cradle." The lead sinker now lay on the edge of the desk. Merlini placed it on the phone cradle. "It will ring now."

"And it would go on ringing as long as the sinker is there or until you hung up." Doran looked at the switchboard phone lying on Rosie's desk where Merlini had left it. "But you didn't hang up."

"There is," Merlini said, "more than one way to skin a cat." He returned to the switchboard, clicked the hook, and dialed again. And again Courtney's phone rang.

"Hocus pocus," Merlini said. "Abracadabra!"

The phone rang a second time, then started to ring once more. What happened in the middle of the ring was almost as startling as though the dead man had moved. The lead sinker jerked suddenly with a life of its own, jumped off the phone, rolled to the edge of the desk, and fell to the floor.

The ringing stopped.

For a moment Gavigan and Doran simply stared. Then Gavigan moved, striding across the room. He picked up the weight and examined it. This got him nowhere. It was just a lead weight.

"Okay," he said. "I give up. How did you manage that—from the other room?"

"It may," Merlini said, "be just about the oldest trick in magic. Far older than the girls vanishing underwater at the Hippodrome. It probably dates from the days of the witch doctor and medicine man. And the modern form of the gimmick is one the Hi-Fly Rod and Reel Company sells."

Merlini took the sinker from Gavigan, then knelt and picked up something from the floor that was nearly invisible against the beige carpet.

"Fishline," he said. He wrapped its end several times around the sinker and placed the sinker back on the phone cradle. "It crosses the room and goes out under the door to a reel in Rosie's bottom desk drawer. She knocked the nail polish bottle off her desk purposely—an excuse to reach down behind the desk, yank the line, and dislodge the sinker."

Merlini gave the line a jerk; the weight fell from the phone cradle. "Not being tied, it came loose, and under cover of putting away the rest of her polishing equipment, she reeled it in."

"Okay," Gavigan said, "that wraps it up. After she killed Courtney, she set the fishline-sinker gimmick, then phoned McCall and got him over here as a witness to testify that she was sitting innocently at her desk when Courtney was killed."

"And your arrival," Merlini added, "gave her an unexpected and even better witness to her innocence."

Doran scowled thoughtfully at Merlini. "When you pretended

just now to call your boy genius you actually dialed Courtney's outside phone instead. And Rosie's phone call to her girl friend was also phony."

Merlini nodded. "Just the sort of telephone trickery that a switchboard operator would dream up. She made one phone call appear to be two. Her outgoing call to a phantom girl friend and Courtney's incoming call from a mysterious stranger were one and the same. Her description of the movie she had seen was a report to a dead man."

"And then," Doran added, "Rosie the Dish dished up Panama Harry as a red herring. Since he's on the lam he's not likely to come forward and deny her story."

"And who," Merlini asked, "would believe him if he did?"

"But there's one thing the D.A. isn't going to like," the Lieutenant said dubiously. "You've pinned this on the person with the least motive. One of the boys reported that Mrs. Courtney got a divorce decree in Reno last week, and that Rosie told a girl friend that she was in line to marry her boss. Why, just when his wife steps out of the picture, does she want him out, too?"

"She might," Merlini said, "if she discovered that his promise to make an honest woman out of her was one he didn't intend to keep."

"We'll find that out right now," Gavigan said. "When she sees this alibi of hers fall apart she'll talk. Doran, tell the photographer I want pictures of that casting reel in her desk drawer. It's Exhibit A."

"Wait, Inspector," Merlini said. "That would be the wrong picture. She pulled another cute one—an impromptu stunt that may be unique in the annals of the Police Department. At least, I never heard of another murderer who gave Exhibit A to a Police Inspector hoping he'd take it away from the scene of the crime off to the wilds of Maine. The reel in her desk is one I found in the sample case there on the files. The one she really used . . . "

Gavigan took the spinning reel from his pocket and glared at it.

"If I ever do get that vacation," he growled, "I'm going to spend it on a desert in Arizona. Somehow I don't feel much like fishing."

"Q"